Lost Lake
A Jippsy Russ Adventure

By Brian Wolfe

Copyright

LOST LAKE A Jippsy Russ Adventure

First published by BrenWolfe Publications 2014

BrenWolfe Publications
Text copyright © 2014 by Brian Wolfe
Publisher Name: Brian M. Wolfe
ISBN: 9780991705504

Visit us at : www.brenwolfe.com
and www.jippsy.com

Acknowledgements

This book would never have come to fruition without the tireless effort of my wife and partner Stephanie Brenhouse, whose editing and writing talents turned this wonderful story into a great read.

I also have to thank all of my children Alicia, Brittany, Trevor, Zenith and Mekhi, for their encouragement, and specifically Zenith for his last minute editing. Thank you guys. I love You!

For the Wolfe family and anyone else who loves a great campfire story.

The News Report

"Mom, Flash Gordon is coming on! Can we turn on the radio? This is the episode where Flash crash lands in Africa and meets Jungle Jim. I remember this part from the funny papers. Pleeeease???"

"Have you brushed your teeth and gotten into your pajamas?" his mom, Bella, asked, knowing full well that he probably had.

"Yeah, mom," Jippsy answered, anxious to get to his show. It was a routine they had played out since he was just a little boy, and even though he was already fourteen years old he still hadn't given up this one particular tradition with his mom.

"Ok. Turn the dial and get it to your station."

The radio dials were made of ivory - smooth alabaster dials that always felt cool to the touch. Jippsy usually felt a sense of remorse when he thought of the poor elephant that had been mercilessly hunted down across the Savannah by some blood-thirsty hunter. He could always picture the hunter in his safari outfit, but could never see the hunter's face as it was always obscured by some ostentatious hat. The hat, of course, would have been fabricated from the skins of his bounty. Jippsy always felt badly for the different animals that must have met their miserable demise at the hunter's hands, only to wind up perched atop his head. This time, he imagined a hat made of crocodile skin, with a zebra-striped band encircling it. That hat represented the hunter's ultimate trophy, and it pronounced his dominance over all living things.

Jippsy pictured the black-and-white of the band shining in the sun, the two colors blending to create a silver prism, as the light reflected and refracted the full color-spectrum. In his mind's eye, he would watch as the intrepid hunter took aim and fired. The grey beast would hear the hunter's shot and its unfamiliar violence would stir the elephant's survival instinct. But for some reason Jippsy always imagined the elephant turning defensively *toward* the sound and bearing down upon its source in a roaring gallop. Its trunk would swing wildly skyward and release a cry that alerted the others in his herd to follow suit, and charge!

Jippsy imagined two white Range Rovers as they spread out across the field. Only one of them had been close enough for a hunter to fire upon the elephant, and now stood in the path of the docile-animal-turned-raging beast. It would lower its head as it closed the gap between them, just before it smashed its finely honed, long curvy tusk into the side of the vehicle. The impact on the Range Rover is so great that it reels across across the plain like a log rolling toward a river. The driver, and the passenger riding shotgun, jump from the moving vehicle just in time and land in the fields. A moment of triumph for the elephant!

Probably not unlike what I feel when I score a goal for my hockey team, Jippsy thought to himself. The feeling of ecstasy that would sweep over him and his team ramped up their adrenaline. They would pump their fists in the air and whoop and holler. *But then we're not fighting for our lives,* he thought with relief. He would imagine the great elephant as it prepared to battle again – the anger and ferocity in his glossy stare, the huffed-up flapping of its ears, its stance just before it begins to gallop, directly into its ominous fate. He could practically hear the 'Thump', though, as the hunter's bullet hits its target.! The elephant's eyes fix on the shooter as blood starts pouring from his chest. He stares him down, his normally passive eyes now slipping from ferocious to horrified all at once. The beast won't charge again - his body simply cannot comply - as six gentle tons immense power fall to the ground.

How many ivory buttons do we really need? Jippsy pondered ruefully.

Jippsy hated looking at the radio but he loved listening to it. The radio announcer came on the air as he settled into his favorite old armchair - his father's favorite – but Jippsy was the man of the house while his father was in the city. Jippsy mimicked the announcer as he introduced the show: "Flash Gordon will be brought to you by the good people of Good Year. 'The only tires with wings'." He had heard that introduction so many times... So he wasn't at all prepared for what came next.

"We interrupt this program to bring you a special news report. The notorious gangster known as Dutch Schultz has escaped the federal marshall's custody while en route to the Federal Court Building in Malone, upstate New York, where he was to appear in court on charges of tax evasion."

Dutch Schultz was infamous for his bootlegging operation and his involvement in organized-crime. The announcer continued, "He is considered armed and dangerous and is travelling with another man, known as Otto Berman. They were last seen fleeing the area in a black 1931 Lincoln K heading north towards the Canadian Border. We are asking all citizens of New York, the Tri-state area and our listeners in Canada to be on alert, stay indoors, and report any sighting to your local authorities. We now return to Flash Gordon."

"Mom, do you think Dutch Schultz could come here?" Jippsy asked him mom excitedly.

"I don't think so, Jippsy. We're pretty far from where they last saw him, and why would he want to come here to Brébeuf, Quebec? To be honest with you Jippsy, I've read in the Star that Dutch does business with some shady people in Montreal and we *are* still 80 miles north of the city, nowhere close to where Dutch seems to be going but I can assure you if he comes to Canada the Mounties will get him - don't they always get their man?" Jippsy's mom laughed to herself.

The Getaway

"Hurry up! Get in the car; we have to hide the dough!" Dutch didn't like slowpokes and Otto knew this. Otto raced around the Lincoln as though he was being chased by a bear through the forest. His arms were flapping and flailing, like a chicken about to have its head cut off, and his feet felt like they were moving in every direction. He was becoming untethered, and the fear would have transfixed him on the spot if Dutch had not been yelling at him. At the time he was struggling to maneuver the two large leather valises into the boot of the car. And then he heard the sirens. He was out of time, and they'd just have to take the chance that the bags didn't get thrown from the car. He mustered what strength he had and heaved the valises into the back seat of the car.

Otto was not a large man, so the job was actually difficult for him. His small stature - he was only 5-foot-three and weighed no more than 125 pounds soaking wet - was not made for what he called schlepping and hauling heavy objects. He was a frail man at the young age of 33, his slicked-back hair curled under his fedora at the back, giving the impression that the hat was made with the curls attached, and made him look like a dark-haired Harpo Marx. His pale face, wide cheeks, and slivered dark red lips made him look like a scare crow, and no matter how many times he told Dutch, "I'm a numbers man, not a baggage handler," it didn't faze Dutch. In fact he liked it when Otto complained - it gave him a sense of family. But now no one talked – they knew what had to be done.

Dutch drove with all the calmness of a Sunday

morning stroll in New York's Central Park. He had nerves of steel, but that did not preclude the fact that there was danger all around, not the least of which was the blinding sun glaring in his eyes, making it practically impossible to see.

"One more hour and we'll be in darkness," Dutch observed. "If I was going south I wouldn't have this trouble, but Mexico is too far and we got no friends there. We need to get out of this clearing quickly. We lucked out with this weather."

It was a clear June night, the sun still shining high enough that there was no hiding place and, to top it off, they were in the middle of this godforsaken town and everyone already knew who he was. Despite the rampant thoughts of danger swirling through his head, he was thinking clearly. He thought inwardly, *I have to get to the Canadian border by 11 o'clock.* That was the time Dutch and the boys from Montreal arranged to make sure the border patrol was clear. A little whisky and some extra cash to buy the missus something always did the trick. They had 3 hours to make it to the border.

Otto finally calmed down while Dutch did the driving, but Otto still had the Tommy gun in his lap, a constant reminder that at every bend they were the prey. Every cell in his body felt like it was boiling; he could hear his heart in his ears and feel it reverberate throughout. *How could Dutch be so calm?* he wondered to himself. *The man is not human. Trouble could come from any direction, although the sirens were getting further and further away, and all of Dutch's liquor-running competitors, Lucky Luciano, Big Al, and Myers himself, had a pretty good feeling that Dutch was on his way out and that he was carrying the loot with him.* The thought didn't encourage Otto.

The road finally opened up out of this sleepy town into a two-lane road that weaved its way through all the outlying farm towns, and that would lead them to the border.

As they were passing the Maiden Lane Movie House Dutch gave a little nudge to Otto. "I wanted to see that movie."

"Which movie?" Otto asked incredulously. *How could he think about movies at a time like this?* Otto thought to himself.

"You know, Anna Karenina." he said, nudging Otto two more times, raising his eyebrows, intimating that he was up for a movie with a little sex appeal. Otto didn't even notice the sign. Instead, the Tommy gun had become an all-consuming symbol of his eventual untimely death. He couldn't take the racket in his body any longer, and just as he looked back at the theatre...

Ratattataatatatat! Ping. Ping. Two bullets ripped through the trunk and nestled in the back seats. "Otto what was that?" Dutch spit out. But he knew. Dutch swerved left thinking they were under attack, and Otto's body became a battering ram, his head swinging violently to the left, hitting Dutch right in the gut. Dutch groaned, but now his adrenaline was pumping and he didn't feel the pain rise in his chest. His thoughts flashed momentarily to the seriousness of the situation; he imagined the headlines in tomorrow's papers announcing Dutch's failed escape and subsequent death, alongside his associate Otto Berman, while attempting to flee the country with 13 million dollars in the trunk of his car. Well, 13 million if some shady copper didn't get greedy. Dutch yanked the wheel to the right so fast and furious that his elbow hit Otto right over the eye; it was sure to leave a shiner the next day, if they were actually to live that long, thought Otto cynically for the umpteenth time that day.

Yelling over the screech of the tires as Dutch gave it all sixes, "It sounds like a Chicago typewriter, Dutch".

"I hear that, where did it come from?" Dutch seethed.

Otto spun his head around again, this time as far as his body could contort, and saw just from the light of the setting sun what looked like a Cadillac Sixteen convertible with three dark shadows in the car about a half mile back.

"I think its Myers' boys," Otto screamed over the roar of the engine and the sound of the tires screeching on the pavement. "Let's get the hell out of here - fast! Myers doesn't know we have the money, but I'll bet he's willing to take a chance." Dutch sped away and was able to put enough distance between them to render the guns useless to any of them, but they were still in sight. At least the coppers weren't after them anymore; they never knew what hit them on the way to the court house.

On the corner of Broadway and Maiden Lane stood the newly constructed building which housed the post office and Courthouse – it was a majestic building typical of the art deco era; the designers called it "modern classical" with long, squared white columns surrounding the building - a modern tribute to the Roman Empire. Dutch, however, perceived it as his coliseum, and he was about to fight off the lions. He was ready for them, but this time instead of arming himself with a leather shield and brass sword, a 1927 Ford truck, normally used for hauling milk crates but used by Dutch's gang to run barrels of hooch, would be his weapon of choice. This time the barrels were empty and ready to inflict chaos on impact. The Ford sign on the front grill hit squarely at the window of the first police cruiser, causing an eruption that resonated like thunder striking steel, and sending the

11

cruiser reeling onto its side, glass and metal flying in every direction like shrapnel from a grenade, almost hitting the innocent bystanders on the steps of the courthouse. Just as the Ford was gearing up to strike the next cruiser Dutch smiled, but the coppers' eyes were popping out of their heads, all their training rendered useless, as they were immobilized with fear.

Suddenly the two bulls riding in the Ford lunged out of the car as fast as their bluchers, military boots which looked like heavy, blunt-toed oxfords, would take them. The shotgun rider grabbed Dutch out of the car and Dutch immediately ran to the other car he had waiting for him across the street. The barrels did their job as they rolled off the truck and directly into the dozens of other barrels that lined the road blocking the other coppers. They hit parked cars and shattered glass everywhere. People coming out of the courthouse ran back into the marble-surfaced foyer, paying no heed to the mop-up job the janitor was doing, and paid the price for their haste as their feet came right out from under them, and their heads and backsides struck the black and white marble floor.

Dutch, the ego-maniac who thought of himself as a modern-day Napoleon, believing he was above the law, was cold and calculating, yet charming when he wanted something and had followers from both the underworld and regular folk. Being the Beer Baron of New York certainly paid off both in hard currency and favors.

"Hurry up Otto!" Dutch growled as he shook his head, and thought to himself once again, *He is such a slowpoke.* But at this time Dutch's curiosity was so overwhelming he couldn't help but look around and take in the war zone that he had created: people screaming, police sirens wailing in the distance, everywhere dozens of 4-foot barrels strewn, shattered, and broken, lining the street and courthouse lawn, even on top of cars. He thought sardonically that terror is the Lord's greatest weapon. With his ego fully fueled and the urgency of their departure ever-increasing, Dutch bellowed, "LET'S GO OTTO! No time to waste," and before Otto had a chance to settle into the front passenger seat, Dutch jammed his foot down on the accelerator without a second look back.

"Ok, Dutch, you could've helped," Otto was practically whining now, "I had to move all of the luggage into the boot from the other car; it's not easy." Beads of sweat were streaming down Otto's white skin, something Otto was not used to as a numbers man - you just didn't work up a sweat pushing a pencil.

I love when a plan comes together, thought Dutch with a sense of satisfaction. *I have to hand it to The Rock*, he thought inwardly. *That hood sure knows how to dot his I's and cross his T's. Sometimes it paid to have good connections in bad places.*

Swerving back and forth across the road, Dutch figured he could stay out of the path of the bullets that they could still hear coming toward them from a distance. Dutch was growing aggravated, "Goddamn sun! I can't see a thing." But he kept on swerving and as he saw the car gaining on them, he realized they couldn't see him either. Every time a car came by he ducked into the lane of the oncoming traffic. *This just might work*, thought Dutch, if he would slow down just enough.

"DUTCH! Truck!" shrieked Otto.

"I know," Dutch blistered irately. "Don't worry. Just point that goddamn gun and fire back as I go into the other lane. I'll let you know when. Got it?"

"Yeah, Dutch. For god's sake you're going to get us killed," Otto was now in a panic.

"No I'm not. Now just do what I tell you." Dutch spotted a truck coming toward them.

"Perfect timing," he thought to himself. The truck was an old Model T Ford. It seemed to Dutch that everyone in these parts owned one. "Ford knows how to make a buck, that's for sure," Dutch mused.

"Otto, on the count of three, you start firing." Otto didn't answer, and there were too many distractions for Dutch to turn his attention to Otto. "Hey! Otto! You there?" Dutch couldn't wait for an answer. "One!" Dutch slowed down to about 60; the Cadillac was gaining. "Two!" Down to 50.

"We're getting fired on Dutch," Otto's pleading voice rang out. Otto stuck the rifle out the window just as a bullet whizzed by his Tommy's muzzle.

"Stop whining and fire. NOW!" Otto had been Dutch's numbers man for almost five years, and had witnessed plenty of violence, and had fired a rifle as a teen when he visited with his cousins on his uncle's farm. The power of the rifle and chunk of bark it stripped from the tree he hit by accident – an easy ten feet off his mark – had solidified for Otto the notion that a professional career would surely be his best bet. It took every fiber of courage in Otto's body to take aim, and as he opened fire the Cadillac started swerving left toward the oncoming traffic, then right, skirting the grass along the side of the road that borders the trench, and finally onto the grazing fields for cows. Every swerve brought at least one tire off the road, and as Dutch tucked his car behind the Model T on the oncoming side of the road, Otto flipped himself back into position in his seat, but the rifle got stuck in the window opening with his finger still on the trigger. The unsteadiness of the car, combined with Dutch's erratic maneuvering jostled his trigger finger, forcing another round of fire to blow into the sky.

The driver of the Cadillac tried to maintain control while gunfire and chaos seemed to be coming from every direction. The sun was a constant irritant. "I can't see anything," the driver said to anyone listening. The backseat became a swirling tea cup ride from the Coney Island amusement park, the two thugs were being slammed from side to side, metal rifles waving, crossing, and clanging together in the air like gladiators sword-fighting, battling to the death. "Watch out you schmuck - get your finger off the trigger or you're going to kill us," shouted the burlier of the two. As if on cue the gun started spitting bullets through the roof, shards of metal raining down on them and burning torturously into the exposed skin on their faces. One bullet shattered the Cadillac's windshield, and from the corner of the driver's eye he saw the shimmer of the gunfire as it flashed from Dutch's Lincoln, and just as the next round of gunfire erupted they all ducked.

1922 was Ford's biggest selling year for that model since its inception in 1910, as more and more people were recognizing that travelling by horse and carriage was becoming antiquated, and were trading up for faster, stronger and less taxing means of transportation. It had become the middle-class means of movement across the country; the modern era influencing a new generation what with worry-free cars, dance clubs and movie theaters, women's rights and organized gangsters like Dutch, but lastly and certainly not least, men and women driving around a two ton weapon. The automobile was a machine capable of travelling at speeds previously unknown to humans on a scale smaller than a train or plane, fired by a highly combustible fuel. Flames fired into an engine that powered those tons of steel forward at 40-plus miles per hour, and everyday thousands were being killed by the latest number-one-killer in the nation: the automobile driver.

This time the Model T was being driven by 16-year old Shawn McDonald, a strapping young man, who stood 6-feet tall, and easily weighed in at over 230 lbs. He dreamed of playing hockey for the Montreal Canadiens, but could just as easily have made his way into the motion picture industry. He possessed a confidence uncharacteristic of most young men, and while his physique could be imposing, his sweet-natured smile and striking blue eyes could be instantly disarming. He was charming, and still boyish; he idolized Elmer Lach, the captain of the Canadiens, adored his family, and loved the satisfaction that came from working on their orchard, but he just couldn't push back his overwhelming need for adventure. His curiosity was stronger than his dad's wrath when he stepped out of line, but Shawn knew his dad loved him and would never hurt him, even if it was for his own good. That day, he knew his dad had already taken his truck into town, and would likely already be at George O'Reilly's grocery store on Broadway unloading the barrels from the previous day's haul of cherries. His dad had insisted Shawn stay put, but Shawn knew his dad would end up being there all day and he just wanted to get a glimpse of that infamous gangster, Dutch Shultz.

Shawn took the only road that could bring him into town, promising himself he would only go by the courthouse for an hour. He had heard from many of the townsfolk that the court case would take place in the evening to discourage the press from travelling into Malone for the day, the drive back to New York would be long, and late at night without any lights, other than their headlights to guide them, the ride could be treacherous. Besides, there were no established accommodations for visitors in Malone.

As he drove toward town, his head bumped against the roof at every pothole He was humming and counting the cows as had become his custom while driving past the farms flanking the road. Tracts of grazing fields went on for miles, a sight that calmed Shawn and awed him with its expanse, as if the fields were truly unending. He was up to 37 cows after only two minutes, at which point he started his mental calculations: *It'll take me twelve minutes to get there; I've already counted thirty-seven in two minutes; twelve divided by two equals six. Thirty-seven times six is - let's see, two-hundred-and-twenty-two, plus six times seven is forty-two. Two-hundred-and-sixty-four cows. OK. I don't have to continue this - I know already. Damn that's a lot of cow shit at the end of the week. Glad we grow cherries.*

Finished with his cow counting, Shawn turned his focus back to the road, and just in time. As he spotted the car hurtling toward him adrenaline started coursing through his system; Shawn cursed aloud, "Whoa! That car's swerving - what's going on??? Shoot, that other car's swerving too. Is that gun fire? That looks like the black Lincoln they said Dutch was in!" he yelled out excitedly. "What the hell is going on here??? Whoa! He's headed straight for me!" Shawn's hands tightened on the steering wheel, which normally felt smooth and solid, but now felt moist from the sweat of his palms and remarkably flimsy, considering that its durability might very well make the difference between keeping control and crashing outright. "Whew - that was close. Bastard! That was way too close. I better get out of here." A brief glimpse into the rear-view mirror and he could see that the Lincoln had tucked into his lane. He could see the distance growing between them, but that glimpse lasted one second too long, and as Shawn adjusted his view forward he was immediately back to a heart-pumping reality as he spotted the next car heading straight for him. "That other car is out of control - oh jeez – NOOOOOO!"

Shawn jammed his foot on the brake pedal, pulled up the emergency brake and the car veered toward the ditch on the side of the road. All sense of propriety lost now, he was trapped in a frenzy of desperate reactions. "SHIT! I'm going to tip..." Pump, pump... His feet hit the brakes like rapid-fire. He covered his eyes and turned the wheel hard to the right, opening his eyes for what might be his last opportunity, only to take in a sight he would never forget.

"Hold on!" yelled the driver of the Cadillac, "we're going to crash!" The driver jammed both feet on the brake, and the car skidded, fish-tailing over to one side of the road, then to the next, jerking the passengers around in the back seat like ragdolls. Their bodies tensed and braced for impact as they realized what was about to happen. As the Cadillac skidded horizontally across the road, its speed was too great, and in tune with the deafening sound of metal screeching against pavement, Shawn watched the surreal scene as the Cadillac rolled roof-over-chassis, not once but twice until it righted itself rather ominously directly in front of his father's car. His shirt had soaked right through.

Dutch and Otto never did figure out exactly who was after them, but they were not about to forget there was another enemy out there. They passed their time like most travelers; they watched the cows as they drove along in silence, and kept a sharp lookout for problems until the sun finally went down.

It became apparent that *whoever* was chasing them no longer mattered, as two hours had passed without a sign of anyone trailing them. They had travelled in utter silence until Dutch suddenly blurted out, "There it is!"

"There's what?" asked Otto, confused.

"The sign," Dutch answered abruptly, annoyed that Otto could be so dim.

Otto looked up and read it in his mind.

You are now entering the Dominion of Canada
Bienvenue/Welcome

Just then Highway 55, which crossed through New York, became Highway 10 - sixty miles to Montreal.

Dutch was all business now, "Ok Otto, let's see if the Canucks came through." Otto gripped the machine gun but wouldn't put his finger on the trigger. He had been having thoughts all night about how he may die, and the anxiety was so overwhelming that he started cracking up while daydreaming. He thought to himself, *I'm probably going to bleed to death after shooting myself in the foot...* He laughed aloud, and it was a crazy laugh, tinged with the pain of stress and fatigue, making him sound like a Hyena rallying its clan to make a kill. Otto nervously checked his watch. 11:10pm.

"SHUT Up!" Dutch flared. "You never know if the guards are at the border or if they disappeared for a while. I want to make sure we get into the country just like when we're moving our booze, without anyone knowing our whereabouts."

For the first time during the drive Otto sighed, just enough to help him relax. No border patrol, no cops, no Mounties – not even a light from the farm houses that hugged the road. The farmers were busy this time of year, planting their seeds for the season; most of them worked very late hours trying to use every bit of daylight at their disposal in order to make sure they could survive the coming year and whatever Mother Nature dared throw at them.   At this time any farmer, whether they had electricity or not, was lights out, because in just a few short hours they would be back at it again.

The Rock

The last few years since the depression had been so bad that many farms were completely abandoned in favor of work to be found in the city. Montreal became a boomtown and it didn't hurt that all of the East Coast was getting their alcohol from there. Companies like Seagrams, Molson's and so many other liquor companies thrived and were hiring very knowledgeable farmers. No other family in Montreal had thrived better during this period than the Rothmans; it was believed that Dutch took his orders from none other than Chaim "The Rock" Rothman.

"It looks like The Rock came through Dutch," Otto said with relief, because the alternative would put Dutch in a really bad mood, and the both of them in danger.

Dutch sounded relieved too, "Yeah, what do you know? It's good to have rich friends in low places."

Otto came from one of the new middle class merchant families that were growing in leaps and bounds in New York, like the Gimbels, the Macys, the Bloomingdales, the Saks' and so many others that sold to the masses. But the wealthiest class belonged to a group of families that never really declared their income to the IRS or Canada's Department of National Revenue; they ran their businesses as if they *were* the government. And nobody ran the show better than Chaim Rothman (or The Rock, as the authorities referred to him). Nothing seemed to breach this man's control; he was soulless and heartless - all the necessary ingredients of an autocratic dictator.

The irony was that, by all appearances, The Rock came across as a gentle, warm-hearted man; his wavy gray hair fell across his forehead with a spit curl, and his face seemed so young and fresh for a man of 52 that he could have easily passed for a much younger man, were it not for the gray hair. His eyes were wide and warm, a Caribbean blue that entranced you, but that's where the façade ended. Just like the Caribbean Sea, where danger lurks all around, where sharp corals, jelly-fish and sharks exist innocuously until you stumble into their path, The Rock was not to be trifled with. He was quick and merciless. At 5' 7" and 150lbs The Rock was no shark, but to keep fit he played basketball twice a week at the Y, and swam every other day except Saturday. If life hadn't turned his world upside down when his dad left them when he was 12, he would probably have been a gym teacher or a coach somewhere. He spent the next 10 years working to make sure there was food on the table for his sisters and mom and it just wasn't enough money from regular work. He turned to a life of crime, and because of his intelligence and cold-heartedness he became the boss of all the bosses.

The Rock ran all the families in Montreal and some in New York, and no booze would make it past the border without The Rock's stamp of approval; bootlegging was one racket, but where The Rock kept most of his power was in protection. And right about now, this was exactly what Dutch needed. The Rock knew Dutch was making his getaway and would be at the border between 11:00 pm and 1:00 am; he had to make a deal to get him into Canada.

Gerard went to see The Rock at his home and headquarters and was sweating like a pig. The Rock never contacted Gerard directly; Izzy, the warehouse manager, was always the go-between. Gerard got off the trolley at

Park Avenue near Mount Royal Street and looked admiringly at the mountain, lush with greenery of every kind. As he walked up the road with the mountain to one side and magnificent homes on the other, he noticed the maples, their leaves fluttering in the gentle breeze, causing the midday sunlight to blink through the foliage like flashes of lightning. Under normal circumstances Gerard would have appreciated the simple magnificence, but it was only disturbing today, as every nerve in his body was hypersensitive. He had no idea what The Rock would want with him and he feared for his wife and new baby. Gerard had worked for The Rock for almost 5 years and he knew one thing for sure, The Rock has no mercy. Gerard took a mental inventory of the last few weeks, and wondered nervously what he had done to warrant a visit. *All I do is manage the warehouse stock*, he thought with dread. *Nothing I can think of. Nothing at all...*

He walked up the 30 steps of the grand mansion on Maplewood, one of the most prestigious streets in Montreal, in the borough of Outremont (so named as it sat beyond the northern side of the mountain), Nestled on the mountains within the city were the magnificent residences that housed the Prime Minister, artists of all kinds, academia teaching and researching at Mcgill University, old money and new business barons. But at the top of Outremont was the grand mansion of The Rothmans. Gerard couldn't help but snicker at the thought that he was visiting the King at his palace. *A lowly jester like me would never get an audience with the King*, he thought to himself. He had arrived.

With each tentative step he took, the scent of the white and purple lilacs lining the stairs overwhelmed his senses. He was in awe of everything he saw: the marvelous cedars that flanked the walkway leading to the mansion, ornately trimmed in the most unusual spherical designs, the enormous silver maples that towered over the house, clustered like a grove, affording the mansion the illusion of a plantation home, the boulders, set so naturally among the beautiful flower beds and lush lawn, resting solidly as though they had always been there. Every element perfectly placed, but somehow not contrived, so natural and real yet magnificent that he felt himself set apart from the scene, an intruder in this Eden-like setting.

The house was immense; there must have been at least 25 rooms, but the design of the house was quite simple, having been built just at the turn of the century. The designers had opted for a classic Tudor style, primarily built of multidimensional stones in hues of grey, red and soft brown, the stucco painted a creamy off-white, the accents painted in a deep brown tone that helped to enhance the effect of the landscape elements. New money was buying up the mountain properties, and they expected the best – the most elegant styles for the most elegant tastes, and opulence was in style, but Rothman's mansion was elegant and understated, in such a way that it was one of the most envied properties on the mountain. The land was fenced-in by 10 foot walls built of the same stones as on the façade and it sat atop the mountain like a castle overlooking its domain. Looking beyond the house and towering maples, Gerard could see the Laurentian mountain range 45 miles away – the views were simply spectacular.

Gerard reached the front door and slowly lifted his head, allowing his eyes to scan the full height and the width of the mansion – he was dwarfed by this property, this artistic rendering of an English lord's mansion. Unfortunately, rather than offering some respite from his effort-strained panting and nervous anticipation, this started him shaking even worse. He couldn't understand what was happening to him physically, but he felt weak and dizzy. Crouching down, he placed his head between his legs and tried to breathe deeply and compose himself. A few moments, that's all he needed to reorient, and loosely gather his chaotic thoughts. Straightening himself up he reached a shaky finger toward the doorbell and pressed the brass button to the right of the immense oak doors. The door opened, and a young man wearing a light grey wool suit with black slicked-back hair and shiny black shoes, answered the door. "Aah Monsieur Gascon," he said in his thick French accent from France, Monsieur Rothman will see you in his study. Suivez-moi s'il vous plait." He started to follow the doorman, and although he was terrified he couldn't help but take in the paintings everywhere. *The Rock must be a collector*, thought Gerard. They walked over the marble foyer floor for what seemed like several minutes, every step seemed to go in slow motion, his stomach knotting up, his heart starting to seize and the rest of his body revolting; he just wanted to wretch and let it all out, his senses were screaming; "Run, Gerard, run!"

The shiny-shoed butler stopped before two rich dark brown oak French doors and slid them open without knocking. As Gerard watched him leave all he could remember about him were those bright black shoes which seemed to gleam like a chandelier lighting his way through every room. He gave a nervous smile as he thought sardonically, *It's always the butler who did it.* And suddenly Gerard was pulled right back to reality.

"Bonjour Gerard". The Rock's voice was deep and coarse. And frightening. There was no hiding the fact that French was not The Rock's first language – English for sure, maybe with German or probably Yiddish hidden in the back of some of his words.

"Allo Monsieur Rottman,"– Gerard spluttered. The

French had a very hard time with the TH sound.

"Would you like some tea?" asked The Rock. Gerard thought to himself facetiously, *Even the Jews drink tea like les anglais.* "Non, merci, Monsieur Rottman," he replied hastily. The only thing that would calm him down was the swill his père called cider, but to Gerard it was just poor man's moonshine; if it didn't make you blind, you lost all inhibitions with one shot of the jug. He remembered fondly the distillery his père had set up at their home in Joliette. He seemed to be having difficulty focusing on the here and now. *Focus Gerard!"* he scolded himself.

"Ok, Gerard, why don't you come and sit down on the couch." The Rock interrupted Gerard's reverie. It wasn't a question so much as a polite order. Gerard looked around the room and saw more of those fabulous paintings. Many of them illustrated some great sporting event in history, captured in graphic detail by magnificent painters of their era. The one that caught his attention was hung behind an antique desk which took up almost the entire width of the large room and was positioned just in front of a black and white marble fireplace. It depicted a matador slaying a bull, and what struck Gerard, although he could never put words to it, was the divergent reaction of each – the look of resignation on the bull's face and the matador's look of exultant triumph as he pulled the blood-soaked sword from the animal's limp body, blood dripping from the gently-curved tip. Gerard shivered.

As they both sat on the red leather couch, Gerard was impressed by the supple feel of the leather as he slid in, while the heady smell of the leather conjured up images of wealthy men smoking cigars and talking jovially over snifters of brandy. Perhaps this was as close as he would ever get...

The Rock sat back comfortably but Gerard just couldn't settle into any position that was remotely comfortable, so he opted instead to sit on the edge. "Not everyone appreciates art; each piece represents triumph or failure - as in life, Gerard, we either fight like the bull or run like a chicken and you know what ends up happening to the chicken." The Rock could not have been more clear.

As Gerard tried desperately to conjure up some saliva to swallow – his throat was so dry - in walked Shiny Shoes. Gerard recognized the gleam of his shoes long before he walked through the opened the door.

"Right, here's my tea. Are you sure I could not persuade you to join me? It will calm your nerves."

This time Gerard's physical discomfort outweighed his mental discomfort and so he reluctantly, but with great relief at the second offer, agreed. "Ok, Monsieur Rottman – merci." The Rock added three sugar cubes and a little milk – *Juste comme un anglais,* thought Gerard. Unlike the English, Gerard did not take anything in his tea.

"Where were we – ah, yes, art. I didn't always appreciate art; only after I bought this house."

Were the rumours true? Gerard wondered. Did The Rock buy the house or did he just make sure the owner signed over his deed and perhaps the paintings came with the house? Either way it didn't matter because, in the end, The Rock always got what he wanted. *Maybe I am the bull,* Gerard ruminated; he was, most assuredly, trapped in The Rock's stadium.

The Rock moved a little closer to Gerard as soon as Shiny Shoes left the room. *Here it comes, Gerard,* said the little voice inside his head.

"Well, Gerard, I have a little job for you – I want you to go down to the Lacolle border tonight around sunset, say 8:00pm, and have a discussion with the border guards. Take Louis with you – he can be especially effective with that baseball bat of his. This is a routine visit, and I do not want Izzy to find out we spoke. Otherwise, mon ami, you better be a very fast chicken. Farshstaize?" Everyone who worked for The Rock knew that what he was asking was, "Understand?" In Yiddish.

Lacolle

It was 15 minutes past eight when Louis and Gerard arrived at the Plattsburgh/Lacolle border crossing. The Mounties saw them coming and knew there was something they would have to do for The Rock - or else. Louis pulled over and shut the ignition at an old farm house, which straddled the Canadian and American border, and that for years now had acted as the Customs House. The house was surrounded on both sides by vast corn fields, rolling hills, and green pastures, and the smell of cow manure wafting densely around them. For a city kid it stank like shit, but country folk were so used to it that they thought it was the sweet smell of success. The smell was an indication that the farm was doing well - the cows were grazing, milk was being produced and they had food, shelter and a few dollars to send their children to school.

The Mounties watched through the dust-coated windows as a giant humanoid opened his car door and emerged from the car. He approached the house with a lumbering stride. They both agreed it belonged in a freak show or a Barnum and Bailey Circus. They spotted Gerard, but he was neither imposing nor remarkable in any way, and so the Mounties kept their attention focused on the incoming menace. They could hear the creak and sag of the porch as the giant stepped onto the slightly raised platform, closer now to the door, the awning overhanging the porch barely tall enough to accommodate his imposing height. The giant grasped the handle and pushed the door harder than even he had intended, causing a rush of air as the door created a vacuum that swirled the dust around the room.

Louis was 6-foot-5 and sure to be 350 pounds; he wore overalls just like the farmers because it was the only thing that allowed him to keep his pants on over his immense beer gut. He wore big brown boots like a farmer and always carried a baseball bat on a string like it was a billy club. He was not to be messed with. He stepped over the threshold and into the little ramshackle house, floor boards creaking under each step he took, as though the floor was about to give way and he would be swallowed up by the earth. He stopped, glared around the room, looked at the map of North America on the wall above the Mounties' puny pine desks, turned to the officers, and in his low French Canadian accent said, "Oo's en charge?" The more senior Mountie, already standing, waved his hand with authority, and looked up into Louis' wide hazel eyes, then slowly scanned his furry face. His mind wandered momentarily, envisioning this giant as a fur trapper from the Hudson Bay Company back in the 19th century, although he couldn't look at him very long without wanting to run for his life.

Gerard knew that no man could stand up to Louis; they would need a very big gun to bring this moose down. He just let Louis do the talking - ok, not talking per se, but rather intimidating...

"The Rock wants you to shut down from 11:00pm to 1:00am cette nuit." Close da lights et don't look outside and you weell let any car pass wit'out making notes. Comprends-tu?" Louis had this odd habit of finishing all of his sentences in French, asking if the Mountie understood. He actually spoke 3 languages - French, Patois and English. His mother was the daughter of a Louisiana slave-and-plantation owner, who, after the civil war, moved to Montreal looking for a more accepting way of life. The Mounties working there were mostly English, as were most Quebecois near the American border and they all understood French. But the unspoken word was the world's most prolific language: the communication of fear.

This hamlet was still The Rock's domain, and he had to make sure business went smoothly at the border. He therefore ensured that all the families along the border made it through the tough economic times, and eventually they became his suppliers for whiskey and cider. Border guards, farmers and even the local folk knew who he was because he had helped many of them through the depression.

Gerard offered each of the Mounties a bottle of whiskey, along with a somewhat menacing reminder. "'Ere is a leettle someting for your trouble," as he passed the senior Mountie an envelope, "and as usual 'der will be a leettle Christmas bonus for you to get some-ting nice pour vos femmes. Joyeux Noel, eh! N'oubliez pas ce que je t'ai dit." *Don't forget what the giant said*, the Mounties both thought to themselves. *Not a chance!* His face moved closer to the Mountie; pock marks riddled his face, but you couldn't see through his light brown skin and fuzzy beard unless you were up close, and if you were it was dangerous. "Don't forget what I tell you," he insisted one last time in his heavy French Canadian accent.

Although The Rock was known for his ruthlessness he could not escape his fancy for science fiction and was a fervent listener to Flash Gordon. Chaim had a ritual: he sent everyone away, turned on the radio, and readied himself with a glass of brandy and a Cuban cigar. With the doors closed, he finally sat back comfortably and closed his eyes. This was his ultimate escape. He could relax now that he had ensured that

Dutch was set, and he was happy to help his long-time business associate and friend.

The show was about to start, and The Rock knew every word the announcer would say, having listened for so long and with such interest. "Flash Gordon will be brought to you by the good people of Good Year. 'The only tires with wings'." He was not surprised but admittedly unsettled by what he heard next: "We interrupt this program to bring you a special news report. The notorious gangster known as Dutch Schultz has escaped the federal marshal's custody while en route to the Federal Court Building in Malone, upstate New York, where he was to appear in court on charges of tax evasion." The Rock listened carefully to what the announcer had to say, inwardly acknowledging his involvement in and proximity to the news story, but taking the situation seriously as it could definitely impact his business.

The announcer continued, "He is considered armed and dangerous and is travelling with another man, known as Otto Berman. They were last seen fleeing the area in a black 1931 Lincoln K heading north towards the Canadian Border. We are asking all citizens of New York, the Tri-state area and our listeners in Canada to be on alert, stay indoors, and report any sighting to your local authorities. We now return to Flash Gordon." The Rock settled in to listen to his show and forget his concerns.

Jippsy

"Wow! Flash and Dale got out of it this week. Those lizard men were real Dumb Doras - they actually thought they could capture Flash. He's the smartest spaceman in the galaxy."

"You really like Flash, don't you Jippsy?" his mom asked from the kitchen.

"Yeah mom, he's the bee's knees, a real big six." Jippsy's mom had no idea what he was saying. Kids these days had the most perplexing jargon!

"A big six?" she asked confused.

"You know, strong and fast like the new 6-cylinder cars. You have to get with it mom! It's not like in your day when everyone was driving around in a horse and buggy..." Jippsy said teasingly.

"You kids and your crazy expressions! I can't imagine what the world is going to be like when you're an adult. As it is I can barely understand what you're saying. You and your friends think everything is an adventure – what about responsibility, doing your chores, helping your parents. Eh? You're lucky you are sooo cute!" she answered as she walked into the living room and planted a kiss on his warm cheek.

Jippsy tried playfully to avoid her kiss, but there was no getting away from it, and besides, he didn't really mind – she was a great mom and Jippsy really loved her. Still, he couldn't help but act grown up, "Awww, c'mon mom!"

"Ok, kiddo. Let's get washed up and get to bed. Tomorrow is another day and I'm sure there's an alien you'll have to capture or an invasion to ward off, or maybe you'll be hunting for treasure with an evil pirate."

His mom was so silly! "Sure mom," he said with a snicker.

"Good night, my baby. Sweet dreams..." She kissed him lightly on his forehead; that always makes him smile. He never let her know this, but he secretly enjoyed their nighttime ritual – it reassured him that she was always on his side. He closed his eyes reluctantly, and yet sleep overtook him without delay.

Montreal

"I see the city lights, Dutch, and there's the bridge." Otto felt tension at the sight. "There's no way onto the island of Montreal without going over some kind of bridge, unless you can swim, and coming over the south side means going over the Saint Lawrence - 2 miles long across with very fast currents and treacherous rapids." Otto's mind was churning. Since the 16th century the Saint Lawrence had been in a battle with man and man had been losing: ships, canoes and even cars had capsized into this raging river just to get across her. The ice bridge worked great in the winter when walking or taking a horse, but cars were a different matter.

By the late 1800's the need to ease traffic on Victoria Bridge, which had originally been intended as a rail-only bridge, had brought about major discussions with respect to the construction of a new bridge. The plan was to replace the wintertime ice bridges and the ferries, which connected the city to the South Shore. The Dominion Bridge Company was contracted to erect the Jacques Cartier Bridge; construction started in 1925 and the work was completed in 1930. It was a magnificent bridge, which spanned 5 lanes and extended 3,400 feet in length.

Man had finally won and no one was more satisfied about this great feat and thing of beauty than Dutch himself. Once he was successfully over the bridge, he and his money would finally be safe.

Kchunk - kchunk – kchunk - the tires bounced over each steel plate that connected the segments of the bridge, causing both Dutch and Otto to jolt up and down as though they were riding horseback. They eventually made a full left turn onto Wellington Street heading west. Otto's head filled with the smell of the myriad lilacs which hugged the riverside. On the other side of the road were large red-brick box warehouses, ominously present with their 2-storey smoke stacks rising up through the belly of each warehouse, spewing foul waste into the summer sky. On the side of the first building that came into sight hung a sign announcing the Montreal Piano Company, its sweeping black lettering contrasted against the white-washed background. Otto couldn't help but think that, for such a beautiful city that could fill your nostrils with perfume the moment you arrive, this place also housed the meanest son of a bitch he has ever known.

Otto looked for the sign for Montreal Shirts and Blouses. "There it is. It's the fourth building down, Dutch. Dutch turned right onto the cobblestone driveway that went right up to the front steps. As he approached the front of the building, at a pace no faster than walking, a figure - clearly male - emerged from the steel front door. Dutch squinted to see the silhouette, through the blinding light of his headlights as they reflected off the steel door of the building.

Dutch turned and spoke quickly to Otto, "Otto, hold your gun up out the window, and make sure he sees it." Otto rolled down his window slowly, eased just the tip of the rifle onto the ledge of the window opening, and trained it at the unknown man. This time Otto was sure of himself; if someone was going to die now it wasn't going to be him. The man saw the gun, felt his Adam's apple strain against his neck as he swallowed hard, took a single step and saw the car blink its lights 3 times. He knew that was the signal, and dared not make any sudden moves; he didn't know how trigger-happy they may be or how scared or tired they were, so he put up both his hands, forgetting that this was not the signal. Just then Dutch flashed the lights 3 times again. Otto put his finger on the trigger this time and yelled, "Hold it. You there, what's the signal?" The man's arms were up straight in the air and, hands trembling now as he crossed one arm over the other making the letter X, he held his arms there for a few seconds.

Otto turned to Dutch, "So is that the signal?"

Dutch answered nonchalantly, "I guess so..." and laughed out loud like he'd never laughed before, tears of laughter rolling down his face. The man put down his arms and walked down the eight concrete steps while holding onto the iron railing. He came to the bottom of the stairs, and slid his left thigh against the car, his beige pants unavoidably brushing against the dirt from the side of the car. His blue denim shirt was soaked from nervous sweat and was now beginning to stink, but he didn't care; he knew this was the best position from which to duck in case of trouble - especially from the man in the shotgun position. In those brief seconds, he flashed to his beautiful wife and their new baby. *I have to give my son a better life than this*, he thought to himself. *All those near-misses and now it may come again. What is so important that The Rock doesn't want anyone to know about this night*, he couldn't help but wonder...

Otto watched him come around the car, took his finger off the trigger and redirected the gun, pointing it out Dutch's window. "Watch out Otto! I don't want to get my head blown off - make sure you're pointing that thing at the other guy." Otto started to appreciate the feeling of power, and now understood why Dutch was such a ruthless asshole who cared about people as much as he did ants. It was power that Dutch wanted and the feeling of it, a feeling that most people simply couldn't understand.

The man looked inside the car and saw Otto's Tommy gun pointed right at him, and this only fueled his nervousness. Otto could see the sweat around his armpits, even in the dark, and the fragrant smell of the lilacs was being overwhelmed by the rank smell of human fear. Otto could recall that smell – it was the distasteful stink of an employee who has been caught stealing from Dutch or running a little side business on the company's time.

The sounds of begging for mercy and smell of bodily secretions were too much for Otto and he was relieved those times were over, because Dutch couldn't go back to that world; but what lay ahead might not be much better. Sometimes, better the devil you know.

"Allo Monsieur Schultz. My name is Gerard. Welcome to Montréal. My boss wants you to spend the night here; we have set up accommodations for you and no one will disturb you. I will stay the night here with you and await instructions from Monsieur Rottman."

"Did you say mon-see-ur Rottman?" Dutch turned his lip up in a grin and said, "Ok, Geerard. We will wait for Mon-see-ur Rottman," He was making fun of Gerard. Gerard hated the English, and especially Americans. He believed that one day those people would pay and the French would be in their rightful place as leaders of this country once again, not those maudits anglais (damned Anglos).

"I will go to open the garage doors for you," offered Gerard. Otto followed him with the rifle from the shotgun seat and finally laid it flat on his lap, but only when he saw Gerard go back up the stairs through the large metal door.

"Whew!" said Otto, as he looked up above the 4-storey building toward the quarter moon and watched clouds drift across it. *I don't know how much more excitement I can take*, he thought cynically.

They could hear the chains rattling as the large warehouse doors began to climb up the rail, and could make out a figure pulling on the chains about 40 feet away. A dim light glowed and filled up every corner of the room. Dutch reversed the car and pulled up to the warehouse doors, then brought the car in very slowly while they both looked about, seeing all of the wooden crates of hard liquor and barrels of beer packed up high on both sides of the warehouse and another 75 feet down to the back. They must have been 24 feet high, and once again Otto's nose turned toward another smell, one he knew very well, the intoxicating smell of money.

As if they had been sharing the same sensory experience, Dutch whispered to Otto,

"Otto, smell that! The Rock is in it for the long haul; looks like there is no stopping him, and the coppers here don't give a shit. No prohibition in this part of the world, and all we did was allow the lousy Canucks to get rich."

Gerard stopped, looked back to the car from 10 feet ahead and bellowed to Dutch over the sound of the engine, "Monsieur Schultz, leave the car here. We have a room for you in the back."

Dutch would not stop the car completely, and kept his eye on the warehouse door through his rear view mirror. Just as he started to say, "No...", the door started closing as what looked like a beast closed it with one yank of the chain. Dutch spit out, "What the hell is that? Otto, get out and turn your rifle on that animal." As Otto stepped out of the car, he was able to see the shadow of what looked like a large gorilla.

"What is that thing?" Otto muttered under his breath, as he turned and looked straight at it, brought his rifle up to his face, and slowly put his finger on the trigger once again.

Just as he was about to contract his finger to fire, he heard a yell from behind, "Stop!" Gerard came running up to Otto, while Dutch, who had run around to the front of the car, tackled Gerard into the barrels, which swayed back and forth above them. Dutch looked up, and thought mockingly, "This would be a fitting end: crushed by the one thing that has made me all my money."

Gerard's air rushed out of his body with an audible "Ahh!"

Dutch got back on his feet, and attempted to wipe the dirt off of his suit just as Otto yelled to the animal, "Hold it right there! One more move and I'll pump so many holes in you, you'll look like Swiss cheese when I'm through." Dutch was so proud; his young little numbers cruncher was growing up and becoming a man.

The animal stopped. A guttural sound of French words escaped his mouth, and his hands flew up in the air. "Merde (shit), je suis un ami – a friend. I'm with Gerard. My name is Louis. Please put down your gun." His French patois accent, coupled with his baritone voice made it difficult to understand what he was saying, as he continued, "You are safe here - we have orders to protect you."

"What did he say, Dutch?" Otto was too shaken now to follow.

"I think it's safe Otto, you can lower the gun," Dutch said, almost reassuringly. Otto sighed once more, and lowered the rifle to the cracked red concrete floor. Dutch looked over to Otto on the other side of the car, and from the glow of the incandescent light hanging from a chain above him, he could see the toll this day had taken on Otto. Sweat was shining on his forehead and upper lip, his clothes were rumpled and dirty, and Otto had an overall gray cast to his skin which hadn't been there that morning.

Dutch started to speak as if reciting a poem, "The Rock is an old-time friend and he has enough money to buy and sell The Rockefellers. Trust, I do not have. Faith, I am willing to gamble. From friends I will accept help."

All Otto could think was, *You're just going to get me killed, aren't you Dutch?* Dutch turned away from Otto, while Louis hauled himself up from the concrete, and rubbed the back of his head from the jolt he took right into the barrels. Dazed and seeing stars, he listened to Dutch, not really knowing who he was, but was now in the power position. He finally stood up, gazing in Dutch's vicinity, and tried to regain his full balance.

"I do not understand," said Gerard.

Dutch did not mince words, "It's simple you little Frenchie; tonight we will stay with the car. That's the end of the interview. Farshtaize?" Gerard knew that word quite well and cringed at its meaning each time.

"Oui, Monsieur," Gerard replied with resignation.

"Cut the French, and just call me Dutch," Dutch had clearly started to lose his patience.

"Ok ... Dutch. Louis will stay by the door tonight, and I will go to the nest," Gerard explained.

"The nest?" asked Otto.

"Yes. It is the eagle's nest, or what you might call the dispatcher's room." Louis pointed to the back right side of the room. Dutch followed the direction of his finger to where a glassed-in office hung over the warehouse, accessed via a metal staircase that wound up from the ground. "We call it the nest – for eagle's nest." Both Otto and Dutch understood immediately - they also had their people watching in their own operation.

Louis' voice reverberated around the barrels, "Bonne nuit, Messieurs." He walked back to his station like a yeti traipsing through the snow of the Himalayas and back into its cave. He slumped his body onto the ground, and leaned up against the door, so any vibration would awaken him. As a man of the forest he knew all the signs of any movement around him, awake or asleep.

"Good night Dutch et Monsieur...," and Gerard walked at a brisk pace to the stairs at the bottom of the nest. Otto and Dutch watched as Gerard disappeared further up the stairway until all they could hear was the echo of clanging metal, and then a bright white light seemed to alight as if by magic, even though they knew how, but the illusion seemed to surprise them nonetheless.

"Dutch, I need a drink ... and a lobotomy so I can forget about all of this," Otto grumbled.

"Otto, you don't drink, but you can get up and walk away now, or you can wait until we are completely safe; I'll give you your 3 million as promised and then you can put a hole in your brain however you like." Dutch was serious about letting Otto leave if he had lost his nerve – the last thing Dutch needed was dead weight – but he expected Otto would stick it out.

"Ok, Dutch. I'll wait." Otto had resigned himself to finishing what he had started.

Dutch didn't miss a beat and laid out his plan for the night, "Then get in the back seat of the car - I've got the front, so give me the gun." Otto reached over the car hood and passed the rifle over to Dutch, who continued, "You get some shuteye; you've got 2 hours. I'll wake you at 2:30. You'll let me sleep until 4:30, then we either see what The Rock has in store for us, or we high tail it to Toronto next. Oh yeah, don't forget to get those bags in the boot."

Both men got into the car; Otto opened the back door, moved the heavy bags to the trunk, and fell abruptly onto the back seat. The final ebb of adrenaline released the tension in his body, as exhaustion ultimately engulfed him, visions of Model T's, lilacs, and guns swirled through his mind only briefly, and then nothing.

Dutch was relieved and immeasurably pleased that the day had unfolded with him still able to think, breathe and feel, but, looking back on the day's events grimly, the realization took hold that he was still not out of the woods. Sauntering around the car, he took inventory like a shopkeeper counting his supply, muttering numbers to himself, *Thirteen? Shit! Thirteen bullet holes - they should call me Lucky, not that idiot Luciano. I'm still here boys, and if I don't come back alive, you'll feel the wrath of my ghost.* Dutch felt reassured that even if they did get him, he had put it out to the universe, and his energy would carry that curse to whoever tried to take his money. But that gave him an idea.

Dutch practically ran around from the back of the car to the passenger side, opened the door, and reached into the glove compartment as he sat down at Otto's side. He grabbed the black leather book, Volume 13, that Otto was always writing in, and started flipping through page after page, annoyed at having to find a blank page among all the full pages. The other 12 volumes had been stored safely in the boot of the car, each page filled with line after line of dates, numbers, receivables, borrowers, bribes, excuses, relationships – a coded who's who in the underworld and its ties to the local community as well. The Bible, as Otto referred to it, had information about everyone they had ever come into contact with.

Otto spent most of his time holed up in his tiny apartment at 113 West 125th Street, Room #13. There were no available apartments on 113th Street, a numerical obsession that guided Otto's spiritual side and, although a genius, Otto was prone to superstition when it came to the number 13. Perhaps his fondest memories of childhood had to do with the number 13 or the fact that 13 was a lucky number for Jews. Dutch knew the real reason, when it came to social cues and understanding people: Otto was a moron, and that's why he could never be the boss. Manipulation was how one became powerful, not number crunching.

Although a brilliant mind, Otto turned to a life of crime; he felt, however, that not every criminal associated with organized crime was interested in violence, and what he did was just business, as he was always heard saying, "Nothing personal, it's just business." He was a trained accountant, capable of solving very complex mathematical equations within seconds. He developed a system of betting that no one had been able to figure out and had made Dutch extremely wealthy. Otto Berman's mind worked like a machine of sorts, calculating new ways to shark the idiots, but he was very meticulous in documenting his codes and only 2 people knew the betting and information code, with only one written description, safeguarded in a vault in a very secretive place.

"Ah! Finally, a blank page." Dutch was not fond of the cryptic nature of his employee as it left him powerless and reliant upon Otto, but he was masterful in making him money, more so than just bootlegging, and, if need be, he would be able to set up all over again, once they got back to the vault.

He pulled out his pen from his wrinkled pinstripe jacket pocket. *A good pressed suit is what separates us from the rabble*, he thought, *and now look at me. Oh well, 13 million can buy a lot more suits.* Dutch smirked as he imagined Otto trying to calculate exactly how many.

Friday June 21, 1935, the longest day of the year, he wrote, and thought to himself, *and feels like the longest day of my life.* He continued to write, "I, Dutch Schultz, being of sound mind and body, bequeath all of my worldly possessions to my only daughter Rebecca Francis Cooper of Saratoga Springs New York, who does not know me, but I am a very aware of her." And then he directed his writing to Rebecca, "Although I did not know you and that makes me sad, your mother is the only one I will ever be and have ever been in love with. It was for your protection that we did not know each other. I hope this letter finds you and you will be able to live a life full of adventure and luxury.

The following items were mine and are now yours:
- A 1931 Lincoln [which Dutch immediately scratched out, recognizing that the car was now riddled with bullet holes, and with the money she would inherit she could afford to purchase any car she desired.]
- My home in Westchester
- All of my money, which includes 13 million dollars to be found in my car or somewhere nearby [not knowing what was in store, he thought best to give her some indication that he will try his best to hide it before anyone else can get to it.]
- More money to be found in the secret vault – the location of which I cannot divulge in this letter but I will leave you with one clue: Follow the Books.

He tried to rip out the page, but then thought it best just to leave it in the book after all, gazing momentarily at his Mont Blanc pen then tucked it away in his breast pocket, and patted it as though it was a trusty revolver. He remembered fondly the customer who had 'given' him the extravagant writing instrument, Mr. Lewandowski, who was always a good customer, paid on time, never won a damn lottery, drank what seemed like a case a week, and just couldn't stay away from the ponies, and that was his downfall. Week after week, more and more money on credit, and the pen was a real beauty; wood carved with just a hint of ivory at the top to give it that special Mont Blanc snowpeak design - it was truly worth it, but Dutch just about had to take the man's shorts to get all of his money back, along with the usual interest.

Drained and exhausted, trying to push his weariness away, a hum started to overtake his sense of hearing, as though a hummingbird's wings were fluttering in his ear. He slowly guided his body across the front seat, no longer caring about his already rumpled suit.

His sleep had been disturbed, his dreams dragging him back to the day's events, numbers interspersed in his visions. *What did they mean? Why so many numbers? Where am I? Is this heaven?*

A loud knock shook them both to the core, and suddenly all synapses fired at once, their hearts pumping erratically, causing them to bolt upright in unison, and practically knock the rifle to the floor.

"Wake up, Messieurs," Gerard said cooly as he attempted to get their attention by banging on the hood of the car. He didn't want to get too close to them in case they had a gun or a knife, and instinctively felt he would be on the losing end of this go-around. His encounter with them the previous night led him to believe they would be like wild dogs being woken by a cat. He spoke quickly, "I just heard from Monsieur Rottman. He told me..."

"What time is it?" Dutch interrupted, shouting out the window.

"It is 6:30 Monsieur Dutch," Gerard replied in his

heavy French Canadian accent.

Both Dutch and Otto got out of the car at the same time - each from their respective passenger side - Dutch still holding the rifle, but loosely now, as he realized he did not do a good job on watch, and forgot to alert Otto to take his turn. Suppressing a smile, he mentally acknowledged that, for the time being (you could never assume things wouldn't go haywire) he was among friends. Standing now, he tried to stretch his body as unassumingly as possible; the previous day's excursion and the deep, but cramped sleep on the front seat had taken their toll on Dutch's body and he could feel the strain on his back and neck. He went over to stand above Gerard while Louis remained stationed next to the garage door at the back of their car.

"What did he tell you?" Dutch asked summarily.

"'Ee wants you to go to a safe house until the heat settles down; the fuzz are everywhere looking for you. They know you crossed the border last night, the gendarme went to see the boys at the border and they sang like canaries. I am sure The Rock will have something to say to them – but my guess is that they took their families as far away as they can go, maybe Newfoundland or Vancouver." As Gerard said this, his facial features intimated that nowhere would be far enough to escape The Rock's reach – or his wrath - but Dutch thought, nonetheless, that running as far as possible was exactly what he would do if The Rock was looking for him.

"I 'ave for you some coffee," Gerard offered, holding up 2 cups to Dutch, who turned and passed Otto both the rifle and a cup of coffee, then took the second cup for himself. "I'm afraid it is black, we do not 'ave sugar or milk, and the baguette..," but Gerard was

47

interrupted once again by Dutch.

"Oh...that *really* hits the spot." They both drank their coffee heartily and quickly, forgetting about the baguette, and then both slid back into the car. Dutch sat behind the wheel and started the engine, thinking to himself with relief that at least no bullets had hit the engine. The baguette bounced around on the hood as the engine roared to life and Dutch yelled out the window, "Gerard could you hand me the bread? And where is this joint?"

"'Ee wants you to go to his house in the Laurentian Mountains, so you must go through the city. You will take boulevard Saint Laurent about two miles back in the other direction from the bridge you crossed, follow the riverfront, then turn left onto this road, and continue all the way down across the city about 16 miles to the north end bridge - it is called Pont Lachapelle. You will 'ave to go along the Fleuve Saint Laurent, excuse me, Saint Lawrence River West by turning left from boulevard Saint Laurent along the north shore for approximately 6 miles to the bridge, then turn right and take the bridge." Otto was listening very carefully as his brain was a sponge for information; Dutch knew this and did not say anything or ask any questions. Gerard continued, "Once at the bridge go over Ile Jésus, and continue on this same road – it is Route 117, for 80 miles to a village called Lac Mercier. You will see a wooden sign with white lettering on the side of the road about 1 mile before the exit; it says Village Lac Mercier. Take this turn until you hit the lake. It is, I would say...aaah...about 10 miles - you can't miss it. Follow around the lake going right for another 5 miles. There is a large log home with a gated entrance on your left, and there are no other homes within a mile of this place. We have people up there - you tell them, you were sent by The Rock.

Otto's mind, still taking notes, was already ahead of Gerard, and he didn't wait for Dutch and asked, "What then?"

"La Roche," Gerard continued, then corrected himself as that was the name the French workers often used to refer to their boss ,"I mean The Rock will think of something. This is the safest thing for you to do now." Gerard said this with absolute certainty.

"You will need gas," Gerard observed, "Come around the back of the warehouse with the car, we have a pump there. And I will you give you another 10 gallons in 2 cans just in case you run out. This will get you to the lodge."

"Will we need a code? Otto asked, thinking ahead. Otto's mind was always conjuring up figures and puzzles for the next caper.

"You can just tell them La Roche nous a envoyé – it means The Rock sent us. They don't speak any English up there even though most of the big homes are owned by the wealthy English of Montreal. Gerard secretly hated anything to do with the English.

Otto imitated Gerard's mouth and facial movements, as he realized that talking in French meant your mouth did not fully open with each syllable; it was more like scowling, as though you had just tasted a lemon, causing your facial muscles to distort and retreat to your ears. Otto got it.

Louis opened the garage doors, and Dutch backed the Lincoln out of the warehouse, as he saw the sun for the first time in what felt like a lifetime, it made him realize the urgency of their escape; he imagined that if he was caught, it would be straight to jail for him, in solitary, and that could never happen. He knew madness would overpower his thoughts and he would feel compelled to kill himself. He thought idealistically, "If I'm going down, it's with guns blazing, wearing a face-splitting grin. Otto looked at him, puzzled, but decided it wasn't worth asking.

With the Lincoln fully fueled, Otto found it hard to concentrate with the two reserve gas cans in the back seat. He could feel the fumes wafting in front of his nose, and every time he took a breath his stomach began to revolt. He finally had no choice, and leaned out of the side of the car just in time, as his stomach projected its limited contents onto Saint Lawrence Street. He caught random glimpses of the merchants setting up their shops, opening the gates in front of their windows, storekeepers hauling their wares onto the cobblestone streets, in an attempt to entice passersby to buy that one last item they didn't really need. But this was a post-depression economy and everyone knew nothing would come easy.

A little boy selling newspapers for the Montreal Gazette hollered above the hum of activity on the road, "EXTRA! EXTRA! READ ALL ABOUT IT! Dutch Shultz Escapes Police – Headed for Montreal." The pedestrians on their way to work, normally in a mad rush, stopped and flocked to the newsie like pigeons around a handful of seeds thrown to the ground. People flicked open their newspapers to the see what had happened, and were thoroughly involved in the story.

Otto overheard one reader say, "He's in a Lincoln like that one," and on cue dozens of people looked toward their car to see Otto, his head wagging out of the window as he gasped for air.

Then another observed, "Hey! Doesn't that look like..."

"Wait a minute!" another man was heard saying. "It IS him," as he looked back at the paper, then back again at Otto.

And then another called out, "Je pense que c'est Doutch."

"Yeah! It's him. There's the guy travelling with him; see, it's right here," he said, as he pointed excitedly at the picture in the paper.

The door of Saint Laurent Bagel opened and out stepped a tall, lanky man who could easily see over a crowd. He was an actor with the Saint Lawrence Players, and had stopped in to grab a quick sesame seed bagel, which was now halfway inserted into his mouth, above which sat a large Roman nose on his overly-tanned face, and a head topped with wavy light brown hair. He heard the crowd beginning to rumble about seeing Dutch. He immediately added his two cents to no one in particular, "Maybe we should alert the cops."

Then he saw it - a constable's hat above all the working men's various hats - on the corner of Marie-Anne Street and Saint Lawrence, about 1 block south of where he was. An orator by profession, he called out to the constable, "Officer! Officer! Officer!" But to no avail. He was a good actor, but even he could not project his voice over the roar of the city noises.

He ran down the street in the direction of the constable, determined to catch up to him, and dropped his precious bagel. He stopped momentarily, debating whether to retrieve it, as it was always the highlight of his day, but decided that the sighting of a criminal mastermind was of greater importance.

He apologized profusely as he shoved people aside, "Sorry. Sorry. Excuse me, Madame," and finally, stepping off the curb and stumbling away from the congestion, the tall man found his footing and his voice. Once again he started to yell, "Officer! Officer!" With all his bravado, and in a majestic voice which easily reached the back of the theatre during performances, he managed to attract the officer's attention, who turned immediately to determine what required such urgent attention, and spotted the tall man running down the road toward him like a man possessed.

The officer took an almost patronizing approach, "Just a minute there son, what's the rush?"

Although trained to breathe just right when performing, the tall man could not catch his breath now. All he could manage was, "Dutch..." in a puff of effort. More breaths between words, and then, "Dutch Schultz."

"Yes, yes, what is it?" The constable reached out his hand and placed it on the man's back, as he was bent over trying to catch his breath. "Dutch what?" the constable asked curtly.

And then in one complete, mustered-up breath, "We think we saw Dutch's car go down Saint Lawrence just after St. Viateur." It was a relief to get it out.

"That's nonsense," replied the constable, now condescending to the tall man.

"No sir! Ask those people down there," the tall man responded, pointing up the street to where a crowd assembled on the corner 1 block up."

"Ok. Let's go talk to them and I will call it in." The constable decided rather unfortunately that the seemingly impossible was, in all likelihood, not possible.

As they walked up the street together, the constable tipped his hat to the ladies as they passed him. The constable was clearly in no rush, and justified his nonchalance with the assumption that people always see what they want to see, especially when sensational stories like Dutch Schultz' escape have them riled up. He could still remember the townfolks' crazy behavior when the Lindbergh baby disappeared; He was assailed constantly by people claiming to have seen the baby, or who and where the kidnappers were hiding out. As they strolled up toward the crowd, their movement and energy was undeniably that of a single organism. A loud, excited mob, intent on conveying their message, shouted one after the other.

"Constable! Constable! Officer!" they shouted individually and in unison.

"Yes, yes - what is it?" he asked with a tone somewhat akin to annoyance. Then he turned and pointed with authority toward the actor, and in a sarcastic tone he questioned the crowd, "This man thinks he saw Dutch Schultz... Did anyone else see him?" he asked with undue ridicule as he peered skeptically at the faces in the crowd. They all nodded in agreement, much to the constable's surprise.

"I saw him," shouted a business man on his way to his accounting firm.

"Well, we saw his car," said an older man with a scruffy beard and weathered face. By the looks of his clothes and the apron he wore that was rife with oil stains, and the logo on his shirt, he was a laborer for an oil distribution company.

"There was a man with his head sticking out the window, and he threw-up right in front of us," piped in another.

"He looked like this man," said the oilman, pointing to the picture in the paper.

"I saw it."

"Me too!"

"So did I - it was Dutch. For sure it was Dutch. I saw bullet holes in the car. There were two men riding up front," this from another in the crowd.

The reality of the situation was finally starting to overtake the constable's reason, so he started to question the crowd, "Ok, rather than all of you shouting out at once, by a showing of hands, who saw this man?" he asked and, taking the paper from the oilman, tapped his index finger against the photo. Without having to count, he finally conceded that a sighting had very possibly taken place right here. He continued his questioning, "Who saw the man really well?" An attractive woman stepped forward. She was wearing a form-fitting floral print summer dress, beneath which one could tell she was not wearing a bra, and clearly all the men were more interested in her, as their thoughts drifted away from Dutch and instinctively to her. With every step she took toward the constable all he could think was that this woman could stop traffic anywhere. He was happy for this, and with a confident gate also came a confident description, in full detail, of what had transpired the past few minutes.

"I can tell you for certain THAT was the man from the picture." She was adamant. The constable, taking a pencil and pad from the side pocket of his uniform, licked the pencil to get it more moist, even though it did not require it, and asked the woman, "Which way was he headed? And could you tell me anything more about the car?" He wanted to stay in the company of this woman as long as he could, but grappled with the thought that he had better get to a phone fast and call down to 1 Police Headquarters immediately.

What the constable knew for now was that Dutch Schultz was headed west down St. Viateur, off of Saint Lawrence, in the same car as described by the newspapers and on the radio, a black Lincoln, and it looked pretty dirty, and was apparently riddled with bullet holes.

After celebrating with Louis over a cup of coffee and his favorite croissant from Boulangerie Fairmont - Gerard even loved the smell of the butter on the roll - he started to gather his things in the nest, when the phone rang. "Merde!" he swore in his constant colloquial French. He answered the phone. "Oui," he spoke into the receiver as he picked it up, the word sounded like 'why'. "Oui, Monsieur Rottman. Oh, non - dans les journaux, merde! Oh, excusez moi." Gerard was dismayed to hear that Dutch's escapade had made it into the newspapers. A silence washed over the room as Gerard listened and nodded. The Rock must have been giving Gerard instructions, Louis thought, as he overheard only Gerard's very limited side of the conversation. Gerard finally answered into the receiver, "Oui. Ok," he agreed, his head cocked against the phone while staring at the floor. He hung up the receiver, snapped his head up and spun around to Louis.

Both his French and Louis' were so accented in their respective dialects it was almost impossible to understand the words they were saying to one another, but Gerard's facial expression said it all. "Louis," Gerard said in a rush, "Let's go – the fuzz know that Dutch is in Montreal. La Roche wants us at the Lachapelle Bridge to make sure Dutch gets over the island safely. We have to wait all day and check in at sundown even if we don't see him, and if we do to call right away."

"Dutch, the word is out. I heard some kid yelling it on the street. "We have to get out of here." Otto was overwhelmed, and was getting increasingly agitated as every moment slipped by.

"I heard," Dutch answered, all business now. "Get your hands around that gun again. We know the route, so let's find somewhere to hide until the heat cools down." Dutch and Otto slipped through the side streets of Outremont, awed by the wealth and majesty of some of the buildings, extravagantly enveloped by perfect gardens, tended to by professional groundskeepers. They marveled at the meticulously sculpted cedars, the overgrown, fragrant lilac trees, and the exotic spray of wild flowers painting the neighbourhood's expansive lawns. Clearly this must be where The Rock lives, they thought to themselves. They couldn't imagine any place more resplendent or expensive, and Otto couldn't help but muse, "This sure beats the big apartment buildings lining the sky in Manhattan - I definitely prefer this...". Dutch, on the other hand, didn't care about things like that - money and survival were his raison d'être, and right at that moment he was more concerned that there was a trap closing in on them. As they made their way further down the mountain and onto McEachran Street heading north, they came upon a road that doubled as a tramway line, swarmed with people queued up waiting to be transported to their places of work.

Otto remembered his instructions well, "Take this road Dutch." Dutch turned left onto Van Horne Avenue, a major artery traversing the west end of the island. They drove along Van Horne for another 4 miles, passing through less and less congested areas. Now most of the homes were townhouses, attached or two homes semi-detached with less manicured gardens, more commercial establishments, shops, and food markets. They thought to themselves that this must be where the workers lived. As they passed a street called Decarie Boulevard, Otto recalled that Gerard had mentioned this was a major throughway north to south. There was nothing else for another mile or so until they suddenly came to an impressively ornate sign that announced:

Hampstead Golf Club, est. 1922 Members Only

Otto was stunned, "For god's sake, what lunatic planned this? This city already has two mountains smack in the middle of it, forcing all the roads to wind around. Then there are enclaves of homes that radiate around a circle. And now a golf course in the middle of it all!?" Otto was puzzled by the city's abstract design, yet impressed with its overall beauty, the lack of slums and the charm of hearing different languages spoken throughout the city.

Inasmuch as he appreciated what he saw, Otto was still intent on getting out of the city intact, and addressed Dutch, "We have to get to that bridge; we've travelled far enough west Dutch, we have to head north now. I think I saw another artery 1 mile back, so let's go there."

Dutch pulled the car as far onto the side of the road as possible, admiring the golfers as he did so. They were lined up just behind the clubhouse taking their practice swings, with nothing but leisure time on their hands. *I don't have that luxury right now,* he thought ruefully to himself. As he turned the wheel to reorient the car onto Van Horne, the tires slipped on the gravel road until he righted the car, and he drove until he reached Decarie Boulevard. The sirens were unmistakable.

Dutch was clear about what had to be done, "I hear sirens everywhere. We're going back to the golf course - they would never think to find us there. The parking area looks like it's well enough concealed that curious golfers probably wouldn't realize we were hiding in the car."

Lost Lake

"Mom, I'm heading outside." Jippsy couldn't wait to get on the move.

His mother had other plans, "Are your chores done, Jippsy?"

"Yes, mom," Jippsy answered with all the peevishness of a teenager. Jippsy thought back to the morning and how he couldn't sleep; he was up at 5:30 – the crows roosting in the trees surrounding his house were so noisy - all morning nothing but "Caw! Caw! Caw!" those insufferable crows talking to each other, fighting, or reveling over a deer carcass, leftovers from a wolf pack's take-down.

Jippsy normally started his chores by 6:30, feeding the chickens in the coop, and then milking the cows before letting them out to graze in the field. He gave the pigs their slop, and then his final chore was to open the valve for the irrigation system to make sure their crops were well maintained. Jippsy's dad was so proud of him, since the irrigation system was his idea after all. Jippsy secretly enjoyed seeing that everything was in tip-top shape. But the best part of his day was breakfast – his mom made his favorites...eggs sunny side up, toast, and bacon-bacon-bacon-bacon. Jippsy loved bacon!

Jippsy opened the porch door, which was rarely closed, allowing more air to circulate through the house, and sauntered onto the wrap-around porch, every footstep resounding with a creak of the floorboards, his stomach percolating as it always did when he ate bacon. He could tell that the sun was going to be strong that day, and he could already feel the humidity seeping in. For

Jippsy this was the best weather to go swimming down at Lost Lake.

Jippsy called out to his baby sister, "Dodo! Let's go. Everyone will be waiting already down by the creek." Jippsy hated waiting, and would have been there already if his mother hadn't insisted he take her along. "Dodo, are you coming or not?" Jippsy kicked the air at nothing in particular, almost like a nervous tic, just to let out his frustrations, and felt his worn-out leather shoe slip off his foot. He stared at his feet, and muttered to himself, "Damn! Dad's old shoes are so big on me, but at least they're better than my last pair; you could see all of my toes, and there was no way mom could fix those." He took a deep breath to try and stifle his impatience, raised his hands in the air as if to stretch to the sky, and then made his way down the stairs onto the dirt road that led away from the house. Jippsy yelled back toward the house, "Dodo, that's it! I'm leaving."

Right on cue, the porch door swung open and out walked his sister, "I'm here! Don't get your knickers in a wad." Their mom said that all the time, but it was funny hearing it come from Dodo. Dodo was always wearing the latest fashion, even if she was just going down to the lake; her white summer dress with orange butterflies no longer fit her loosely, the scalloped lace collar would no longer close up with the buttons, resulting in a V-neck opening, exposing part of her chest. She had a similar shape to her mom but not as filled out. Her legs were long and well-tanned, and evident since her dress could no longer hide them sufficiently. Although Jippsy and Dodo were only 11 months apart, his baby sister's maturity was starting to show, and it was obvious that they were not kids anymore. Dodo had just turned 13, and she had started to lose interest in finding buried treasure, travelling to prehistoric times through the jungle, or just plain hunting for rabbits; now it was all about boys...who was strong, smart or cute? Jippsy thought to himself, *Yucch! My sister is interested in boys. I can protect her from the forest, although she's just as capable, but boys are going to be a problem - I know.*

"Hey Dodo, did you hear about that Dutch Schultz gangster last night?" Jippsy thought she might still be interested in some real-life drama,

"No. Who's that?"

"Dutch Schultz is only one of THE most scary gangsters around, and they think he's headed for Montreal. Well, we'll never know what happens to him...he is still very far away, I guess."

"Let's meet up with Frankie," Dodo said casually, but with a hopeful smile. Jippsy didn't catch on. "Jippsy, is dad coming back tonight?"

"I think so. At least I hope he does."

Dodo was concerned, "Do you think he did well this year?"

"I'm sure he did, and if not he always has the cherry brandy he sells in winter." Jippsy was worried too, just a little, but he had faith in his dad, and also, he didn't want Dodo to worry.

Jippsy knew his dad would prefer to ponder over his kegs of cherry wine that lined the walls of the warehouse where he spent most of his leisure time, rather than play catch with Jippsy or listen to the radio. He really loved his brandy-making business, but complained about his customers. "Not the nicest sort," he would say, in his Italian-accented English.

As they walked down the dirt road away from the gate of the big house, the signature red-painted barn stood out like an ink splotch. Just beyond the big house, and a short walk from the road, the fields extended back as far as one could see. The family owned 3197 hectares, and dad would often find cause to remind anyone who would listen that he had earned every one of those three-thousand-one-hundred-and-ninety-seven hectares. Otherwise, no one would remember how big the land truly was. Jippsy fully appreciated their property, and he never ceased to be awed by its expanse. He habitually took a mental inventory of the land, in its seasonal states, and on this clear day he took in his dad's pride and joy, the cherry orchard. It spread out just behind the house; the white blooms had erupted in the month of May, and its simplistic beauty overshadowed the showier nature of any other blossoms. Thanks to Mother Nature, the harvest had come and gone successfully, having picked 100 pounds of cherries per tree. Jippsy's dad had to make 4 trips to carry it all to the city; he should have been finished selling it all by now. Jippsy thought how the cherry harvest was the best part of the year, ready by mid-June, leaving them to concentrate on the vegetable harvest in July, and finally the apples in late summer. Jippsy was impressed by his dad's vision and efficient use of their land; he felt it would occupy and sustain his dad, and his family, for years to come...and then it will be up to him. Jippsy longed to help his dad, but he worked so hard, and Jippsy wasn't convinced that he wanted to be a farmer. He imagined being a detective like one of Dashiell Hammet's hard-boiled characters, or he could become an inventor like Thomas Edison or maybe fly airplanes for the RCAF. But a farmer? Maybe he could be successful, but would he love it? He hoped that maybe Dodo would want to be the family farmer, but Jippsy was more of a realist than a dreamer, and he thought, *Sure, as soon as pigs fly!* Unfortunately, he thought that out loud...

Dodo immediately questioned him, "What did you say?" Pigs fly? That's applesauce." Indeed, pigs flying was nonsense in every way...

"Oh...I was just mumbling to myself; I was wondering what it would take to make pigs fly." Jippsy was flustered.

"One day that overactive brain of yours is going to lose its marbles, or it's going to get you into trouble, probably double trouble." Dodo loved teasing her big brother, but she knew how smart he really was, and loved him all the more for it. "I'll race you to the creek Jippsy!" Dodo knew she couldn't beat him but would laugh, seeing him get so intense about a challenge.

The creek was only a mile down the road, but you had to go uphill just before descending the final 100 yards to reach the shores of the creek. The creek snaked around the base of the hill for another 2 miles, finally turning into a cluster of small rapids which dumped into Lost Lake; it was the only source of water that fed the next-to-stagnant lake. Lost Lake was surrounded by high brush, bull rushes and towering pine trees, which essentially had the effect of concealing the lake from view but for the fact that the occasional fallen tree proffered a funnel of light which magically brought Lost Lake into view.

It was the highlight of their year, when the kids could finally go swimming in the lake. And Jippsy was wasting no time. "C'mon Dodo! You're not even trying..." Jippsy would push her to her limits.

Sure I am," Dodo yelled ahead, giggling to herself. Jippsy was sooo easy for her to tease, and Dodo knew that sometime in the very near future the girls were going to drive him crazy. "It's too long to run all the way," Dodo continued, as she meandered down the road at such a casual pace - it was making Jippsy anxious. "Jippsy, I can't wait to go swimming either - is everyone coming?" Dodo was most interested in one swimmer in particular.

Jippsy was exasperated now, "How do I know?! Geez Dodo...probably Butterball, Frankie, Capri, and I'm sure Vicky will show up too..." Jippsy said, rolling his eyes at the thought of Vicky tagging along. She really did try so hard to keep up that he felt bad for not wanting her to come along. Oh well, BB, short for butterball, always insisted on getting her to come with them, so Jippsy just accepted it.

Dodo was excited at the prospect of seeing Frankie. She stretched her body skyward, waving her arms in the air. She looked as though she were attempting to capture the few clouds that drifted lazily along the dazzling blue sky. She yawned loudly, the sound emanating from her body, comically resembling the mating call of the moose that inhabited the surrounding forest. Jippsy watched as, with a final melodramatic swing of her body, Dodo seemed to relish some secret thought, a mischievous smile playing on her lips. Jippsy could always tell by Dodo's body language that she was hiding something – especially where Frankie was concerned. He teased her mercilessly, "Dodo, are you calling out to the other moose looking for a mate?" As if on cue, there appeared, in all its majestic glory, a moose, right in the middle of the road...

"Dodo, stop that!" Jippsy cautioned in an authoritative yet calm voice. "We can't make any sudden movements - their antlers can tear us to shreds and we won't be able to outrun it. It seems to be more interested in the creek right now, but if it thinks we are a threat, or if it's the female there's probably a calf around somewhere and it will be very protective of its area. So keep quiet now."

But Dodo simply couldn't contain herself, or just refused to heed Jippsy's entreaty, as another loud yawn left her body. This time, Jippsy was furious, "Great, Dodo!! Now it sees us. You sound like a grizzly, and moose are food for grizzlies." They both watched in shock as the massive moose started kicking forward with its front feet. Jippsy wasted no time, "We have to get up a tree, Dodo, we can't outrun it." Jippsy grabbed Dodo forcefully by the arm, practically tearing the skin from her forearm, and they took off in a run alongside the road until Jippsy spotted a birch they could both climb. Mere seconds later and the moose started its pursuit.

Jippsy was all too aware that if the moose caught up to them they would be stomped by its galloping feet, or speared by its enormous antlers, but, either way, immense pain and suffering would be involved and Jippsy would have no part of it. He let go of Dodo's arm, and clasped his hands together to make a rung for her to climb, as he encouraged her, "Quick Dodo, step up!" Jippsy leveraged his body against the trunk of the tree as support. "Take a running start and I'll hoist you as far as I can..." Dodo could only run a few steps, as they didn't have the luxury of time, and managed to launch herself up to the nearest branch with considerably little effort. She grabbed the branch, wrapping her elbows tightly around the rough bark and awkwardly swung her left leg over the foot-thick branch as she pulled her body over and into a sitting position with all the power in her arms. As she did so, Jippsy took as much of a run as possible, and propelled himself toward and up the tree, jumping as high as he could. He managed to grab hold of the same branch as Dodo and then attempted to haul himself up and over as she had done, while Dodo continued climbing upward.

Suspended in the tree, and in shock, with the moose mere yards away, Jippsy started to swing his body in an effort to get his arms wrapped around the branch. He realized that he lacked the strength and the momentum to get his body up and that Dodo had already climbed too high to come back down and help him. Gravity ultimately won out, as he lost his hold on the branch and fell to the ground, landing on his side under the tree. He started to roll down the embankment toward the creek, and yet his pressing thoughts were of Dodo. "Hold on Dodo!" he yelled as loudly as possible. Now all his senses were heightened; he could smell the freshness of the moss and grass, feel the twigs and rocks as he tumbled over them, saw the sunlight cascade intermittently through the dense forest, but mostly he could hear the heavy breath coming from the moose, as it drew in ragged breaths and prepared to charge the tree in which Dodo was sheltered.

The tree was easily over 100 years old, and had certainly never borne a shock as it did at that moment, as the moose charged and rammed at incredible speed straight into the body of the tree. This old tree had withstood lighting strikes which tore off limbs, 100-mile-an-hour winds which attempted to uproot it, and earthquakes which shook it from its roots to its uppermost branches, but the moose, in a single blow, had managed to carve a gash into the trunk which spanned an impressive 18 inches in height and 6 inches in depth.

Dodo held onto the branch with all her might, and with every new attempt by the moose to dislodge her, she began to resemble, more and more, a rodeo rider on a bucking bull. The tree shook violently back and forth, swaying under the incredible power of the moose's thrusts. She was determined to hold on – for dear life – because they would both make it through. The moose finally started to stagger, almost tripping backward on its long legs, suddenly realizing that it no longer needed to charge the tree, as another forest enemy lay sprawled on the ground at the bottom of the hill. The moose spied Jippsy through the trees, near the creek.

Dodo could see the sweat on its back, foam clinging repulsively to the sides of its face, anger the only emotion she could discern. It sprung forward without delay, the sounds of the undergrowth crunching with a sickening sound beneath its hooves, as it crushed dead branches and any other living thing in its path. Dodo watched in horror, unable to find her voice, as the giant beast tore through the trees, bellowing madly, its legs a blur, antlers lowered, snapping branches and trees that came between the moose and his target. Dodo knew that Jippsy could not escape what was about to happen, as there was nowhere for him to turn, no tree to climb, no shelter from this looming danger. The moose was fully in charge mode, its massive head as near to the ground as possible, ready to strike, bowl over his enemy and summarily stomp its prey to death. As though suddenly aware of his impending fate, Jippsy found the narrow window of opportunity still available to him, and managed to spring, rather impressively, to the side, and then rolled into the creek, just out of reach of the moose's 6-foot antler spread.

The moose's anger and frustration was evident, as its crazed shrieks pierced the otherwise calm of the forest. Its antlers reeled backwards violently, and Jippsy tensed as he watched the moose's head swing from side to side as though attempting to shake off a swarm of pests. Jippsy, convinced the moose was about to attack again, braced himself, as he was completely out of options. But the crazed moose continued to shake its massive antlers, and Jippsy could now see the source of its distress: rocks were bouncing from the moose's face and head. He scanned the trees and the embankment, finally catching sight of Frankie, clutching his slingshot, much to his relief.

Frankie quickly tucked another rock into his slingshot and took aim; he breathed in deeply holding that breath a moment, then sent the rock flying in a beautiful arcing trajectory, hitting his target squarely between the beast's raging eyes. As he bent to retrieve another rock, Frankie yelled a warning, "Get out of there Jippsy!" Jippsy wasted no time before taking off in a run, inasmuch as one can run while stuck in a creek. He could feel the water sloshing in his shoes as his hands played across the surface of the cool running water, his eyes scouring for just the right place to bend and retrieve a handful of weighty rocks to launch at the moose, and to keep up with Frankie's slingshot. He raced back up the embankment to Frankie's side, his chest on fire from the exertion and adrenaline coursing through his system. Almost as one, they both took aim, Frankie stretching the elastic to its limit, his right eye closed to better sight his target, his arm shaking from the force. Another deep breath, a moment's pause, and they both let loose their respective projectiles. Frankie managed to hit the beast on the neck, wasting no time to grab another rock from the pouch resting over his left hip, as he cheered himself, "Got 'im again!" Frankie's exultation over his strike was short-lived as Jippsy's pitch sailed right between the moose's antlers and directly into the beast's eye, causing it to flee in a sudden burst of panic and indignant resignation.

They jumped up and down, their fists pumping in the air, Frankie holding his slingshot skyward for the gods in the heavens to anoint him king. Jippsy was overwhelmed with relief – and gratitude, "Thanks, Frank, I owe you."

Frankie's chest was pumped up and beating hard, proud of himself, "Nothing you wouldn't have done for me Jips old boy. That was one screwy bull. It was pretty nifty though."

Jippsy couldn't help but laugh now, the adrenaline easing only slightly, the panic of the experience starting to ease, "You bet your ass," and, calling out to the skies, "Dodo, you ok?"

"Where's Dodo?" Frank inquired excitedly.

"She's in the tree," Jippsy told him nonchalantly.

"What do you mean, she's in the tree?" Frankie asked incredulously. Frankie looked inquiringly through and up to the tops of the trees; a slight breeze rustled the leaves, momentarily obscuring his view, until his eyes finally came to rest upon the tell-tale streaks of white that glinted through the moon-shaped leaves of the white birch. "Is that her?" Frankie asked aloud, doubting what he perceived. Frankie looked to Jippsy for corroboration, but Dodo's scared yet smiling face gazed down from her perch, her focus entirely absorbed by her hero, Frankie. She was beaming now, as her stress and fear dissipated. She started to make her way down, branch-by-branch, while Frankie jumped over the creek to get back to the road.

Jippsy followed Frankie's lead - although thrilled with their victory, he was still drained from the rush of adrenaline and almost fell back into the creek. He climbed the embankment on all fours, toward where Frankie had run, eager to help Dodo. Frankie hoped Jippsy wouldn't reach them quickly, as he did his best to covertly ogle Dodo's long golden legs as she made her way down the tree. Her dress hitched up every so often, affording Frankie a slightly more rewarding view, and although his motives were (mostly) honorable, even he knew the road to hell was paved with good intentions. Lost in thought and desire, Frankie forgot his purpose in standing beneath the birch, but the sound of Dodo's voice released him from his reverie, "Aren't you going to help a lady down?" she asked in her most playful voice.

As she lowered herself from the last branch, she jumped in such a way that Frankie had no choice but to catch her around her small waist. Frankie was keenly aware of her hourglass figure; he relished the position he was now in, and he lowered her to the ground as slowly as humanly possible in order to set this moment to memory. He seemed to have no control of what his body or brain was doing, and he heard himself say aloud, "I gotcha. Here you go."

Too fast for me, Dodo thought to herself disappointedly. He could have let go of her but left his hands to linger around her waist momentarily, as he resisted the urge to smother her with his arms and lips.

What's wrong with me? He wondered to himself in a daze. She was looking up at him, her emerald eyes gleaming, both inviting and coy at once, and in that instant he felt a wave of electricity surge through his blood. All he wanted to do was kiss her on her soft pouty lips and run his hands through her golden hair. He abruptly let her go as though touching her had burned his fingers, but his hand brushed against the silky flesh of her arm, and he was lost. He laughed nervously, and backed away, his eyes locked on hers, her eyes entranced by his. Frankie knew someone else might have witnessed what had just happened, and while he was confident now that she understood what they felt, he questioned whether anyone else would.

"Thanks again, Frankie," he heard Jippsy say as he finally reached the road from the embankment, still on all fours. Frankie turned guiltily, and looked down to meet Jippsy's eyes. He extended his right arm, his slingshot tucked tightly into his back pocket, and Jippsy reached out to take hold of Frankie's hand. "Up you go," Frankie encouraged, as he hauled Jippsy to his feet to face him. Jippsy grunted as he was pulled up, and Frankie couldn't help but get his licks in, "You guys sure know how to start an adventure!" Frankie chuckled nervously – he just couldn't help but feel guilty.

Jippsy, having settled somewhat, realized someone was missing. "Where's Caprice?" he asked curiously.

"She's coming, but still way behind... I heard all kinds of commotion, and it's usually pretty peaceful in the morning. I came running along the creek when I heard the noise. The rest you know. It's fate, eh?" Frankie grinned sheepishly.

"You and your screwy beliefs, Frankie!" Now that Jippsy was feeling more like himself, he was back to the usual bantering that went on between them.

"It's fate, I tell you. I was *meant* to save you two," Frankie insisted.

My hero..., Dodo thought to herself distractedly. *He's so handsome,* was all her brain would process as she just stood there, utterly transfixed by Frankie's presence, hanging on his every word, watching the movement of his lips, enjoying his cockiness and the effect on her body when she heard his voice. All she could do was smile brilliantly, trapped in her statue-like pose, as though Medusa had turned her to stone, which perhaps she had become, because no matter how Jippsy tried, Dodo could not be broken from her trance.

"Dodo. DODO! Do you hear me, Dodo?" Jippsy couldn't get through. And yet her eyes were alive, Jippsy could see, as he realized that she was hungrily taking in every detail of...Frankie.

She felt flushed as she noticed how Frankie's undershirt clung to his stomach, accentuating his muscles, so much like a washboard, how his dungarees, cut-off at the middle of his strong thighs, exposed his shiny copper skin. His shoulders and arms were strong and confident like a farmer boy's should be, and he hated wearing shoes, so it was not unusual to see him without them, as he was at this time. To Dodo, his face had been sculpted by Michelangelo himself, his dark wavy hair woven by silkworms, and his eyes more deep and inviting than the turquoise oceans she had seen in magazines. No museum, no art gallery, no magazine displayed a work of art more beautiful to Dodo than Frankie. She could feel herself melting, her thoughts blurring, as she descended into this catatonic state where the rest of the world slid from view, and yet her body stirred and her every sense was aflame, but just for him, as only a woman could understand.

Jippsy would tolerate no more of Dodo's nonsense, and walked over to stand beside her, shaking her shoulder as he called her name, "Dodo...Dodo...Dodo!"

"What?" she asked gently at first, and then again more harshly, "WHAT!" as she realized her reverie had been interrupted.

"Let's catch up to Caprice," Jippsy answered her, more disconcerted than ever. They all started walking, in no particular hurry, down the clearing that had been cut between the tall pines. No one spoke, and the silence was comfortable as Jippsy, Frankie and Dodo left one other to their own thoughts.

Was it forever or just minutes? Jippsy wondered to himself. He felt tired and somewhat confused, as though a lifetime had just passed and yet the entire event had unfolded within minutes. He couldn't wait to see Caprice – just thinking about her brought him back to himself – she always had a way of making him feel right. As much as he wanted to see Caprice, though, he knew a swim would help relieve the tension he felt creeping through his body; a swim would not only be refreshing, but would definitely rinse off the filth and dirt that now clung to him, along with the unfortunate stench of fear. He kept vacillating between OK and anxious. His mind was spinning again, *I almost died here. Shit...that was too close.*

I'm going to have to start carrying a weapon on these walks. As he made his way along the road, he scanned the roadside for something he could use to keep any kind of predator or enemy at bay. *What can I use?* He saw vines on the ground, and thought about the ropes they used for the horses. *Yeah, that could work. I could snap that from a distance and that would startle anything coming near. No, it would take me too much time to learn how to use it. I like Frankie's slingshot, it really did the trick. No, then we would always be competing to see who was a better shot, and Frankie would always win, and he would be impossible! Forget it. I'll just have to use my head to stay away from these stupid situations.*

But something in the trees caught his eye, and he abruptly jumped off the road and ran into the forest. Halfway between the road and the creek, he had spotted a branch, its bark chewed away by chipmunks. It was tan colored with creamy streaks throughout, and stood out like it was placed there on purpose. Like Excalibur, King Arthur's legendary sword, Jippsy imagined that whoever took possession of the mighty staff would forever be able to protect all who were within its presence. He second-guessed himself, thinking that it was simply too corny to carry around a glorified stick, but he simply had to have it.

He picked it up without hesitating and inspected it more closely. He noticed it was as wide around as a baseball bat, and, testing that theory, he swung the stick with all his strength, several times in succession, gauging its properties. The stick weighed about half that of a baseball bat, but had a solid feel in his hands. Where he gripped it, the stick was slightly thicker than an average baseball bat handle and it was rotted. He picked up a rock and scraped away a knot that protruded from the shaft of the stick. It wasn't soft inside, which was a good sign that it wouldn't disintegrate easily should Jippsy have to strike something. He held it in his right hand, and with a forceful backhand swung the stick so that it whistled through the air. *For sure*, Jippsy thought to himself, *This could be enough to inflict damage if I get into a bind. Problem solved.*

Jippsy had been lost in thought, and hadn't really been listening to what was going on around him. As far as he was concerned he had found the sword of the stone. But he suddenly picked up Dodo's voice, "My brother thinks he's a swashbuckling pirate." Well maybe that was just right...

Jippsy ran back toward Frankie and Dodo with his new weapon in hand.

"That's a nifty branch you got there, Jips," Frankie affirmed.

"Yeah, I think I'm gonna keep it, and see if I can bone it so it won't chip." Jippsy was excited that someone else recognized the quality of his new weapon.

Frankie, however, knew that Jippsy was trying to measure up even though he didn't think he had a chance. But Jippsy was his buddy and buddies have to stick together and help each other out.

"Jippsy!" The sound of his name resounded in the clearing, a sound both sweet and inviting. Even though he was still daydreaming about his weapon, hearing *her* call his name suddenly roused him from his thoughts in a most pleasant manner.

"Hi, Capri!" Jippsy couldn't mask the excitement he felt upon seeing her in person, as she walked down toward them from the top of an incline where the road turned sharply. Jippsy thought to himself that it was impossible to see what was coming down the road, and if you weren't familiar with its twists and turns in a car, well, wrong place at the wrong time and it would be 'goodbye Charlie'. Then the next thing you'd know you'd be hugging a tree.

"I thought I would meet up with you guys instead of waiting down at the lake." Capri was getting closer to the gang, closer to Jippsy.

"Hi, Capri." Dodo hadn't noticed yet how weird Jippsy was behaving now that Capri had arrived.

"Hi, Dodo." Capri was equally unaware of Jippsy's behavior.

As she reached the bottom of the hill, Capri quickly took in the ruffled appearance of her friends and brother. "Wow! What happened to you guys?" She could see Jippsy's shirt and short pants were caked in mud, his shoes soaking wet. "You could've just walked beside the creek instead of in it." Her sassy mouth got the best of her, despite the serious looks all around.

Jippsy opened his mouth to explain, when Frankie piped in. "I saved them," he boasted in that arrogant tone of his.

"What are you talking about Frankie?" Capri was so used to Frankie's truth stretching that she didn't hesitate to discount his tall-tale this time.

Frankie persisted, and this time it came out in a blur of words. "Dodo and Jippsy were attacked by a moose - you should have seen the rack on this one - it was about to spear Jippsy and trample him to death, but I pulled out my slingshot and fired one after the other until it bowed to me in surrender and ran off."

"That's amazing, Frankie," Capri answered, drawing out the word 'amazing' while she rolled her eyes in disbelief. Capri knew all too well that his mouth was usually ten times the size of his bravado, and that she would get the true story from Jippsy later on. It was always easier, and better for everyone around, to leave Frankie in good spirits instead of getting his goat, which she did often enough. Capri reached out and gingerly touched Jippsy's left arm, somewhat alarmed despite her reservations about Frankie's version of the morning's events, "Oh my god! Are you alright?" Jippsy and Capri were about the same height, and their eyes met easily; their mutual attraction was evident, to them at least, and in that moment they both wondered was it something they would act upon?

Jippsy couldn't stand the thought of being molly-coddled, especially by Capri, and in a reflex he nonchalantly swiped the hair away from his eyes and continued walking toward the creek.

Dodo certainly didn't mind Frankie telling Capri of his heroic deed, of how he protected her from the great beast. She imagined listening to him retell the story over the course of their ever-romantic lifetime together; it would be the epic story they would tell their grandchildren about his bravery and love. Suddenly aware of how swept-up she had become, she chastised herself, *Oh my god Dodo, get a hold of yourself!*

Jippsy couldn't wait any longer; he decisively stabbed his staff into the ground and started walking toward the creek at a steady pace. "Let's go to the lake and see if Butterball is there yet - I have to get into the water." Everyone fell into line with Jippsy's plan and started to follow him without hesitation.

They made their way quickly, up the hill and over the bend, until they came upon it. Jippsy needed no more incentive than having glimpsed the edge of the lake. Maybe it was the day, the encounter with the moose, his proximity to Capri, but he made a bee-line through the forest with only one thought in his mind, *This time I have to conquer it!* He was a boy on a mission.

Her sweet voice couldn't carry through the trees, as she called out in a panic, "Jippsy don't!" It was Capri's voice, which was lost in the woods, lost to Jippsy. Frankie and Dodo strolled together as though no one else existed, catching only faint hints of the others' silliness.

"Don't worry, Capri, Jippsy has to do what he has to do. Even you can't stop him," Frankie knew how to provoke his sister's wild side – and it worked to his advantage - another few moments alone with Dodo while Capri's attention was set to challenge.

"Oh yeah? Watch me!" Capri yelled cheekily as she started after him. She didn't know how to back down. "Anything he can do, I can too...," she yelled as she pushed the branches of the small bushes out of her way, running ever faster to catch up to him. "Wait, Jippsy!" Capri entreated; she had to get his attention. He turned back, but was unwilling to stop. He was so close, just another ten yards ahead, and he could make out the clearing. And then, of course, perched forty-five feet above the water level, and jutting out from the forest like the pride of the land, was Lion's Head.

He had never jumped from this height before although he had swum past it many times. *One day...* he had always told himself, because he recognized that taking that jump wasn't about courage - it was about sheer stupidity; if he didn't jump from just the right spot, and in just the right way, well, it would be game over for him. But if, just if, he hit the right spot, he would fly right into the deep. Jippsy imagined the fall to be breathtaking, and he imagined how it must feel to be like the osprey, soaring as they looked for prey in the waters below, their remarkable grace as they dove and plunged. He longed to feel the drop and the weightlessness, invigorating and sublime. And suddenly, it was so clear to him. All he had to do at that moment was pick up his speed. He felt that surge of adrenaline, starting to course though his body again, and he was acutely aware that this time it was all or nothing.

I'll show them I'm not afraid, he thought brazenly, throwing the branch aside, as his strides lengthened, and his speed ramped up. All that nervous energy came rushing back, and it was impossible to stop now. He felt the cold and unyielding rock as his feet finally hit the ledge, the last message his senses would transmit, as he lost all awareness of the sounds, the smells, the sights that normally pervaded the forest. It was impossible to stop then, so without another thought he leapt, and in that moment there was nothing, an empty space that no sense could perceive. His body was overwhelmed by the pull of gravity, his brain temporarily rewired, defenceless, his breath caught and expelled with a force he could never have imagined - a shriek borne of such pure exhilaration. He was, indeed weightless and weighted all at once, and he had surely never known such a cathartic release. He was flying! His arms wind-milled, his hands grasped at air, his heart beat in a rhythm that was unsustainable. He felt a stirring in his gut, and he would have sworn he could feel, rather than hear, the steady flutter of the hummingbirds zipping around nearby. Maybe he simply understood them better now. He could hear his name, the echo carrying through his decent, and like vapour his fears dissipated, and he accepted his imminent contact with what lay below, lost in the ecstasy of flight.

His shoes hit the water, carving the path for the rest of his body, nothing stopping or slowing him except the cool water that swallowed him whole, stifling his ability to breathe. Further and further down he dropped, the weight of his fall and the extra drag from his clothing pulling him down so the sun no longer broke through the depth of the water. In an instant it had become so dark that he could no longer see the surface or sense that the sky was above. Jippsy became dizzy as panic crept in, but he still knew up from down; he shook his head, clearing the fear away. He started to move his arms then, swimmers' strokes, dragging the water down with his hands, kicking his feet and using his oversized shoes to his advantage as though they were flippers despite the fact that they were waterlogged and seriously weighing him down. The sun finally broke through the dark water in an amber burst that encouraged him to keep going. Then Jippsy's head broke the surface of the water, his dark hair falling flat on his head, and he instinctively breathed in the fresh mountain air in one solid lift of his diaphragm. He caught a sound, a movement right behind him. A scream, part terror, part euphoria shattered the temporary stillness that was settling over Jippsy as the adrenaline rush ebbed. "Aaaaaaahhhhhhhh!" echoed once more through the peaceful cliff side. Jippsy had no time to look for the source of the scream but already knew what, and more importantly *who,* it was. He ducked back into the water and frantically started swimming out toward the middle of the lake. His shoes slapped the surface of the water with every kick, his arms stroked the water with ease, propelling him forward, as he breathed steadily on every other stroke, until he felt safely out of harm's way, but close enough to reach Capri, just in case... A wave rolled quickly toward him, cresting over him, pushing his body forward and then pulling it back in a violent rhythm. Jippsy stopped to tread water, and see where Capri had landed. He lifted his head out of the water, and flipped his hair from side to side to shake it off his face, swiping at his face quickly to clear the water from his eyes. Those few moments seemed to last forever as he waited for Capri to surface, his anxiety increasing steadily. Suddenly he could see her rising to the surface as elegantly as a mermaid. He hated her, always trying to be

78

one of the boys, but couldn't hide his smile, and the unusual sense of pride he felt considering what she had just done.

"Wow, Capri! You're screwy," Jippsy couldn't help but tease her.

"I'm screwy? I wasn't the one with the idea in the first place," she had to respond. She continued enthusiastically,"Whew! That was quite a humdinger, eh Jips?"

Jippsy was laughing now. "You're not kidding. I was getting the screaming meemies coming down!"

"Me too!" Capri agreed, with as much exuberance as one might expect.

"Hey, you two!" a bellow came over the cliffside. "Are you ok?" It was Frankie.

"We're fine, Frankie," they yelled in unison, laughing at themselves.

"You two are *completely* screwy! Swim down to the sand bar, and we'll meet you there." And then Frankie muttered audibly, "Crazy lunatics!"

"No, just meet us over here," Jippsy insisted.

"Ok, we'll meet you down at the edge, next to the Big Rock," Frankie agreed finally.

Both Jippsy and Capri swam over to the Big Rock, Capri swimming ahead of Jippsy at his insistence.

Jippsy noticed how her clothes hugged her shapely body. He couldn't help himself. The lake was not shallow enough to walk out from the shore next to the Big Rock, as the water had been completely displaced by this erratic boulder. Trees branches jutted out from the land, which Jippsy and Capri used to help guide them to shore; hand-over-hand they used an enormous branch to drag their bodies closer and closer to the edge of the lake until they finally reached Frankie.

"Here, Capri, stretch your arm to me," Frankie

urged.

"It's too far, Frankie... Come closer," Capri pleaded.

"C'mon, Capri, you can do it." So, with a little push from Jippsy, and an energetic swing, Frankie was able to grab her arm. "I got you," Frankie said reassuringly, even as he slipped on the muddy shore. But he held firmly onto the same branch as her and finally pulled her to the shore, his shoes getting soaked as they slid forward into the water. He did the same for Jippsy, and with a grunt and a yank, Jippsy was catapulted to the ground.

"Aah – thanks, Frankie," Jippsy acknowledged for the second time that morning.

"Don't mention it, Jips," Frankie said somewhat smugly, standing tall once again, winking at Dodo.

Oooh my hero! Dodo started swooning, as her thoughts became one-dimensional once again.

"You're a regular Davey Crocket, Frankie. Where's your coonskin hat?" Capri started to tease him.

"Very funny, Capri...," Frankie hated to be taunted, but Dodo was staring at him with those doughy almond-shaped emerald eyes, and his irritation dissipated.

"Let's go," Jippsy insisted, and they were off once again through the dense forest, following the lakefront until they came to the opening where the sand started and stretched for a quarter mile.

I can finally remove these ridiculous shoes, he thought to himself as he pulled off the soaking-wet leather shoes and threw them to the shore as though they were garbage. He knew his parents would be so disappointed, but he shook that thought away, and rushed to the water. They all followed his lead and did the same; shoes hit branches, others were swung inadvertently up into a tree, while another landed just before the shoreline and slid into the water. They went out onto the sand bar that reached into the lake for fifty or so large steps until it dropped sharply in depth by twelve feet. The lake was large but easy to see across. They were all great swimmers and could easily make it across, but their motivation today was purely fun, no work in mind. The lake was usually abandoned, and no one ever went out there with a boat. The lake was just too out of the way for any tourists, and finding it wasn't easy because you couldn't see if from the road, the road itself had been created for and by loggers as far back as the early eighteenth century, but most of the old-growth trees had never been touched around the lake since there was no waterway to move them to the ships destined for England or France. Lost Lake stood alone with no real way in or out, and that was just perfect for Jippsy and his friends.

Jippsy forgot all about his new weapon, the altercation with the moose, and even his exhilarating cliff jump, because his attention was completely riveted on *her*. He watched as her long golden hair flowed down her curvaceous back to just before her bum. Her hair trailed in the water, flowing behind her as she moved gracefully toward the sandbar. She reached the sandbar and, tilting her head back to bask in the sun, Jippsy was mesmerized as the light reflected off the water all around her, highlighting her deep tan and further accentuating her feminine shape. Capri, who had taken to swimming in short pants like the boys, simply couldn't hide how her body had developed - her small waist, rounded hips, and her small but pert breasts that clung to her camisole. Jippsy's eyes took it all in, and he knew that if he didn't stay under the water he would surely embarrass himself.

Capri joined Jippsy where he was swimming off the sandbar, and jumped in next to him; she loved to rile him, and knew no matter what she did, it would stir him up. She made sure she accidentally bumped into him or brushed against him while swimming. Seeing him without a shirt was the highlight of her day, but she couldn't help but compete with everything he did or tried. *I can do anything boys can do*, she always told herself. "What's the matter, Jippsy, don't you like swimming with me?" Capri teased.

"Of course I do," he said sheepishly, as he looked away from her deep dark eyes, as quickly as his brain told him to. Even so, he couldn't help but linger just a little. , but even so lingered as he couldn't help himself sometimes.

"Then why do you take off each time I come near you?" Capri was so mean to taunt him when she knew *exactly* why, but she had to get him to the point where he would blow his cool. "C'mon, Jippsy, I'll race you back to the sandbar," Capri challenged, and without hesitation they both burst out of the water, splashing and chopping at the surface, just to be the first to get to the sandbar. Jippsy, who had great speed, would always be ahead, but his stamina always did him in. He told himself it wasn't going to happen this time, and his kicks became vigorous, but he could hear her nipping at his heels.

Ten more yards, he encouraged himself, but he could feel her there, at his waist, keeping pace with him. She was so close now that once again his mind wandered, as images of her beautiful body and shining smile distracted him. *Shit! She's right next to me*, he thought, frustrated, and then furtively splashed her face to distract her. They were neck and neck. "Darn it," he said aloud as they reached the sandbar at roughly the same time, except that she was standing first.

Still down in the water, Jippsy looked up the length of her legs, as she stood right in front of him. She audaciously stepped closer to where he was lying and put her foot on his back, as though he were a hunting conquest. He grabbed her leg abruptly and twisted it as he pulled her down to the sandbar.

"You didn't say anything about standing," he contended. She fell almost on top of him – yeah, they both would have liked that.

"That's how we always see who wins," she countered as her hand swiped at the lake and sent a spray of water in his face.

"Well not this time!" he glowered, as he splashed her one last time in a defiant rage and swam off again. A satisfied grin spread across her face as she acknowledged having won. She ran over to where Dodo and Frankie were lying on the sandbar, and splashed them out of their daydreams. They had spent their time lazing in the water, watching as the small waves Dodo and Jippsy stirred up gradually reached them, and then coasted over them at regular intervals. Although they never said a word to one another, they were both clearly entrenched in the same daydream.

They had all been lost in time, but hunger finally seemed to awaken them all at once.

After swimming and frolicking in the hot sun for what felt like just a moment, Jippsy looked up to the sky and noticed the sun was almost right above them. "Wasn't Butterball supposed to be here? He said he was bringing the egg sandwiches." Jippsy knew Butterball's mother would always make them something to eat because she hated the thought of anyone going hungry.

"Let's fish instead," Frankie suggested, always eager to kill something or see it suffer before he devoured it. "We can make a fire here," he started to say when Jippsy stopped him, his hand in the air.

"No, Frankie. Let's wait to see if Butterball shows up and we can save the fire 'til later on."

"All right, Jips, but let's go and eat on top of that

screwy rock you jumped over today," Frankie was excited now at the prospect of eating.

"Ok," Jippsy agreed eagerly, "We can eat there." *Back to the scene of the crime*, Jippsy thought, an amused smile taking over his face.

Dodo saw his smile and had to speak up. "But no jumping this time!" she admonished, pointing her finger first at Jippsy, then at Capri. "You two almost gave me a heart attack!"

"Yeah! That was pretty fantastic, Jips. I bet you felt like Flash Gordon going off into space and landing in Lizard World!" Frankie was impressed, but a dark envy started to settle in.

"Sure, Frankie, it...," Jippsy started to say, but was interrupted by Capri.

"It was like being Amelia Earhart," she piped in.

"Cut it out, Capri," Jippsy said spitefully.

"What's the matter, Jippsy, don't like being compared to a woman?" Capri was making it personal now.

"No, Capri, that's not it, it was nothing like that..." Jippsy replied, so frustrated now that he wanted nothing more than for Capri to leave. *She makes me crazy!* he thought to himself. "How could someone so beautiful be so infuriating?" he would always hear his dad say, and Jippsy finally understood why.

"Ok," Jippsy changed the subject, "Let's do that. But first we have to wait for Butterball." Jippsy wondered what was taking Butterball so long, but, more importantly, *Where was the food?* He couldn't stop thinking about those amazing butterball cookies his mom was sure to send with him. Round little bites of splendiferous goodness - Jippsy was testing out his vocabulary. Those sweet cookies with powdered sugar and nuts inside suddenly became Jippsy's obsession. *I could eat a hundred right now,* he thought.

The friends had long ago bestowed the name Butterball upon Roberto Fried when Frankie had observed one day that anytime they played or went to his house, he was either eating or offering those amazing delicious cookies. It certainly didn't hurt that he was overweight and that his cheeks were round and rosy like Santa Clause. His hair was blond and his skin was so white he was pasty.

Poor Butterball, Jippsy reflected. *We always make so much fun of him, but he's so funny to be around, and it's just so fun to say that name.* As if on cue he heard, "Hey Butterball!" almost in unison from the rest of the gang. And sure enough, there he was in the clearing just in from the road. Jippsy jumped up from where he had been sitting on the grass to go see his younger friend.

"Hey you guys," Butterball announced as he came in from the covered forest swinging a woven basket on his arm. He stopped and set the basket down on the beach just before where the sandbar started to jut out. He called out to his friends, "I brought some good-ies," stretching the 'ies' in order to get them all interested. Butterball knew from a young age that you could always win over people's hearts with good food, and if anyone knew what tasted good, it was Butterball. His love of food had become legendary; there was a time when he would sleep over at his cousin's farm and they would have to lock up the ice box with chains anytime Butterball stayed over - he was a raider of the worst kind!

So today, knowing he would be meeting his friends, he had his mom whip up some egg salad sandwiches; she packed up the cucumbers and carrots (definitely not Robert's idea), some homemade chips his mom made from the potatoes they grew - deep fried in lard, they were the most heavenly golden slices - and lastly, and always the most coveted, those delectable butterball cookies. Butterball imagined them to the stuff of dreams and, looking up at the sky dramatically, he thanked god that they even existed. He spoke to the skies gratefully, *Thanks, Mom, you're the best!*

"What you got there, Butterbaaall?" Jippsy teased, stressing the 'ball' just to see what kind of mood he was in.

"Ok, Jippsy," Butterball answered somewhat deflated. "I know you like the sound of that word – it doesn't bother me." But his tone was irritable though calm, and his intention was clearly to impress upon his friend that he preferred his given name to the nickname he had been attributed.

"Ok, BB, you got it." Jippsy appreciated where his friend was coming from, but continued to use the shortened nickname.

Coming right up behind Jippsy was Capri. "Hi Robert," she said in her sing-song voice. He always liked Capri; she was never disingenuous and didn't make fun of him all the time. She was also great to look at, and perfectly symmetrical. *God must have broken his mold after her*, he thought to himself.

"Hi Capri," Butterball answered more enthusiastically, "I got you your favorite, egg salad."

"Oh, Robert, you're the best," she said, truly pleased, and gave him a kiss on the cheek. "Hey!" Jippsy exclaimed jealously, "How come I didn't get a kiss?!"

"You got a heck of a lot more just swimming next to me, didn't you?" Capri teased. Jippsy walked off and sat down next to the basket, flushed and embarrassed.

"Oh, Jippsy, you're such a baby..." Capri mused, as she sat down beside him Indian-style. Butterball went to sit down as well; he opened the basket and handed sandwiches to both of them, reached into the greasy newspaper wrapping and retrieved a few chips for Capri, whereas Jippsy dug his hand into the paper and pulled out a handful.

"Dodo, Frankie, come and have some grub," Butterball called over to them where they were still sitting on the sandbar.

"Ok, Butterball!" They both called back in turn. "You bet we will," they both said together, laughing.

Frankie stood up right away, and put his hand out to help Dodo up off the sandbar. "Thanks, Frankie," she said sweetly, as she took his hand graciously. He yanked her right up off the ground like a ballet dancer throwing the prima-donna ballerina into the air. She was as light as a cloud. They took their places beside the others, and once again Butterball handed out the sandwiches. "This is a real party," Jippsy said as he smiled contentedly. The others stared at him curiously. He realized they didn't understand, so he clarified, "It's just something my grandfather used to say whenever we were with a group of people, other than our own family, of course."

"Ok, Jips old boy, if you say so," Frankie answered in a condescending tone. But when he actually thought about it, he liked the idea, so he raised his chip to the sky, toasting the day's excitement and the great food, and they all joined in, raised their chips together and laughed.

The Bridge

"Otto, go into the clubhouse and see if you could use the telephone. I have The Rock's number, so write this down," Dutch said brusquely. Otto pulled out a pen from his breast pocket, and his notepad from his front jacket pocket, where he always kept it just in case he had a brainstorm. He realized that they hadn't even removed their jackets as they had been in such a rush that they hadn't taken the time - and finally noted that he felt sweaty, stinky, and now down-right uncomfortable. So he removed his jacket, and threw it in the backseat, believing he would look less conspicuous this way, even though most of the men showed up in their suits and changed in the locker-room.

"Ok, boss, I'm ready," Otto said at last. Dutch gave him the number, which Otto wrote down even though he knew he would remember it. Dutch knew that Otto could be trusted to find out where their next move should take them. "Dutch, what if someone recognizes me?" Otto was clearly anxious, and needed reassurances.

"Keep your hat low and your eyes down. I can't go in, they'll definitely recognize me since I've been in the papers for the last couple a years," Dutch answered, knowing that he couldn't take the chance himself.

Otto started to walk from the far reaches of the gravel parking area, from under the sagging weeping willow that hid most of the car. Enough golfers had shown up during the course of the day, so parking that far away from the clubhouse would not be unusual, especially to take advantage of the shade during the hot summer hours. The players from the early tee-off were probably at the 19th hole by now having lunch or a little nip before retreating back to their places of work. *Otto shouldn't look too conspicuous,* Dutch reasoned with himself, *as long as he can keep his head on straight and doesn't panic - especially if he happens to glance at the newspapers, which they're sure to have at the bar.*

Dutch watched as Otto walk up to the clubhouse, and cringed slightly as Otto tipped his hat in acknowledgement to the golfers who greeted him. Otto clearly looked out of place next to the golfers in their knickers and argyle socks. *Oh boy, this is going to be gut-wrenching. I wish I had a drink right now; a beer would surely hit the spot or, better yet, some whiskey.* Dutch was surprised by how nerve-wracking it was to be waiting in the car. Otto entered the clubhouse – no issues so far.

Otto's eyes scanned the building. Three steps up from ground level was a one-story ranch house with a deck that encircled the circumference of the clubhouse. Many of the players waited on the deck to watch their fellow golfers and business associates finish up on the 18th hole. Once players had reached the deck, the competition was over, and there was always a glad hand extended, in congratulations or consolation, regardless of individual style, attitude or the extent of the bet. The 19th hole was the place for a display of good sportsmanship, laughter and good-natured ridicule. Otto never fully understood this kind of camaraderie and didn't give it too much thought. As he opened the ranch door, to his left he noticed a group of names on the wall, all engraved on a large plaque:

Dedicated to the Men of the 14th Regiment Blackwatch of Montreal
Who gave their lives for King, country and liberty

There were many names there, including MacDougall, MacFarlane, Aubrey, and Baron. There were dozens of names on the list. *I guess they also knew what it was like to just try and make it through one day*, Otto surmised. He just had to make it through this day; to Otto, he felt as though his future had never been so uncertain.

As Otto entered the room he couldn't help but notice the high ceilings, as his eyes were drawn upward toward the immense beams crossing the great span of the open room, which was packed with men drinking, smoking, and reclining in massive leather-tufted armchairs, newspapers opened in their laps, rejoicing with their fellow golfers. Twenty-five feet ahead of him was an impressive bank of windows that spanned the entire wall and afforded the golfers an incredible view of the greens. The surrounding landscape was magnificent, an eclectic mix of tall trees, shrubs and flowers, clearly tended-to and designed to impress. *Ah, to be one of them right now. Is the money really worth it?* Otto was starting to doubt. To the far right beyond all the tables was the bar. *They'll know where I can find a telephone*, he thought hopefully.

Otto walked slowly around the small square tables and low leather chairs, making sure not to look at anyone, when an older man with long red whiskers stood up suddenly and bumped into his knee. The old man apologized in a heavy Scottish accent, "Aaay, hope I dinna hurt ye sonny. Eh, you look familiar, do I know you from somewhere?

Otto was quick to answer as he pulled his hat a little lower over his brow, "No, I don't think so."

But the old man persisted, "Yerr from the mill arren't ye; yerr Tom's boy."

Otto was desperate to get away from the old man,

but couldn't move forward past him as the old man was intent upon pursuing a conversation.

"No. I don't know Tom," Otto replied hurriedly, so stressed now that he could barely contain himself.

"Oh. Sorry mate - thought ye werre someone else. I was sure I'd seen ye beforre. Anyway, have ye played today? The greens are quite smooth." His Scottish burr rolled his r's with such emphasis that Otto was mildly amused hearing the old man despite his intense stress.

"No. I won't be playing today, just passing through," he answered more aggressively than he intended as he quickly moved away from the old man and started making his way towards the bar. *Just another 5 steps* , Otto thought to himself, *and there's no one at the bar – that's good.*

The bar was long, and beautifully handcrafted, with a worn-in mahogany bar top and deep brown leather-bound edges which matched the leather chairs in the bar. "Excuse me," Otto called out to the barkeep, who was cleaning the counter at the far end of the bar, "Do you have a phone?"

"Sure, it's down the stairs next to the lockers," the barkeep answered with a friendly wave toward the entrance where the stairs were located.

Otto didn't stay put even long enough to say 'Thank you', and bolted from the bar in the direction the barkeep had indicated. He spotted the same stairway, right at the entrance, which he had originally assumed led down to the lockers. *Damn! I have to get past everyone once again*, Otto thought with mounting frustration. *Ok*, he encouraged himself, *here goes*. Otto weaved his way once again through the many tables, as he stared intently at the maze of wooden flooring that carved a path toward his destination. He felt like a rat in a laboratory experiment. He managed to make it to the stairs without incident then made his way down a flight of thick wooden railway-tie stairs. He spotted the phone immediately as he reached the bottom step. *There it is*, he thought with relief. The phone was hung just to the right of the entrance to the lockers, and Otto couldn't help but think how he would give anything to take a shower right now. Instead, he put his nickel in the slot, and the operator came on the line. "Cambridge 649, please," he said quickly to the operator.

"One moment please," the operator answered in a surprisingly military tone, as if she were completely lacking emotion. Otto heard a ring, then a pause, another ring, another pause, another ring. "Come on, come on," he muttered under his breath.

"Allo. Rottman residence," answered the voice on the other end in a heavy French accent.

"You are connected, sir," the operator interjected, this time with greater interest, as she immediately recognized the name of the party at the other end.

"Oui? Allo? Oo is theess?" the French voice at the other end inquired.

"May I speak with The Rock, please? I mean Mr. Rothman," Otto quickly corrected himself.

"Oo shall I say ees calling?" inquired the French voice, who then tried hard, but ineffectually, to cover his accent.

In a hushed and muddled voice, "Tell him it is Dutch and Otto, and hurry, damn it!"

"One moment, please," answered the voice in a hurry.

"Yes! Where are you guys? You were supposed to call in hours ago," The Rock answered without any preamble, and he was clearly incensed.

"We had some trouble getting out of the city," Otto answered both apologetically and in defense of their situation.

"I know. It's all over the radio. Where are you now?"

"We're at a golf course. What should we do now, Rock?" Otto didn't want to sound stressed, but he couldn't stop the tremor in his voice.

"I have my guys stationed at the bridge; they'll clear the way for you. You got that? So be sure to get to the bridge by 4:00 today - you have one hour to get there, you got that?"

"Yeah, yeah, Rock." Otto was feeling a little more reassured that they would make it through.

"Keep following the route you got from Gerard," The Rock added in.

"Got it, Rock, but there's a lot of heat. Can we get to the bridge following Decarie north?

"Yes, that will work, but it'll take you about 45 minutes to get to the bridge, so go now."

"Got it," Otto was ready to hang up and get a move on.

"Call me the moment you get to the cottage," The Rock insisted.

"Got it, Rock. Thanks again."

"Don't thank me; just get out of there alive. I'll meet up with you two in a couple of days. Goodbye." Without waiting for a response from Otto, The Rock hung up.

Otto's mind was in a tizzy. *How the futz are we going to get out of this alive?*

Otto was not known for his athletic ability, but he nonetheless leaped two stairs at a time to reach the exit then ran across the parking lot. He no longer cared who was looking; *All these mooches with their multi-coloured knickers and flashy argyle sweaters,* was all he could think. Dutch slumped down in his seat, even more troubled than before, as he watched Otto run across the parking lot, practically tripping over the azaleas. Otto called out to Dutch in a loud yet whispered tone, "Let's go now! The Rock has everything taken care of at the bridge."

Dutch started the car without hesitation, and as Otto jumped into the passenger side, Dutch started to back out of his parking spot, almost causing the door to slam on Otto's hand. "God damn it! That almost took my fingers off!" Otto was on full adrenaline now.

"Otto," Dutch's voice was impatient and hurried. "What's the plan?"

"Easy does it, Dutch. Go back to that street called Decarie; it will take us to the bridge, about a mile back." They sped off, flying past all the beautiful homes along Fleet Street, until they made a left onto Decarie. Once more, the tram was stopping and picking up passengers at every intersection alongside them. This time no one paid them any mind. Otto sighed as the tram finished its route a little ways down from where they turned north off of Van Horne Street. Otto watched as they passed more fields and the odd farmer. Otto was clearly on the lookout, and spotted the sign before Dutch. "There it is, Dutch."

You Are Now Entering the Parish of Saint-Laurent, Established 1720

There was just a smattering of factories, houses and farms as far as the eye could see, but at the end of Saint Laurent, heading north, was the Lachapelle Bridge, and all Otto could think was that they had to get there in the next 30 minutes. "It's our only way off this godforsaken island," Otto said to no one in particular.

Police Headquarters

"Police Headquarters. Constable Richard Laberge," she heard the voice say.

"This is the operator calling. I would like to speak to the person in charge."

"You can speak to me, Madame," Constable Laberge replied courteously.

In a carefully organized manner, the operator explained that she was following the protocol precisely as, she had been instructed by her superiors. "As you may be aware, if we believe there is an emergency we are expected to call the police immediately after transmitting our call." She continued, "I connected a call to a well-known gangster, The Rock Rottman, and the caller mentioned the name Dutch. I read about him in the paper this morning, that he was..."

But the operator didn't have an opportunity to finish as the Constable interrupted her. "Yes, yes, we know of him. Go on," the Constable said with calm impatience.

"Anyway, the caller identified himself as Dutch and Otto. Monsieur Rottman told him to go to the bridge and he will arrange everything. That is all I heard."

"Thank you, Madame," the Constable offered. He wanted to tell her that people were entitled to their privacy when using the telephone, but thought it best to let her keep spying as they needed as much help as possible against all the gangs. "Anything else at all, even a little thing that you overheard, could help us immensely."

"Let me see...wait, I remember he said something about four o'clock," answered the operator.

Looking at his watch he exclaimed aloud and rather loudly into the telephone, "That's in forty-five minutes!" As the rush of knowledge spread, a hopeful thought occurred to him and he asked the operator, "Or do you mean tonight?"

"No." she replied rather confidently, then continued, "I'm certain they meant right away. They only had an hour to get to the bridge," she added.

"Anything else at all?" The Constable asked, in a hurry now to end the conversation and get moving.

"No... No. That's it," the operator answered with a slight hesitation now, although she felt a certain pride at having aided in the case of the notorious gangsters.

"Ok, then. Thank you, Madame," he said, in a hurry to get off the phone. "Call back if anything else jars your memory. Ask for Constable Rick Laberge. And again, thank you."

During the morning roll call, the Commander mentioned to be on the lookout for Dutch Schultz's car. "U.S. authorities are very anxious to get him back - preferably alive," the Commander explained. "You've all seen the pictures, at least in the papers this morning, and you all know that his car was seen on Saint Lawrence - full of bullet holes. He was last seen heading north. We will be watching every access off the island...bridges, trains, planes, any means of transportation for that matter. I have spoken with the Mounties, and they will be watching the bridges and roads off island, so it's up to us to circulate with all of our cruisers, cavalry and foot patrol throughout the city. The Mounties have also asked us to provide them at least 2 cruisers at each bridge, so we will camp out there on 24-hour shifts for at least the next 3 days. Is that understood?"

"Yes, Commander!" came the enthusiastic reply from the assembly.

"Very good. The Lieutenant will give you your assignments. Dismissed!"

Rather than call up to the Commander, Constable Laberge preferred to convey the information personally. The Constable was an eager young man; with a square chin, beady eyes and short light brown hair, he easily fit into the lineup of young officers working at the precinct. He ran up the inside front stairs of 1441 St. Urbain, the stairwell now brilliantly lit up by the afternoon sun, thanks to the windows so auspiciously located as to allow the sunlight to infiltrate the police headquarters and provide natural light almost throughout. He took the stairs, two-by-two, and felt his feet light as air as he soared up the three flights.

The Commander peered through the glass panes of his office as he heard the urgent knock on his door. "Yes!" the Commander called out with rough authority. "Come in, Laberge."

"Commander...I just...received...a call..." the young Constable started, panting heavily between words.

"Laberge, I don't have time for stammering," the Commander barked, clearly impatient. This whole Dutch Schultz affair was obviously taking its toll.

"Yes, sir," the Constable answered, determined now to spit it all out succinctly. "An operator from Bell Canada just called to inform us that she overheard a call made from Dutch Schultz to The Rock Rottman. She overheard The Rock giving instructions to make it to the bridge and that he would take care of everything." He was relieved to get it all out in a single breath.

The Commander rose from the rickety wood chair behind his desk, and addressed the Constable, "Go get me Lieutenant Shaugnessey." The Constable knew when to run, and immediately left the room, calling down the hall before reaching his office. "Lieutenant," the Constable panted, "the Commander wants to see you right away."

They both hustled up the hall to the Commander's office, where he stood in front of his desk, twirling his pen around his thumb and index finger. He didn't wait for them to enter before handing out orders, "Call down to Dorchester, Laberge."

"Dorchester, sir?" the young Constable was uncertain as to the Commander's meaning.

"RCMP Headquarters, Constable."

"Yes, sir!" This was quite exciting for the Constable, a departure from the usual, for sure.

"Tell them we have it on good authority that Dutch is going to cross a bridge; they'll know what to do," *I hope*, he told himself. "In the meantime, Elliot," the Commander continued now, addressing the Lieutenant informally, as they had both joined the force at the same time, although the Commander had surpassed the Lieutenant with incomprehensible speed, "Get two more squads to each of the bridges." The Commander then turned his attention to the Constable, who was staring fixedly at the floor rather than at his Commander. "Laberge, Laberge!" he heard the Commander saying, but his concentration had been purely focused on some tidbit of information he seemed to have misplaced or overlooked. "Laberge!" he registered his name now, the shouting finally reaching through.

"I.., I...was just thinking there was something else..." the Constable managed to spit out.

"Well, out with it man," the Commander said irately.

He put up his hand to stifle the Commander, and by this time the Lieutenant was mesmerized by the young Constable's disobedience. But then the Lieutenant noticed the Constable's glowing smile as that parcel of information finally came flooding back.

"By 4 o'clock, pardon, 1600 hours, sir, 1600 hours,

that was their deadline. That's what The Rock told them." The Constable was elated now, for having remembered that critical deadline.

"Are you sure?" the Commander was suspicious now of the Constable's ability to communicate vital facts.

"She was quite sure, sir," the Constable replied. He could tell the Commander had his doubts, yet he kept his resolve.

"Shit, Constable! Pay more attention – this is time-sensitive information you failed to share." The Commander turned immediately to his right-hand man, "Elliot, get on the phone immediately and get those cruisers out on the double." Recognizing that the Constable was young, but eager to please, he addressed Laberge with greater consideration, "Good job, Laberge. Pay a little more attention to detail from now on... Now get back to the desk - no one else is watching the fort." Laberge turned back, with a sweet and sour taste in his mouth. He knew he could be a hero if given the chance, but it was still very prestigious to be the desk Sergeant.

The Lieutenant was back in the Commander's office, reporting his progress, "The RCMP are sending more men, and we've got 2 cruisers going to each bridge, with other cruisers on the roads at Papineau, Lachapelle, Cartier and Champlain. We'll get them sir," the Lieutenant said with conviction.

"Good job, Elliot. We'll see what happens at four o'clock, won't we." The Commander was much more practical than the Lieutenant.

"Yes, sir," the Lieutenant replied reluctantly.

The desk phone rang, and the Constable answered immediately, recognizing, finally, how being in receipt of information could be beneficial to his career advancement. "Constable Laberge speaking," he said earnestly into the receiver.

"Constable, I'm so glad it's you. This is Mary from Bell Telephone. We spoke earlier." She hoped that she had been taken seriously.

"Mary? The operator, of course... Yes, Mary, have you intercepted another call?" *This could be the break I need* – we *need*, he corrected, as he thought to himself.

"No. No, I haven't," she replied, "but I remembered something else. Dutch, or this Otto person, mentioned Decarie north."

The Constable glanced at his watch with alarm. *Merde! 15 minutes until four*, he thought to himself. "Anything else Mary?" he asked hurriedly.

"No. This time I'm positive nothing else was said," she answered with certainty.

"Good job, Mary. Thank you," he answered without waiting for a reply, and promptly hung up on the operator.

The Constable called up to the Lieutenant, "Lieutenant, the Bell operator called back, said she remembered Dutch or Otto mentioning Decarie north. It's the Lachapelle Bridge!" The Constable could no longer contain his excitement at this most relevant bit of information.

"Right! My god - that's in fifteen minutes! Good work, Laberge." The Lieutenant summarily hung up.

The Lieutenant's next call was to the Mounties. In his mind, Elliot was convinced they had missed their window of opportunity. *We're too late...what's done is done*, he thought to himself. *They'll have to dispatch to the Laurentians office in the event Dutch gets past the bridge, and then it's no longer Montreal's worry. Well, at least the Mounties always get their man, isn't that their motto?* He laughed inwardly, all the while hoping his men would be the ones to drag them in. *All we can do now is wait*, he told himself.

Escaping the City

"Otto get your hands on that gun - we're going to have to go blazing through," Dutch insisted as he sped up the boulevard.

"You think so, Dutch? The Rock insisted he had it covered." Otto wanted to believe, had to believe that The Rock would come through.

"Even so, it's over Otto, and this is our only chance to get outta here. If they're watching this bridge, then they're watching everywhere, which means we have nowhere to go. We have to get off this island."

Otto took a resigned breath, and pulled his jacket and the rifle from the back seat. He slipped his jacket on hoping it would help protect him from bullets, and realized how ridiculous that seemed, but he needed to believe in something. Although Otto wasn't a religious man, he recognized the wisdom of the adage that there were no atheists in foxholes, which was surely where they were, and so tilted his head to the skies and prayed.

The sun was still high in the sky, streaming rays of light directly through the driver's side window, causing Dutch to lose much of his peripheral vision. He was gaining speed as he headed north on Laurentian Boulevard toward the bridge, passing more of the same empty trucks with workers sitting, standing idly, or just enjoying the beautiful weather with a bottle in hand. A passing thought flashed through Dutch's mind, *Aaah to be free with the wind in your hair after a long day of labour, just lounging around in the back of a pick-up, no worries except, 'What is the missus making for supper?'* He forced his thoughts back to reality. *Concentrate, damn it, this is no time to be daydreaming. All hands on deck,* he warned himself.

He was approaching the bridge now; he squinted his eyes to mitigate the effects of the sun, and as he did so he spotted the two police cruisers parked on either side of the bridge. "The cops are letting everyone go through," he said to Otto without losing visual contact with the cops and the cruisers at the bridge. "We just have to hide behind one of these trucks and hit it when we get there."

Otto was speechless, and Dutch expected nothing else.

The sound of sirens washed over them like waves, threatening to swallow them right down into the ocean - one wave, then another and another still. *This won't let up until we're either dead or captured*, Otto thought to himself as he tightened his grip on the Tommy gun, his only life preserver.

Otto was finally attuned to the situation, and Dutch's voice came through clear and direct, "On the count of three I want you to just spray bullets wherever you can, but make sure that any cars parked at the entrance of the bridge are riddled. You got that Otto? Stick that gun out there and shoot to save your goddamn life!"

"Ok, boss. I got it." And he did.

The sirens were getting louder; Dutch realized how fast the coppers had to be travelling for their sirens to be piercing the relative quiet of this sweltering summer day, and with such intensity. On either side of the cars that were blocking the lane to get onto the bridge, Otto spotted two men who suddenly ran behind their cars. There were two trucks directly in front of Dutch and Otto, and one sputtered intermittently, each time imitating the sound of a gunshot; it was enough to make Otto jump every time it did. Dutch started to count, "Ok, Otto...One," and Otto rolled down his window, then, "Two," as Otto's hands shook, but his mind was sharp and he clutched the trigger, then, "Three! Shoot anything and everything, Otto," Dutch yelled over the sound of the bullets rattling out of the Tommy gun.

Dutch, meanwhile, swerved around the first truck and floored it. Ratatatatatatatatat. "Again, Otto," Dutch yelled. Ratatatatatatatatat. "Again!" Ratatatatatatatatat. This time, the two trucks began to wobble as the terrified drivers, unsure of what exactly was happening, did their best to get out of the way of the car with the Tommy gun blazing out the passenger window. The first truck turned his wheel so hard that the momentum of the back wheel caused the entire truck to flip on its side, effectively launching the men in the uncovered back into the road. The truck continued on its path of destruction, careening into the cruiser parked on the right side of the entrance to the bridge, and the two vehicles exploded in a bright orange flame, and then the black smoke started to billow and weave its way around the cars.

Dutch had no time to swerve around the bodies that now impeded the road, and felt a bump beneath the carriage of the car. He was positive it was the cargo they were carrying, and his throat filled with bile at the thought. The other truck was able to right itself, and stop with a penetrating screech as metal and stone ground together, and then came the unmistakable sound of tires blowing out as the spray of bullets from Otto's gun hit their mark.

"Pass me the rifle," Dutch yelled over the calamity. Bullets came hailing in from the left and ripped through the windshield, narrowly missing Dutch's head. "Shit!" Dutch spat out, and Otto quickly handed him the rifle. "Hold the wheel, damn it," he yelled at Otto. Otto kept the wheel as straight as he could; he wasn't as worried about the bullets flying toward them since they were only coming from Dutch's side. He still kept his head below the dash, just high enough to see the road. Dutch opened fire on the cruiser. Otto thought he saw Dutch smile while shooting up the entrance of the bridge, and surmised that Dutch felt a renewed confidence. Otto thought to himself, *If the last bullet didn't get him, maybe today wasn't the day. Maybe we have a fighting chance.* The bullets continued to fly, and ripped through the steel body of the car, the rubber tires, anything it could find to stop their trajectory. As they finally passed the car that had been blocking their way, the two men who had ducked behind their respective cars suddenly turned and jumped over their sides of the bridge. They would be lucky just to land in water, Dutch realized, but what lay beneath was of no concern to him.

Kchunk... kchunk... kchunk...those familiar sounds were music to Dutch's ears. *We made it*, he thought with relief, *we're past that damn bridge.* On the mainland, sirens were still chasing them down, but Dutch knew he had enough gas to get him to his destination, and so he ran that old car as fast as it could go. He had had the motor retrofitted with the latest innovations for this very reason. Escape.

"Giuseppe, that car behind us is awfully close," Jippsy's grandfather, Papa, as he was known to everyone, said with concern - although his thick Italian accent always stressed the importance of everything he said.

"I see that, Papa. I'm watching him too... Papa hold on!" Giuseppe Sr. shouted over the roar of gunfire, sounds his Papa recognized all too well from his tour in the Congo. Giuseppe Sr. was always proud to hear his Papa's heroic tales about how he fought against the rebel army that had been trying to overthrow the Italian government there. Giuseppe Sr. pulled the steering wheel of the truck to the right as fast as he could to get out of the way of trouble, not even thinking of the consequences.

He was shocked as all of the passengers riding in the back of the truck immediately ahead of him were launched to the ground. He had no time to think, and simply uttered aloud, "Oh my god!" as he slammed on the brakes and then yanked the wheel to straighten the truck out from skidding. They pitched back and forth as though they were a boat rocking in the water. His Papa made the sign of the cross, as he prayed and braced himself for a collision. Giuseppe Sr. suddenly realized that his passengers, who were riding in the open back of his truck, were being thrown from side to side. The sound of bodies slamming against the wall of the open-air truck made him acutely aware of the important cargo he was carrying. His tanned, weary face was a mask of consternation and strain, which now highlighted his crow's feet, wrinkles which normally gave him a kindly appearance given his happy-go-lucky demeanor. Instead, the stress was apparent, his face aged and broken, as he attempted to fight off a horrendous crash. The tires were blown and the metal rims, as they scarred the pavement beneath them, drove home a piercing sound he had never heard before. Giuseppe Sr. was able to stop the car, his passengers suddenly thrown against the front of the cab with a thud, which in turn slammed the front seat forward, sending Giuseppe Sr.'s chest full force into the steering wheel, as his head struck the windshield. His head was throbbing; he tentatively reached his hand up to his forehead and then, clearly in shock, he pulled his hand away to stare at the blood on his fingers, as the blood slowly trickled down into his right eye. He slowly scanned the scene and took in the other sights and sounds surrounding him - the bodies on the ground, sirens wailing, his men groaning in the back, the bullet-riddled vehicles. "Everyone all right?" he called out from the window.

"Oui, juste un peu blessé, mais tout le monde est correcte," he heard one of them reply. *Yes, just a little hurt, but everyone is fine.* His Papa hadn't said a word, and he turned to look over at him, slumped over in the seat beside him.

"Papa...you okay?" But his Papa didn't answer. "Papa...Papa!?" he said, with panic creeping in. He shook Papa's shoulder, hoping to revive, lightly at first, and then more frantically in the hopes of startling him into consciousness. "Papa, Papa, please wake up," he begged desperately, and shook him more vigorously. "Oh my god, is he dead?" he asked aloud as he slid over to the passenger side, but the gear shift was blocking the way for his feet to slide over, so he bent across the seat as far as he could reach. He put his ear close to his Papa's chest; he thought he could hear a heartbeat, but his own heart was racing, his adrenaline still coursing so fast that he couldn't be certain. Still, he held fast to his Papa's shirt, and as tears welled up and clouded his vision, he started to give up any hope of movement, when a slight moan escaped from his Papa's lips.

Relief washed over him, and, wiping his eyes, he pulled himself back into the driver seat and sat back, trying to concentrate on a plan. He couldn't help but think of his family in Brebeuf – his beautiful and loving wife, a constant reminder of all that was good in life. He flashed back to how they had met.

His leg felt like it was missing, and he hesitantly reached his hand toward his lower body, and placed it, with relief on his leg. *It's still there*, he thought thankfully, his heart racing, his head spinning, *but why can't I feel it?* He tried rubbing his thigh, it was completely bandaged up above the knee, and considerably larger than his other undamaged leg. He looked around the open room, as white and sterile as possible given the fact that the makeshift hospital was nothing more than a tent filled to overflowing with injured soldiers. He realized he was one of the lucky ones – cries of pain and despair surrounded him, and in his confusion and desperate need to understand what had happened to him, he joined the chorus, "Doctor, nurse, anyone," he begged. He became keenly aware that the tent was filled with the smell of rot, and it was too much for him to bear; his body tightened and, beyond his control, threw itself over the side of the bed to release the yellow bile from his stomach. He felt slightly better, but felt desperately alone and disoriented.

"Are you feeling better?" asked a soothing female voice. Her Italian was not very good, but he understood what she meant.

"I speak a little English," he replied, his mind distracted from the immediate issue, as his attention was drawn to the absolutely beautiful woman who had approached his bed, and diverted his attention away from the misery surrounding him.

"I have felt better," he said hoarsely. He tried to clear his throat; he couldn't take his eyes from her face, and didn't realize he was staring as he took a mental inventory of every feature he could see - her long dark curly hair that dropped over both sides of her face, showing her widows peak at the top of her forehead, smooth skin and small ears, her cheeks were apple rosy, a straight symmetrical nose, but mostly, the slant and vibrancy of her soft green eyes as she smiled brilliantly at him. *Is it possible to feel love at first sight?*, he wondered to himself. Her smile was truly dazzling; her pink lips accented her mouth like a statue in Florence, her smile, a beacon of hope. He noticed her bright white teeth, and chuckled to himself as he thought sardonically, *She can't be from Britain...* She had turned to pour him a glass of water, and he took in the sight of her backside, round and firm, the slimness of her waist, her legs, what he could see of them below the uniform. She was heavenly in every respect.

"Do you know what happened to me?" he asked, reviving somewhat from the enchantment of this beautiful girl.

"You were hit by barrage of grenades; I think you were one of the lucky ones. You just get some sleep today - the doctor says your leg will recover and will be fully functional," she said in such a soothing voice. He didn't want her to leave his bedside.

"I was at Caporetto..." he started to say, just to keep her there.

"I know," she said softly, "All of you were. I'll come back a little later to see you," she promised, and then turned to leave. He watched her walk away until she was completely out of sight.

"Grazie," he said aloud, as he lowered his head onto the pillow and slipped away to a happier world, this time with her.

"Giuseppe – you ok?" he heard a familiar voice seeping into his consciousness.

"Yes, yes. Did I just nod off?" Giuseppe asked hesitantly, as he refocused his attention out his window and took in the worried look on Giovanni's face. Giuseppe was relieved to see his best worker alive and seemingly well. "Giovanni, Papa needs help..." Giovanni wasted no time – he jumped off the truck's side-runner, and strode quickly over to where the police had stopped their cruisers just beyond the heat and hazard from the truck that was still blazing.

I must have dozed off...I remember looking over at

Papa. He turned now to check on his father. "Papa, wake up," he pleaded.

Giuseppe could hear Giovanni, "Police! Police!" He was pulling on the policeman's shirt trying to drag him over to the truck. Giovanni didn't speak much English. "Help!" was pretty much all he could say, and the policeman nonetheless allowed the young man to drag him over to the truck.

The constable checked inside the passenger side, reaching through the open window to see if the old man had a pulse, which, sure enough, he did. The Constable turned his attention to Giuseppe, "Are you alright?"

"Yes, officer, but my Papa will not wake up," Giuseppe replied, somewhat relieved that help was there.

"We will get him an ambulance, don't you worry," the Constable said reassuringly. "I have to check on some of the other men," he added hastily and disappeared back into the chaos.

By the time the firemen arrived, the fire had all but dissipated, as it had nothing left to burn. They were able to put out the many smoldering embers with pumps from the river, and all that remained were two charred skeletons of steel fused together, and if there were bodies in there they were now ash. The wounded were transported to the Montreal Jewish General Hospital. Thankfully none of Giuseppe's men were seriously hurt except for Papa. He sent the boys back to the farm after locating a mechanic in the area willing to sell him a spare. He gave specific instructions to his right-hand man, "Giovanni, let Bella know I'm fine and that Papa is in the hospital. We don't know what it is yet, but they say he seems to be in a coma. She's a nurse - she'll know what that means. Tell her I will call shortly." They were all happy to leave the scene of such disaster.

On his way to the hospital, sitting with his Papa in

the back, he couldn't help but recap all that had happened, all those bodies on the ground, men jumping over the railing of the bridge to their death or at least a rough go in the river, a fire that seemed to reach as high as the suspensions above the bridge, sirens everywhere, a man that wherever he went, violence, mayhem and dread seemed to follow. *I hate that son of a bitch, I hope they catch him and hang him.*

Incroyable

"Louis, did you see that?" Gerard was in awe.

"Oui, Gerard. Mon dieu, c'est incroyable!" and, my god, it WAS incredible, replied Louis. Louis was a man who had never been, nor had he ever needed to be, afraid. He thought he had seen it all in his line of business; he had seen men executed, had taken part in shootings and torture, and believed that they were, at the heart of it all, no different than animals. The stories his family used to tell about the suffering they endured, and their attempts to escape slavery made him hate all men, and he no longer cared one way or the other, but it never precluded the incredible fascination he had for destruction, and this was one sight to behold. *Yes*, he thought to himself, *we had burned down some buildings, but that was easy, just a little gasoline and a match.* But a truck going head first on its side, men falling from its bowels and a thunderclap of steel meeting steel, engine to engine, that explosion mushrooming to the sky gave him a resolve that god truly wanted him to be his eyes to witness all that was Sodom and Gomorrah.

Louis was lost in thought, and utterly bewildered. He only heard every second word coming from Gerard in his grating voice, "...to go."

"What do you mean, 'To go'? Louis asked.

"Time to go," Gerard repeated. "La Roche want us to follow 'dem," he said in his thick French-Canadian accent. Louis held onto his bat as though it was a stuffed teddy bear, staring straight ahead. As he realized they were going to have to go through the wreckage, his senses perked up. He wanted to feel the action, and his anticipation of more ruin made his heart beat faster, while the surge of his emotions brought out the best in him. A warrior at heart, could never really have worked for the good guys in that day and age. *I could never amount to my full potential with laws and rules*, he thought to himself. Gerard sped forward from the side of the road, just outside the purview of the gendarme who would have been able to see them from the bridge. He sped past the two cop cars, just barely missing the truck and the growing fire and followed Dutch. He knew where he was headed so he was able to keep a safe distance. He heard the sirens coming to a stop just after they reached the other side; they didn't chase them and he found that odd. *Could that mean there is more to trouble to contend with up ahead?*

Bodies in the Street

As the police arrived from headquarters, they could see men lying on the street. They had heard the entire incident from miles back and knew instinctively where they were headed. They increased their speed as they recognized the urgency of the situation. Once the top of the bridge came into view they could see that it was covered in black smoke, evidence of the fire burning out of control. But nothing had prepared them for the sight of dozens of men strewn about bleeding and moaning with the heat of the wreckage scorching their bodies.

The police cars stopped fast, skidding sideways before the bodies and the wreckage. Without giving any thought as to why this had happened, the officers jumped from their cars to help get the victims to safety. "This one is still alive!" called out one of the officers. "Help me get him to the cruiser for now." Two officers picked him up cautiously, not knowing the extent of his injuries and gently lay him down on the grass next to the road.

Another officer heard a man calling out to him, "Officer, officer, please - in the truck..." There was a man unconscious in the truck, and while it seemed to be out of harm's way from the burning wreck, they didn't want to take any chances and moved the passengers and driver to the safety of the grass next to the cruiser.

The men in the cab spilled out and went to help their buddies. It didn't matter what language they spoke; Italian, French and English were all interspersed in the frantic dialogue that went on, but somehow they all knew what was expected and worked together to get all of the men on the road to safety.

As the police and those men who could walk

113

helped the others, sirens from the fire engines and ambulances came all at once. The firemen from Station 21 in nearby Ahuntsic were first on the scene and next came Station 19 from Saint-Laurent. Seven men immediately set up the hoses and trucks and used their diesel engine to pump water from the river to douse the fire.

The fire took over three hours to extinguish, and they made sure that the surrounding areas, which were covered in leaking gasoline, would be doused sufficiently so some fool couldn't toss a lit cigarette and start it up again. There were no reporters, nor any photographers, just the stories that would be told by the thirteen wounded, by the families of the nine dead - including the four Mounties and four police officers - as well as the twelve firefighters who arrived on the scene, and nine more witnesses who had escaped relatively unharmed.

Once all the wounded were being treated, and the scene somewhat under control, one of the police officers went back to Firestation 21 to make a call to Lieutenant Shaughnessy. "Lieutentant, I just came from the bridge. It was utter mayhem."

"What happened officer? And where's Dutch?" the Lieutenant asked expectantly.

"He escaped, sir," the officer answered with resignation.

"What do you mean he escaped?" the Lieutenant asked menacingly.

"He's travelling north on Route 117. That was about forty five minutes ago, sir," the flustered officer explained.

"How did this happen?" the Lieutenant was turning a deep shade of anger-induced red.

"Well, you see sir..." the officer started to explain.

"Never mind! I don't have time for details now. You say he is heading north...did anyone think to try and follow?" the Lieutenant demanded.

"We were too late sir. He was long gone and there were bodies everywhere," the officer said for effect now.

"What do you mean bodies everywhere?" Now the Lieutenant was starting to appreciate the dire circumstances.

"Well, sir, there was this big crash, a fire at the bridge and bodies and, er, bodies every-..." the officer started to explain.

"Oh, forget it, sounds like a long story. Just tell me, where do you think he is going?" The Lieutenant needed a new plan now.

"I don't know, sir," the officer replied solemnly.

"Ok, Constable, you report to me right away. Come back here now," the Lieutenant ordered.

"Yes, sir, right away!" the officer answered promptly.

"One last thing: what happened to the Mounties, Constable?" the Lieutenant wanted to know exactly HOW bad.

"I think they're both dead, sir. We couldn't find them at the bridge, and one of the cars burned up in the fire," the officer explained with great remorse.

"Ok, Constable. Come back to headquarters now. I want to hear everything, but right now we have to get Dutch." He hung up immediately.

His frown made his eyes disappear beneath his eyebrows. *Those god-forsaken...,* he thought to himself, but couldn't think of an appropriately derisive word at that moment, as his fingers dialed up Dorchester. He stared out of his office window at nothing in particular. He could still see the sun resting high in the sky. With an abject sense of frustration, he thought to himself, *Today could have been just an ordinary, beautiful day. We didn't need this son-of-a-bitch upsetting our town.* The phone only rang once before being answered.

"RCMP Headquarters," said the female voice.

"Yes, hello. This is Lieutenant Shaugnessey of the Montreal Police," said the Lieutenant in a surprisingly softer tone than usual; he was somewhat taken aback by the fact that a female had answered the phone. *A female Mountie?* he thought to himself.

"Yes, sir," the female RCMP officer replied professionally, "I recognize your voice. How can I direct your call, sir?"

"Get me Major Knowles," he replied immediately.

"One moment, Lieutenant," replied the female officer without delay.

"Hello, Elliot," answered the concerned voice on the other end, "Have you heard anything?"

"I just got word, and it's not good - he escaped. Apparently there was an accident and a fire at the bridge, and your boys are nowhere to be found as of yet. I suggest you contact Ste-Agathe and get a squad up there as soon as possible." The Lieutenant wasn't going to waste time on niceties.

"Right. I was just thinking that," said Knowles, his gears already spinning, worry over the missing officers and their families taking precedent over the pressing issue of Dutch's escape.

"Call me back once you have the full story," Knowles requested. "In the meantime I'll dispatch a squad immediately."

"Sure, Knowles," answered the Lieutenant tersely before hanging up.

Knowles' nephew was in one of the squad cars that had been dispatched to the Lachapelle Bridge. "Olivia! Get me Ste-Agathe," he yelled from his office. Her desk was toward the front of the large building on Dorchester Street. The headquarters had recently been relocated to this brand new art deco building; it was 5 stories high and clad in grey stone like many of the newer buildings in Westmount. There were only three offices per floor, toward the rear of the building, and Knowles' office was located on the third floor. The art deco flair had been incorporated into the large open areas which occupied the majority of each floor, and accommodated row upon row of Mounties seated at their individual desks deciphering codes, studying Communist activities, monitoring the international smugglers, and synchronizing measures for action against terrorist threats. The head office was located in Montreal and all was coordinated from there, whether an event took place in St.John, Newfoundland or in Victoria on Vancouver Island. They had the most sophisticated telephone system in all of Canada and all operations were borne and conducted from this building.

In this particular case, they had been forced to contend with one of the most influential, cunning and ruthless gangsters to-date, and in their own backyard.

Olivia, despite being located at the far end of the floor, heard him loud and clear over the constant racket of voices talking, planning, and shouting – after some time on the floor it had all simply become white noise, the background music that played during her hectic work day.

"Your call to Ste-Agathe, sir," he heard her say through his office telephone.

"Benoit, Bonjour c'est Knowles," he greeted the commanding officer at the Ste-Agathe police station, and continued speaking in French despite his overpowering Manchester England accent, "Benoit I'm sure you're aware we're tracking the whereabouts of Dutch Schultz and his sidekick Otto Berman."

Benoit replied in French, "Yes, we heard this

morning that he's in town, but I didn't know you were tracking him."

"Well we have been, and he slipped through, crossed the Lachapelle Bridge just about forty-five minutes ago, and he appears to be heading up in your direction. If he doesn't have car trouble, we think he will go up to The Rock's," he said in English, "At Lac Mercier. An operator intercepted a call that was made from Dutch to The Rock. Get your people on the lookout for a –," but before Knowles could finish his sentence, Benoit interrupted him.

"I know - a 1931 Lincoln, bullet holes in the car, two men, etc... We heard it on the radio last night and there was another report this morning," Benoit replied efficiently.

"Lastly Benoit, I am sure he is packing, so you make sure your boys are full up, you understand?" Knowles wanted to be sure that there were no further deaths or casualties.

"OK, Knowles, we'll dispatch cruisers up and down the 117, and officers to stake out The Rock's place. I'll report back as soon as I have something. Salut."

"Salut et bonne chance," he offered. *Goodbye and good luck.*

Laurentian Mountains

"What time is it Butterball?" Jippsy asked.

"Oh, come on, Giuseppe. Do you like that, or do you prefer Jippsy?" Butterball was sounding irate.

"Very funny *Butter*ball," Jippsy retorted, stressing the word 'butter'. "What's wrong with your name? It's a compliment - those are the best cookies in the world!" Jippsy tried to calm him down.

"I know, but it makes fun of my belly too," Butterball answered, sadness in his voice.

"No it doesn't BB. Robert is too formal, and you don't look like a Bobby - that's what they call their cops in England." Jippsy loved the trivia he learned from reading.

Butterball ignored the last comment. "It's four," he answered, "Satisfied?"

"Yep," Jippsy answered smugly.

"Hey, look!" Butterball said excitedly. "There's Victoria."

Victoria was coming up the road, and called out to her friends, "Can I join you guys?"

Victoria barely had the chance to get the words out before Butterball happily called out, "Sure, Victoria!" Victoria was three years younger than Jippsy and generally a nuisance. She wasn't very strong, just a little 11-year-old redheaded girl that always had to be helped along during their adventures.

"Hi, Vicky," said Caprice, who always had a soft spot for this girl; she was generally very quiet, but not in a sad way. She was more of a curious sort, and would stare off every now and then, almost as if calculating something.

"Hi, Capri," she answered back in her small voice. Vicky was certainly no tomboy in her little summer dress.

"Let's go, Jippsy - and grab a branch," Frankie called out from where he and Dodo were still sitting back taking in the sun's rays. "I have some twine, so we can make ourselves fishing rods."

"I'm coming too," said Caprice.

"Me too!" Dodo piped in.

"OK, then, we might as well all go," Jippsy said authoritatively. They all went off into the forest to find the best branch - not too brittle or the fish would snap it, but sturdy enough to create resistance.

Frankie liked the peace and quiet of fishing, but more importantly he loved the hunt. The moment he had a serious muskie hooked - at least a 15-pounder - it was a fight to the death. He craved the challenge, always wondering to himself, *Will it pull me in the water and try to drown me - I'll refuse to let go - or will I yank it out of the water with no way of it catching its breath again?*

The five of them spent the next hour sitting at the beach casting their lines as far as they could. Jippsy instructed Caprice how to twirl the twine, "Do it quickly, but be gentle, letting the line in and out depending on the fish's reaction. Let the fish think he's off the hook, and let him go a little so the hook gets in a little deeper, then reel him in again. If you let him pull too much he'll snap the line."

"This is the life, eh Jips old boy?" Frankie was really in his element.

"Sure is, Frankie," Jippsy answered, knowing Frankie needed to feel validated whenever he thought or said anything. But Frankie was having some great success, and since Jippsy really did respect that he felt the need to acknowledge it, "Frankie, you're a machine! Five bass and two perch - wow! Supper is going to be delicious." Jippsy was starting to get hungry again.

"Now all we need is some ice cream," said Butterball, licking his lips.

"Only you would think about ice cream, eh Butterball?" Frankie asked and then started to laugh.

Butterball tried to deflect Frankie's unyielding taunts by getting the group to laugh, "That's right, Frankie, I'm the only one who likes ice cream."

"Ah you, you..." Frankie stuttered and then trailed off as he started to grow annoyed by Butterball's quicker wit. He rarely came up with a good comeback. "At least I'll never go hungry," Frankie finally managed to say after a delay, as he lifted up the line of fish triumphantly.

"Neither will I," said Butterball as he pointed disparagingly at his own stomach and then smirked as he jiggled it in front of Frankie. Jippsy burst out laughing, while Capri tried to stop herself, but she had to succumb as her eyes started watering; she couldn't contain it any longer, as from the bottom of her stomach came a hysterical roar of laughter that swarmed the area like an angry hive of bees. Eventually even Frankie couldn't control himself.

"Oh, oh, oh my stomach," Caprice managed to squeak out between gut-wrenching bursts of laughter, "Make him stop," she pleaded.

Jippsy snorted loudly, and the gang burst out laughing even harder. "I can't," he just barely managed to say, "He's just too funny!"

They carried on like this for some time, teasing one another so that the laughter, as it died down, sparked up again until they had exhausted themselves, and then finally went back to fishing.

"I could spend a lifetime here," Dodo said dreamily. Jippsy, Caprice and Butterball had had enough of her swooning and decided to pick her up and dump her back in the water.

"In you go, Dodo," the three of them said almost in unison as they picked her up. She started thrashing around and yelling, "What are you guys doing? I'm finally dry," she whined.

"Oh, don't worry. I'm sure Frankie will make a fire," Capri teased.

"Yeah, Frankie will dry you up," Butterball piped in.

Then it was Jippsy's turn, "Oh, wait, what will Frankie do? Oh yeah, Frankie will come to the rescue," he said mockingly.

Dodo got the point, but she was irritated now. "You guys are sooo mean. But you're right - Frankie will get you...especially if I ask him to."

"Bring it on sister!" Capri said with a grin.

Dodo hit the water with an impressive splash, and while the water at the sandbank was not deep, it still had the desired effect. Frankie saw it all, but was consumed with his fishing, since he wanted to double his take before they had to get back.

Route 117

"Looks like we made it, Dutch. You ok?" Otto asked, noting the look of consternation on Dutch's face.

"I'm peachy!" He answered acerbically. "We haven't made it," he continued with irritation. "We still have to get to the lodge. You remember the instructions, right Otto?"

"Yeah, of course boss - just follow this road, Route 117, for about two hours or so, and you'll see the exit in about 80 miles. How are we for gas?"

"We don't need to fill up yet, and I don't want to stop," Dutch answered, all business now. The road took them through one forest after another. Scattered here and there, for the first thirty miles, were low-lying hills, and cows grazing in the unending fields. Otto noticed that all of the cows were standing - a good sign that it wouldn't rain. It could have been a relaxing drive in the countryside, but at sixty miles an hour, and running for their lives, neither one of them could appreciate the beauty and tranquility surrounding them. An hour passed and they started to enter the mountains. The road they were travelling ran alongside the North River that went as far north as Lac Mercier and as far south as the Saint Lawrence River that surrounded Montreal. The Laurentian Mountains, although not as famous as The Rocky Mountains, were considered the world's oldest standing mountain range. Rising up more than thirty-eight hundred feet above sea level at its highest peak it spanned either side of the Saint Lawrence Seaway.

The lakes, mountains, rivers and rich soil just north of Montreal brought avid fishermen, hunters, and weekend swimmers, and opened up trade for loggers and trappers to send their massive pine, oak, birch, beaver pelts, moose and deer hide to be transported through

Montreal. The constant traffic of goods resulted in Montreal becoming North America's first trading post, and an ongoing successful transport hub for all of North America. The rich soil and abundance of maples made the St. Lawrence River valley a grower's paradise for fruit, and, hence, spirits, most of which were exported to the United States by none other than The Rock's company. It was here and in New York where Dutch was able to prosper. Although he had never visited this particular area of his distribution network, this was where it had all started.

The first car to pass them was a non-descript grey car with red Canada plates, not the blue Quebec plates they had seen on every other vehicle. "Otto, did you see those mooks staring at us?" Dutch didn't like the idea that they might have been spotted.

"Yeah, Dutch. Both of them knew we were trouble," Otto answered warily, concerned that this might impact their next move. Dutch glanced in his rearview mirror, and immediately knew they were, once again, up shit's creek.

"They're stopping and turning around. Feds I bet, not those local keystone cops. We're going to have to pick it up a bit. How far until the exit, Otto?"

"About ten miles, Dutch." Otto answered and started to get nervous all over again.

"Here goes," Dutch said, with a hint of excitement, in contrast to Otto, and pushed his black-and-white saddle shoe that much closer to the floor. He felt the leather strain as he pressed his foot in a position it didn't normally go. The speedometer's needle crept up - sixty five mph...Otto checked the mirror on his side, and they weren't gaining...seventy mph...he could no longer make out the leaves on the trees, and they still weren't gaining...eighty mph...and every bump sent their bodies bouncing against the roof...but then suddenly the other car started gaining a little. They had been travelling faster than ever before, and the car had never been pushed to this limit. Otto couldn't believe what was happening, and blurted out, "Dutch, they are actually gaining on us!"

"That's impossible!" Dutch yelled over the roar of the engine and the sound of the car's tires as they rolled hard against the pavement. His sweaty palms on the wheel locked on even tighter, and he thought to himself, *Faster, damn it, faster*, in an attempt to will the car to barrel along at an even greater speed. His foot hit the bottom and finally rested on the floorboard; he felt the car go beyond its limits as they started to descend a hill. Neither of them could see what was on either side, and so they focused on the bottom of the hill where there was a sharp bend to the right. At the speed they were travelling Dutch knew it was highly likely they would flip, but he didn't want to slow down. He glanced quickly into his rearview mirror, and spotted two cars - the grey car that had given chase and further beyond what looked like another black car.

Otto thought to himself, *Dutch has the devil on his side and he's just the kind of guy to cheat death, but I don't feel as lucky*. He spoke up, "Dutch you better slow down, or you won't make that turn."

But Dutch had run out of patience and snapped at Otto, "I know! Shut up."

Dutch shook his head. He had no time to wipe the sweat beading down his forehead and into his eyes. "Damn it!" he yelled as he pulled the car into the right lane as he spotted an exit ahead. He eased his foot off the accelerator as he thought to himself, *Maybe we can fool them just before the turn.*

"This is not the way!" Cried Otto over the engine's

roar. Dutch didn't bother to acknowledge Otto's pleas. "Dutch. Dutch! Where are you going?"

"Shut up and let me...," Dutch started to say when a gunshot rang out. Otto slouched down once again, while Dutch raised himself off the seat and rammed his foot down onto the floor once again.

They picked up speed, and at the very last second Dutch yanked the car back onto the main road and away from the exit. He made it somewhat into the lane and started to push the steering wheel to the right with all his might in order to counter steer the car into place. The car skidded one way, then the another, and suddenly they were on the overpass of the Petit Train du Nord, a train that brought goods, mail and passengers to and from the city. Otto felt like a popcorn kernel about to pop; his body was being catapulted in different directions as the car skidded back and forth, back and forth, until Dutch finally brought it back under control. He had no choice but to slow down or they would have gone right over the overpass. He hoped their pursuers would have the same difficulty.

"Otto," Dutch yelled, "Grab one of the canisters of gasoline!"

"What?" Otto yelled incredulously.

"You heard me...get in the back and grab the canister and shove it out the door. Then I want you to shoot it."

"Are you crazy? At this speed...," Otto started to say.

But Dutch interrupted him to set him straight, "It's that or die. We have no choice..."

Otto jumped into the back, then glanced over at the speedometer - eighty, eighty five, he was mesmerized, incapable of doing anything other than stare at it until Dutch brought him back to reality, "Otto, move it!" Dutch shouted irately.

He opened the back door and let it just sway back and forth. "Don't do anything screwy now, Dutch," Otto half insisted half pleaded, "Hold it...hold it still..." He picked the canister up and pulled it over his lap then shoved it unceremoniously out the door. The metal canister clanked and rolled, spilling its contents as they had intended, but Otto could not reach the door to close it. Dutch didn't care, and yelled to Otto over the ramped-up noise, "Now fire, Otto!" With the door still flapping open, Otto jumped back into the front and grabbed the gun that was at his feet, stuck it out the window, grimaced while trying to take aim at the canister and started to fire in a spray that hit the can and the road. Sparks flew everywhere along the road and with a brilliant burst the flames finally engulfed the canister, spreading rapidly to the dry grass and shrubs on the side of the road. Smoke rose from the flames, encouraged by the breeze, the elements seeming to aid Dutch and Otto in their escape.

Somehow Dutch managed to keep his speed steady at eighty five miles per hour, the gas gauge rapidly dipping lower and lower as heavy black smoke clouded the road. *This will slow them down,* he thought to himself with momentary relief.

Otto let out a sigh, but refused to voice what he was thinking, *Damn those coppers! This is getting really tiring,* as a shot hit the back of the car.

"What the hell!" Dutch started to swerve while Otto spun around to spot the source of the gunfire. "We're not out of it yet, Dutch," Otto growled.

They heard another shot fired, but it didn't hit. Otto instinctively put his hand over his head and slouched. Dutch peered over at him with disdain, reminded once again of Otto's cowardice. "Otto!" he bellowed, "Pay attention!" Otto sat back up reluctantly.

"Are we near the exit?" Dutch asked as he realized another car was gaining on them. "Who the hell are these guys?" he growled. The situation was spiraling out of control as more shots were fired. Dutch took his eyes off the road and looked at Otto. "We have to get out of here or we are goners...," he finally said aloud.

Ding - another shot ricocheted against a large boulder just ahead of them. They both saw the spark, and then a sudden spray of glass as the windshield was ripped open. Otto slumped over towards Dutch, who in a fit pushed him and yelled, "Otto get up - I need your eyes on the road!" When Otto refused to move, Dutch started yelling more anxiously, "Otto! Get up now! Otto! Damn you, Otto! I can't believe..." Once again Dutch pulled his right hand off of the wheel for a second and this time pushed Otto's head, but as he glanced down at him, he saw the clean bullet hole right through the middle of his forehead. *Oh my god, oh my god*, he repeated desperately to himself. He was panicked, and refused to look at Otto, regretting how he had thought Otto a coward. He needed to get control of his emotions and regroup because his panic was as much about the loss of his friend and associate as it was about his now seemingly dire circumstances. He breathed in slowly, but it didn't help as a surge of panic resurfaced. *Otto, damn it...*, he whispered to himself as tears welled up in his eyes. "What the hell is wrong with me?!" he shouted out, the sound of his agony dissipating into the vacuum of noise that had overtaken the car. He became acutely aware of his surroundings, and it served to distract him from his consternation and fear. *Trees, trees and more trees, this whole damn country is nothing but trees, zipping by like a big blur of green. I have to get out of here*, he thought to himself as another shot whizzed by not hitting anything, but this time a ricochet coming from the front was extremely dangerous

- he knew that now. He slammed his foot back down on the gas pedal, touching the floorboard of the car, hoping to get even more speed out of the engine, but at ninety miles per hour he was travelling as fast as any man has ever gone in a car. He heard another shot.

If A Rifle Is Shot in the Forest, Can Anyone Hear it

"Did you hear that, you guys?" Jippsy asked, but they had, and all of them perked up. Jippsy quickly grabbed his shoes, and urged his friends into action. "Come on guys, let's see what it is!" he encouraged, as the anticipation of another adventure ramped up his energy.

"It must be a hunter," Frankie said, somewhat disinterested as he continued to casually cast his line back and forth hoping to pick up another perch.

"No, Frank, it doesn't sound like a rifle," Jippsy countered.

"How do you know? Are you Davey Crocket?" Frankie started with his taunts.

"Very funny, Frank. I know the difference. My dad lets me use his rifle to hunt, and THAT is definitely not a rifle shot." Jippsy stood his ground, confident that he was one hundred percent right.

Frankie didn't care. "Well, you go ahead - I want to stay. I really don't care."

"Ok, then. I'm going," Jippsy spat out, then turned around and ran for the road. Capri didn't hesitate and immediately ran after him, calling out, "Wait, Jips, I'm coming too." Jippsy knew she couldn't resist an adventure, even if it was make-believe or turned out to be nothing. Butterball also yelled after Jippsy, and started to chase the two of them, eager to leave Frank behind and join his friends. He tripped over his shoes, almost hit the ground, but managed to right himself with a quirky flailing of his arms. "Hold on...I want to come too," he called out breathlessly.

"Me too!" Vicky said confidently in her quiet voice.

Jippsy and Caprice waited for them at the road, and Jippsy took control, "Ok, guys, let's head back towards Big Rock." Capri walked just behind him with Vicky and Butterball almost skipping every second step, just to keep up. Vicky was anxious to find out what it was too - any excuse to get away from Frankie and Dodo - but more importantly she could be with Jippsy, watching as he walked ahead, his wet shorts dripping down his tanned legs, hitting those terrible shoes, her mind wandering to another time... *One day we'll be together and have the clothes we want to wear not the ones handed down by some distant family members*, she thought to herself. He wasn't wearing his shirt, and his copper-skinned back accented all the muscles, while his hair was a wavy wet mess. *Those green eyes he and Dodo share, I hope those will be passed down to our kids. I hope they get his small straight nose and that divot in his chin, just like he got from his mom. He'll make a very handsome man*, she thought giddily.

"Why are you guys walking so slowly?" Jippsy was getting aggravated, and turned back, his face contorted while trying to hold in his rage. He started to let them have it, "Come on Butterball step it up. Capri..." but Jippsy's words were interrupted by a single sharp wave of sound: PING! "Did you guys hear that? It must be another shot!" Jippsy's senses started picking up more information. "I can hear a car too," he blurted out.

Butterball's mind was always at the extreme end of make-believe, "Maybe it's a gangster and the cops are chasing him," he said thoughtfully, as he remembered the radio broadcast he had heard last night. "Hey, Jips, did you hear about Dutch Schultz? It was in the paper and the radio - they think he's in Montreal," Butterball continued excitedly, although a little afraid it might also be true.

"I know, screwy eh?" Jippsy remarked.

"Yeah! Maybe it's him," Capri piped in, and because she couldn't help herself her sarcasm stabbed at him, "Sure, Butterball, and maybe pigs will fly..." she snorted derisively.

"Come on, Capri, what do you know? You're a girl," Butterball retorted.

"So, BUTTERball, you challenging me?" Capri retaliated, always up to the task.

"No. But I bet you don't listen to Flash," he was leading her on now,

"So...?" her irritation was clearly apparent.

"So you don't think it's possible that a man can fly to the moon?" Butterball responded with his seemingly outlandish fantasies.

"Are you totally screwy Butterball?" Capri answered and started to twirl her finger next to her temple to show that Butterball was crazy.

"You see – no imagination," Butterball finally said, as he tried to find the fastest way out of this conversation.

Jippsy had been ignoring their conversation as his mind wandered. *What if it is Dutch?* Jippsy thought to himself. But something pulled him from his personal thoughts. "I hear a car coming!"

The Chase

For the first time since this had all started Dutch was feeling trapped. His mind was reeling and his thoughts were scattered as though Otto had somehow buffered some of the stress and pressure. *How do I get off this road? Green more green*, kept repeating through his thoughts. "There!" he yelled out with hope, then muttered to himself, *There it is...a break in the road. If I pull off at the last minute I might be able to lose them.* Craning his head just to get a glimpse of his pursuers, he realized he had to let them get a little closer if he was going to pull this off. Dutch slumped down in his seat, but seeing Otto just lying there conjured up images of the past. He had no time to dwell, but couldn't stop himself from feeling sorry. "This is for you, Otto," he said to his friend as though he were still breathing, and gathered up the balance of his will as Dutch imagined this was the final showdown. He continued speaking with Otto, "I'll help your family once I get out of this," and allowed one last mournful thought to creep into his head; *I'm ready*, he thought to himself, as he prepared his body and his mind. He knew the bullets would be flying, so he kept his foot sturdy on the pedal and his eyes riveted above the dash. No sooner had this thought escaped but a piercing shot ripped through the back of the passenger side and put a hole right through the last gas can. He could hear the can emptying out onto the floor, but had no time to worry about that. *Steady, steady*, he used the words to count in his head. *Almost there*, and then with a jerk, "Now!" he belted out the word and yanked the steering wheel forcefully to the left. He could feel the change in the

133

ground, and a cloud of dust soared into the sky as if a herd of cattle were on the run. The gravel road rumbled under the tires, and the car skidded from side to side skirting the ditch each time. He could feel the excitement welling up inside, his mouth getting dry, his heart pounding, and the bile from his stomach lurching up through his esophagus. He shrieked - a sound he had never heard himself make – and then allowed the tension to subside somewhat as he gathered his wits. The car slowed enough to allow Dutch to see what was happening behind him.

The driver of the pursuing car jerked his hand instinctively to the left so as not to let the perpetrator disappear. He felt as though he was chasing his prey and his keen senses would be enough to guide him to the kill. He underestimated, though, the torque of the beast he was riding; any horse could make that turn on a dime but a four thousand pound hunk of metal did not have that kind of flexibility. The car spun one hundred and eighty degrees at first, and threw the two bodies askew. Then, just as suddenly, there was a moment of calmness as the two bodies, now clumped one atop the other, no longer felt the centrifugal force of the spin. It was just long enough to allow each man a glimmer of hope, but it was short-lived as without hesitation the car spun again so fast that it flipped on its head and continued to roll, the crunch of the vehicle as it bounded from roof to side to tire to side over and over, the intermittent screams of the men as their bodies whirled inside the car - upside down, right side up, there seemed to be no end until the car came to a halt, and there was no further movement nor any sound at all.

Dutch twisted in his seat in order to see if he was still being followed, but he was already too far away and now completely unaware of what had happened to the vehicle pursuing him. At this point, though, he no longer cared, and so he just kept on driving. Although he was acutely aware of his surroundings and his faculties were still intact, he now needed more information to assess his next move. He had to rely on his senses now more so than ever; he tightened his face with a mock smile in order to open his ears, and squinted to block the extra light from burning his eyes. His nostrils flared in disgust from the overwhelming smell of gasoline, but he no longer heard gunfire. He could only hear the sound of the tires crackling over the pebbles on the road. Dutch saw a flash to his left and turned to look in the direction of what might have been more trouble, but all it took was that momentary distraction coupled with the intense sunlight for him to miss that he was about to send the car flying over and down a small hill. The car - metal, rubber and cargo - lifted off the ground, and then forcefully back down with a thud of tremors that bounced the car up and down like an insignificant rubber ball. Otto - who was not bleeding at all from the hole in his head, as if the bullet were a cork in a wine bottle - was sent flying around the inside of the car like a rag doll flopping and lifting off of the seat into a nearly upright position only to return again to the seat and slide ever slowly towards the floor.

The Lincoln's speed increased down the hill at an alarming rate, and Dutch couldn't keep his feet securely on the brake as the car lurched and jumped down the hilly road which suddenly started to snake to the left toward a grouping of trees that he couldn't help but notice. His mind raced, but he gathered his wits about him, shoved Otto away as best as he could, and held the wheel firmly as he was literally holding on to save his life. The ground came up fast and the speed with which the car was travelling made it seem as though the trees were hurtling straight toward him instead of the other way around. He pulled on the steering wheel, a hard left, squeezing the wheel tightly as though that extra pressure would give the car more traction, but the car's back tires began to skid out, which caused the Lincoln to slide horizontally, and slowed its speed somewhat. *Thank goodness*, he thought to himself, as the ground started to slope upward, further slowing down his imminent crash into the trees. Dutch started to have better control of the car and was able to straighten the wheel and right the car. He could breathe easier, looked around and into the rearview mirror to be sure there was still no car behind him. *I am in the clear*, he surmised, but still not willing to take any chances he put his foot back down to the floor.

The Crash

Frankie and Dodo heard it that time, as the lake had a way of amplifying sound as though they were right next to the source. But what they heard was not just gunfire, but what sounded like metal clanging together. They shot up together in a start, like a track and field athlete at the gun. "It sounds like a car crash of some sort, Dodo...hurry!" Frankie said, running while trying to get his shoes over his feet. Fortunately he was too good of an athlete to stumble, and he was off, Dodo chasing after him. He knew Dodo would follow, but did not want to delay what he could potentially see.

"Frankie, wait up!" she called after him.

"Come on, Dodo! Hurry, girl!" he yelled back, not really caring whether she was near or not.

Her rage had started to build and she could not hold it back. Her breathing started to quicken, as the blood pumped through her chest and face. She recognized the feeling; it was a Russo family shortcoming, and if Frankie could see her, he would know she was furious. She did not like being left behind. *That selfish bastard!* he fumed. *How could he just leave me behind?* Then she shook off the thought, gathered her things, and chased him up the road.

Frankie spotted them at Big Rock. "Jips, old boy! Hey Jippsy!" Frankie called out, then Dodo interrupted purposefully, "We're back here, wait up..." She could see Jippsy reaching for that stick he found earlier up on Big Rock, while the rest of them were waiting for him back at the road. "Hold on, dammit!" she yelled not caring if anyone heard her cussing. They started to run even more furiously, and she and Frankie quickly made their way to where the others were standing.

Dodo was doubled over panting, and anxious to recount what they had heard, but Butterball beat her to it, and excitedly told them what they had heard. They waited another moment for Jippsy, who was running back with his stick in his hand waving it up and down, pumping it to help him gain speed. Capri stood staring at the ripples on his stomach, as his muscles flexed and his proud chest showed the beginnings of chest hairs. As she watched him she felt warmer than she had all day. This whole day had been a sea of mixed emotions for her, but she waved off the thought as though trying to get the hair out of her eyes.

He was breathing so fast that she could clearly see his heart drumming against his rib cage. "Let's go," Frankie insisted as his impatience became apparent, and he started walking up the hill.

"Hold on, Frankie. Let me catch my breath," Jippsy entreated.

"Come on, Jippsy. I'll help you..." Capri said mockingly and grabbed up his arm, linking them together as she pretended to help him along.

"I'm ok now - you can let go, Capri," he said brusquely.

"Sorry, Jippsy. Forgot you have your trusty staff to help you." Capri was rest-fallen but refused to let it show. "Ok, Moses, are we just supposed to follow you for forty years now?" Capri taunted.

"What are you talking about Capri? Just follow me," he said with a sneer.

"I hear a car coming," Vicky said.

"I hear it too!" Butterball chimed in. "It sure is coming fast too. We, ahh, better get off the road...hurry! There it is!" Butterball's widened eyes told the whole story - they didn't have to wait for the words.

"Everyone get out of the way!" That was the last thing they heard Frankie say before they all hit the ground, and then it appeared like an alien spaceship from above, the chassis of a car soared directly over them and landed with a series of bumps before it careened out of control as it headed straight for Big Rock. It razed everything in its path like lava from a volcano, as it knocked down the small birch trees lining the road, then over a dead fallen pine. The car rocked back and forth, and no one seemed to be in control of the car, the person inside having given up hope at this point.

They had all fallen on the road like a succession of dominoes, but the pain of falling on the gravel road was instantly forgotten as their mouths fell open in astonishment, their eyes fixated on the car clearing a path to Big Rock. They all had the same thought: *Was it going over*? Vicky calculated the probability in her mind, Butterball wanted to cover his eyes though he could not, Frankie hoped it would go over, muttering, "Come on, come on. Go. Go! You can make it…" Both Jippsy and Capri wanted to run over to see who was in the car and why they were going so fast.

The Landing

His breath stopped, and he was unable to even feel his heartbeat. Over another hill, and this time there was no stopping his flight; where and how he would land didn't matter anymore – it was out of his hands and only God was in control, he thought.

Reality seemed to slow, replaced by moving pictures at high speed. *Rebecca, I wish I knew you. Your mother was the only woman I ever truly loved. Those days I spent with her were the happiest of my storied life.* Like a dream he became lost in the retelling of the story as if living it all over again.

There she was at the ticket counter at the Saratoga Race Course. I watched as all the men lined up to go to her wicket, one after the other. "$1 on General Tom," they would say.

"Here's your stub sir. Good luck," she would always say. But they were suckers. They were never going to win anything...

"You're a fine tomato, ain't ya?" She was constantly put on the spot or propositioned. She would look up to the sky as if questioning god. How did you even make these people? she wondered.

"Next?"

"$2 on Sassafras. Hey, baby, how 'bout we visit a speakeasy after the race?" another poor slob would ask.

"Looks like you just came from there," she would reply coolly as she handed him his stub. She had nothing but disdain for these losers. She had to snub them one after the next - married men, old men, young men, of every size, shape and colour.

140

"Boys, you stay here," I said to my entourage. I walked up to the wicket, and I could hear people whispering around me. They all knew who I was. There was one more man in front of me before I reached the counter, and he seemed innocent enough; not too tall, brown leather jacket, white shirt and tie. The fedora was a little ratty, but he looked like he was clean shaven, probably had a job.

I heard him say in a quiet tone, but not too abrupt, "Hey, sweetie, I'm a pretty good kisser. You look like a woman who likes to cuddle strange men. How about a go after the race?" My blood boiled over - I had heard enough. I spun him around and told the so-called man with a job that that was no way to talk to a lady. He jerked my hand away and told me to mind my own business. "I'm talking to the lady."

I politely told him not anymore, but just to make sure he stopped, "Here's one right for the kisser," I told him and belted him right in the mouth. Then I laughed to myself that that guy wouldn't be doing much kissing for the next little while.

She didn't see, but my boys whisked the man away to make sure he learned to stay respectful all the time. "I'm sorry miss. In fact, I apologize for all these mooks." Those were the first words I ever spoke to her.

"Thank you, sir. How can I help you this afternoon?" she asked in her angelic voice. "One thousand dollars on Grey Minstrel in the third," I told her.

Her eyes widened. "Sir, I can't take a bet like that. I have to check with my superior," she replied, almost apologetically.

"Sure. You go ahead and do that. In fact, I'd like to make it up to you on behalf of all these thugs. How about I make it two thousand? One thousand for me and one thousand...," I had started to say, but hesitated as I stared into her blue eyes, trying very hard not to look at all of her. I knew all the other men did, and didn't want to be seen by her as one of 'them'. "What's your name?" I asked instead.

"Mary", she answered with reservation.

"Mary what?"

"Mary Cooper, sir," she answered plainly.

"Then that's what we are going to do," I said.

"Do what, sir?" she asked perplexed.

"I'll make a deal with you Mary, Mary Cooper. You come with me to my box to watch the race and I'll place two bets each for one thousand, one for you and one for me." She smiled, that kind of smile that said, Maybe my luck might actually be changing, but instead she smiled coyly and asked, "How do I know you'll pay me?" And this time she stared me straight in the eyes.

"I'll give you the stub as soon as the race is over." I could tell she was interested. Besides, I knew a woman like that couldn't just be handed a one liner.

I also knew that she would have to ask her superior, that she would have to get up and go over to him, and although chivalry was something I honored, having a good plan was more important, and all was working out according to plan. She got up and I could see that what I had imagined was hidden behind that wicket was exactly what I had anticipated. Her body was magnificent – in every way. She spoke quickly with her superior, and a satisfied smile gently curled her beautiful lips upward as she nodded appreciatively. She walked back and I was mesmerized by the sight of her, and the sound of her high heels, as they clicked rhythmically on the old barn wood floor, in perfect time with the sultry sway of her body as she moved toward her seat behind the wicket.

"My boss said it was ok," she said demurely, and

she beamed that magnificent smile in my direction.

"Well, then, shall we go?" I asked, extending my arm in the direction of my box.

"Don't you want to make your bet first?" she asked, both bemused that I had forgotten, and eager that she might actually come out of this a winner.

"Of course. As I said before, one thousand, two times." I handed her a stack of bills as thick as her arm.

"Here are your stubs, sir," she said as she handed me the two stubs with Grey Minstrel bet to win in the third.

"Call me Dutch."

"Ok," was all she answered, her eyes wide as she finally realized who I was. She placed the CLOSED sign on her counter, pushed in her chair, and pulled her long curly hair away from her face. She didn't have short hair like many of the women that year - she was different. Her eyes were a deep ocean blue, and her dark hair created such an interesting contrast – it was no wonder men threw themselves at her. Her skirt and sweater didn't hide any of her assets; her bare legs seemed to be tanned, indicating she was a beach-goer, and her small ankles gave me the impression that she could fit into any fashionable shoe of the season. What a dish, I thought. She walked behind all the other tellers, many of who were men, staring at her from behind their chairs as she walked down the lane and out the door toward the green exit door.

They walked up the painted green steel stairs at the outer rim of the stands, which led up to the boxes. They were followed by his bodyguards and closest friends, many of whom were wealthy merchants and bankers in the area, Dutch made friends with his overwhelming generosity, and especially in a small town like Saratoga, this was no exception. Mary noticed the wives or probably mistresses of the men that were joining them. They were all so beautiful and they seemed to be dressed as if they were at the Kentucky Derby itself. *I'm not one of them, she thought.* Dutch was just a few steps behind and he noticed her looking at the women, sizing them up. He leaned in close to her and spoke softly so no one else could hear or decipher the movement of his lips. "That's right, kid, you're not one of them. That's a good thing." Dutch could see her hiding her smile, and he knew there was something about him she liked, no matter how hard she needed to hide it. She told herself it was about the money. Five-to-one odds and I can help my mother properly.

Dutch had never recounted the story to anyone about how they had met, her feelings for her mother, or why she had gone to the box with him. Later on, she had told Dutch that her mother was sick - not sick in the way you can simply take medicine or have an operation, but since the Depression and her dad leaving, her mother was unable to work or cook or even feel love. She would never smile. Her mother was a corpse trapped in a live body. Those were the words Mary used to describe her. Mary had to start working at whatever clerical job she could get. The pay was very good at the racetrack and a friend of hers had told her that with her looks she would easily be able to get a job. She had offers from many men along the way, but most were just losers. This guy seemed different – a man who would actually come to her rescue, not just try to get some action.

She had been working there for nearly two years and had never been in the stewards boxes - this was reserved for the very wealthy of New York and now she could possibly make five thousand dollars; that was enough money to set them up for life and get the proper help her mom really needed, even if they had to hire a headshrinker.

She felt the palm of his hand on the small of her back. She was surprised but not upset. "Why don't we sit here?" she heard him ask as he guided her to a small table with two dark leather bucket chairs placed conveniently overlooking the whole concourse. From here she could see the jockeys mounting, readying themselves for the next race. A man appeared at the table, and Dutch turned his attention to the waiter. "Milo, could you get the lady..." He paused, and looked back over at her not really sure what she would want. "What will you drink Mary?"

"How about a beer?" she responded decidedly.

"That sounds great. Milo go get everyone beer - I think it's a great way to celebrate the best in sports."

Milo came back more quickly than she had expected; they stored Dutch's beer in an icebox hidden behind a wall just in case of a raid. There was never a raid, though, as Dutch's business helped the economy of the area. So the police had no interest in busting up the local speakeasies, and certainly not the racetrack, as much of their income was subsidized by the industry, of course, all of the illegal activity was controlled by the chief of police himself, but the Feds were a different story, so all was kept hidden.

"Hey, this beer is really cold," she commented cheerfully. He remembered her face as she said it, with a look of surprise and happiness that glowed all around her when she smiled. He couldn't take his eyes off of her even when the race started.

They watched from the best vantage point. They were at the oldest racetrack in the United States and this was their most important race of the year. All the best horses from across the country came to Saratoga, accompanied by their owners, jockeys, handlers, trainers, and even a few lackeys to clean the manure each day, all in order to see who was the fastest. The stands, boxes and grounds were packed for as far as the eyes could see, everyone anxious to get a look at this year's big winner, and be part of one of the area's greatest events.

The stands could hold twenty thousand people, and Dutch and Mary were seated in what the locals referred to as the Turret. The Turret was quite large and located at the far end of the long building. It was rounded with a pointed roof, which gave it the appearance of a turret at the edge of a castle. The rest of the building ran the length of the track right up to the finish line where the building was embellished with three more rooftop points. People not only lined the stands but flanked the track along the rail. *There must be fifty thousand people here*, she thought in awe, as she had never had the opportunity to witness a race in such a manner, let alone the time to observe the action and customs on race day. Today was the most important thoroughbred race in the raceway's history.

The day was clear, with not a cloud in the sky; there was a slight breeze, and it was warm - so warm that the smell of the paddocks wafted completely around the track. *There's no other smell like it*, Dutch thought to himself. *The smell of desperation is unmistakable...*, he thought disdainfully, as he felt the tension and fear pouring forth from the overcrowded stands, rife with men, women and children so hungry for the win that could finally set things right. The jockeys appeared to be having difficulty with their horses as they rode them toward and loaded them into their respective stalls at the starting gate. The pressure had reached a boiling point and no one – not even the horses – was unaffected. Handlers did their best to quickly ease their charges into the stalls, but Number 9, with his checkered blue and white markings, was particularly disturbed by something.

The shouts from the crowd were not helping the three year old. The horse bucked and bucked trying to rid himself of the one hundred and ten pound pest on his back. The jockey's kicks became fiercer as the whip slashed across his horse's hind leg. The jockey waved his free arm at the handlers to help him down, shouting obscenities at them to "Get this beast under control." They could not even get close. The horse's whining was upsetting the others in the starting gate.

"This has to stop now!" Dutch yelled aloud to no one in particular, growing impatient, as were the other fifty thousand fans.

"Look!" Mary responded to his agitation, as she pointed just beyond the bucking horse. Dutch leaned over toward her, followed her arm to the tips of her painted fingernails, where he spotted a man, clearly the horse's trainer, with the stock of his rifle braced upon his shoulder, ready to take aim. They were in shock - this could never happen at such a grand event. The man's rifle was pointed directly toward the raging beasts head.

"Oh my God! What is he doing? What if he hits the jockey?" Mary's stunned voice cracked as the words left her mouth. The handlers ran and took cover while the jockey tried desperately to gain control of his steed. She could almost make out the trainer's finger closing in on the trigger. An eerie silence had overtaken the crowd, their voices lost to their emotions, as a communal gasp sucked the air out of the concourse. The anticipation of the race was easily forgotten, as this was the most extreme event most spectators had ever witnessed: life or death.

"Shoot him!" a heckler called out.

"Run!" a woman's voice shrieked. The gun fired with an explosive shock that rippled through the air, but the whip trained on the horse's hindquarters had snapped at the bequest of the woman's frantic scream. It was a mere split second before the rifle rang out, but the horse catapulted forward just as the bullet tore through its tail, effectively sending the horse racing with blind fury through the raceway. The jockey held onto the reins for his life until he was able to reel the horse in like a fish on a line, ever so slightly pulling back and releasing the horse, subduing the bewildered beast until at last he could yank him to a halt. The audience stood hollering and cheering as though Number 9 had won the race when in fact his life had been spared. Mary was no exception as she too stood, cheering, relieved to have seen the horse being trotted back toward the paddocks. The roar and exultation of the crowd reminded many of the hullabaloo that ensued when the Yankees had won the pennant in '28. Everyone seemed to have regained hope and had forgotten about their individual plight.

Moments later, as the din died down and the audience started to take their seats, the announcer came over the loudspeaker, "Ladies and Gentlemen! Now for the race you have all been waiting for." All eyes turned to the starting gate as if nothing untoward had happened. There was one unoccupied stall but no one seemed to care anymore. The gun sounded, the gates swung open, and the riders flew out of their stalls. There were always odds-on favorites in any race, and this race was no exception, but the horses didn't break off into smaller groups, but ran as a single stable, tucked together, hooves pounding mercilessly in the dust as they reached the turret in mere seconds. Their strides seemed longer, faster, more urgent, as though the commotion at the starting gate had whipped them into a frenzy of competition.

Mary was thrilled and animated as they passed, and yelled excitedly, "There he is!" as she jumped up from her seat. She recognized her horse immediately, having spotted him in the middle of the pack, the only one with a grey coat. *Just like me*, she thought, *not brown or black like all the others, my hair long and flowing, not short or tied back, dying to be free, but trapped in a race.* She looked around the room noticing all the other women in the room watching, but with no real investment. Yes, she was most certainly different.

"Go Grey!" she shouted at the top of her lungs, her heels leaving the carpeted floor as she jumped up and down, as she did her best to help him win by the sheer force of her will. The horses started to break off into smaller groups, some pushed ahead, while others fell behind.

The announcer's voice spurned on her enthusiasm, "It's King ahead by half a length coming around the first turn, Iron Whisper behind, Dakins next, Jonny Boy and Grey Minstrel tied for fourth, and finally we have On the Fairway, Browney Shine, Little Moe and Casper White."

"Come on Grey," Dutch's entourage started shouting, as they had all bet on Dutch's horse, believing he might actually have something to do with the winner. Mary's enthusiasm was infectious, as the men waved their hats and yelled louder, cupping their mouths to project the sound, as though anything could be heard distinctly above the screaming hordes. The entire building, and the audience at the rails had joined in at the top of their lungs with cheers, chants and prayers that God would grant them this one last chance, but Mary's was among some of the loudest.

"King still has the lead," the announcer continued, "Iron Whisper still a close second, as On the Fairway pulls up on the outside with Grey Minstrel just a nose behind. What a race, as On the Fairway picks up speed, pushing past Iron Whisper who's now in third, with Grey Minstrel still holding on the rails. With one last turn, one more furlong left and this is the final stretch."

"Go Grey! Go Grey!" Mary was screaming at the top of her lungs, loud enough so they could hear her at the starting gate. She could feel her throat starting to tighten as it became raw and raspy, but she didn't care...this was the most exciting thing that had ever happened in her twenty-one years, and it was so liberating to finally let go after three long years of struggle and strife.

"King is slowing down, as On the Fairway now takes the lead, King has dropped to second, no third, as he falls behind Iron Whisper. Grey Minstrel seems to have taken this as his cue – Grey Minstrel is pushing ahead on the rail overtaking King, no, wait, Grey Minstrel is now in second. He is half a length behind the lead."

She could see the jockeys hammering at the beasts with their whips for that little bit more, counting on the animals to feel that pain and kick them into another gear.

"Go Grey! Come on Grey! COME ON GREY!" The shouting and energy pulsed through the room. The rest of the field had slipped too far back to still be in contention so the audience took up cheering for one of the two horses still in the race.

"Grey!" "Fairway!" The yelling was so out of control that the announcer's voice was muffled by all the noise, but they were neck-and-neck. "It's going to be a photo finish," yelled the announcer.

"Go Grey!" she yelled as the horses crossed the finish line.

The hooting and hollering stopped, and the crowd hushed as the announcer's voice filled the concourse, "Ladies and Gentlemen, we have a photo finish, and we have On..." She moaned in disappointment as her body slumped down into the leather chair. She had been hoping so badly.

The announcer continued, "On the Fairway. No. Wait - excuse me - the winner is...GREY MINSTREL by a nose! Thank you Ladies and Gentlemen..." and the announcer went on to state a bunch of numbers, but Mary heard nothing else after 'Grey Minstrel'. She was up on her feet, cheering and jumping for joy. In her excitement she grabbed Dutch, wrapping her arms around him, as she planted a warm, enthusiastic kiss right on his mouth. She felt his pouty lips full of need, desire, and something else, and she gave in to her body instead of her brain. They kissed for what could have been forever as they both felt themselves drawn into something greater, something deeper, something neither one of them had felt before. It wasn't just the crowd or the race or the win.

This is crazy, she thought, and let him go as though he were on fire, although what she really wanted was to hold him there and to be held by him for eternity. He smiled, a beautiful, genuine smile, and without looking away from her eyes, he grasped her hand in his and placed the winning stub into the palm of her hand.

Her smile warmed his heart. She knew she would never forget that day, but she didn't know that neither would he. *He* could never forget that day because it was the start of the best year of his life. *I love you, Mary!* escaped his lips, although she couldn't hear him.

Shrapnel

"Don't go down there yet - it could blow up." Jippsy cautioned while holding onto Frankie's arm. He knew the curiosity would be too much for Frankie - he could be a little too impetuous.

"Can you see anything, Jips?" Frankie was dying to run down.

"No, Frank, the trees are too dense, but I was waiting for the splash," Jippsy said ruefully.

"Yeah, me too. It would have been something, eh Jips, old boy?" Frankie replied with a hint of malice in his voice.

"Let's get help," Dodo insisted.

Jippsy stood in front of them all and took charge. "We go down together, slowly and not without a plan," he ordered confidently.

Vicky, who was usually very quiet and reserved, and certainly not one for broad announcements, was now bold, confident and self-assured. She did not want anyone going near that car until she was heard. "I bet there's gasoline spilling out and if there's a fire it could blow up the car. Parts could start flying like a grenade blowing shrapnel." She was keenly aware of this fact, as her dad had been hurt by shrapnel in the 'Great War', as he always called it.

"Ok, Vicky, we'll wait a few moments. Is everyone agreed?" Jippsy asked the group, appreciating her plan of action.

"No!" they heard Dodo say as she wiped the dirt from her dress while getting up. "I think we should tell our parents."

"Absolutely not!" Jippsy countered without hesitation, and continued, "Once they get here we'll never be able to see what it is. They'll have police here investigating for months before we could ever get close." Jippsy refused to miss this opportunity, and knew that Frankie would back him on this. He looked each one of them in the eye to determine their resolve. He caught Frankie's eye, then nodded toward Dodo to enlist Frankie's help to keep her onboard with their plan. Finally, he leveled his gaze at Dodo and announced with an air of absolute command, "We're all in this together. Am I making myself clear?"

"Crystal!" answered Butterball and Vicky in unison as though they were soldiers in Jippsy's army. Frankie and Capri nodded their heads in agreement, while Dodo reluctantly shrugged her shoulders and went along with the consensus of the gang. At least they had all recognized who was in charge and that they were to follow his lead.

"I think Vicky is right; we should wait a few moments," Jippsy truly appreciated how smart she was and that he should pay closer attention to her opinions. Frankie and Capri were clearly cut from the same adventurous cloth and would have to be somewhat restrained.

Their curiosity was killing them, but without timepieces they had to look up to the sky and try to gauge how much daytime they had left. Jippsy could tell by the position of the sun and the length of the shadows that it was around six pm. *Sundown is coming in three hours and that's the last chance we are going to have to investigate before the world knows about it, if Dodo has anything to do with it*, he thought to himself sheepishly, even though he knew it was the right thing to do.

The Death of Dutch's Car

Dutch stirred, momentarily disoriented, having passed out from the solid blow his chest had sustained as his car struck a tree at the end of that terrifying slide. He took a mental inventory of his physical and psychological injuries, but other than a number of throbbing bruises everything seemed to be in proper working order. He tried to open his car door but it was jammed. He watched as sparks streamed from the engine and noticed a small flame flickering just under the hood of the car where it had popped open from the impact with what was now just a stump with the limbs and branches collapsed on the ground. Trees surrounded him in every direction, and as he looked from the sparks and flames to the forest of trees he realized that if - or more likely when - the sparks or flames reached the gas that had spilled a trail of pungent flammable liquid down the path his car had carved, he'd be part of an inferno. What he needed now was to gather his faculties, money, and the books, and high-tail it out of there. *I can't carry both valises*, he thought regretfully as he looked in the direction of his deceased right-hand man. He wanted to be as quiet as a mouse, and while he wasn't sure if he was being pursued, he knew that someone would surely see the smoke rising from the car before long. He leaned warily toward Otto whose body was now crumpled on the floor of the car, and steeled his resolve.

"Sorry Otto", he whispered as his hand reached into Otto's jacket to check his pockets. Dutch wanted to be sure Otto didn't have any of the books. He moved from Otto's jacket to his pants, maneuvering him as though he were simply rifling through his luggage, focused solely on the task at hand, and not thinking about the man who used to inhabit the body. He was just a cold corpse, Dutch surmised, not anyone he knew anymore - his spirit had left and in its place was fodder for the next animal on the food chain.

The last book Otto had been working on had been in one of his jacket pockets, and Dutch remembered there was another book in the glove compartment. *The rest of them must be in the valises*, he presumed.

He had to jam his body against the driver door repeatedly, and his shoulder took the brunt of the punishment and bruising. He imagined the pain was nothing compared to being engulfed in flames, and made sure he forced his way out. The door finally gave and he fell out onto the soft mud and sticks that lined the forest floor. He heard a hissing sound and momentarily thought it might be a snake, until he realized the exhaust pipes were releasing the last of their contents. The pipes must have burst along the way, and turned to survey the destruction his car had caused; it looked as though a meteorite had carved out a path, burning and devastating anything in its way. *Wow! That car has seen me through many lives*, he mused. *I'll be sorry to leave her. Sorry, Rebecca, this is not something your dad will be able to leave for you.* He looked to the sky, hoping his thoughts could be transferred through the cosmos directly to her, even though he knew it to be just a bunch of hooey - or was it? It couldn't hurt to leave a little room for doubt, just in case.

He stumbled around to the back of the car in a desperate haste; the trunk had already flown open because of the impact. He sighed with relief when he realized that the two leather valises were still intact. The fire seemed to be growing- he could hear the flames crackling from the undercarriage of the car. *No time to waste*, he concluded, as he wrapped both hands around the handle of the first valise and pulled with all his might. Clear of the boot, he released the valise – he really had no choice as it was far too heavy for him – and it dropped to the ground with a thud. It was heavy but manageable if he dragged it. The other valise would be impossible for Dutch as it was much heavier - three times heavier in fact - since they had been split up as per Dutch's instructions. He had never expected to have to carry them himself, but this time he had no choice and dragged the last valise with all the remaining strength he could muster. "I...wasn't...expecting...huhgh...to carry...them...myself!" he said aloud, not caring whether or not he would be heard.

He dragged the two-hundred-pound valise one hundred yards deeper into the forest, after throwing the other one as far ahead of him as he could, and finally hid on the ground behind a dead log covered in moss. It was far enough from the car, and out of sight; he hoped to catch his breath, and figure out what to do next. He could once more feel his heart drumming against his ribs, his breathing labored but steady, his inner thoughts stifled momentarily. But that quasi-peaceful state was immediately interrupted by a voice, "Gypsy?"

Dutch stilled and carefully leaned over the log to get his ears pointed in the direction of what sounded like kids. They couldn't be too far considering how clearly he could hear their chatter. He slunk down further beneath the log and planned his escape. *The last thing I need is for anyone to see me*, he thought contritely, considering that there were children now in the picture, and thoughts of his own child filtered through relentlessly.

Brebeuf

"Operator could you get me Brebeuf party line 744?" Giuseppe Sr. tried to keep calm as he had the operator dial his home.

"Of course sir, one moment please," the operator replied politely.

Ring...ring...ring...ring   –   pause   -   ring...ring...ring...ring. That was the cadence of the party line ring at the Russo residence. They shared their telephone line with three other families, and each residence had their own distinct ring tone in order to know the call was for them.

"Hello?" she answered on the second ring.

He heard that angelic voice with the British accent, and felt an instant relief. "Bella, it's me," he said with a gush of emotion.

She could hear the tension and desperation in his voice. "Giuseppe!" she breathed with both concern and relief. She preferred to use his full name, and besides she could never find an appropriate nickname for him. "Are you alright?"

"I'm ok," he answered untruthfully. In fact, he was heartbroken about his father.

"How is Pappy?" she asked, her voice full of worry, knowing well enough that he was not ok.

"They don't know yet. He's still in a coma. He doesn't have anything broken. His heart is fine they said." He tried to find more words to describe what was wrong, but none were coming to him. "He won't wake up, Bella," was what came out finally. She could hear it in his voice - he was very attached to his father, and she could tell

157

when he was scared and on the verge of tears. "Bella, I love you!"

"I love you too, Giuseppe." He had to get off of the phone; just talking was too unpleasant for him. He could not talk about it any further; even the soothing voice of his beloved wife was not enough to vanquish his immediate sorrow.

"I have to go now. I will call you shortly and let you know how long I will have to stay here and what is happening with Papa. Goodbye."

"Bye, my love," she whispered soothingly. She recognized his need to get off of the phone, even though she needed to know more.

Bella could tell his world was coming down on him. They had experienced many difficult circumstances and overcome their fair share of adversity, but this felt different. She wanted to hang up the phone and scream, but she simply clutched it to her chest and slowly slid down the wall crying. Bella was not normally prone to overt emotions, but her tears fell in a flood over her cheeks as she imagined the worst-case scenario, *What if it had been him*? She had been preoccupied by that question all day, ever since Giovanni had returned, recounting the events that took place at the bridge. She had almost fainted on the spot just hearing the news, and as she had listened to the details of the story, not wanting to miss a word, she could feel her body pulsing with adrenaline. What seemed like hours must have been moments. Giovanni finally finished telling his account of what he remembered; she thanked him for his bravery and loyalty then ran into the house not wanting to show any of her staff her vulnerability at that moment. She ran across the hall to their room and threw herself on the bed, blustering until she could not control it any further. She could not live without him was all she could think that afternoon.

She couldn't do anything since she had found out, but tried to stay busy any way she could - cooking, mending, or tending to her garden - whatever she could do with her hands was medicine enough. He was in her mind and occupying every corner of it. Pappy was sleeping they has said. She believed that was ok, that his body would rest until it had healed sufficiently, and then he would wake up. She truly believed that if you listened to your body, and focused on the positive, you could help yourself recover. *But it could have been Giuseppe...*, she kept thinking, and once again the tears would start welling up. She could believe in all the science in the world, but it couldn't change her feelings - she was too afraid to lose him. She would never admit to anyone, even though she knew it to be true.

Her thoughts traveled back to the last time she had sensed him helpless, alone and afraid. He had been lying there in the tent city in the valley. The rain had just stopped beating against the canvas that, like a percussion drum, kept a rhythm for the nurses and doctors. They counted on that drumbeat to keep them moving rather than give into exhaustion. That day they had treated or pronounced dead one soldier after the next; the Germans had been relentless that day, like shooting fish in a barrel - it wasn't fair that so many men had to die. Tens of thousands... *I haven't thought about that day until now. Life has been so good for both of us. We have a love that cannot be explained, and I just can't lose him.* She peered closely at the floor, as though it held some mystery, but she was lost in thought as her mind wandered back and forth. She pictured him again, in that hospital bed, just another soldier that made her soft heart ache, but he seemed different somehow. Maybe he reminded her of someone else - she couldn't really put her finger on it.

They were all young and striking, some a little more injured and hurt inside, others joking to protect their fragile core. These men would be scarred for life even once the stitches, cuts and bumps went away. Giuseppe seemed to understand his place and role. At the time she thought he must have been an officer. Many of the wounded gathered around him during his stay, feeling comfort and confidence in his presence. His rank, although only a sergeant, she found out later, did not stop him from holding counsel with some of the wounded officers. He was, to them, an honorary officer, and although he did not have any officer training his instincts seemed to be able to decipher some of the enemy's tactics.

I saw him watching me and I was sure he was hoping I would visit more and more. I remember sitting at the end of his bed after his tenth day, as he was holding court once again. I was going to say good-bye even though I did not want him to leave, but it was time for him to go home - wherever that was.

A bug walked by her foot, and she watched it in a daze, not willing to move to squash it before it got into the food in the kitchen. She drifted back to her memories.

She sat next to him on the bed, and it was unusually warm that day in October; the tent flaps had been lifted to let out some of the stench and allow the breeze to carry in some fresh air. The sunlight seemed to lift the soldiers' spirits as it shined brightly throughout the tent. It had become easy, necessary even, to ignore the sound of men crying, but her heart was sinking - she didn't want to see him go. She loved their talks, and the way his Italian-accented English rolled off his tongue like a song. She was in love and they hadn't even kissed, but she was not going to let him go without a true memory of her.

"This is my last break before you leave," she said wistfully. "I won't see you when you go..." she remembered telling him, her words barely able to escape her mouth, as her heart was in her throat.

"My Bella, this is only the beginning," he said to her, and leaned closer to where she was sitting. He took her hand in his, and looked up into her translucent green eyes, which were clearly swollen and bloodshot from crying. *Was this for me*, he wondered hopefully. But in his heart he knew that what they felt for one another was the only reality amid this horror they were witnessing. He knew they would be together. "I will come back for you," he swore, as his free hand reached up gently to caress her neck just below the base of her hair. He gently squeezed her neck, and could feel her tension easing with that small gesture; it was just enough pressure to maneuver her head a little closer to his, whereupon he kissed her, gently feeling the softness of her lips, the sweetness of her mouth. But they were hungry for more; their lips, at first only slightly parted, now furiously sought out the passion that had been growing since they first met. Their tongues danced and darted, and they tasted blood as Bella nipped a little too aggressively, wanting him as she had wanted no other man, and knowing this feeling might never come again. They kissed furiously, without abandon as all around them whistles and catcalls resounded, but fell on their deaf ears as they were lost in this one true moment of bliss.

The other soldiers had seen it coming; in such close quarters it would have been impossible to ignore the signs, and they had hoped that they would give in to their growing attraction and affection. Bella and Giuseppe didn't care about anyone or anything else at that moment.

Bella shook herself from this memory, a smile lingering on her lips as she remembered that first kiss, the moment that sealed her love for this man. Sunlight streamed through the window, warming her through-and-through, reassuring her that the man she loved was alive and well, and that they would survive this together, as they always had. She stood up, determined now, her will recharged and intact, a single thought on her mind. "Now where's that bug?" she asked aloud, and thought to herself, *Because the next time it crosses my path, it won't be pleasant.*

Valises

"Ugh, this is damn heavy," Dutch moaned as he attempted to drag the valises foot by foot. He realized this wasn't going to work out. *Oh - the gun!* e suddenly remembered. He left the luggage up against a white birch tree whose roots had grown over the rocks that covered the ground; it had the look of an octopus grabbing its prey with all of its tentacles. He bolted back toward the car without giving any thought to the terrain beneath his feet. The black tip of his saddle shoe jammed into an exposed root and sent him reeling forward face first to the ground. *Futz! Damn it!* he muttered to himself, as he recalled that he was probably not alone. He had heard some kids earlier and did not want to draw any attention to his whereabouts. Back on his feet, not worse for wear, he returned to the car where his old pal was still slumped on the floor. This time he didn't give him a second thought; he had made his peace. He surveyed the car, the flames and the fire, but felt that the rifle was his lifeline. He spotted it in the back seat next to the gas tank. He grabbed the nose of the rifle through the open window, popped it up into the air using only his right hand to catch it, then turned and headed right back to the money. He was safely out of sight from the road and the car, but he had to get these kids away from here. He patted his trusty Tommy gun, as he spoke to it, "You've gotten me out of a few pickles today, old friend."

Dutch on the Loose

"Jippsy, we've waited long enough! Let's go see what happened," Frankie insisted, his patience wearing thin.

Jippsy gauged the others' readiness then pronounced, "Ok, Frankie, lead the way." They all followed Frankie, but Jippsy kept in mind what his grandpa had always taught him: never enter a situation with someone else until you understand their motives. Is this person hurt? Do they need help? Are they escaping from something? Are we in danger? He let his mind wander as he peered up to the sky. He could tell it was going to be dark very soon - the sun was no longer the intense ball of fire it had been earlier. It was only six o'clock, and they had hours before sundown, but Jippsy could already see how dark the forest had become as the trees swayed gracefully in the breeze, the treetops glowing in the remaining sunlight.

Dodo ran in front of Jippsy and stopped everyone from continuing toward their intended destination. "Wait" she said, "It looks like it is going to pour. Maybe we should head back."

"Come on, Dodo, stuff like this doesn't happen every day in Brebeuf," Frankie said, dismissing her as he surged ahead.

"Jippsy, take a look at this..." Frankie said enthusiastically as he pointed to the car.

Caprice ran ahead to get a closer look, with Jippsy following right behind, and the others on his heels. The car was whistling. "What's that sound?" asked Butterball. "That's from the radiator," answered Vicky.

"How do you know?" Butterball asked dismissively. "You're just a girl." Vicky knew he would say that, but she also knew so much more than he did and didn't really care what came out of his mouth.

"I'm smarter than you Butterball," she said condescendingly, "That's how. The radiator cap must have popped off." It looked like steam whistling out from the hot engine.

"So it's not smoke?" asked Capri inquisitively.

"I don't think so," Vicky answered, "But you never know. I wouldn't get too close, especially to a car that slashed through a forest. It may not be the only thing causing that smoke."

"Who cares?" Frankie called back as he ran ahead, his need for adventure clearly trumping all common sense. He was within yards now of the smoking car.

"Where are you going, Frankie? It might be on fire," Jippsy called to him as he followed Frankie closer to the wreck. He had to make sure everyone was safe.

"It's Dutch's car." Frankie asserted with confidence.

"And how do you know that?" Caprice asked him curiously.

"I remember the description - look over there...those are bullet holes," he answered knowingly as he threw his arm out and pointed to the back of the car, where they noticed the trunk hatch was open. "I wonder what was in there?" Frankie pondered, intrigued by the whole adventure.

"If it IS Dutch's car, he may have a gun," Jippsy said with a renewed awareness as he grabbed Frankie's arm. "Let's go there carefully, and make sure the girls are behind us, Frankie," he proposed as he held him back as though Frankie were a dog who had just spotted a cat.

"Forget that," Capri said.

165

"I'm ok with that," answered Dodo.

"Me too," uttered Vicky, while Butterball said nothing at all and merely fell in line as the other three walked up ahead.

The wind wound a path down to the ground and whipped up the dust from the road into the trees, pelting pebbles against the trunks. "It feels like freezing rain does in the winter, eh Jips?" Butterball observed critically – he was no fan of the winter, preferring, instead, the warmth of the sun and the carefree time the friends shared.

"Sure does, BB," Jippsy answered tersely, barely opening his mouth to let out the words for fear of getting dirt in his mouth. He glanced at the sky once again, and knew it was going to rain and that it would be a big one.

Pesky kids, Dutch fumed, aggravated at the prospect of having to shoot at, or simply shoot, some kids. *Anything goes in the jungle*, he reflected, all the while picturing himself as a hunter watching his prey. He didn't dare to stir, allowing, instead, his body to remain calm, his heartbeat to pump steadily, his breathing effortless yet controlled. He heard the hawks off in the distance, their screeching growing in intensity, until the sound had wedged its way into his head, driving away the peace he desperately needed to maintain his concentration. The wind picked up, and he could feel the humidity as it descended through the trees toward the forest's floor. Dutch lifted his head angrily. *What more could this day possibly heap upon me*, he lamented, as he focused his eyes with the sight at the end of the rifle, ready to pounce.

A loud clap startled them; the thunder was right above them, but there was no sign of lightning. "It's going to rain any second," Dodo said nervously. This day had started to be too much for her.

"I know, Dodo, don't worry about it. We've been wet all day anyway. If this wind keeps up..." he started to say, but then realized he wasn't yelling loud enough for her to hear as the wind caught their spoken words and blew them indifferently through the trees. Jippsy adjusted his pitch and continued, "it will be over and done with by the time we..." he tried to say, but he couldn't even finish his sentence as the wind howled through the forest completely overtaking any effort he made.

"Maybe Dodo's right, Jips," Butterball practically shouted into his ear.

Jippsy jumped in front of everyone, threw out his hand and yelled, "Stop!" He pushed back on Frankie's chest as he stepped closer; Frankie was intent on marching everyone forward as fast as he could possibly walk.

The wind continued to whip and howl, but Jippsy yelled above the noise, "Whoever wants to stay should stay right here until we get back," and he motioned to the ground. Both Dodo and Butterball were happy for the opportunity to back out - they didn't care about bravery and they weren't curious about what lay ahead.

Coppers, Kids and Bullets

Dutch's aim was impeccable – he had had plenty of practice. His resolve was without doubt, and his morals were clearly unscrupulous, and while he would have, under normal circumstances, tried to keep the kids out of the picture, the law of the jungle now prevailed. He knew it was kill or be killed and like a switch in his brain survival mode had kicked in; he no longer saw children in his scope, but rather a group of lesser beings that stood between him and freedom. "Any closer now... Come on you punks. Take my money, will you?" he spoke aloud since the noise of the wind had made it easier to protect his cover. Somewhere deep down he knew these kids were no threat, but he couldn't risk the exposure or any more loose ends.

A violent clap of thunder suddenly shattered and rolled through the heavy air, the sound erupting piercingly in Dutch's ears. The shock tore down his spine, his body clenched against his will, and his trigger finger, already in position, reacted by depressing the trigger as Dutch unexpectedly jerked in reaction.

Dodo and Butterball had just taken their places on the ground when the thunder broke. They shuddered from the sheer intensity of the impact as it echoed through the air. They could feel the charge all around them, felt the hair stand on their arms and heads. Unable to hear one another over the roar of the thunder they stayed quiet. Jippsy turned back toward the car and pointed with his finger as if to move on. He would set the pace this time. *Easy – let's take it easy...* he thought to himself. A moose encounter, a cliff jump, gangsters, crashing cars, fire, thunder and lightning – this day had become surreal, each event a lure to draw him in, wondering what would happen next.

"Coppers, kids, bullets, car crashes... Now I have to fight against god!" Dutch laughed at the insanity of it all. Still crouched behind a fallen log, he could feel the ground beneath his pin stripe suit. Although he was normally quite vain, he didn't care for much at all right now. His thoughts were all about survival - the ultimate match. He lifted up the rifle, and carefully set it back on the log, his right eye sighting the kids. He noticed they were approaching more slowly; the kid in the lead was pretty smart, but not smart enough, Dutch mused as his finger found that sweet spot on the trigger once again. "Come on kid, one more time."

Car Bomb

They had barely moved forward when the air around them erupted once again, but this time with a ground-shattering Boom! A torrent of fire ripped upward from the car, as the flames that had been licking the engine of the car finally found the fuel that it leaked all over the surrounding area. Although the gas was an excellent accelerant, the air would help the fire bind to anything and destroy everything in its path. The kids were only fifteen feet from the car and were thrown backward in a tumble on top of one other. Their arms, legs, and bodies twisted together in such a jumble that neither Dodo nor Butterball, who had also been bowled over by the force of the explosion, could determine what belonged to whom.

Butterball was the first one to jump to his feet. He could feel the heat of the fire, and smell the reek of the fumes as they stung his eyes and nose. He ran to the others, no longer concerned about his wellbeing. "Let's get out of here now!" he shouted to them, as they squirmed on the ground making sure all of their parts were in working order. Vicky was on the bottom, beneath the other three who were much heavier than she. Butterball put his hand out to Jippsy, and yelled at him over the roar now of the fire and the vicious wind that seemed determined to carry the flames outward. "Jippsy! Grab my hand!" Butterball found Jippsy's ridiculously oversized shoes and stepped on one of them to give him better leverage, then hoisted him up with all of his might – which wasn't enough to haul him up. His face twisted and contorted at the effort. "Aahh," he grunted and lifted with all his might once again. Jipssy was able to get to his feet this time, somewhat dazed and unbalanced, and uncertain what to do next. He heard Butterball yelling in his ear. "Help me with the others." Jippsy took stock and realized he was ok, but the reality of what had just happened suddenly struck him. He had to get Capri to safety! He looked for her, and saw that Butterball was already helping Frankie to his feet.

"Capri, give me your hand. Capri get up," Jippsy urged. She was lying on top of Vicky, who looked like she was asleep. Capri was moving, but not getting up. Jippsy leaned down to try and lift her up under her arms, but she wouldn't budge. "Butterball!" he yelled out over the sound of the fire, the wind rustling in the trees, and tremors of sound rumbling in the distance. The noise around was infuriating, and his yelling was to no avail. He screamed Butterball's name with everything he had. Butterball turned to see Jippsy pointing anxiously at Capri. He was struggling to get Frankie over to where Dodo sat, obviously in shock. He was dragging Frankie as best he could – it was a chance they hadn't moved more than several feet from where Butterball and Dodo had stopped. It was a struggle but he reached Dodo, and as gently as he could, Butterball dropped Frankie to the ground beside her. Clearly neither of them had their wits about them - Frankie would be no help at all.

"I'm coming," he yelled back knowing full well that the sound would be lost amid all the noise. He ran back the ten feet and saw Jippsy trying to grasp Caprice from under her arms, but then noticed Vicky, who wasn't moving at all. Butterball uttered a small prayer.

"Help me!" Jippsy pleaded. Butterball didn't try to rouse Capri, as he knew that a trauma could play tricks on the body. "Grab under her arm. 1-2-3. Now!" They each had a grasp on an arm and lifted her up. She moved unsteadily with the boys holding almost all of her weight between the two of them. When they made it back to where Frankie and Dodo were sitting dazedly, Butterball practically dropped her on top of Frankie then turned to run back to see what happened to Vicky.

Jippsy noticed that the flames didn't seem to be spreading. The fire was burning from inside the car, out the side windows and through part of the roof. The engine had not caught fire and the windshield was actually still intact. *I hope it rains*, he thought, *otherwise this whole area will become ash.*

Jippsy didn't wait for Butterball to catch up. He was worried that the engine would explode before they had a chance to escape. He reached Vicky and dropped to one knee; he could feel a small rock digging into his knee cap, but he scooped her up into his arms without any further thought except, *Please be ok, Vicky.* She was limp, and he carried her toward the rest of the gang. He didn't want to set her down, and instead put his head down to her chest, turned his ear, and listened closely. The chaotic sounds around them made it impossible to hear, but he pushed his ear closer against her ribs, and he thought he felt her heartbeat. He stayed like that for another moment, then resignedly admitted, "I can't hear anything damn it!" He lifted her higher toward his head, and his arms started shaking from the strain. He put his cheek next to her mouth to see if he could feel her breath, but he still couldn't tell. He jostled her one more time in an attempt to keep her from slipping out of his arms then brought his head back down to her chest. This time, there was no mistaking it...there it was...he could feel her heart beating, the pressure coming back to her lungs that forced his head up and down.

He almost cried on the spot, but instead he talked

to her, "Thank god, Vicky, you scared me." He talked to her as though she was completely lucid, even though he had no idea if she could hear him or when she would come to.

He sat down with Vicky up against a pine tree, feeling the sticky sap on his back while she was still in his arms.

Vicky, in the meantime, had a very clear picture of what was going on: the vivid orange of the flames and the emerald green of the forest were a striking backdrop for her fairytale. She was trapped in her stone tower, the mote murky and black, as it reflected the foreboding sky. "How will I get down?" she lamented as the fire started to rise higher up the tower. "I can't jump - there's no escape." The dense smoke cleared just enough for her to see movement on the field that surrounded the tower.

He was astride a massive brown horse with a striking auburn mane. The man was tanned and tall, sitting high in the saddle, with a strength that was evident given his masterful command of the beast he was riding. "I have come for you my fair maiden," he proclaimed, his magnificently deep voice weaving its way through the noise of the raging fire. "What, pray tell, is your name, my beauty?" he asked of her.

Her eyes were radiant with joy at the sight of this handsome man, her golden red hair glimmering as if she herself were ablaze.

"Victoria," answered the small voice from above.

"Ahh, Victoria...such a beautiful name for a beautiful maiden," he remarked, his voice music to her ears.

"Vicky, Vicky, wake up," he said urgently, his voice strained.

"Victoria," she said proudly in a whisper.

"Yes, you're Victoria." She heard him say, but his

voice was not so deep.

"What?" she croaked as her eyes opened.

"You're ok," Jippsy answered with relief.

"What, what happ-?" she started to ask, her voice still caught in her throat.

"An explosion," Jippsy interrupted, not wanting her to talk too much right away. "Are you ok?" he asked, his voice full of concern.

"Yeah, I guess. I passed out. Pretty screwy, eh?" she answered playfully. His laugh shook them both, as he realized he was still cradling her in his arms.

"You bet," he answered. "You had me scared."

"I'm ok. It was just a quick nap." She couldn't help but smell him. "It was..." she couldn't think of the word to describe what she had experienced, but she knew she wanted to remember this moment, the way he smelled, his arms wrapped around her, the fire crackling around them, and the impending storm. She was speechless, and this was new for her, the girl who always had something to say. *Maybe* comforting *would best describe it*, she thought, and nestled thankfully into his arms until the dream had to end.

Turkey Shoot

The bullets cut through the wind's resistance, their trajectory right on target, but just as Dutch's finger flexed on the trigger, God exerted his will once again, this time with a thunderous eruption that caused him to jerk the gun skyward in reaction. The bullets soared far over their heads, their rapid-fire racket concealed by the natural chaos that tore through the sky. He looked skyward again, his lips pursed and his face contorted as he did his best to contain the anger that threatened to overtake his senses. "Every time I try it seems there is a divine intervention," he called to the powers that be, and laughed at the thought that he was completely at the whim of nature. *I have to Forget about them and move on*, he thought to himself. He watched as they scurried and rallied, believing the explosion had been enough to curtail their curiosity. He wasn't happy about his decision, but he had resigned himself to his fate, and clearly there was a higher power looking out for theirs.

He scanned his immediate area, looking for the best escape route. To his right stood a giant boulder that stretched into the water; behind him was a dirt trail that led down further into the forest; to his left was a hill that was out of the question; ahead of him were the kids, and his best chance for survival. *I can't go back that way...that's suicide - I can't let anyone know I'm alive. Hostages?* he wondered to himself. *Not the answer if I can't transport them, and there'r too many of them. I guess there's only one way.*

He looked back into the forest and then to the two suitcases as another thunderous sound shook the ground.

Despite the forest of trees and the abundance of leaves he felt a raindrop hit his nose, then his chin. *Just what I needed*, he thought, as the clouds finally loosed their contents and the rain poured down torrentially. The intensity of the rain doused the fire, sending a mushroom cloud of smoke to rise above the trees. It left the car no worse for wear than when it had crashed; the fire hadn't burned long enough to heat sufficiently and so the materials had not broken down into liquid, ash or gas.

It was impossible to see through the rain dropping in sheets. The ground became slick as the water mixed with the leaves, and turned the dirt to mud. The sloping terrain became a natural slide, and Dutch reckoned this was his best chance, so he grabbed the lighter of the two suitcases and swung it down the hill, hoping the momentum created by the gravity would take it even further. The other one would be trickier. Water was splashing off of the log, creating a stream that ran down to the rock face of the boulder. As he searched for the suitcase handle his feet slipped on the mud and he fell, hard, into the suitcase and sent it sliding down the heavy stream of water and straight toward the lake. He cursed loudly as he fell and realized what was happening. He covered his mouth – a little too late – in the hopes that his voice hadn't somehow carried back to the kids. He jumped after the suitcase in a dive that sent him sliding, head first, down the incline. He felt like the penguins he had seen in pictures, sliding down an ice cliff. But that thought was fleeting as he took in the rock directly in his path. Maybe the suitcase would hit first and he would slide into the suitcase, but either way he was headed for an impact. He put his hands over his head instinctively in an effort to protect himself, but then saw how quickly he was approaching the valise and grabbed at it desperately with both of his hands. But the desire to save his money quickly waned as the urgency of the situation dawned on him. He searched for anything to grab onto that would stop him from sliding right into the rocks and splashing into the lake. Jagged stones ran the entire length of the hill and his suit was quickly being shredded, along with his skin. More of the same awaited him at the bottom of the hill where the rocks were larger and far more likely to cause some serious damage. He swept his legs sideways to see if he could turn, but it was no use - he was going too fast and his body was carrying too much weight for his arms to be able to stop him now. He couldn't breathe. All he could do was brace himself for the impact and the subsequent fall, and when it came the rocks wracked his body and tore at him, and then with the seeming insignificance of a ragdoll he was tossed over the rocks and into the water below.

The water enveloped him; he was out of air and couldn't swim. He needed to find the surface, and would have called out to the kids to help him if he could. There was no way they would come, though, as they couldn't have seen or known what had happened to him. He was sinking, and it occurred to him what it must have been like for those men he and his boys had sent to their death in the Hudson. Nothing could help him now. His arms were losing their energy, the weight of his clothes becoming unbearable, and he could only see darkness. He thought of his daughter.

Suddenly he felt something solid beneath his feet, and found the strength to push against the boulder in an effort to force his way up, but to no avail – all he encountered was more resistance, and more rocks. More rock meant another way up perhaps, and so, with his adrenaline flagging and his oxygen almost completely depleted he slid his other foot onto the next rock until finally locating a small crevice jutting out from the boulder. He could see he was close to the top, if he stretched, maybe...just maybe he could hoist himself out of the water. With a last desperate attempt he pushed up with the tips of his toes and his head broke the plain of the water.

He breathed in furiously, feeling the burning of the water in his lungs, his exhale a torrent of coughs that almost sent him back into the deep. He hugged the boulder, not wanting to let go, his fingers digging in deep past the moss until he reached stone. He held on while his body rejected the abundance of water he had swallowed. He almost let go as he retched and came dangerously close to smashing his skull against the rock. At no time did the money ever enter his thoughts. He was lucid, although light headed. He couldn't speak, and the water in his system didn't soothe him as it normally would on a hot summer's day. This felt more like pins and needles burning and stinging inside his chest. His coughing continued until the feeling began to subside.

As he watched the water cascading over the face of the boulder he could make out the exact locations of the cracks and crevices that caught the water and changed its direction. If he was careful he could use them as handholds to help hoist himself up. He realized that it would be impossible to do if he kept his jacket on; somehow he had to get rid of it. He was positive that if he were to fall back in the lake, he wouldn't make it back out again. He carefully removed his right hand from the hold he had on the rock and, moving his arm behind his body, wriggled his shoulders in an attempt to loosen the jacket from his arm, playing at the hem of the sleeve with his fingers. All he succeeded in doing was losing his balance, and concluded it wasn't worth the risk.

He brought his arm back around, reached up to a red vein in the stone, and stuck his fingers deep enough in the crevice for the water to be sidetracked from its course, causing even more water to splash in his face.

He shook his head in an effort that clear the water from his face and eyes, but it just kept streaming down. Below the water line he moved his right foot along the large stone, precariously balancing on his left. He slid his foot up along the boulder, its slimy wall scaring away any hope he may have had, until he found another crevice large enough for his shoe to fit inside. His hope was restored, and in a single motion his whole body worked in unison to lift itself up above the water to just beyond his shoulder.

The rain began to subside, and he felt the heat on him once again. The sun seemed to be punching a hole in the sky now, enough so that the light was able to hit the rock directly and warm the water now trickling down the sides. He reached up further and found another crack, felt the moss and polished granite that seemed to cover the sides, but inside the crack, were small stones as sharp as baby shark teeth. He could feel them digging into his fingers, and feel the warm liquid run down his fingers; he knew they were bleeding.

His body was now half way up, but he was unable to find another crevice or bump. He searched more frantically now. *There has to be something*, he thought with abject frustration. He had to find something, *or learn to swim really fast*, he thought mockingly.

"COME ON!" he yelled up to the sky, indifferent to whomever might hear him. "There!" he cried with joy, his throat now heeled from the retching. He shoved his left foot into the crevice and heaved himself upward, his elbows anchored onto a plateau. Just to his left, sticking up right out of the rock, was an evergreen gone orange. Even though Dutch wasn't a believer, he couldn't help but think of the irony; as God had revealed himself to Moses through the burning bush, perhaps he had taken notice of Dutch and was sending him a sign. He grabbed at the bush as he said a small prayer. "Baruch Hashem," he said, thanking God, not wanting to miss a chance to make up for his non-believing days. He hauled his body out of the water and out of immediate danger.

Henchmen

"Gerard, I think we lost 'em," Louis said with relief. He was losing his patience and that was never a good thing with Louis.

"Where's he going to go, Louis? There's only one way down this country road." Gerard wasn't so confident.

"That's gun shots, Gerard. Slow down." Louis didn't want to get caught in the crossfire.

"Of course. I don't want to catch up to them just yet, and that sounds like a Chicago typewriter, Louis. There it goes again. Well I guess we're on the right track after all, aren't we Louis?" Gerard said almost triumphantly, his small face smirking from ear to ear. He didn't want Louis to catch on, but this was going to be his payday once and for all. Then he reconsidered, and smiled animatedly. *Come to think of it, I don't really care what Louis thinks*, he thought to himself.

Gerard was at the wheel, and his own wheels were turning. In fact, he was not especially interested in Dutch's welfare. He slowed down, and was replaying the incident earlier that day at the bridge. *Why have an altercation with the cops?* he wondered. *It's probably a shootout and we might even get killed. If there's a roadblock at the bridge Dutch will never come out of it alive. All I have to do is lay low and let Dutch get arrested or killed. The Rock would never find out what really happened; we just have to lie and tell him there was a shootout, that there were too many cops for just the two of us to manage. The Rock only sent us, but I'm sure he's hiding something that has to do with Dutch. They slept in the car after I offered them a bed to sleep on - there must be something important in the car,* he concluded, once again sporting that devious smirk, *and I am going to find out what it is.*

"Ok, Louis, we're going to follow the trail of destruction that a guy like Dutch leaves everywhere he goes." They figured they were about 2 miles behind, judging by the speed they were going and the sound of the gunshots.

"There Gerard - up ahead. I see smoke," he said, pointing to the exit on the left. "Look...look, there's an overturned car."

"We're going to take that exit, Louis," Gerard said.

"How do you know he didn't go straight, Gerard?" Louis was clearly not convinced.

"Just a hunch, Louis. I can't see why that car would be overturned exactly at the exit, unless Dutch pulled a fast one on him." he said with confidence. The wind seemed to pick up, and the clouds were rolling in fast. Gerard glanced out his window, and felt the wind lifting the car when it hit broadside. *That's quite a gust,* he thought.

Gerard slowed down, anticipating a tremendous downpour at any moment. He could hear the thunder crashing through the skies, shaking everything in its vicinity. Louis was getting a little jumpy in the car; he didn't mind the rain but the noise would send him scurrying as a child - and even now.

Louis and Gerard fell silent. There was something about this day, and this storm that was brewing added to the surreal atmosphere. Both men were silent, processing their own personal interpretation of the day's events to-date, when a thunderclap blasted through the sky shaking everything in the vicinity. It startled the two men who had become lost in their own thoughts. "Did you hear that thunder? It actually sounded like gunfire!" Gerard remarked with amazement.

"That's what I thought, Gerard," Louis agreed almost plaintively. Then realizing how he must have sounded to Gerard tried to make light of the situation. "Pretty *screwy*, eh?" he added snidely in his throaty French accent. "As les anglais always say..." Louis added for effect.

Just as Gerard took the exit, the car started bouncing on the dirt road, throwing the two of them every which way. Gerard was having difficulty concentrating on the road as the bouncing car brought back his vertigo, rendering him unable to focus for a few moments. He tried his best to regain his composure and shake off the feeling, but hadn't realized he was heading directly for the woods.

"What are you doing? Go left!" Louis barked in his guttural voice. Gerard yanked the wheel to the left and the wheels responded instantly, but the weight of the car and the speed they were moving forced the car to skid sideways. They were no longer headed straight for the trees but were likely about to sideswipe them, which would still be quite disastrous. Gerard decided that quick action was needed and gunned the gas pedal to the floor hoping this would force the car forward. The sudden acceleration created a cloud of dirt under the wheels until the rubber of the tires gained some traction. The car surged ahead, much to the relief of the two men. "Good thinking, Gerard, mais qu'est ce-qui c'est passé?" *What happened*? Louis questioned suspiciously.

"I didn't see the road!" Gerard responded defensively. "Why don't you help me instead of criticizing? Keep an eye out and let me know what's coming up, d'accord?" He had to specify his needs with Louis, as he didn't always catch on.

"Ok, Gerard, I can do that," Louis agreed in his

simple way. "I think it's raining Gerard."

Gerard shook his head. "I can see that...it's on the windshield," Gerard sneered. "Just look out and let me know the turns on the road," he said, exasperated. He had barely gotten the words out when an explosion ripped through the sky making them both duck.

"Qu'est-ce-que c'est ça, Gerard?" Louis implored.

Gerard let out a low whistle. "Look," he answered simply, as he pointed toward the smoke billowing up above the trees and seeping out onto the road, obscuring any chance of seeing the source.

They were still moving at a steady pace when Gerard's premonition came true; the rain came down like he had never seen before. It was as if all the clouds in the sky had accumulated in this one place. "Merde! Je ne peux rien voir." Gerard couldn't see a thing. "I have to stop. We'll wait here and investigate the explosion when it calms down." He pulled to the side of the dirt road just before it dipped. The smoke seemed to transform from fire to steam in seconds, and they could no longer smell the rank odour of burning fuel.

Otto Body

Frankie was pacing. He was thankful that Vicky was all right, and looked around at everyone just sitting there, scared and confused – they had no idea what to do next. He, however, knew exactly what he wanted to do and couldn't contain his burning curiosity any longer. He ran the few yards distance to the car, which was still steaming from the rain. He marveled at how the Lincoln had actually stayed fairly intact, and that the smell of gasoline had mostly dissipated. The rain was letting up so it was easy to see everything in the car. Jippsy gently set Vicky down on the ground and ran after Frankie. He was worried about him - he would probably make a great soldier one day, he thought, but tactics were not his strong suit. Once Jippsy was on his way, Capri ran after him as well. The others waited to see if it was safe, and Vicky was still a little startled from the explosion but kept a keen eye on the action.

"Frankie? Be careful!" Jippsy yelled out, then realized he didn't have to scream as loudly now that the rain had subsided. "The car may still be dangerous," he continued. As he reached the car, he could feel the heat against his skin as it emanated from the metal.

"Nonsense, Jips old boy, come take a look at this." Jippsy reached the car only seconds before Capri, and the three of them walked carefully on the mud-soaked ground, cautious not to trip on anything and get thrown against the car. They approached the car from behind, noticing that the trunk was open and now full of water. They didn't see anything unusual, so Frankie went to the driver's side, while Capri and Jippsy went around to the

185

passenger side. It was Capri who saw him first, then Jippsy who peered over her shoulder as she stood there with her mouth agape. Frankie looked through the driver-side window. "It's a man..." Capri finally quavered, a trace of delight in her voice; she and she alone had found something fantastic that none of them had ever seen before.

Frankie took off his shirt and wrapped it around his hand – just in case the handle of the car door was still too hot – because nothing was going to keep him out of the car now. As he opened the driver-side door, it creaked and whined, seemingly determined to remain closed and keep the contents of the car secure. He reached in and pushed against the man's head. The body was burnt everywhere, and although it was fairly intact it was charred, the skin having partially burnt off, exposing bone in some places. Frankie noticed a hole right in the middle of the man's forehead. "Hey Jips, look at this," Frankie said, as he pointed to the man's head lying on the charred leather seat. Jippsy opened the passenger door after tentatively tapping the door handle to be sure he wouldn't get burned, and immediately pulled his head back as though having been slapped. The stench was so powerful that both Jippsy and Capri took a step back.

"What is that smell?" she asked disgustedly. "It smells like cooked game and drying hides."

Jippsy recognized the smell. He fondly remembered tagging along with his dad's workers when they went hunting; they would usually bring back a deer worthy of a feast, which they cooked on an open fire. Back home they sometimes took one of the pigs from the farm and slow-roasted it on a spit. The meat was tender and juicy and would even fall off the bone. Jippsy remembered Giovanni always saying, "It's all in the basting, my dear Jippsy," in his Italian accented English, as he carefully tended to the preparation and cooking of the pig with his 'special' sauce. He never would tell Jippsy his secret.

Frankie snapped him back to attention. "I think he was shot in the head with a gun - it looks like a bullet hole." Jippsy and Capri moved closer again, Capri had to hold her nose, while Jippsy tried to think of pleasant smells and not breathe in too much. He couldn't understand how it was not affecting Frankie. The man's clothes were completely burnt off. Jippsy gave only a fast look and then stepped back. "I guess you're right, Frankie. Let's see what else there is to see."

Frankie was mesmerized by the body, not by the person, he didn't care who it belonged to - and he wanted to know what had made it stop. He knew for sure it wasn't the fire, but by the looks of the outside of the car, it must have been the bullets.

He checked all around the corpse as much as he could from his side, but that wasn't enough, so he ran around the front of the car and tripped on a root, which sent him reeling in the mud. He stumbled but righted himself almost gracefully, and ran to the passenger side. He slid over onto the seat and moved the body without any concern whatsoever. The smell, although overpowering to anyone else, aroused his morbid curiosity, and the lure of a dead body simply intoxicated him.

The fire hadn't charred the body's skin as badly as Frankie would have hoped. He maneuvered the body, moving the arms and checking his back. He even looked in his mouth. Jippsy pulled Frankie back from the body. "A little respect, Frankie," he suggested.

But Frankie shook Jippsy off his arm. "Get lost, Jippsy," he snarled, incensed that his investigation was being interrupted. "I want to check this out."

"Fine. Suit yourself, but don't be a pig about it, eh?"

187

Jippsy still had morals and beliefs after all.

Capri went around to the back of the car again. "Hey Jippsy, look at these," she said as she pulled the trunk down, but the latch holding up the boot snapped and dropped the hood onto the back of the car, which caused it to roll off, just about landing on their soaking wet shoes. The two of them jumped back quickly, and Capri tripped on a log behind her. Jippsy was right next to her and managed to get a hand on her back to stop her from falling any further. "Thanks, Jips, old boy," she quipped, making fun of the way Frankie always said it – "Like he's a proper English gentlemen," she always teased.

"No problem, Cappy," Jippsy chortled, another one of Frankie's favorites.

"What did you want me to see?" he asked curiously.

"Look at these..." she answered, as she pointed to the hood of the trunk which now rested on the ground. They stared at all the bullet holes in the back of the car. "Someone really wanted this guy dead," she said too loudly.

"What do you mean 'dead'?" Dodo asked. She was scared but definitely curious.

"It's ok, Dodo," Jippsy called out reassuringly. "Nothing to worry about, everything's fine here." The last thing Jippsy needed was for Dodo to get upset and want to leave.

"What did you find?" Butterball called out, also not realizing the rain had subsided. "Everything's ok," Jippsy called back. "Stay there - we'll be back in seconds," he promised, knowing their level of tolerance. "Dodo you stay there and make sure Vicky is resting," he prompted, wanting to make sure his sister didn't move from there. He knew well enough that her curiosity could get the better of her and she'd end up with night terrors. The explosion had been enough.

Jippsy bent down and saw what looked like a black book sticking out from beneath the toppled hood of the trunk. He was sure no one else had seen it, but to be on the safe side he didn't pick it up right away - he pretended to tie his shoes instead. He knew that if Frankie found it he would want to continue to search for more treasures and wouldn't give up until nightfall. He picked it up slowly and carefully shoved it in the front of his short pants. The book dug into his skin but didn't hamper his walking. He hunched slightly so it wouldn't bulge, and if anyone asked he would say that his back hurt a little from all of the activity that day.

He would show Capri, Butterball and Vicky, and only then would he show Frankie. He knew that once the book was in Frankie's hands he would have a hard time getting it back. There really was nothing else to see; a bullet hole through the front windshield, more bullet holes around the frame of the car, a charred gas can and, of course, a disgusting dead body with a bullet to the head.

"Frankie. Frankie!" he said a second time with more seriousness in his voice. "Let's go. This is really for the Mounties."

"I know, Jips'" he said resignedly. He knew they would ruin their discovery with all of their new techniques to find out whom the body belonged to, and where the car came from. They'd never get close like this again – at least not until the whole thing was over and the body had been removed.

"Have you guys had enough of an adventure?" Dodo asked with a clear disinterest for the entire scene.

"Sure, Dodo," Capri answered. "Let's go back for dinner. It's getting late enough and we're all tired and dirty." Dodo not always trusted Capri's judgment and readily agreed.

"Sounds great to me!'" Butterball chimed in enthusiastically. He was actually hungry and had had enough excitement for one day.

"Figures..." he heard Frankie say snidely.

"Shut up Frankie!" Butterball fired back.

"I just saw a roasting-" Frankie started to say, but was interrupted as both Capri and Jippsy snarled, "Shut up Frankie!" and sandwiched him between them so he wouldn't say anything stupid in front of Dodo.

"Ok. Ok! You guys are such babies," he snapped. He didn't know what else to say because he realized they were right to stop him from saying more than Dodo needed to hear.

The five of them started back up the road Jippsy looked at Capri and nodded his head toward Frankie. He wanted her to keep a close watch on him. He needed to lighten up the mood and Butterball got the ball rolling by asking Jippsy if he thought the body in the car was Dutch Schultz. "I don't think so," Jippsy answered matter-of-factly, much to Butterball's relief. "We did see a body though. The poor man must have died in the crash. We better tell the Mounties so they can investigate," Jippsy continued.

But of course Frankie jumped in, "Yeah and he-" he started to say but Capri elbowed him in the ribs. "What did you do that for?" he hissed. She glared at him and murmured for him to shush. "Ok. Ok! Geez..." he said and shook his head.

Vicky walked slowly but assuredly. She was curious but obviously worn out, and wanted nothing more than to be home. Butterball and Dodo knew there was more to the story than they had seen themselves, but didn't really need to know more for the time being.

"Jippsy, what do we tell our parents?" Butterball was uncertain what to do next.

"Tonight, nothing. We'll meet here tomorrow morning, look around a little more until lunch and then we'll tell them." He thought this was a good plan – in case there was something important in that book. "Is everyone agreed?" Jippsy asked the group. Frankie broke in first and happily agreed, followed by an always-willing Capri. "Butterball?" Jippsy asked and raised an eyebrow at him.

"Sure..." he answered warily.

"Vicky?" Jippsy asked somewhat less enthusiastically.

"Whatever you say Jippsy," she muttered, plainly tired.

"Dodo?" Frankie asked as he looked at her, knowing it would be the hardest for her. *I'll have to watch her*, he thought.

Dodo hesitated but ultimately agreed to go along. She was one of the gang after all.

Jippsy knew that he needed to go back, especially after reading the book. He was positive it would give them clues as to the identity of the mysterious charred man. This was turning out to be better than listening to Flash Gordon on the radio.

They walked on, and as Jippsy considered all of the events of that afternoon: the car, the body, the bullet holes and the news reports, he became more and more convinced that, in fact, it was Dutch's car. *The make of the car is the same, the bullet holes, the New York license plate...it all adds up*, he reasoned with himself. *But weren't there two of them?* he wondered. *And if there were, where's the other body?*

191

Gerard and the Car

The rain had dissipated enough for them to resume their chase, up and down winding roads of dirt and gravel. As the sun beat down it dried the gravel, causing a mist to rise up along the trail. Louis, meanwhile, could feel his stomach sink with every pitch over a hill.

"Eh, Gerard, mon estomac," he complained. "You're going to make me sick."

Gerard glanced over, and could see his associate turning white - or in his case a cream colour tinged with green.

"Hold it in, you pansy," Gerard practically spat at him. Louis didn't like that kind of talk, especially directed at him.

"'Oo are you calling a pansee?" he asked menacingly, his voice an octave deeper than usual, Gerard noted. Clearly he had touched a nerve.

"Ne t'inquiète pas, Louis," Gerard calmly told him not to worry. "It's just an expression."

"Well, cut it out...I don't need to be insulted by you."

"Ok, Louis, how about this one? Don't get your knickers up in a wad," Gerard scoffed, obviously not too concerned about Louis' penchant for violence.

"What does that mean?" Gerard asked curiously. For some odd reason he was getting a kick out of the ribbing; his telltale smirk made that apparent.

"It means don't worry about it for god's sake." Gerard responded with a bit more force than he had intended.

Louis turned his head toward the window and

watched as the trees shot by in a blur.

Down another hill...

"Eh, là! Watch out for 'dos kids!" Gerard was startled by Louis' sudden warning, as he broke the silence. Gerard swerved the car to the left pulling them completely to the other side of the road.

"Maudits enfants!" Gerard shouted while raising his fist in the air at those lousy kids.

"There's the smoke, Gerard." Louis was certainly doing his job right, riding shotgun as the lookout. Gerard glanced back at the kids suspiciously, wondering if they knew something. But he had no intention of stopping; he had to see if that was a car, and if so, was it Dutch's?

One more turn, then down a steep embankment and there it was... Louis could see the car from the road, and Gerard slowed their car to a crawl, pulled off to the side and saw what looked like a huge rock that appeared to dip right into the water.

The car was smoldering, steam spewing out from the car in all directions, literally enveloping it in a cloud. *The rain must have put out any flames*, Gerard surmised. Louis and Gerard both took in the sight of what was clearly Dutch's car, with all of its doors still opened, and the trunk cover on the ground. Gerard and Louis got out, and started to make their way toward the wreck, until Gerard remembered something critical... Gerard stopped dead in his tracks and put his arm out to stop Louis from advancing. It occurred to him that Dutch and Otto may not be dead, and that they had rifle.

"Louis, wait," was all Gerard could say before Louis brushed past his extended arm and continued down the slope toward the crash site. Gerard watched him go, wanting to see what would happen, but knew he couldn't do this alone, not just yet.

"Get down, Louis" he called out. "They may have a

gun." Louis fell to the ground with a thud. Neither of them heard nor saw any movement near the car or in the forest. Louis got up from the wet ground, covered in mud now, but he didn't mind - he loved the outdoors. Gerard wiped his hands over his pants then tried to whisk it off of himself but to no avail - the mud was too wet. As they cautiously approached the site, Gerard motioned for Louis to go to the left to the passenger side, while Gerard, gun in hand, went around to the driver's side.

Once they reached the car, he peered in to see if there were any signs of life. Nothing stirred, so with a sigh of relief Gerard lowered his gun and poked his head into the car. He was immediately assailed with the putrid smell of what he knew now to be rotting charred flesh. He recoiled with a sour taste in his mouth and an equally sour look plastered on his face. Louis was aware of the stench as well, but was much more accustomed to more primitive odors. Gerard could see one of them lying dead on the front seat dead with what looked like a bullet hole in his forehead. "Louis, check the trunk," he called over to him. Louis reached in awkwardly but found nothing.

Dead end, Gerard thought to himself. "Let's get out of the rain and back to the car for a minute." The light was still good but wouldn't be for too much longer. They both made their way to the car through the path carved out by the crashed vehicle. Once inside, Gerard could think more clearly. *The kids*, he thought to himself, *they must have seen something*.

The Black Book

The kids left behind the chaos of the enraged moose, death-defying jumps, car crashes and gangsters, and made it safely to the comfort of their individual homes. Jippsy and Dodo had barely walked through their front door when their mom came running - clearly relieved to see them - and wrapped her arms around them both, pulling them in close to her. It was clear from her actions and the look on her face that something had happened.

"Mom, what is it?" Dodo asked as they both wriggled out of her embrace. They could tell now that she had been crying. "Is Dad ok?" she asked a little less calmly. "MOM. What's going on?" Dodo insisted, as she became frantic for news. This time, however, Jippsy waited patiently to hear what was going on.

"Dad is fine. They were..." she swallowed back the sorrow that crept into her throat preventing her from talking. "They were in a car accident in Montreal."

"You mean Dad and Grandpa?" Jippsy asked although he already knew the answer from the distress in his Mom's voice.

"Yes. He's in the hospital. They think he has a concussion, but he hasn't woken up." She managed to blurt out the last couple of words in a flood of emotion. She was thankful they were safe – especially that her husband was safe. She went on to explain to them that their grandpa was sleeping and that their dad would stay in town until he had to come back to work. There was no need to go into detail right now, she told herself reassuringly.

Dodo wasn't worried about her own welfare anymore and went to hug her mom, wanting to take care of her. But now her mom looked closely at her two children.

"Why are you guys so filthy?" she asked, changing the subject

Jippsy finally spoke up. "We'll wash up," he announced, but said nothing more. He, too, was worried and scared. He loved his grandpa, and there was nothing he could do from here, except wishing and praying, but thought perhaps there was something back at the crash that could help them. He kept thinking that maybe there was something in that book.

Dodo went to bathe first. She scrubbed with all her might, trying to wash off every unpleasant reminder of the day. Dodo couldn't help but think that she would love to spend a lifetime with her knight in shining armor, but that he was going to be trouble. *He is too curious and doesn't spend enough time thinking about the consequences. It's going to get him into trouble*, she thought to herself. *But how can I protect* him? *Thank god he was there today...*Jippsy *would have been a goner.*

She slipped on her nightgown, and went back to the kitchen to help her mom reheat some dinner while Jippsy washed up. They ate quickly and mostly in silence as they were all far too drained to talk. She decided to get right to bed, told her mom she was really tired from swimming, and went to her room. Sleep came easy, but she awoke repeatedly throughout, not completely remembering why. She woke the next morning not feeling rested at all.

Jippsy followed her lead and went to his room early as well. He didn't tune into the radio as he usually did at night. *They must really be exhausted*, their mom thought to herself. *It's usually a fight to get them off to bed, especially when Giuseppe's not here.* She was actually quite relieved for the break.

Jippsy could hear Dodo from across the hall, waking up from time to time, stirring in her sleep. He knew the day had been a lot for her, but that she was remarkably strong when she had to be.

He turned on his lamp, and the yellow light glowed along the pine walls in a soft gold. There was still enough light from the setting sun to highlight the streaky red clouds that lingered as the rainclouds swept past Brebeuf, blowing west toward Ottawa and beyond. The clouds shifted and the sun came back to life, just in time to illuminate a blood moon. It was a beautiful thing to behold, and something Jippsy would normally have spent the night pondering, but tonight his attention could not be diverted.

He sat up straight in bed, comfortably settled on top of the soft quilt his mom had made for him. He carefully studied each page, reading and re-reading every word and every line, trying to make heads or tails of what seemed like gibberish. Names, symbols, and numbers, those were clear enough, but it seemed to be some sort of code, which he spent much of the night deciphering. He could barely keep his eyes open, let alone continue to make any sense of what the pages contained. As he went to put the book on his nightstand he flipped through the pages and watched as the indecipherable information flew past until he reached the last page. He was so tired he barely registered the change in format and handwriting, and was about to toss the book on his nightstand when something clicked.

Jippsy literally bolted right back up, realizing the last page did not have the same style as the rest of the book. His bed was pushed up against the wall, which allowed him to sit comfortably for all those hours, but this time he just sat straight up, his legs crossed Indian-style even though it was awkward for him as his muscles were too tight and large to stay in that position for long. He opened the book to the last page, and there it was in bold letters: "I, Dutch Schultz, being of sound mind and body, bequeath all of my worldly possessions to my only daughter Rebecca Francis Cooper of Saratoga Springs New York, who does not know me, but I am a very aware of her." Jippsy perked up, his neurons firing all at once, his brain now a hive of activity, and read every word slowly - he couldn't believe his eyes.

"Thirteen million?!?" he said it out loud but not loud enough for anyone to hear, straining his voice to yell it out in a whisper. "Thirteen Million!" Again out loud, "There's thirteen million in that car..." Then it dawned on him, *If that's Dutch's car, where is the other guy? Oh my god, we could have been shot!* "We were soooo stupid," he said aloud, as he talked to himself, no longer concerned about who might hear him. He leaped from his bed, and started pacing around his room. He stared thoughtfully from his window - the sky was black but the moon was lit up like a headlight on a car. He could see shadows cast by the trees in front of their house, and the only sounds were those of the chirping crickets drowning out all of the other sounds on that hot, humid night. He knew the owls were on alert for any moving creatures, but the noise of the crickets drowned out all of their hoots, which he could normally hear.

He didn't know what to do; his dad never prepared him for this kind of adventure into the wilderness. He thought back to all the novels he had read, and asked himself, *What would Ellery Queen do?* As he considered how Ellery Queen would solve those cases, he realized it was just a matter of looking for the inevitable clues. He was excited. *That's it*, he thought. *That's how we'll do this*... He skipped with child-like enthusiasm around his room, until it occurred to him that he couldn't tell anyone about what he'd found, otherwise he would never have a chance to find the money.

He jumped back into bed and closed his light. He knew he would have trouble sleeping, but figured he could relax in bed and hash out a plan. *Oh my god...thirteen million dollars is just two miles away. This is screwy!* He laughed and kicked his legs in the air. *Ok Jippsy*, he thought to himself. *Calm down. Calm down. First thing...who* can *I tell? I have to tell the guys - they were part of this, but how do I get Dodo to stay back? I can't trust her now. I need Frankie, but he is such a moron sometimes. Capri? Yeah, she's great; she'll be very useful. Butterball, not so much, but he's a lucky bastard sometimes, and Vicky...she's sooo young, but awfully smart and she has a mathematical mind. She'll definitely be an asset. Next, I have to give everyone a job. Keep your mind off the money*, he told himself. *Thirteen million...this is screwy. How?* How*? This is* **so** *hard; how do I keep everyone occupied and not milling about with their own agenda?* The moonlight shined though his window with an intensity that made it possible for him to to make out every slat of wood as he stared at the ceiling trying to piece this puzzle together. He counted each: *one, one, two, three*... His mind travelled back to the crash site. *Is it possible the other man had time to get out of the burning wreck, and take the bags of money? But thirteen million, how could one man carry all of that? If he did carry it, how far could he really get?*

The Boulder

The rain came trickling down, a far cry from the bullets of water that had pelted down against his body on the rock. He had rolled over onto his belly on the large rock in order to protect his face from the stinging effects of the rain, and his jacket and pants were a tattered mess. Survival was no longer the chief factor, and reality came back with a surge of clarity and purpose. The money. *Where did that end up?* he wondered. He raised himself up slowly on the boulder and removed his jacket. He checked his pockets, but all he found was the pen from that kindly old man. He carefully slipped it into his front pocket, gliding the clip onto the fabric in order to secure it.

He looked toward the car, and didn't see anything to cause him any concern. *Those kids must have decided to go home during the downpour,* he supposed. *That's a relief.* He recalled having thrown one bag down the hill, while the other bag had slid down the muddy hill. He figured the best vantage point to see up the hill was from the shore of the lake.

Where is it, damn it? He stood on the tips of his saddle shoes, using his right hand to shade his eyes from the light and rain and narrow his field of vision. "There!" He pointed excitedly at the bag where it had landed down by the edge of the rock, in the bull rushes, just the tip of the valise touching the water. *The bag must have been stopped by those marshy bushes; that must be the heavy one,* he concluded. *Now where is bag number two?* He stayed on the rock, scanning left and right, up and down for minutes, but failed to spot the second valise. Frustration and panic started to rattle him. "Damn it!" he spat out audibly. "I have to find it." He went back toward the car, and noticed the doors were open, the trunk blown off. *Those kids must have been snooping around here, and if they found it, they'll surely tell the coppers.*

He ran around the car like a man obsessed until he realized how uncharacteristic this behaviour was. He slowed his pace, composing himself, and then walked calmly to the rear of the car where this leg of his journey had started. He breathed in slowly, taking his time to consider his exact steps from the time he went to retrieve the bags. He retraced his steps and located the log where he had been hiding, then recreated the act of throwing the valise. Following the trajectory, he ran down the hill where he spotted it almost immediately and ran to reclaim the lighter of the two bags. *Thank goodness*, he thought with overwhelming relief. He picked up the bag, which by then had been even further weighted down by the rainwater it had absorbed, and only then remembered the major obstacle he now faced. *How the hell am I going to manage this*? he wondered irascibly.

I have to bury them and come back, he concluded. *It's the only way.* He dragged the valise down toward the lakefront, when he realized that if he could somehow manage to get them across the lake, no one would find them. *No that's screwy*, he said aloud, laughing to himself. *I've seen more than my share of this lake.* He reasoned that he could probably float the valise along the shore if it was shallow enough. He dragged the valise the final twenty yards down to the lake, so that the two were within just a few yards of each other. He noticed it was starting to get late. The rain had stopped, and while the sun was still out, it was casting very long shadows along the lake, which meant sundown was approaching.

He couldn't see far to the west as the trees were blocking his view, but he realized once he knew that one direction, he wouldn't be lost. He walked along the shore line and, while his feet were muddy and wet from the swampy terrain, he was still able to maneuver among the plants and bushes, until he reached an expanse where he felt he could safely leave the valises. It was murky with an assortment of broken branches and tree roots sticking up from the bottom of the lake. Dutch's mind whirled with different possibilities as he realized that time was running out. He ran up and down the shore, one hundred yards, two hundred yards, even further until he finally saw it – a narrowed section where the water receded enough to show a sand bar.

He ran back along the shore, slashing the high bushes with his arms and jumping over exposed roots. He felt light as air and able to reach a speed he never would have thought possible given his general lack of athletic prowess. He felt a sense of euphoria he had never before experienced. He imagined himself an Olympic athlete, hurdling over the obstacles in his way, at least until he couldn't get his feet high enough as he jumped over a small pine tree and a birch that were tangled together. He tripped and was sent reeling forward with no time to brace himself. He landed with a terrific thump, scratching the entire right side of his face on the exposed roots.

He rose slowly, taking a mental inventory. *Nothing broken*, he noted with relief, then started to reach his muddy hands toward his face, but stopped and thought it best to wipe them on his pant legs first. He gently felt his way along the right side of his face and pulled his hand away only to find it covered in blood from a stinging cut along his cheek. He shook his head muttering, "No time now, damn it." He started running again but he stumbled once more, this time from the intense pains shooting up his right side and through his spine. He bent forward and shifted his weight onto his left leg, hoping to alleviate the pain in his upper body, which it did, but realized he could not run. He limped back slowly, trying to breathe steadily, searching for that ideal log. He stopped suddenly and turned back to investigate the source of his fall. He felt pleased that, as luck would have it, his fall had perhaps revealed what he most needed at that time. He crouched in a catcher's position next to the two logs, pulled on the pine and they both moved together. He pulled harder, and felt the pain shooting through his body, but grimaced and groaned through the agony and pulled ever harder. The logs moved with him, and finally detached from another as he managed to move them from their resting place. He rose in order to pull the two logs by their branches, one in each hand, and pulled with all his might. Little by little he was able to reposition the logs, intense pain washing over his body, although he did his best to ignore his body and remain focused on the task at hand.

The bulrushes, ferns, saplings and tall grass rustled with every heave. Once at the water's edge, he was ready to test the logs to see if they could, in fact, float and provide the support he needed for the valises. Dutch was no engineer but assumed by their sizes and weights that they should do the trick.

He stood parallel to the water's edge, and gave a hearty yell as he thrust the first log up and out of his arms and into the lake, catching the butt end on the shore. *So far, so good, he thought.* He repeated the same action with the second log and was pleased once again at the results. Both logs were positioned side-by-side along the shore, roughly two feet apart. He limped over to where the heavier valise lay, and dragged it along the shore, which was practically impossible now given the added weight as lake water seeped into the leather, not to mention his injury. He managed to haul it over the first log then went around the other side to pull the valise up and over the second log with a gut-wrenching yell.

He looked around for anything he might use to lash the two logs together so they wouldn't drift apart, even though he was confident the weight of the valises would be enough to secure them. He saw nothing but plants, trees, and shrubs. There were no vines in the countryside – oh how he missed civilization. He remembered the jacket he had tossed away, and climbed back up along the big rock, groaning from the pain in his side, retrieved the jacket and returned to the lake. He searched for a sharp rock he could use to help him rip the fabric. He couldn't help but think what a shame it was to destroy a beautiful pinstripe suit from Brooks Brothers just to use it for its basic threads; it seemed sacrilegious, although necessary nonetheless.

He found a reasonably sharp rock along the shore, and wasted no time as he dug the rock into the fabric. He tried to stab at it to no avail, then lay the jacket on the nearest boulder and swiped at the fabric, but without success. The rock was too small to work effectively. "Damn it!" he spat sourly. He searched his body for anything else that might work, and as he passed his hand over his belt he smiled triumphantly. He unbuckled the belt and swiftly pulled the leather out of the loops with a single tug. He walked gingerly over to the makeshift raft, the pain gradually intensifying as time went on, and ran the belt around the logs. The belt fit perfectly and he was back in business.

"Ok. Next..." he muttered to himself. He then used the jacket sleeve to tie around the log closest to the shore. He used the jacket as a tether to guide the makeshift raft along the shore. *That will do!* He thought with satisfaction. *Why didn't I think of this before rather than worry about my pants falling down?* "Now the moment of truth," he uttered under his breath as he pushed the logs out into the water, and watched as his contraption settled steadily into the water, the ripples glimmering in the light as he dragged it along the shore to settle the next valise onto the raft. He wanted to jump for joy, but could not - the pain would be excruciating. Instead he pulled it slowly and cautiously along the shore, conscious of every step, unwilling to trip or let go of his cargo.

What The Rock Don't Know

Gerard walked through the clearing the car had carved out, while the incident at the bridge played through his head. He could have helped Dutch escape or at least taken care of his pursuers. *Why should I risk my life for him or The Rock?* he wondered. If he had helped Dutch, then maybe he wouldn't be able to help himself. He believed that what The Rock didn't know wouldn't hurt him. *I could get my hands on that money and go as far as humanly possible with my wife and kid*, he thought with anticipation.

"Louis, check the car," he called out as Louis approached the deserted vehicle. If there was someone actually still hiding in the car then Louis would get hit first. "I'll cover you," he promised as he pulled out his revolver. He really didn't want anything bad to happen to Louis but it was better to limit the possibilities. *It's him or me*, Gerard thought ruefully, but Gerard knew who had to come out on top.

"Eh, Gerard. Y'a juste un corps. Je pense qu'il est mort." "Let me see if he's dead," he continued in French. He was sure enough that it was Otto. Even though the face was almost unrecognizable and the clothes burnt to a crisp, there was no mistaking that the body did not belong to Dutch. His sense of surprise and the memory of him alive just a few short hours ago were overshadowed by an odd sense of elation and opportunity. *There's money out there*, he thought to himself. *And what better opportunity could I have than right here, right now?*

They searched all around the car, but Gerard knew that the valises were missing. He also knew that Dutch, alone, possibly injured, couldn't have gone too far. If they approached under the guise of a rescue, maybe they could get close. *Which way did he go*, Gerard pondered as he scanned the forest, the steep hill, the surrounding area for any clues that could lead him, *them*, to Dutch. He wondered about the gun, and whether he might have been picked up on the road. *Maybe he went into the forest*, he thought. *Or maybe those kids know something...*

He stopped and cupped his hand around his ear to try and pick up any sounds above the din of chirping crickets and the rustling of leaves from the faint breeze. But all he could hear were forest noises - nothing out of the ordinary as far as he could tell. Louis, born of the forest, and a skilled tracker, did not relish the idea of following a man with a machine gun, but said nothing and simply followed Gerard's lead. Gerard, he observed, was not especially familiar with nature, nor was he particularly comfortable in this environment. Louis noticed with great amusement how Gerard fumbled around the car like a clown act directly out of Barnum and Bailey's circus.

Louis could see that Gerard was not wise to the natural world. He watched as Gerard searched around disjointedly for what must have been an hour until he waved to Louis to join him back at their car. Louis complied. "This is what we're going to do, Louis. We're going to hide out here until tomorrow, and then we're going to follow those kids - I'm sure they'll be back. And I'm positive they must know something. We'll report back to The Rock once we find Dutch," Gerard lied.

"Oui, ok," Louis answered, always a "Yes Man". But maybe not much longer...

Buried Treasure

Dutch was about three hundred yards from the big rock, standing on a sand bar. The last part of his plan was underway. "I made it," he said triumphantly as he fell, exhausted, onto the sand, heedless of the pain, but grimacing as it shot through his side. "I must have broken a rib," he said aloud. It was almost comforting to hear a voice, even if it was only his own. The quasi companionship renewed his confidence, even if it was just an illusion. He looked down at his once-white shirt, now stained to match his environment, brown, green and grey...a camouflage of sorts. His cuffs were unfurled, devoid of the gold cufflinks that had efficiently adorned them. His clothes were ripped and tattered as though he had been stranded on a deserted island for months. He gently pulled his shirt over his ribs to find the source of the pain in his side. It was evident, just at a glance; his skin was red and mottled, with shades of blue and purple starting to emerge. He touched it delicately, pressing slightly, and could feel that the area had hardened somewhat and was tender to touch. "Damn it! I must've broken more than one rib...". He had to put this out of his mind. What were a few broken ribs compared to his very survival? He turned his attention back to the task at hand.

"I have to find something to dig with..." he said as he scanned the area immediately around the sandbar. He remembered the rifle, but realized he hadn't seen it since he had fallen in the water. *Forget it. There has to be something close by, maybe a branch or a flat rock. I'll have to work through the night,* he thought to himself. He found a reasonably sturdy branch and picked it up, knocking it into the ground to test its resistance. He could feel the air cooling somewhat, as the sun had disappeared from the sky. The abundance of clouds and overgrowth of trees made it difficult to know for sure but he assumed that it was close to sundown. As he made his way along the shoreline, just a few feet in, he came upon a clearing. There were no trees and hopefully no roots either. "It's close to the shore - I may get lucky...yeah, lucky like Luciano. What are you saying Dutch? Just dig!" Although he found talking to be helpful he was worried he might be losing his marbles.

Dutch carved out a perfect square in the ground, large enough to fit a valise. He planted four small sticks on each corner of the square in order to show the perimeter and continued to stake out the plot. He figured if he did it this way he would still be able to feel his way around when the sunlight ran out completely. He started to dig, ignoring the pain and focusing on the end goal, his survival. But there was a bigger picture...getting away with it. As the night wore on, the humidity never subsided, but he continued to labour ignoring the setting sun. The moon had risen without Dutch realizing, and while it had hung majestically in the sky, radiating a soft orange glow, it had eventually diminished in size until it was no more than a small but luminescent white orb. It lit his way for most of the night until the shadows of the trees blanketed his vision. In just a few short hours one hole was successfully excavated with the use of some solid branches and a rock which doubled as a scoop. The soft soil close to the shore made for an excellent location to execute his plan.

The hole was as deep as the valise with a few extra inches to spare. He dragged the valise off of the raft and onto the sandbar and pulled it only inches at a time. Sweat poured from his neck and face, and his fatigue was overwhelming, as gravity pulled at him. His motivation for this exercise had waned and would have reached zero had it not been for the searing pain at his side - a constant wake-up call, reminding him that this was about his survival. He thought that many renowned athletes had played with fairly serious injuries and had hustled on to victory on sheer will alone. He sank the valise into the hole and it fit perfectly. He covered it with the remaining dirt and moved on to the next hole.

The dread of having to start again weighed heavily on him. "I need to sleep," he slurred, talking aloud in the hope that the sound of his own voice would encourage him to keep going and to stay awake. He couldn't listen to his laboured breath any longer.

He returned to the second valise, which still rested on the raft floating along the shore. It was the heavier of the two, and the thought of heaving and hefting onto the shore had become a more daunting task than he could mentally or physically absorb. His jacket was still tied to the raft, and so he tied the other end to his wrist and sat down. Exhaustion overtook him; his eyes closed involuntarily and his body, tired and racked with pain, simply fell sidelong onto the soft undergrowth. Darkness swept over him as he succumbed to a dreamless sleep.

He awoke to the sound of crows off in the distance. Their caws were fervent and determined, each louder than the next, as they relished their discovery, vigorously fighting one another for every morsel. He shook his head, not wanting to picture what he believed they were probably feasting upon. He realized he had slept through the balance of the night.

It was morning, but it must have been very early. The sky was light blue, and the sun had risen sufficiently to sparkle off of the lake. The clouds had dissipated and the promise of another beautiful summer day unfolded before him. Unlike the stark dreariness he had felt as the darkness of the night had crept in, the beauty of the dawning day gave him hope.

The pressure of the jacket sleeve tied around his wrist was an abrupt reminder of his urgent purpose that morning. He sat up, stiff from his night on the forest floor, and turned his attention to the raft and its cargo. To his shock and outrage he realized that the raft had floated off!

He searched frantically, hoping that it had only drifted away recently. His eyes were still blurry from exhaustion as he squinted to focus with whatever light his retina could absorb. He couldn't find it. He thought maybe it might be along the shore, but he couldn't see far enough to make out anything distinctly, so he barreled through the pain of his broken ribs and launched himself onto his feet, his adrenaline momentarily overriding the intense pain from his ribs. He ran to the big rock, remembering it had the best vantage point. Sure enough, he spotted the raft across the lake where it was swaying along the shoreline. It had lodged itself next to a birch that had grown parallel to the lake as it stretched itself out for several feet as though trying to reach across to the other side.

He ran with abandon through the forest along the shore, his pain once again piercing into him with each stride. He was mindful of the ground beneath him as he ran past the sandbar, carving out his own path through the forest, as he made his way to the other side. The light had completely transformed the lake area, and had illuminated the leaves dotting the surface of the lake with flecks of golden light. The raft was now in plain sight; just a few hundred yards around the bend and he would be there.

The water was higher on this side of the lake, and there was no real beach or sandbar from which to retrieve it. The bag was still resting on the raft, which floated against the tree, not quite at the shore. Another ten feet, he guessed, and the only way to reach it, he realized, was to climb out onto the horizontal tree. He stamped his foot on the ground like a child, cursing. *Damn it!* he fumed. *When it rains it pours...* He reached the tree but realized he wouldn't be able to reach it without using something to latch on. He picked up a long stick and saddled his way across the trunk, pushing his way along mere inches at a time. He could tolerate the pain radiating through his body, but the fear of making one false move and plunging back into the lake had him terrified.

Dutch grimaced hard, and braced himself, as he reached forward and wrapped his arms around the tree trunk. He leaned hard against the branches of the tree. The stick became an extension of his right arm as he reached out to the raft and slowly dragged it with him toward the shore. Dutch moved ever so slowly, and never took his eyes off of the stick that anchored that large sum of money to him. He worked himself backwards now. Failure was not an option. The raft seemed to drift with ease.

His jacket sleeve was still tied around his wrist in anticipation of reattaching it once he had rescued the raft and the valise. Even though he knew better than to look down, he couldn't resist, and peered into the depth of the lake below. Without a doubt, he knew that if he slipped and fell he was a goner; the pain in his side would make it impossible to struggle against the pull of gravity this time.

He managed to turn around on the log and jump to shore with the stick still firmly in his grasp, and the valise at the other end. "Whew!" he breathed out with relief. "That was a close one." He lay on his left side along the shore just next to the tree and reached for the handle of the bag. He grasped it and brought it closer to him, finally placing both hands on the valise to pull it to shore. He pulled as hard as he could but realized that it was an exercise in futility. There was simply no way he had the strength to hoist it from that position given its weight and his injury.

He had to change tactics, so he lay again along the shore, reached for the valise with one hand while he held firmly onto the base of an evergreen with the other hand. He struggled through the intense pain, slowly heaving the valise and pulling against the tree as he did so. Little-by-little he was making headway. "Heave!" he grunted. "Heave!" he made more progress. "Again!" he barked through gritted teeth. "Heave!" he cried as each grunt and exclamation marked another inch or two. "One more," he labored. "Heave!" he muttered through clenched teeth as he inhaled the words rather than let them out. Relief came in a sudden wave as the valise finally made it to terra firma. He rolled onto his back and breathed in rapid-fire bursts of air, like a panting dog. He finally let go of the valise.

Now that the bag was on dry land, Dutch knew every moment was precious. He started his search for a perfect burial site and he located it just a few feet in from where the horizontal tree lay. The digging took just as long, and while the sunlight helped him see what he was doing, it also intensified the heat, making it more difficult to work quickly. He went back down to the water repeatedly, unconcerned about its quality, and drank until he was full.

Before burying the bag, he reached into the bag and pulled out book number 12. He pulled his favorite pen from his shirt pocket and noted the location as best as he could remember. He wrote it in code and then determined that he would have to mark the trail inconspicuously in case the book wound up in the wrong hands.

Dutch's Last Will and Testament

They had agreed to meet at the crash site after breakfast. Jippsy often woke with the sounds of the morning infiltrating his dreams. This morning, however, he woke readily from a dreamless sleep, anticipating the adventure that lay ahead. The birds were camped out in the trees surrounding his home, chirping loudly, and the sun had started to rise, already warming the day. Today Jippsy had every intention of setting out before anyone else, and investigating that site before the others realized what was at stake.

"Jippsy, what are you doing up so early?" Jippsy's mom asked as he walked briskly into the kitchen.

"Good morning, mom," he said as he bent to kiss her on the cheek. She was sitting at the breakfast table drinking her morning tea.

"Is dad going to call today?" he asked with concern.

"I'm sure, Jippsy," she answered hopefully. "What are you doing today?"

"Oh, you know the same, I guess. We'll probably be going swimming again."

"Sounds like fun," she said thoughtfully as she recalled her childhood back in England. She had been a fortunate child with loving, indulgent parents. But her life here, with her husband and children, outshined even that happy upbringing. "Is Dodo coming with you?"

"Sure, mom," he answered reluctantly as he looked around for some bread and butter.

Instinctively she smiled and said with a laugh in her voice, "The butter is already on the table, son."

"Thanks, mom." He truly loved his mother...the

way her smile lit up her whole face, and how he never doubted her love and support. She was so proud of him all of the time.

He reached into the cutlery drawer next to the sink, pulled out a bread knife and cut a sizeable chunk off of the loaf she had baked yesterday. He continued to stand as he slathered on the butter, not wasting any time as he wolfed down his small breakfast, so intent to rush out of the house.

"Slow down, Jippsy, you're going to make yourself sick," his mom chastised.

"Thanks, mom," he mumbled with his mouth full. He really just wanted to leave as inconspicuously as possible. He finally decided he should just take the bread with him, and placed the dirty knife in the sink.

"Jippsy...?" she drawled his name, eyebrows raised, a smirk on her face, as she assumed he knew what she was going to say.

"What?"

"You know what." He looked from the sink to the table.

"Ahh," he groaned. He just didn't have time for this. "Could you do it mom? I'll do anything else you ask when I get home."

She had known it was coming, as if they had rehearsed this same scene for years. He really was such a good boy. "Sure, sweetie," she answered with a smile. "Off you go."

For the second time that morning he bent down and kissed her on the cheek. "You're the best mom ever!"

She grinned. "I know." She rolled her eyes and laughed.

Jippsy ran out of the house like a man possessed, jumped right down from the porch to the ground as the front steps were superfluous, and kept on running. He stopped suddenly as he remembered that he had placed his newfound stick against the porch next to the steps. He ran back, picked it up and off he went.

He calculated his time while running. *If I go at this pace, I'll be there in ten minutes.* He knew that the crash site was easily a thirty minute walk. Running up the hill would be a cinch, but if he continued at this pace he would have to slow down anyway when he started down the hill. It would be too treacherous in his bare feet as the momentum and gravity pulled his body faster down the hill, his feet barely touching the ground, his arms flailing every which way. He needed to focus and maintain control to make it there in one piece. He raced on.

He made it to the last descent and could see that there was no one there yet. He reached the bottom and followed the new path carved out by the burning car. He approached with a little more caution this time, as he knew for sure there should have been two people in that car and that one had escaped. He seemed to be alone, and the only sound he could detect was the drumming in his ears from his heart.

He stopped just before the car, and tried to listen again, but his heart continued to pound in a frenzy, and so all of the forest sounds were muted. He stood there thinking about what he was going to tell everyone. He had decided not to bring the book; it was too important, and certainly dangerous in the wrong hands. He didn't want anyone else to see it just yet.

He looked around the car, and then inside where he could see that the body had been hideously disfigured as some of the birds and perhaps other forest denizens had made their way into the car. Jippsy took the time to close the windows and doors, inasmuch as that small act would help to preserve the rotting body, so that the police could possibly identify it before it was too late. He would give his gang of friends a small window of opportunity to further investigate before they would tell the Mounties.

All that money couldn't have disappeared, Jippsy thought to himself. *Dutch wrote that he had it with them. Maybe they dumped it on the way...* But then it occurred to him that if Dutch or Otto was still out there, then maybe he was traveling with the money. Jippsy smiled. *He would have to be moving pretty slowly, given the weight.*

He could hear someone coming from the road, but wasn't overly concerned as he turned to face whoever was approaching.

"Still twirling that baton of yours I see, eh Jips, old boy?" Frankie, of course...

"At least *I'm* not pretending I'm King David with that slingshot of yours."

"That sling shot saved your life yesterday, you dumb Dora."

"Who are you calling a dumb Dora? You big oaf!"

"Ok! You boys cut out the crap. Hey, where's Dodo?" Capri showed up, all smiles.

"She'll be along," Jippsy told Capri reassuringly. He could tell Capri still liked the company of other girls, even though she acted like one of the boys.

"We saw a car down the road - looked like a couple of guys were sleeping in it. I wonder what they're doing here?" Capri asked innocently.

She couldn't see it, but Jippsy's eyes were dilating. His heart had started racing again and his throat had suddenly stopped producing any moisture. He tried to cover up his anxiety by reassuring her, but he was worried. "Don't sweat it, Capri - probably just a couple of homme d'affaires looking for work at the farms." Since the depression people had scattered everywhere looking for any kind of work. "These guys are lucky...at least they have a car to sleep in," he added flippantly.

"Yeah. Come to think of it, they looked pretty scruffy," she agreed.

Dodo came down the road walking alongside Butterball and Vicky who had come along as well. "Hey everyone!" Dodo called cheerfully as she waved. Frankie was thrilled to see her; her dress didn't fit her well, and that only added to Frankie's happiness, his grin belying the look of innocence he attempted to affect when Jippsy poked him in the side.

"Hey, just remember that's my sister!" He insisted, as a good brother should. He just felt it had to be said.

"Hi everyone!" Butterball called out enthusiastically.

"Hi Butterball," they said in unison as if it was a long-running joke.

"Hi Jippsy." Vicky approached and singled him out as they reached both Frankie and Jippsy.

"Hi Vicky. How are you feeling?"

"Last night all I could do was sleep," she said. She was so cute with her red hair and freckles, Jippsy mused.

"Ok, kiddies, let's get this show on the road," Frankie said condescendingly.

"What show is that Frankie?" Dodo asked with a smirk.

"Our mysterious adventure, of course."

"Which is?" Dodo asked with more seriousness than the exchange warranted.

Jippsy lifted his hand in the air, his other hand still firmly grasping his walking stick.

"Hold on you guys, I have something to tell you."

"Sure, Jips, old boy. Out with it," Frankie prompted.

"Yeah - what is it, Jips?" asked Butterball.

He didn't know how to tell them without divulging his secret, so he lied. "I heard that our boy Dutch over there," he started, and cocked his head toward the car and continued, "was hauling a whole lot of money in this car when he escaped from custody."

They all started asking questions at once, but only partial sentences were reaching his eardrums.

"Are you kidding...?" Butterball started to say.

"..you talking about?" this from Frankie.

"How much?" Vicky piped in, more interested in the facts than conjecture.

He held up his hand again as if this were the signal to shut up. It seemed to work well, this trick he had adopted from their teacher who always managed to stifle her students when they became too rowdy.

"Wait a minute, let me finish." He had to come out with it. He realized he couldn't lie to save his life. It was something he knew he had to work on. "I found a book yesterday lying in the back of the car. It was filled..." he started to say but was interrupted.

"You what? And you didn't tell us," Frankie snarled.

"Let him finish," Capri interjected as she grabbed Frankie's arm to quiet him down. She knew that physical contact generally worked to manage Frankie's outbursts.

"Thank you, Capri. I didn't look at it until last night. I thought we had had enough adventure for one day and I wanted to make sure you were all well rested without more things to worry about - especially you, Vicky. Are you rested today?"

"I am," she replied almost reluctantly, but he had a point.

"Are you ready for this adventure?" he asked with enthusiasm.

"I sure am!" He knew he could count on Capri to get behind his nutty schemes. "What did it say already?" Capri couldn't contain her curiosity any longer, and quite honestly she was becoming impatient with all this ego stroking.

"Where's the book?" Frankie asked somewhat menacingly.

"I left it at home," Jippsy answered to the groans of the gang. "You'll understand why in a second. It says there's **thirteen million dollars** in the car," he said almost in a whisper which had the effect of capturing their complete attention and silencing each and every one of them. They were hanging on his every word. "The last page was written by Dutch Schultz as a last will and testament for his daughter in Saratoga Springs. She doesn't know he's her father; she's also only 2 years old now. The problem is that the rest of the book is nothing but symbols and numbers - everything seems to be written in some kind of code." He didn't go on to tell them about the occupants of the car.

"Wow! So you mean that money is here, Jips?" Butterball asked excitedly.

"It seems so, Butterball."

"We didn't see anything in the car, though," Capri noted with disappointment.

"I know...that's the whole mystery. Somehow we have to find it." They were speechless. "Oh yeah - one more thing...there were supposed to be two people in that car." Jippsy said ominously.

"What do you mean two? We only saw one guy and he was dead." Frankie never failed to mention the obvious.

"I know, Frankie, that's part of the mystery too. It's possible that one of the guys, either Dutch or his partner, got away. I don't think either of them would have left the car with all that money still in it, so either they dumped it somewhere before they crashed or the other guy dragged it with him someplace."

Jippsy looked at Frankie, who was counting on his fingers, "We're six..." he started to calculate.

They were all trying to do the math, but Vicky piped in confidently, "Two million, six hundred thousand each."

"Oh my god, that's more money than Santa Claus," exclaimed Butterball, and they all began to laugh.

"You're funny, Butterball," Vicky barely uttered through her nervous laughter.

"Here's the way I see it...we can split up into three groups, and meet back here at noon. We all know how to read the sun..." Jippsy had started to share the plan he had formulated while making his way to the crash site that morning.

But Frankie interrupted as he suddenly remembered what Jippsy had said at the beginning. "Wait. You said you would tell us why you left it at home."

"Yeah, Jippsy, why?" Capri piped.

"Just in case," was all he answered.

"What do you mean, just in case?" Dodo asked fearfully, although she had a pretty fair idea what he was about to say.

"In case someone else is looking for it," he answered reluctantly. "They may not even know about the money, but if they catch us with the book, they'll know immediately." They all nodded their agreement.

"Isn't it dangerous Jippsy?" Dodo was still hopeful that someone would take her side without everyone thinking she was a nervous Nelly.

"No, Dodo, you'll go with Frankie. We're just looking around a little bit." He was trying hard to reassure her even as he had some serious doubts himself. He didn't feel comfortable putting anyone in danger. "If anyone's uncomfortable with this idea then go home now, but at least wait until noon to tell the cops, ok?"

No one spoke up. He was seriously worried about his sister, but he figured Frankie wouldn't let either of them down, and that he would protect her at all costs.

"Capri, why don't you and Butterball pair up and I'll go with Vicky," Jippsy stated rather than asked.

Capri understood right away and took the initiative. "Butterball you lead the way," she said, and winked at Jippsy.

"Uh, sure, Capri," he said with trepidation.

"I'm just fooling." Capri laughed and swung her arm around Butterball's shoulder. "We'll go together." She turned her attention to Jippsy and asked, "How do you want to do this, Jips?"

"Well, we know no one came toward us from the car, and we got here right after the crash, so I think it's safe to say that wherever it is it's not back toward the road. They all looked inquiringly from the car to the road, and then nodded their agreement. The words had barely passed through Jippsy's lips, though, when Vicky interrupted.

"I don't like this plan," she voiced with uncharacteristic resolve.

"What do you mean? I haven't even started." He had a plan, and Vicky was already throwing a monkey wrench into the machine before he could even get it started. Typical!

But she continued to resist, "Well, I think we should all stay together."

Butterball instantly seconded the idea by raising his hand. "If something happens and we're two kids against one adult, I'm not very confident of our odds. But if we're all together, we would be able to help each other better."

"I kinda have to agree with Vicky," Capri added in.

"Nonsense! We can take on anyone," Frankie said

with a bravado that would get them all into trouble, especially since he never considered the consequences of any of his actions. He loved the idea of an adventure, especially if he could be alone with Dodo without Jippsy around.

Jippsy looked at all of their faces, his own face a mask of confusion while theirs showed confident resolve, with the exception of Frankie's look of excitement, of course. He decided that if they were all of one mind and Frankie was of the other, it was probably best to go against Frankie's drive and agree with Vicky, who was generally quite practical.

"Sounds good, Vicky," he finally relented. Ultimately, even though he believed his plan was foolproof and that they could cover more ground in smaller groups, he accepted that he hadn't taken the real potential for danger and his friends' fears into consideration. "Well, I suppose there's no reason to have a vote since we already have a majority," he said finally. It was just as well, he concluded. This way he wouldn't have to battle it out with Frankie, who always tried to push his agenda and get his own way.

They had wasted enough time discussing the plan, and it was time to get moving. "We'll go toward Lost Lake, along Big Rock, and fan out from there along the shore. It's downhill and the easiest way to lug anything heavy." He tried to hide the grin that surfaced as he contemplated the idea of hauling millions of dollars. In the interest of satisfying the gang's sense of fairness he thought it best to confirm their agreement with that plan.

"Unless anyone has any other ideas?" he asked with a hint of sarcasm in his voice which didn't go unnoticed. But no one spoke up, so that was that. Jippsy didn't waste time and started off toward the lake, his eager friends in tow. Frankie and Dodo walked next to each other, and Dodo was clearly uncertain what to do; she knew Frankie would try to break off from the group, and that she would have to keep him reined in somehow. Nothing worked better, she thought, than good old-fashioned women's charms. Her mind wandered, conjuring up the stories of women like Delilah and Cleopatra, and their abilities to weaken the resolve and fortitude of ancient heroes; these magnificent stories were prevalent throughout history. But for Dodo, a girl on the cusp of womanhood, no stories were as powerful and compelling as those of beautiful, intelligent and irresistible women who exercised their charms and secretly controlled the most powerful men.

Vicky walked next to Jippsy, who had taken the lead several steps ahead of everyone else. "Thanks, Jippsy. I think this is better. And safer," she added in for good measure.

How come this girl is so smart? he wondered to himself. "No problem, Vicky," he acknowledged as he playfully reached up and mussed her hair. She immediately shook her long red hair so that it would fall back away from her face. "This is what I think, Vicky..." He wanted to share his thoughts with her. "I think he made his way down along the shores of Lost Lake - it would be the only logical place to try and drag the bag or bags of money if they're still with him."

"Jippsy, have you given any thought to the fact that he doesn't want you to find him, and that he could be very dangerous?" she didn't want to hide her thoughts from him, even if it meant upsetting him.

"Yes," he replied curtly, and with that terse answer she knew this was the end of their conversation about whether or not they should venture forth.

Capri and Butterball trailed behind the other two couples.

"Capri, are you scared?"

"A little, Butterball. You?"

"Yeah. I don't want to meet this guy Dutch."

"Me neither, Butterball, but what about all that money?"

"What good is it...if we're dead?" He was always so dramatic.

"You're right, butterball. Want to go back?" she asked hesitantly.

"No. I'm just hoping he gets away," he answered decidedly, and that abruptly ended their conversation.

Ti-coq

"Did you see those kids, Louis?"

"Oui, Gerard. What about them?"

"Those are the kids we saw yesterday," he answered with frustration. Louis could be so dense sometimes.

"How do you know, Gerard?" Gerard rolled his eyes at that question. How could a man who was supposedly a remarkable tracker lack the most fundamental recall for details?

"Because I have eyes, stupid," he mumbled under his breath. He looked to the sky and mouthed, *Of all the people who could have entered my life, why him?* He turned back to Louis. "We're going to walk from here, and I want to follow them, **but**," and this he emphasized, "I DO NOT want them to see us, so we have to stay very far back. Much better if they encounter Dutch first; we don't want any witnesses."

Louis was growing increasingly uneasy with Gerard's lead. He could sense that something was up and that they (well, Gerard, at least) weren't really there to help Dutch at all. *There is something that Ti-Coq is not saying,* he thought to himself. *I'll go along with him until the right moment.*

Moses Atop the Mountain

At Big Rock, Jippsy stopped, raised his right arm and held his walking stick high in the air so everyone could see above his head. They all stopped in unison, so much like an army on patrol that it made Jippsy smirk as he gazed toward the lake. Frankie was the first to speak. "What's going on, Jips, old boy?" Jippsy gritted his teeth at Frankie's constant use of that moniker.

"Before we go on..." he started to say as he turned his attention back toward his friends, but then paused, somewhat for effect, but also to reflect upon the approach he wanted to take next. He had spent some time the night before contemplating and calculating what actions his friends would take, and, by consequence, what actions he should take to keep them all united. He said nothing more as, with a dramatic flourish, he pulled a knife from the pocket of his shorts. With a flick of his hand he opened the switchblade and they all stared at him in a stunned silence. Wasting no time, since he had their full attention, he promptly announced, "I would like to propose that we all join together as a secret group, the Rouge River Gang, named for the famous Rivière Rouge that runs through this region, and delivers us the water that sustains our farms. Our gang will consist of the group we form here today, each of us devoted to one another's safety, as we pursue our adventures and protect our secrets. We will not go forth without the complete acceptance of all members' and their express dedication to this cause. I declare this rock to be the birthplace of this society," he added as he moved toward the birch tree whose roots were inexorably wrapped around and through the rock.

"This tree and rock symbolize our unique bond,

through which we are *stronger together*." He liked the sound of it, turned toward the tree and carved his initials and the date deep into the bark. He passed the knife to Frankie next, whom he knew would be eager to follow suit, and Frankie did exactly as Jippsy had anticipated. In fact, after he carved his initials just underneath Jippsy's he added the saying just above. They were wondering what he was writing and jockeyed for position behind Frankie, who handed the knife to Dodo knowing she would go along just to make him happy. She carved her initials and the date under his, and passed along the knife, whereupon the others each took their turn solidifying their bond. *Stronger Together*, indeed.

It took them some time, but the spirit of the ceremony did exactly as Jippsy had predicted; they were now a cohesive unit, not unlike a band of brothers brought together by war. They were now a secret club united by a shared cause, operating with a simple set of rules. Jippsy knew this would not necessarily be enough to glue them together, and that there also has to be a code of conduct. For that, he knew he could rely upon Capri, and probably Vicky, to help develop the club's code of ethics. "Perhaps, Capri, you might be able to think of some rules for our club, and I know you'll have something to say about it too, Vicky." A knowing smile crossed her face; he understood her well, and she knew it.

"Sure, Jippsy, I'm sure we'll come up with a few, but for now how about we get on with the hunt, I, er, mean, ah...mystery, well, whatever you want to call it," Capri answered somewhat at a loss for words.

"Yeah, Jips, old boy, where to next?" Frankie always was the eager beaver.

"Well, like I said earlier, we have until noon, and then we have to tell our parents or the police. The money has to stay between us – as well as the existence of the book; you all signed your names swearing to uphold our club's secrecy. So, I'm asking you all to keep this a secret until we all agree it doesn't have to be any longer. For now we should only tell them about the car. Do you all agree?"

"Agreed!" Frankie said conspiratorially as he threw his arm around Jippsy's shoulder. "We're a team." Jippsy thought about shrugging Frankie's arm off his shoulder as he wondered ominously what he had just gotten himself into. "Ok, Capri? Dodo? Butterball? Vicky? We have to stick together," Frankie continued with uncharacteristic team spirit.

At that point, though, Jippsy would take what he could get and thought, *Way to go, Frankie!* as he looked hopefully from friend to friend.

Each one nodded their agreement, and Dodo proved to be especially supportive as she realized how important this adventure was to Jippsy.

"Ok, everyone, let's look around Big Rock first and then make our way down the shore," Jippsy reminded them of their plan. The mist of the morning hung heavily around them as the sun heated up the moisture that clung to the ground from the night's rain. They couldn't see very far at first, and it seemed as though they were making their way through a cloud. Jippsy tried to look toward the lake from Big Rock, but all he could see was the tree where they had inscribed their names. Behind it was nothing more than a white canvas. He was satisfied his plan was working up to now, we just have to find that money and hopefully not the person attached to it.

Staying together wasn't such a bad idea, he came to realize, after-all, there was safety in numbers. Frankie had his sling shot, Jippsy had his stick, and while neither one would prove useful against a bullet, his satisfaction and excitement had started to wane as paranoia started creeping in.

They seemed to be scrambling disjointedly given that they were unable to see much ahead or around them. "Let's all walk together, so we don't get lost in this pea soup," Jippsy called out, as they could barely see even a few feet ahead of them. "Come to the side of Big Rock," he suggested, and almost as one, they managed to make their way over.

"Jips," Butterball said hesitantly, "What if this guy has a gun? What if it's really Dutch? I mean, he's a ruthless killer - they said so on the radio."

"Butterball, what if we get too close and you're really hungry? He better be the one to run," Frankie said mockingly.

"Very. Funny. Frankie. You're a real card," Butterball answered contemptuously.

"Don't worry, Butterball. The likelihood that he's within even five hundred yards of here is completely remote, especially given the time of the crash yesterday and today's time, the speed at which a man can travel per hour, even through the jungle..." Vicky chimed in, trailing off as she calculated. "That would be..."

"I get it Vicky, thanks," Butterball replied somewhat embarrassed. He actually felt better after Vicky's logical assessment. *She's like a walking professor,* he thought. *How did she get so smart? She's only eleven.*

They slowly they made their way down to the shore, staring all the while at the ground so as not to trip on any roots or loose rocks. Jippsy asked them to keep their eyes peeled for anything at all that could lead them to another clue.

"This is sooo amazing," Capri drawled as she moved ahead of the other kids. She loved the adventure, and clearly couldn't get enough of it, as, in her eagerness, she paced her way ahead of everyone.

"Slow down, Capri!" Jippsy cautioned her. "You might miss an important clue." Jippsy was right, she realized; she wasn't channeling her enthusiasm well. She stopped at the bottom of the hill, and closed her eyes because no matter how much light her eyes were able to absorb, the cloud was too thick to really see anything. She listened to the plodding footsteps and silly chatter behind her, and finally called out,

"Everyone stop!" Her voice reverberated across the lake. She breathed in slowly, willfully encouraging her heartbeat to steady in order to better attune herself with the natural sounds around her.

"What is it?" she heard Jippsy ask as he sidled up beside her.

"Be quiet," she pleaded, so that Jippsy quieted each friend as they approached. She breathed out slowly and allowed her ears to guide her through the forest. She noted with appreciation that everyone had fallen silent, respecting the seriousness of her request. She felt the slight breeze as it rustled through the trees, and her deep-rooted memories developed a reality from the sounds that drifted to her from every angle of her surroundings. Something was clearly unsettled; the land, the water and the living creatures that made this place their home normally existed in a state of harmony, a synchronized landscape tightly woven together by time and the give-and-take of nature. Everything existed in concert, and yet... The moss on the north side of the trees, old forest uprooted with large granite stones stuck to the underside of the roots, suspended in midair by the strength of the roots' ligaments, lay there for many winters until finally too brittle to hold on any longer. This all seemed too fresh; did this happen because of the strong winds yesterday? *Perhaps*, she thought. She felt, rather than heard, the sound of scratching, carried along the breeze.

Must be from the other side of the lake, she assumed. "It's clear, but not close," she said aloud without realizing, and they took that vocalization as their cue, or at least an impatient Frankie did.

"What is it, Capri?" Frankie couldn't hold it in any longer.

"If you close your eyes, you could see the things you hear, rather than trying..." she tried to explain before Frankie interrupted.

"What are you talking about?" Frankie had become impatient, and this kind of mumbo-jumbo talk went right over his head, so all he could do was mock her. "If I could see it, I could touch it," he said snidely. "Let's keep moving," he added brusquely.

Capri kept her eyes closed, while the rest of them decided to follow Frankie, except, of course, for Jippsy, who always had a deep respect for Capri's unusual senses. She ignored the sounds of their footsteps and focused her hearing and thoughts across the lake. A little patience and...there it was again! "What is that?" she whispered under her breath. *If only I could see across the lake.* She opened her eyes and could hear the tempered flapping of wings as a bird flew overhead. Her father was an avid hunter and at her insistence had taken her hunting from an early age. He had taught her to be still and quiet and listen for the sounds of approaching birds, the distinctive reverberation of their wings as they ascended or descended, the fact that they took off, soared, and landed against the wind to mitigate the lift and to better control all aspects of flight. This particular bird, a hawk, she noted, was circling. The sun seemed to refract and made the cloud that had settled above the lake a brighter white, almost blue, not unlike the colour of brand new snow in the wintertime. She closed her eyes once again, and could feel the heat reaching her face. The fog would lift soon, in perhaps another hour.

"It's going to be clear in an hour," she said to no one in particular. Butterball was starting to worry that she was losing her marbles or getting a little screwy.

"You're like Sacajawea," Vicky remarked proudly as she smiled at her.

"Saca-who-ja?" Butterball asked.

"You know, Sacajawea...she was the female interpreter Lewis and Clark hired to take them from Saint Louis to map out the Northwest Passage to the Pacific Ocean. They were the first Europeans, or non-Indians, to make it to the Pacific from the east. She was like their tracker. If it wasn't for her, they probably wouldn't have made it," she said, clearly proud of her insight.

"That's screwy, Vicky!"

"It's not screwy, Butterball. It's the truth! And she did it with her baby tied to her back," she retorted.

"No way - that's just a story." Butterball simply refused to believe it was possible.

"It's not a story," she said irately, incensed that he would question her impeccable grasp of the facts. She gave him an angry shove, unsure how else to make him stop.

"I can feel the sun on my face through the fog - it's going to clear up soon. THAT'S how I know," Capri finally answered.

"You tell them," Frankie chimed in with an approving grin on his face. "My sister knows, that's all there is to it."

Every once in a while Dodo made sure to get too close to Frankie in order to touch him by accident, or in her case on purpose. For her, it wasn't about the mystery. She just couldn't help her desire to be around him. She wasn't paying attention and stumbled carelessly on a root. She was so close to Frankie that she went face-first into the back of his arm, and just barely saved herself from landing on her ass by deftly flinging her arms around his waist, nearly toppling them both to the ground. "Come on, Dodo, you're going to kill me here," he muttered and cursed, aggravated by her clumsiness. A moment's thought, however, and he realized he didn't want to upset her, so he offered her his hand to hold to keep her from stumbling again. Of course, she took it willingly. In fact, she liked the idea so much that she was disappointed she hadn't thought to stumble into him sooner. She smiled thoughtfully.

"Well SacaCapri? You might as well lead the way," Jippsy quipped as he pointed her in the right direction.

"Very funny, Jips, old boy," she said mimicking Frankie, although, truth be told, Capri didn't mind owning this moniker whatsoever. She would be proud to be known as another Sacajawea.

"Yeah, very funny Jippsy," said Vicky also thinking he was making fun of her.

"Thank you. I aim to please," Jippsy beamed.

"How about we stick to your plan, Jippsy?"

"Ok, Vicky. You seem to have all the answers," he teased.

She sent him a look he had never seen on her face before - it was endearing, funny and...hmmm, what was the word he was looking for? Oh yeah...condescending.

He couldn't laugh though, as it would have come across as mean, but he kept it in the forefront of his memory so he could smile any time he needed to. Instead, he made a suggestion as to their strategy. "I do think we should spread out a little bit, all within eyesight of each other, of course. The ground is pretty flat near the water, so we can walk along the shore, but each of us three yards apart. This way we can see all around us and any two of us will be looking in the same spot."

234

"Sounds good to me," Vicky said supportively.

"Let's get moving," Frankie piped in impatiently, having grown tired of everyone's babbling and nonsense. "I feel like I'm in a chicken coop."

"And why would today be any different from any other day?" Butterball quipped, knowing this would get under Frankie's skin. He couldn't help but smirk, and knew that simple joke would aggravate Frankie all day. Frankie stared him down.

"Be quiet Frankie," Capri urged. Even she was losing patience with him.

"Fine!" he barked, resignedly accepting her command. "Ok, *leader*," he said begrudgingly to Jippsy, "Where do you want us?"

"Thank you, Frankie," Capri drawled in appreciation. After all, she did want him to feel like one of the gang.

"I think you should go up top - you'll have to cover the most ground up there. You can also be our lookout in case anyone approaches, since you'll have the best vantage point." Jippsy grinned at Capri, who knew he would like that idea. "I'll stay next to the shore, followed by Vicky, then Jippsy, Butterball and Dodo. Scan the trees once in a while, just in case. Otherwise, the ground is what we're searching.

"What are we really looking for?" Butterball asked even though he figured he already knew the answer...another body.

Jippsy put his hand on Butterball's shoulder in order to reassure him; they spent enough time together to be able to understand each other's thoughts. "It's ok, Butterball. We're looking for anything out of the ordinary, really. Money, a suitcase, clothing perhaps, maybe a...uh, cigarette butt, books."

"Books? Why books? I thought you found the

book."

"You never know, there could be another."

"Keys too." He wanted to say a gun, but knew better. He was pretty sure that if anyone found one it wouldn't be overlooked.

"Ok, everyone, let's get into position," Capri said with authority. She walked down to the water, while Vicky paced off three large steps toward the road. Jippsy and Butterball and Dodo did the same. Frankie had wasted no time and was already starting uphill at that point. Already from his vantage point he was able to see them all and see up to the road. The car was within his sights as well and he hoped that the wind wouldn't carry the scent of rotting corpse toward him – *that* he could live without.

"Ok! All set!" he called down to Capri. They started off at a slow but steady pace. Every once in a while Frankie moved too fast and found himself ahead of them, but he would stop to allow them to catch up.

Their quiet resolve was unprecedented. They were never able to keep quiet as a group when they came here, but now they could hear every sound of the forest...woodpeckers boring holes in the trees, squirrels chattering, the bristling of activity as the forest inhabitants went about their morning. But Capri was attuned to something entirely different... *There's that scratching sound again.*

The fog began to lift just as Capri predicted. They could see the mist travelling along the shore; it hovered gracefully over the water, gently floating skyward to be burned up by the rising sun. They were still unable to see across to the other side. Jippsy loved nature and how everything worked in concert. Vicky could tell, just by the way he walked and the tilt of his head that he was becoming distracted. She kicked a stone in his direction, effectively shaking him from his thoughts. He turned toward her, fully aware of what she had done. *She is just so smart*, he thought to himself.

They had walked roughly two hundred yards. "How far should we go like this?" Butterball asked, wondering if this was how they were going to spend their entire vacation...searching the woods for some gangster and his theoretical loot.

"Quiet!" Frankie shouted to get their immediate attention, and everyone stopped. Dodo in particular was happy to stop as she took inventory of the nasty scratches on her legs from the raspberry bushes.

"What is it?" Jippsy asked in a hushed tone.

"I hear a car on the road," he answered, straining his ears to hear more. He couldn't tell if it was coming closer or was coasting off in the distance. He stood still and listened carefully. The rumblings were definitely getting closer. "All of you go up to that clearing," he called as he pointed roughly one hundred yards ahead near the shore. "Over there! I think you can be hidden well enough from sight." They started to walk, but Frankie felt an impending threat. "Go!" he shouted with urgency. "All of you...now!" he insisted.

Dodo ran down to where the rest of them had already gathered. She 'ran like the dickens' as her mom would always say. It took the others mere seconds to reach cover, but Vicky's short legs made it difficult to maneuver through the brush so she figured she would have an easier time if she ran along the shore.

Frankie didn't join them, and decided to lay low and determine if the approaching car was a danger to them. Sure enough, the car pulled up to within a few yards of where Dutch's car had entered the forest.

Frankie ducked his head as low as possible, and hoped that the hill would hide him. He readied his slingshot; it was his only line of defense from there.

The RCMP

"Regarde-là, Lieutenant!" the Officer said to Simms as he pointed toward the overturned car just ahead to the right.

"Oui. Qu'est-ce qui c'est passé?" he asked the Officer, although he had a fairly good idea what had happened.

The Officer continued in his rural French, "We must have missed that car yesterday as we were trawling up and down the 117. The rain surely didn't help, and it's not much better today in this pea soup."

"I see. Just keep driving," Simms snapped, clearly annoyed by the Officer's excuses. He was definitely not pleased that Dutch had evaded their attempts to recapture him, and that they were no closer to intercepting his car, given the utter destruction he had left in his wake. Simms was intent on riding along until this situation was resolved.

"He must have exited near here. We traveled as far as Lac Mercier, but have found nothing."

He couldn't have just disappeared! Simms fumed.

Benoît Simms was head of the RCMP Laurentian Mountains, a detachment of the Montreal head office that patrolled all the towns along the 117. He was personally responsible for two-thousand-five-hundred square miles of land, home to one-hundred-thousand residents scattered along the Laurentian Mountain chain skirting the St. Lawrence and Ottawa Rivers all the way up to Labelle, almost two hundred miles north of Montreal. It was the largest area covered by any of the other RCMP posts in Canada.

Simms was known to be quite meticulous. A small but fit man with short dark hair cut in such a way that it resembled a rooster's crown, he prided himself as good-looking, what with his chiseled face and clean-cut style. He was a proper gentleman and held a rather prestigious position in the community. Simms was a descendant of one of the 1000's of orphans whose parents had perished of typhoid crossing the Atlantic while escaping poverty, overpopulation and famine in Ireland in 1847. His grandfather had been permitted to keep his family name, as the Canadian government was sympathetic to the plight of these children and did not want them to lose their heritage.

His father and his grandfather were hard-working men who appreciated what Canada had to offer. They attended church, spoke both English and French, and were well liked in their community. Simms's parents had moved to the Laurentians from Montreal when the opportunity presented itself to take over a farm. Simms was only 9 years old at the time and left behind many close friends. It was difficult for him to fit in, particularly with such a distinctly different name. His name at birth was not Benoît, but rather Ben. He eventually became so desperate to belong that he insisted his parents call him Benoît. Eventually, his charm and willingness to please won over the other children. But the name change certainly didn't hurt. Because of his mastery of both languages, and as one of the only children in town who was bilingual, he knew he was destined to do more with his life. When he turned 18 he left the Laurentians and joined the police force in Montreal. His inherent sense of justice in all facets of life was his driving force. He was diligent, levelheaded, and a natural leader; indeed, he stood out in all respects. It came as no surprise when Simms was asked to join the RCMP, and it was a true credit to his character when, at the age of thirty-six, he became the youngest man to ever ascend to the rank of

Regional Superintendent and to be responsible for such a vast and populated territory. He was unforgiving and uncompromising. If he so much as suspected that any of his people were dipping their hands into the kitty or taking bribes, they would be arrested immediately. It had happened twice, early on in his career, and the perpetrators' punishments had been swiftly meted out. They never worked again in law enforcement. Needless to say, Benoît Simms ran a tight ship and no one working for him ever stepped out of line again.

"Officer, head toward the overturned car. Let's go take a look." Simms never called any of his staff by their first names, not even when they were off-duty, and since he refused to socialize with any of them, the need never arose.

The Officer steered the car toward the accident and then onto the side of the road as he pulled up within feet of the overturned car. Up close it was horrific, so much so that the officer, after quickly scanning the scene, had to look away. He could see body parts in the engine, and was overwhelmed by the rancor of the combination of gasoline and blood and guts. The odor of the early stages of decomposition, and the visual and mental carnage he was witnessing had become more than the young officer could bear as he felt his stomach lurch and roil. His hand fumbled for the door handle in a desperate attempt to eject himself from the squad car. It had suddenly become more than he could bear, and with one final sense of relief he clasped the handle, yanked and pushed simultaneously as he unceremoniously launched himself from the driver's seat and purged the contents of his stomach, thankfully on the opposite side of the scene.

Simms stared at the Officer with a mixture of amusement, pity and disappointment. The Officer, his stomach contents fully expelled, sat back on his heels and wiped his mouth, shaking his head in embarrassment. The Inspector, in the meantime, said nothing, exited the squad car, and went to investigate the scene. Indeed, the body was in tatters. He must have been going pretty fast and couldn't make the turn, Simms concluded. He searched the car meticulously, and called out to the recovering Officer, "Officer! Take notes."

He looked up from where he was squatted and finally remarked that the car appeared to be a police cruiser. The Officer stood shakily and went to lean on the hood of his squad car as he pulled out the notebook and pen the Inspector insisted they carry at all times.

"Write the following," Simms called to the Officer. "June 22, 1935. 8:12am. Fog cover. Un-marked road off of the 117 in the direction of either Brébeuf or Huberdeau, approximately 20 miles north of Sainte-Agathe, exits to the west. One police cruiser, crashed beyond repair and recognition. Two men deceased and dismembered, most probably caused by the crash. One revolver, empty. Thank you Officer. Get back in the car."

Simms told the Officer to start the car and continue in the direction they had been headed. "Where are we going, Inspector?"

Simms was clearly upset by this question. "Where do you think?" he asked impatiently. "Just follow this road." The gravel crunched under their tires as he pulled the wheel to get onto the exit. "Go slow. It'll be hard to see through the fog, but we'll follow this road until we find it."

"Find what, Inspector?

"The car, you idiot! I expect more from you, Officer. I'm sure Dutch went this way and you never know, someone might have seen him. We'll follow the road and look for any signs. If we have no luck we'll go back to Sainte-Agathe and arrange to start interviewing these farmers. Someone must have seen something or at least heard this crash."

"Slower," the Inspector insisted.

"Don't you think it's possible he's long gone, Inspector?" "Especially since it's been a full night and more since we last heard any news about him," he remarked uncertainly.

"I'm just covering all the bases, Officer," he scolded. But a few moments reflection softened him; he had always afforded his Officers the right – no, the obligation – to question, and this officer was doing just that. "You may be right," he finally said.

"He could be long gone, that's all I'm saying."

"I know, but like I said we have to cover all the bases," Benoît answered as though trying to appease a child.

"Sure, Inspector," the Officer replied almost sullenly.

It seemed as though they had driven in silence for hours since they had turned off from the main route. The fog had recently lifted, when, roughly ten miles further, at the bottom of a hill, Simms spoke out abruptly, "Officer! Stop here!" The car slid on the gravel as the Officer jammed his foot on the brake obediently.

Simms could see an unusual opening into the woods, which was obviously not a natural clearing. "We're getting out here," Simms said with all the seriousness the situation warranted. "Take out your gun, Officer. If this is what I think it is, we could be in for some trouble."

"Yes, sir."

"I want you to cover me. I'll go down there first. You stay about ten yards behind me." Just before he descended to the bottom of the hill, while he was still on the road, he turned back to the officer and entreated, "Don't shoot me. Look before you fire. Got it?"

"Yes sir," he replied, insulted by the insinuation. *I'm a perfect shot*, he said to himself. Years and years of hunting had given him a keen eye for depth perception and patience.

"That Inspector... One of these days I'd like to give him a 'what's what'," he muttered under his breath.

"Absolute silence from here officer," he heard the Inspector order on his way down, but he hoped the little Napoleon hadn't heard him.

Simms paid careful attention to his footing. Just the snap of a twig or the rattle of the stones under his feet would be enough to alert the enemy. He crept silently down to the clearing. Through the residual mist he could see a car; it looked as though it had been there for years, except no rust had formed and there was no visible natural growth around it. It must have burned, he surmised, to look like that so quickly. As he neared the car, he scanned the area carefully. His senses were alert for any signs of danger, and he was not surprised to see what he determined to be someone hiding down behind the hill. He wanted to draw them out, and was confident he could safely approach the car given the Officer covering him. He made sure to keep the car between him and the suspicious individual lurking below. He reached the car and noted how very quiet it was. He pulled on the handle of the driver-side door, and pried it open as slowly as possible, yet the creaking resounded through the small clearing nonetheless.

Simms peered inside and was instantly assailed by the unbelievable stench. He was not unfamiliar with the smell of a rotting corpse. People often died alone in the woods, their bodies unrecovered for days, weeks, even months. He had witnessed all manner of death, both natural and unnatural. He had been called frequently enough to the scenes of hunting accidents and fires, but the worst experience had been a multiple drowning, where an entire family had drowned, one after the other, in an attempt to save the first child who had succumbed to the water. None of them knew how to swim.

A lot of the townsfolk thought swimming was not as important as farming, but Simms swore he would never leave his life to chance. He learned anything he could about surviving in the wilderness. Bears, wolves, moose, and even mountain lions were dangerous in these parts, and humans were merely prey to some of these animals.

He still had to hold his nose, but didn't want to let go of his revolver just yet.

He held his breath for a moment as he scanned the body. He immediately spotted the bullet hole in the victim's head. *This must be our car*, he thought with satisfaction until the absence of a second body became clear to him. *But where's the other guy*? Then he knew...and wasted no time. Gun in hand, he called out, "You there! Down behind that hill... Come out - we're the police. Officer," he called to the man covering him. "There is a man behind that hill." He signaled to his subordinate to come down to the car. "We have guns and will not hesitate to shoot if you don't come out," was his last warning as he started to move.

Clues

"Hey, Jippsy, look at this," Vicky whispered. She knew Frankie needed them to be extra quiet now. Vicky had been running along the shore when she spotted shreds of fabric caught on a bush jutting out into the water.

"What do you think it is?" she asked as she perched on the tips of her toes in an effort to whisper in his ear. He bent down to accommodate her.

"Looks like pieces of a wool suit," he whispered.

"Could belong to our mystery man," she mouthed to Jippsy, as she definitely didn't want the others to hear her, especially not Butterball or Dodo. She handed him the pieces of wool, which he quickly slipped into his pocket so that the others wouldn't notice.

"Where did you find it?" he whispered. Vicky looked to make sure the others couldn't see and pointed to the location. Jippsy cautiously made his way toward the shore, meticulously scanning the area for more clues. He would tell Capri later on, but he was happy they were now on the right track. Someone was here - he was now sure of it. Capri spotted Jippsy moving slowly back toward the shore and followed him. He had stopped on a mound of soft wet earth that seemed to sink with his weight. She could tell something was up by that guilty look on his face. She spoke softly so no one else could hear.

"I wonder what Frankie is doing up there? He must hear someone coming. We better lay low." Capri saw a dark piece of cloth sticking out of Jippsy's pocket. She hadn't seen that earlier.

"What is that?" she asked as she pointed to his pocket.

"What do you *think* it is?" he asked proudly.

Not *that*," she said with a cringe, as her face flushed, trying to feign disgust. "I mean the rag," she whispered.

"Oh!" he said with surprise, as he realized he had been caught red-handed with their only other clue. "Ok, be quiet," he whispered almost unintelligible. "Vicky found it. It looks like it came from a suit."

"Oh?" she answered, startled and worried.

"Do you think it's... " Capri started to ask, but Jippsy stopped her by bending down and pretending to tie his shoes. He looked her in the eyes and nodded solemnly, then put his index finger over his mouth clear gesture intended to shut her up. "Oh my god," she mimed the words. He watched as her face changed expression and colour as it lit up and then went white like a full moon. It was actually funny, he thought, to watch her face transition from colour to colour. He wondered in amusement what colour Capri the chameleon would turn next? Just like a chameleon, he scoffed, but a moody one to be sure.

It occurred to all three of them that they were on the right path. "We must continue to follow the shore," Vicky whispered to both of them, who had each had the exact same thought. She watched Capri's reaction all the while in order to gauge her tolerance. *Is she even up to this type of adventure?* she wondered. She knew full well that Jippsy and Frankie were up to the challenge, and while she knew Capri talked a good game, was she really ready?

They still hadn't heard from Frankie yet, and while they couldn't see him now, they trusted he was still on guard and dared not to say anything. Vicky had been thinking about the piece of cloth. She whispered to Jippsy that it looked as though the cloth had intentionally been shredded, almost as though it had meant to be used as a lash. The more she thought about it, the more she could imagine what it could be lashed to –something that needed to be hauled, like a bag carrying money, but so close to the water's edge? "A bag that heavy," she whispered to Jippsy, "would sink. Maybe he lashed together a raft..." she suggested aloud, although she was just puzzling through the possibilities. "Brilliant!" Jippsy mouthed as the same thought occurred to him. Capri had come to the same realization as she walked closer to the shore, and scanned around the lake and across.

"I wonder if that was the sound I heard earlier?" Capri asked.

The three of them stood there willing the fog away, but it wasn't happening fast enough. Jippsy waited until they were all close enough, and suggested, "Let's continue along the shore single file. We'll go slow, and Frankie can catch up."

"Sure, Jips," Butterball agreed, happy to be leaving that spot – it was making him nervous already.

Jippsy whispered to everyone, "If you find anything along the path, just remember we have to stay quiet until Frankie gives us the all-clear signal." He tried to wave to Frankie, hoping to catch his attention. He could see Frankie staring intently toward the car, his entire attention focused exclusively in that direction as though he was waiting for the perfect moment to pounce.

They walked single file, along the shore, scanning across the lake, as the fog slowly dissipated. Jippsy was leading the gang, his pace increasing steadily as he knew in his gut that what he needed to find was going to be across the lake, and that it had to be a raft.

"Ok, I'm coming out. Don't shoot," he heard the

quavering voice concede. Simms sighed with relief, and yet he was disappointed.

"Come up here kid," he said in English, recognizing that he must be one of the local farmer's boys. Simms came around from the other side of the car, and could see the boy staring at the officer who still had his gun pointed straight at him. "Officer," he called to his dutiful backup, "lower your weapon, but don't holster it - just in case we are not alone. Come up here boy," he called to Frankie. Frankie walked up to them slowly hoping to buy time for his friends so they could get the hell out of there. He was about to wave them on right before he answered the cop, but to his relief he noticed they had already moved on. *Good old Jips*, he thought, *he's a smart cookie that one.*

"What's your name kid?" Simms demanded as he pulled out the small notebook he kept in the breast pocket of his jacket.

"Frank," he answered tersely. Simms could tell he was a proud boy on the cusp of becoming a man. He flipped to a blank page and wrote 'Frank' in his neat script.

"Ok, Frank. What are you doing here?" he asked gruffly.

"Nothing," he answered calmly. "Just hunting."

"Are you from around here?"

"Yeah."

"Ok, kid," Simms sneered. Frankie could see the cop was getting annoyed. "Enough with the short answers. I want to know it all, and I want to know it all now." Even if the kid knew nothing, Simms would assume he knew everything. Frankie followed the cop's arm as he raised it and pointed toward the burned-out wreck.

"What do you know about this car, and what are you doing here? Or maybe we'll go find your parents and haul all of you down to the police station." Frankie didn't at all like that idea and realized it was time for him to co-operate with the cop. He definitely didn't want his dad to know what he had been up to, or worse get into trouble; that, he knew, would put an end to his fun, and he would spend the rest of the summer feeding pigs and cleaning stalls all day long, and that would be the pleasant outcome of his punishment.

"My name is Frank Cristafaro, and my dad has a farm near here. I come here to fish and sometimes I like to hunt rabbits with my sling shot." He reached into his back pocket and pulled it out - he knew it would lend credibility to his story.

"Spell that last name for me, kid. Slowly."

"Cristafaro," Frankie said as though the spelling should be as obvious as names like Smith or Brown. "C-R-I-S-T-A-F-A-R-O," Frankie enunciated slowly, drawing out each letter as though the Inspector was a child. Hopefully this would give his friends enough time to get clear of the cops.

"Ok, kid, what do you know about this car?"

"It's a car with a dead body, I saw it this morning and I was hiding when you came, because I saw this body with what looked like a hole in his head, I didn't want to end up like him."

"Ok, kid, you tell a good story. What else can you tell me?"

"That's it," Frankie answered with as much sincerity as he could muster.

"Officer, take this boy." The officer started toward Frankie, his pistol finally holstered inside his jacket. Frankie was clearly nervous and didn't know what to do. He turned to look toward the lake, and just as the Officer reached him, he turned and ran like never before, jumping between the trees like a deer running from a pack of wolves. He was faster than any man Simms had ever seen. The Officer pulled out his pistol and took aim at Frank. When Simms realized that the Officer's finger was on the trigger and that he had every intention of shooting the kid, he lunged and knocked the Officer's arm into the air. The bullet exploded out of the shaft, splintering the trees above.

"Holster that weapon, Officer," Simms yelled at the top of his lungs. He could not believe one of his men would react so stupidly. "Consider yourself on record, young man," he seethed. "Get back in the car!"

"What about the kid?" the Officer muttered.

"He's a kid. Let's leave it at that. Didn't you see the way he reacted when I mentioned his parents?"

"No sir."

"He was terrified - he would say anything not to have to go to the police station. He told us the truth, though. It's too hard to lie under that kind of duress." Simms knew this wasn't true, but he needed this Officer back in the car, not screwing anything else up for him.

Simms went back to further investigate the car, but he couldn't note anything more of interest. Any evidence had either been burned, or washed away by the rain. *Is it Otto or Dutch?* he wondered. The police report had indicated that the car had last been spotted with Dutch behind the wheel, but enough time had elapsed that they could have switched places. Maybe the kid *did* know something more. *I'll bet dollars to donuts he does.*

The gang had heard the gunshot, and then the sound of someone running behind them, which made their decision simple: time to run! With Jippsy in the lead, they all took off. Unfortunately for Frankie he could only continue running as fast as his slowest friend, who he spotted trailing behind the others as he closed in on the gang. Butterball was at the rear of the pack, holding Frankie back from really taking off. He waved Butterball forward, urging him to move faster. It occurred to Butterball that if Frankie was running, and not talking or yelling, something really bad must have happened. This thought gave Butterball all the encouragement he needed to get a move on. Frankie caught up to them toward the end of the lake, where the two sides nearly met.

"Keep," he panted, "keep...keep..." he repeated as he tried to catch his breath, "going," he finally said. Then Capri spotted it...the raft on the other side of the lake, halfway down the shore. It was nothing more than two logs held together by something, but she couldn't make out the details. She ran over to Jippsy and signaled to him with her index and middle fingers, pointing first to her eyes and then over toward the raft. He gasped the moment he saw it, and without a word they both dashed off towards it, hoping to get there before the others noticed.

They hesitated when they could no longer run along the shore on the other side; the forest had swallowed up any essence of a path. The vegetation was much denser around this side of the lake, and since they had never visited this side before, at least not from the shore, they were unsure which direction to take, especially as it became difficult to see through to the lake. Jippsy used his stick to try to blaze a trail, but Frankie had caught up to him and grabbed his arm before he could take another swipe. He shook his head and then placed his index finger over his lips, insisting they maintain silence. Jippsy nodded his agreement and the two of them continued on, sidestepping the smaller trees, but always doing their best to keep the lake in sight.

Frankie led the way and motioned to everyone to go deeper into the forest – he needed to tell them what had happened. He stopped roughly twenty-five yards in from the water. They followed obediently.

"What happened?" Dodo asked with great concern. He turned on her angrily and snapped, "Quiet!" This was too serious to start worrying about her feelings.

"That was the cops," he answered in a hush, "and one of them actually shot at me! Didn't you hear it?"

"Yeah we heard it, we ran like the wind after that sound," Butterball admitted.

"He asked me if I knew anything about the car; I told him I was alone and that I saw it this morning while out hunting." Jippsy nodded thinking to himself that Frankie's ability to lie was impressive. "We have to maintain the plan," Frankie continued. "You guys should not get involved with the cops. Don't tell your parents anything now. Got it?" They all nodded their agreement. "As one Rouge River gang member to the others, I swear not to tell anyone anything. Just let me stand up to the cops, if necessary, while we keep hunting for the money. Agreed?" Once again they all nodded.

"Great plan, Frankie," Jippsy said with respect.

Frankie put his arm out, his palm facing the ground. "Place your palm on my hand and swear it." Jippsy placed his palm on his hand, followed by Capri, then Butterball, Vicky and finally Dodo, but only because of Frankie. He was so brave, was all she could think.

"Say, 'I swear on behalf of the Rouge River gang'.

"I swear on behalf of the Rouge River gang," they all chanted in unison then Frankie lifted all of their hands to the sky as a final gesture.

"Ok, let's see what clues this raft holds for us," Frankie said enthusiastically. He couldn't help but notice the shred of cloth hanging from Jippsy's pocket. *He must have already found something*, he thought with excitement.

Frankie took the lead again, checking periodically to see if the cops were anywhere in sight. They were still in the clear...or so he thought. Frankie had asked them all to keep their comments to themselves until they were far away from the lake; they all knew that any noise they made would carry crystal clear across and along the shores of the water – an interesting phenomenon that he had never really given any particular consideration until now. They moved very slowly, and for over thirty minutes they kept up their silence, punctuated every so often by the sound of their feet rustling through the bushes and the occasional 'ouch!' as the spiky plants would dig into their skin.

The cool morning mist had burned away, and at last the sun reflected brilliantly off of any moist surface, lighting and heating even the darkest recesses of the forest. Their bodies were no exception, and Frankie was dehydrated from running scared. He was in dire need of water, and he longed to tell them to start heading toward their stream, but now wasn't the time. The day would disappear before they knew it, and now that the cops knew about the car and the corpse, it was just a matter of time before more of them arrived and put two-and-two together just as the gang had. The cops would be searching the area in no time.

They finally reached the birch tree that jutted out into the lake. Jippsy stepped forward to go out onto the tree to see if there was a clue of any sort on the raft, but Frankie put his arm out and stopped him with his hand on his chest. "I have to go," he said quietly.

"Why you?" Jippsy whispered back.

"The police think I'm roaming around, they don't know about anyone else, and we don't want them to know about anyone else right now. Don't you agree?"

He couldn't argue with Frankie's logic. "Ok, Frankie, from here it looks like something is attached to the logs."

"I see it," he said. Frankie inched his way out onto the birch tree, every now and again looking up across the lake at Big Rock to see if someone was watching. Satisfied that no one was there, he continued. "Can you pass me your stick, Jips? I need to reach down and push the raft to you," he tried to explain in a throaty whisper.

"Sure. Hold on." Jippsy stepped up onto the tree just at the base where it met the shore. He kept one foot on the ground, and straddled the tree with the rest of his body. Frankie turned around, hoping he wouldn't fall into the lake, and held his hand out to grab the stick. He stretched and was just able to reach the end of the stick with his fingertips. He was balanced precariously on the edge of the tree.

I got it, he thought with relief, which he tried to convey to Jippsy without saying the words aloud. Then, with his body wrapped around the trunk, he fell over the side of the tree, hugging it like a sloth until he was in a comfortable position. The stick was perfect, and he was able to dislodge the raft from a branch where it had become trapped. He carefully pushed it to shore, conscious of the fact that one minor slip and he would land in the water with a resounding splash that would surely call attention to their whereabouts.

Jippsy was still holding onto the base of the tree, and grabbed the raft the moment it reached the shore. He recognized the lashing as nothing more than a belt, and so he carefully spun the raft around in the water in order to reach it. He bent down and unclasped the belt, then threw it back to the others.

He slowly backed out of position so as not to fall down the slope and into the water, while Frankie, still straddled along the trunk, gradually inched his way backward toward the shore.

Jippsy was about to turn away from the tree and

toward his friends when he spotted something from the corner of his eye. Had he not been exactly where he was he definitely would have missed it, teetering just under the trunk, held on by friction only. It was the exact kind of book he had found yesterday behind the car. He tried reaching down, but his fingertips merely brushed the leather. He bent down further, but he was too far still to get a good grasp. He saw Frankie making his way back, the weight of his movements causing the tree to sway. If Frankie continued he would surely cause the book to come free and drop right into the water.

"Stop!" he croaked, as he did his best to swallow the word that threatened to come out as a scream. Frankie obeyed. "Can you turn around?" Frankie lay his body back down along the tree trunk. "Careful - don't bounce the tree. We have to get something out from under it and I don't want it to fall into the water."

"Ok," Frankie whispered. With every ounce of strength he had he lifted his body like a gymnast on a pommel horse and carefully spun himself around one-hundred-and-eighty degrees, and then proceeded to inch his way toward the shore where he spotted exactly what Jippsy had seen. Frankie was hovering just above it. He dropped his left arm down in an effort to reach for it as he held on tight with the rest of his limbs. He stretched and pushed his body to its limits, but it was no use. Jippsy simply couldn't take it any longer and jumped into the water. Infuriated, Frankie hissed, "You idiot! You're going to get us caught."

"This is too important to tiptoe about," he called back as he swam up to the tree and reached for the book. Holding it in the air to keep it dry, he passed it to Frankie, who quickly made his way to the edge of the tree. "Give me a hand, Frankie." Frankie leaned his body against the tree and held out his hand, but now couldn't reach Jippsy.

"We can't get you up from here...it's impossible. You'll have to swim along the shore until you reach flatter land." Frankie didn't mind the inconvenience one bit. In fact, it would give him the opportunity to scan through their latest clue.

Jippsy realized that what he had done was pretty foolish, but believed that he had had no other choice. He swam close to the shore, trying his best to stay underwater in order to remain out of sight. About twenty-five yards from where he had jumped in, he spotted an opening where he felt he could easily enough make his way back onto dry land. Unfortunately, this task proved to be much more of a challenge than he had anticipated as he attempted to make his way through the overgrowth of lily pads, fallen trees and marsh. In hindsight, it would have been much easier to continue swimming along the shore until he reached a more reasonable clearing. He had come to regret his decision as he labored through. He felt the pull of the plants as they wrapped around his shoes and legs. He was getting tired and now there was no one in sight from what he could tell. He was on his own.

As he endeavored to move forward the plants seemed to have his right leg in a death-grip. He struggled to break free but was unsuccessful as every effort was met with greater resistance until he realized his foot was undeniably trapped. He ducked under water and could see his foot lodged between a seaweed-wrapped branch and the trunk of an old dead log. He was submerged in no more than six feet of water, but the depth and awkward position of the natural snare made his efforts to dislodge his foot with his hands futile. Jippsy tried backtracking in the hopes he could come back out the way he had entered, but that merely served to tire him as he sloshed in the water and lost his balance.

His foot was stuck, he realized, in part because of the huge shoes he was wearing. He tried treading water, his arms working frantically to keep him afloat as he kicked furiously with both legs. It was all he could do to stay afloat. He submerged himself once again, this time with the intention of untying his shoe and freeing his foot. He pulled at the lace, but it had absorbed so much water that it caused the cord to swell and tighten rather than loosen, and then it ripped free from his shoe. "Damn it!" he cursed. He was stuck for good. *No use trying to lay low now*, he thought ruefully. So he did the only thing he could do. "Help! Help! Frankie! Capri! Anyone!" he called out, acutely aware of the imminent danger of doing so.

He thankfully heard someone call out, "Where are you?" It was Capri.

"I'm in the water, just follow my voice down to the shore." The silence had to be broken as this was his only chance.

"Jippsy?" he heard, and poked his head as high above the water as possible.

"Here! I'm over here," he tried to call more subtly.

"Hold on, Jippsy, we're coming." Frankie made it to the shore first, and easily spotted Jippsy from the flat where he had stopped; he could see where Jippsy had intended to exit the water, just a few yards beyond where he was. Frankie entered the water from the clearing - it came up to his waist. He knew he could swim out to meet Jippsy but became concerned that he would get caught as well. He realized the flora in the lake, combined with the dead trees and branches that accumulated naturally, was just too thick here.

Vicky called to Capri, "Go hold Frankie's hand." The she addressed Butterball, "Butterball, you hold onto this tree, and I'll hold next. It'll be easier for all of us to get back if we have each other. Frankie, can you walk out there as far as you can? If you have to let go to help Jippsy get free, the rest of us will be here to drag the two of you through the marsh. Ok?"

"Got it Vicky. Good idea."

"Frankie was able to reach Jippsy without a problem, but the water was well over his head. He swam out further to gauge what was around, and where they could safely pull free and then came back towards Jippsy's position. "What happened?"

"My shoe...my shoe is stuck," Jippsy panted. Frankie plunged below the water to evaluate the situation. He popped back up moments later and started treading water next to Jippsy. "You have to go underwater and get your whole body down as low as possible. I'm going to lift your foot up. Got it?" Jippsy merely nodded. "On the count of three. One, two, three." And down Jippsy went. Frankie got a hold of his foot, and it was really jammed. He pushed, but had no leverage at all. He swam around for a better vantage and pulled, but his foot wasn't budging. Jippsy came up with a start, gasping for breath, but then fell right back under. He popped back up again to grab another breath. It was clear he was having trouble holding himself above water in this position.

"Capri, could you make it here?" Frankie asked.

"Sure!" Capri answered, ready and eager to come to the rescue, she waded through the marsh, hurriedly pushing the plants and water out of her way until she was able to get to deeper water. She then swam out just like she had seen Frankie do in order to stay away from all the bushes that would impede her progress. The three of them were treading together as Frankie quickly filled Capri in about Jippsy's dilemma. It was obvious to both Frankie and Capri that they would have to fix this problem, and fast. It was obvious that Jippsy couldn't last like this much longer; he was getting too tired to talk and his treading was becoming weaker.

"Jips, you have to take a deep breath, and do the same thing as before. We'll get you free. Capri, I'm going to lift his leg while you try to get his shoe off. Ok?"

"Yeah. Let's go." And with that abrupt acknowledgement the three of them inhaled deeply and dropped under the water. Frankie tried to pull up on Jippsy's leg, but he was struggling so hard that Frankie couldn't make any progress. Jippsy was not faring well – he was splashing his arms frantically in an effort to right himself. He could feel his head getting lighter as his chest and lungs started to burn.

Without the extra wiggle room Frankie's effort should have afforded her, Capri couldn't pull Jippsy's shoe from his foot. She was running out of air anyway and resurfaced quickly. It was then that she understood just how dire the situation was – Jippsy was in distress.

"Frankie, stop!" Capri yelled to Frankie from the surface of the water, hoping he would hear her even though he was still submerged. Frankie could hear her yelling but couldn't make out the words. So Capri did the only thing she could think to do – she positioned herself on her back behind Jippsy, and supported his head and shoulders on her chest. She placed her right arm around his chest to keep him in place and then started to tread hard to keep them both afloat.

Frankie resurfaced. "Frankie, help!" was all she could say as her efforts were entirely focused on keeping Jippsy and herself above water. Frankie took over the rescue position from Capri, much to her relief. She continued to tread water right beside Jippsy's head, and to Frankie's surprise she tilted back his head and put her mouth over his.

"WHAT are you doing?! Kissing him is NOT going to help," Frankie said incredulously.

"It's called artificial respiration, you dummy. We don't have time for this. Just hold him." She pinched Jippsy's nose, blew air into his mouth, and watched his chest. No movement. She tried again. And again, there was no movement. She tried it once more. But still she saw no movement.

"Hurry, Capri, I don't think..."

"Shut up!" she chastised, took a breath, and blew once more. Suddenly Jippsy's chest rose, then his head jerked up as water spewed from his mouth. Jippsy was overtaken by a fit of hysterical coughing. Capri felt relieved and angry all at once.

The others watched in panic, unable to speak at all until they saw he was ok.

"What's the problem?" Butterball yelled.

"His foot is stuck, if we could get his shoe off we might be able to get his foot out."

"Untie his laces," they called back.

"It's busted, and not loosening. He ties it tight so it stays on his foot."

"Try the knife in his pocket," Frankie heard Vicky suggest.

"Right!" Frankie exclaimed, wondering why he hadn't thought of that, but relieved for the reminder. He breathed deeply and dove under the water – he pushed aside his fatigue and focused on Jippsy. He found the knife in Jippsy's pocket and without resurfacing lowered himself to Jippsy's shoe and went to work cutting through the laces. Each segment snapped easily with a single flick of the knife until the lace was in shreds and the shoe had finally loosened. Frankie was now dangerously low on air but was determined to free Jippsy. He wasted no time and slipped the shoe off easily - Jippsy's foot finally came free from the tangled mess as his shoe sank languidly to the bottom of the lake. Capri could feel the strain relieved the moment his foot came free.

"Capri, swim him back to Big Rock. You can't get through these marshes safely," Capri heard one of them yell out from the shore. Capri held him above her, his face to the sun, her right arm wrapped around his chest while she swam them to the sandbar.

Vicky, Dodo and Butterball ran back along the shore and around the lake to meet up with them. Dodo was holding onto the book, and Vicky had grabbed up Jippsy's stick - she thought, somehow, it might give him comfort. Jippsy was lucid yet confused; he couldn't remember what had happened.

"It's ok, Jips, you're fine. You just swallowed some water," Frankie said almost nonchalantly.

"You mean I drowned?" he croaked incredulously. He was clearly shocked that this could have happened to him.

"I guess, but..." Capri started to answer calmly before she was abruptly interrupted by Frankie. The friends were no longer concerned about how much noise they were making – they had obviously passed that boundary some time ago.

"You drowned, old boy," Frankie said grandly as though it was some major accomplishment.

"Frankie!" Capri yelled at him. "Shut up!" she sputtered, unable to mask her anger at him and at the situation.

But Frankie simply ignored her. "We saved you, Jips, old boy," he boasted with satisfaction. Frankie was now pleased enough with himself to finally let it go.

"Thanks. Thanks again, Frankie," Jippsy said with absolute gratitude.

"No sweat. Just wet," he laughed, as he always did, at his own jokes.

"Where's everyone else?" Jippsy wondered aloud.

"They're coming around. They should be here in a few minutes." Jippsy was relieved for the delay. He didn't really feel like moving off the sandbar, not just yet anyway. It was a safe place for him – this patch of dirt was filled solely with memories of good times, and that was exactly what he needed at that moment...until the reason for this particular dilemma crept back into his consciousness.

"Hey wait," he blurted out as he sat up with a start, "where's the book?"

"Don't worry, Jips," Frankie laughed as he noted with relief how quickly Jippsy had rebounded once his attention returned to the mystery. Jippsy was back from the dead. "Dodo has it."

"Phew!" he said, pleased, until he noticed his missing shoe. "I guess I can't go around in just one shoe," he quipped, although he knew his parents would be mad. He untied the remaining shoe and threw it in the lake. "Good riddance!" *I don't ever want hand-me-downs again*, he thought to himself, *even if I have to work night and day for my new shoes, that's what I'm gonna do.*

In all the excitement Frankie had forgotten about the police. He immediately glanced toward Big Rock then jumped up with a start, and ran toward the hill. He didn't see them. *Maybe they didn't see us*, he thought to himself, *but we'd better get out of here because they'll definitely be back.*

Back at Headquarters

"Sergeant, get me Montreal - Lieutenant Shaugnessy."

"Yes Inspector." The Sergeant wasted no time. "Inspector," he called out, "Lieutenant Shaughnessy on the line for you."

The Inspector grabbed the line. "Lieutenant," he said with authority and self-assuredness. "Benoît Simms. I found your men. They were in an unfortunate accident. I'm sorry to inform you that both men are dead. We also found Dutch's car, which appeared to have crashed and burned. Dutch is dead."

Although Shaughnessy was upset about his men, he clenched his fist and pumped it in the air, knowing that this news would be well received from his U.S. counterparts. He was anxious to get off the phone with the Lieutenant and contact the FBI. He listened to the details of their findings, thanked the Inspector and immediately dialed FBI headquarters himself. "RCMP Lieutenant Shaughnessy for Inspector Johnson," he announced with confidence as the operator asked how to direct the call. "Yes, Lieutenant, one moment please," the operator responded with that familiar New York accent.

"Elliot, hope you have some good news for me," Johnson declared as he picked up the line.

"That depends upon your perspective."

"Out with it man," commanded the impatient FBI inspector. He knew something was up if Elliot was calling.

"Dutch is dead," he declared, then explained the scene and circumstances as Simms had conveyed to him.

The Rock on the Move

"We interrupt your regularly scheduled program to bring you breaking news. The notorious gangster known as Dutch Schultz, who had escaped the custody of federal authorities in upstate New York and tried to flee into Canada, was pursued and subsequently killed in a chase north of Montreal. Speaking on behalf of the FBI and RCMP joint task force, FBI Inspector Johnson confirmed that Dutch's burned-out car was discovered in the Laurentian Mountains roughly 60 miles north of Montreal, where much of his smuggling operation originates, and that the body was indeed that of Dutch Schultz. We now return you to your program."

"Get me my car," Shiny Shoes heard his boss bellow from the second floor. He lifted the receiver from the wall and quickly pressed the intercom button to call down to the driver who spent his days waiting around the carport just a few yards away from the main house.

"Monsieur Rottman would like you to bring the car around this instant," he said in perfect French, his manner, as always, professional and uncompromising.

"Oui, monsieur," answered the driver immediately. "Which car shall I bring?"

"Please bring the Cadillac Sixteen," answered Shiny Shoes. "He likes riding in that one, and if it is too hot, you can take the top down. And be sure there is extra gasoline in the boot. "

"Oui, monsieur. Tout de suite." *Right away*, responded the driver as Shiny Shoes smiled contentedly with his decision, released the intercom button and hung up the receiver. He called up the image of the Cadillac from his photographic memory bank. It was a perfect fit for The Rock, custom-designed to meet his very personal needs and specifications, as were all the V16's. Detroit had configured the pedals a little closer to the seat, covered the seats in pristine white leather with red stitching, and even the instrument panel and gear shift had been detailed with ivory. The gorgeous 2-door convertible sportster had been painted Venetian red, the doors emblazoned with the The Rock's company crest, and a gold Madame X hood ornament affixed to the hood. It was by far the fastest car in his fleet and the one in which he took the most pride.

He climbed the stairs that led back up to the second floor from the kitchen. The morning sun reflected gloriously off of the black and white marble directly up to the chandelier, which hung above the foyer. A halo of prism lights twinkled across the foyer ceiling, winking like stars in the sky. He glanced up, beaming with pride at one of his many design ideas. *It catches the light just right. I knew it would be spectacular*! He marched up the rest of the wood staircase, his shiny shoes beating a perfect cadence along the wood steps. He reached the landing and started up the hall, past all of the magnificent masterpieces hung along the wall, and stopped at the door to The Rock's room. He cleared his throat and The Rock looked up, acknowledging Shiny Shoes. "Monsieur Rottman, your car will be ready. I have also asked the driver to make sure there is extra gas in the boot so you will not need to stop."

A knowing grin passed across The Rock's face. Shiny shoes saw it, and preened inwardly. Even though Shiny Shoes was not told where he would be going, it was up to him to determine The Rock's needs.

"May I help you to continue dressing sir?"

"No, not now. I want to continue my exercises." He groaned the last word as he pressed the heavy dumbbells high above his head. The Rock nodded at him to leave the room, even though Shiny Shoes did not need the hint. He turned on his heels and continued on to his morning chores.

The Rock resumed his weight lifting for another ten minutes. It was the same routine every morning. He stood in front of the mirror grimacing at his reflection as he counted off the reps. It was already hot for so early in the morning and his white tank top was soaked in sweat, his black gym short clinging to him. A myriad mirrors adorned the walls of his room so that every wall reflected his straining muscles. His room, although large and majestic, doubled as his personal gym. He appreciated jumping out of bed early every morning, and exercising to the music and news that played on the radio.

His morning routine would never be interrupted by business, but this morning, however, was truly exceptional. His mind was reeling from the news; he couldn't concentrate on the dumbbells as his thoughts kept coming back to the news. He had so many questions... *If Dutch is dead where's the money? What had happened to Gerard and that beast? The radio mentioned nothing about money.* Then he remembered that he had a man in the RCMP up north. He placed the dumbbells back on the floor in their designated spot and walked briskly out of his room. He called out to Shiny Shoes from the landing, "Get me that guy at the RC.." he started but stopped mid-sentence and ran down to his study still dressed in his white tank top and black gym shorts. He shut the door behind him and practically jumped into his chair. His adrenaline was pumping and he felt like a kid running around the house playing hide and seek.

The phone seemed to ring forever. "RCMP Laurentides," answered the voice on the other end of the line.

"I would like to speak with, oh, what was his name?" He couldn't remember. "Hold on please," he asked the operator politely." He called out to his butler, who came to the door instantly.

"Yes, sir?" asked the voice from outside the study door.

"Come in here!"

"Yes sir?" he asked once again.

"What are the names of the people we know at the police station up in the country?"

Shiny Shoes, in his elegant manner, stated their names and gave him a photographic description in order for The Rock to trigger some memory of whom he might be speaking with. The Rock removed his hand from the mouthpiece of the telephone and provided the operator at the police station the name of his contact.

"One moment, sir." The phone went silent for 20 seconds."I am sorry he is not available right now. He is in the field."

"Oh? Where is he right now?" he asked politely. The Rock was doing his best to try and charm the woman on the other end of the phone, using every ounce of humility he could muster. It went completely against his nature and even Shiny Shoes felt uncomfortable listening to his boss pander to the person on the other end of the line.

"Well," she answered, sounding as though she would bust at the seams if she held back any further, "it's very exciting around here." she whispered into the phone. "Dutch Schultz's body was found near here."

"Wow! Really?" The Rock needed her to keep talking. "Where did *that* happen?"

"Just a few miles north, on a small road on the way to Brébeuf," she answered matter-of-factly.

"That's fascinating. I could see why there's so

268

much excitement. What else happened?" he asked enthusiastically, at which point she realized she was talking too much.

"Perhaps he could call you back or you might like to try him at lunch hour," she replied, this time with greater reservation and much more professionally.

"That would be great. I *will* try him later." He put the phone down gently without saying goodbye. Although he would have liked to speak with the mole directly, he was satisfied with the operator's answers. Besides, with thirteen million dollars at stake he would be investigating matters himself.

Fine Tooth Comb

"Inspector, we found something!" His men had scoured the grounds for the last two hours and had found nothing more than what he had observed earlier. He had instructed them to look beyond the immediate vicinity, to set up a perimeter, which led all the way down to the water's edge and up the hill, although he felt uphill would be unwise. After all, any man escaping would try to get *away* from the main roads.

"What is it, Officer?"

"We found *this* behind the log down there," he answered as he pointed toward the river at a fallen tree, carrying the item in question. He approached the Inspector, who was standing next to the burnt-out car supervising the removal of the body.

Simm's eyes must have looked as though they were popping out of his head, because that was how he felt. He had never seen one in his entire career, but seeing it in the hands of his Sergeant brought forth a flood of 'what if's'. Simms knew the Tommy Machine Gun was used by a number of Canadian big-city police forces, but to-date his outpost had not been issued these expensive and powerful guns. He started walking over to the Sergeant to meet him halfway. He couldn't take his eyes off the gun, and wasn't paying attention to the ground. In a scene right out of a slapstick comedy he tripped over an exposed root which sent him reeling forward. He put his hands out just in time so as not to smash his head on the ground, but the sting of the rocks on his palms would be etched in his memory forever. Two officers ran over to help him up, but by then he was humiliated and dirty.

They felt embarrassed for him, but he made light of the situation immediately, joking, "Have that removed!" as he pointed toward the root dramatically. He always did his utmost to maintain his stature and dignity but felt, in this instance, humor would be the only way to save face. He smiled and they chuckled along with him.

"Are you ok, Inspector?" asked one of the officers.

"I'm fine, Officer. Let's see what you found," he said as he took hold of the Tommy gun. "It's a good thing it didn't happen while I was holding *this* thing." He turned it in every direction, feeling it's surprising weight, marveling at the drum magazine which could hold a hundred rounds, then bracing it against his shoulder and sighting down the barrel toward the tree line. In his mind it was a thing of beauty. He was careful not to touch the trigger, although he knew all about the Tommy Gun and how heavy the trigger pull was - he also knew how fast it could shoot off rounds and what disaster it could cause. He had seen the photos of the carnage two Tommy Guns had caused in the infamous St. Valentine's Day Massacre when 6 members of Bugs Moran's gang had been shot to death in a garage on Chicago's North Side. *No...you don't see this kind of weapon in these parts*, he thought as he continued inspecting every angle, *just rifles for hunting, or the odd revolver...maybe even relics from WW1 hanging over someone's mantle, but not this!*

"Fascinating!" he said aloud. "Ok, Officers, keep looking. Keep working your way down toward the lake. There may be more clues that could give us a clearer indication of what happened here." He told his officers that the gun had most likely been thrown from the car during the explosion. They bought it, but he wasn't convinced.

It took four able-bodied police officers to carry the corpse, one holding onto each limb. The stench was so overpowering that even with their shirts pulled up over their noses, they still could not take a single breath without the fumes searing their nose hairs and turning their stomachs. They only moved him a few feet away from the car in order to stuff him gently into a grain sack, which was not an easy task. Although it had been nearly 36 hours since his death, his arms and legs were still in a stage of rigor mortis that rendered them stiff and therefore un-pliable.

Although it would have been routine to take him to the coroner in Sainte-Agathe, Simms was quite confident the bullet hole in his forehead was the cause of his demise. He really didn't want to watch the unfortunate scene of the dead man being stuffed into a bag, and so decided to join the hunt along the trail. Aside from the Tommy Gun the only other clues they found were footprints in the mud, but they could have been made by anyone, even the kid that had been there earlier.

Book #2

They decided as a gang that the best place to go would be back to Jippsy's farm; he needed to rest, didn't have shoes, and the original book was there too. But Jippsy didn't want to show them the book, and he wasn't sure if they were ready for what was inside it yet. Jippsy was concerned that if Frank knew too much he might tell the cops, especially if they were able to scare it out of him.

They hiked back through the forest, so as not to be seen, and by the time they arrived, they were tired, parched, and very hungry. They sat down on the porch while Jippsy went in to find some shoes he could wear. "I'll be right back." He passed the kitchen where he found his mom preparing their lunch. "Mom, could my friends join us?"

His mom looked him up-and-down and smiled knowingly at him. "Of course, Jippsy, it'll be ready in about half an hour. Go find some shoes - I see your last pair didn't quite make it home."

"Yeah, mom," he replied resignedly. "Mom?" he continued, but the tone of his voice was more pleading.

"Yes, son?" she asked suspiciously, not quite sure what to expect next.

"I love you," he said with a burst of pride.

"I love you too, my baby," she answered adoringly. "Are you ok?" she asked, worried now. He wasn't normally so emotional.

"Sure, mom," he answered brightly, in an effort to reassure his mom – she already had enough to worry about.

"Why don't you go and get your dad's boots?" she

suggested. "I'm sure they'll fit right."

"Thanks, mom," he called back as he started out of the kitchen. He was sad, but couldn't share that with her. He had almost lost his life today, and that was something she could never know. His dad wasn't around, and had been gone for so many days that Jippsy could see how his absence was taking a toll on his mom...she was becoming lost without him. *The gang will be a nice distraction*, he hoped.

He found his dad's boots, slipped them on and tied them tightly as he always did, and joined the others. They were sitting on the porch clambering for position to see the book in Dodo's hands, but each page was the same as the next, just symbols or dates and numbers. He was standing between them looking down at the book – he already thought what they hadn't yet figured out. "Dodo, just turn to the last page," he told her with a confidence bordering on condescension. Jippsy was positive it would be different, and sure enough there it was, written above some of the other writing in bold blue ink. She read it aloud.

The words floated from her lips like the verses of a song. The gang had never heard such prose, at least not from a man known as a mobster and a killer. As she read his words, Jippsy pictured a man sitting at the edge of the lake, tattered and beaten by his pursuers, exhausted from having to protect himself from the elements, finding himself in the position of having to bury his treasure. He could picture this man as he reached into the far recesses of his mind to conjure up clues so that no other man could find what he had given back to the earth.

As Dutch wrote those words, he entertained images and moments from his life - his childhood forsaken to support himself and his mother when his father abandoned them when Dutch was 14, and then his meteoric rise within the mob. It was a long way to go for Dutch, who went from a petty thief who did time in prison, to a notoriously brutal gangster. Whether he was running booze, rigging numbers games, or fighting tax evasion charges, Dutch was a winner – at least until this moment. He knew; his body could no longer fight the inevitable. The pain was so intense it took every effort for him to focus on finding the right words just so that he could finally let go.

Salty tears across the lake
Falling from the course I take
A crocodile birch grows strong and hard
Not one but two maybe three from a yard
One hundred rocks and sand form my sky
Heaven above while I lay and die

Where downhill the big rock shades
Toward the sand where the water fades
The thoroughbred runs but the 8th pole
And the trees reach across the swampy hole
The setting sun alights upon the crocodile
As I close my eyes and rest awhile

"What the hell does this mean?" Frankie spat.

"Frankie, don't swear!" Dodo reacted quickly – she definitely didn't want her mother to hear.

"He must have been one screwy guy, eh Jips?"

"I guess, Butterball," Jippsy answered, but was distracted thinking of Dutch, and what a desperate state he must have been in. Jippsy had to unravel this mystery. There was meaning in what Dutch wrote, and he couldn't have gotten very far from where they had found the black book. *So where did he go? And where was the treasure?* He read the clues again, hunched over Dodo's shoulder. He could see Capri and Vicky were doing the same.

"What do you think it means?" Dodo asked looking around at each of them.

"It's a clue," Frankie finally piped in. "This has to be about where he hid the money. Guys! We have the map!" Frankie announced as he jumped to his feet, grabbed Dodo and pulled her up and into his arms as though she weighed nothing. He swung her around on the porch, and as they skipped around Butterball and Capri clapped to the rhythm of their dancing.

Vicky was deep in thought, as was Jippsy, whose mind was running a million miles an hour. His thoughts kept racing between his mom and dad, the situation with his grandpa, and how finding the treasure could solve all of their problems. *We have to find it!* he thought with resolve as he smacked his fist into his hand. The gang was so caught up in their activity that no one noticed Jippsy at all. He was relieved that they were preoccupied. *I have to decipher this riddle,* he thought to himself. He had a feeling about some of the lines, but others simply struck him as odd. *What's the 8th pole?*

Every Man Has His Price

Only Simms knew there should be two bodies, while the rest of the policemen on the investigation were beaming with pride. They had found the infamous Dutch Schultz, the investigation was over, and in time the history books would recount how the RCMP des Laurentides were the ones to bring Dutch to a halt for good. He had his deputy assemble a roll call back at the station. He stood at the entrance inside the small barn wood cabin all of his men knew as headquarters. He started to speak in his usual authoritative manner, "Gentlemen, I have informed the FBI and the Montreal police and it is now on the radio across North America that the hunt is over. Dutch Schultz has been found and is no longer in charge of a syndicate that has caused many people hardship, and cost some their lives. I would like us to take a moment of silence in honor of the brave men who lost their lives in pursuit of this man. Let us all remember and take pride in the fact that their deaths were not in vain." The nine men in the cabin all bowed their heads in silent prayer following the lead of their commanding officer. "Thank you, men."

"I do not feel we need to assemble back at the crash site, therefore I ask that you all return to your regularly assigned duties. Our U.S. counterparts will be arriving shortly and I will escort them to the site." In reality, he knew the FBI would not be coming, and yet he felt it necessary to ward off any kind of suspicion. Although he may have been acting paranoid, he knew there had to be something more to this puzzle. Namely, where was the second man? Did they have something of value? Dutch would not leave the country empty-handed – of that he was sure.

"Excuse me, Inspector?"

"Yes, Sergeant?"

"Will you be requiring my assistance to go with you?"

"Oh, um, no, Sergeant. Actually, I'd like you to man the station. I'll manage just fine. Thank you." His smile was disingenuous as he attempted to express his gratitude. The Sergeant wasn't convinced, and couldn't help but question his Inspector's motives. He nodded thoughtfully at Simms but his mind was ticking away with a variety of scenarios – and none of them were flattering to the Inspector.

Why would the Inspector want to go back there? The FBI are certainly not coming...they never do. Maybe **that's** *why the crooks are always coming up to Canada,* he surmised. *The Inspector is definitely not one for investigating on his own; he prefers to have one of us doing the dirty work while he takes all the praise. Something's different here - maybe there* is *something more at the crash site. Wait a second...that's* got *to be it! Dutch must have brought some of his loot when he escaped. After all, a filthy rich gangster like that – he wouldn't run with nothing.* He thought for a moment and it became clear. *I have to follow him without being caught. If I could somehow get my hands on that loot, it would be my ticket off of this force, and I could retire a country farmer instead of working for this Napoleonic jerk.*

He watched as the Inspector started to make his way out of the barn after ensuring that all of his men were back at work. He was visibly distracted and unaware that one of his men was onto him. *There he goes,* the Sergeant remarked to himself. He made sure to wait until the Inspector made it to the main road. In those few extra minutes of waiting his hands started to tremble from a mix of anticipation and fear. *What if I'm caught?* he worried. *How will I explain myself to the Inspector? Maybe I'll just go to the washroom first.*

He took his time in the washroom, collected his thoughts and steeled his courage. The Sergeant walked out of the washroom and through the station house. He made sure not to make eye contact with the few remaining officers, and casually exited the building. No one stopped him as he left, so he slipped into his car and made his way onto Highway 117. He didn't see any cars on the road until a magnificent convertible Cadillac flew past him doing at least fifty miles per hour. It was moving so fast it was as though his car was standing still. *These vacationers are always in such a hurry to get up here,* he thought ruefully, *it doubles our work in the summer just having them around. I wish they would just go to Cape Cod or Old Orchard like most Montrealers do.*

The Sergeant turned off of the highway, onto the gravel road, and continued at a very slow pace. He didn't want the sound of his tires alerting anyone to his presence. After what felt like hours coasting along the winding gravel road, he was about to round a corner when a moose came dashing across the road. He pulled his foot off the clutch and jammed both feet onto the brake. The car slid for several feet and came to a stop then stalled. The moose merely looked at him defiantly through his windshield, daring the Sergeant to take him on. The Sergeant had encountered moose before and sat patiently, albeit angrily at the inconvenience, as the moose glared at him. They remained there, locked in a standstill, until the moose lost interest and finally decided to continue on his way.

Relieved, the Sergeant put his foot on the clutch, the car into gear, and turned the key in the ignition, but the car wouldn't start. It wouldn't even turn over. "What the hell!?" the Sergeant fumed as he slammed his fists on the wheel. He tried again and again, hoping something might catch, but then he didn't know much about cars, and ultimately gave up. Frustrated, he decided to put this time to better use and explore his surroundings. He got out of the car and stood under the hot sun with the door open. The sun was fairly high now, and had warmed up the gravel road well beyond the actual temperature. His uniform already felt heavy and uncomfortable, so he removed his jacket, tossed it onto the seat, and bent to crank open the window to allow the air to circulate. He hoped that the car would start later and didn't want to sit in a stiflingly hot vehicle.

He started walking along the road, under the cover of the trees in order to stay as cool as possible. "How far have I *gone*?" he asked no one in particular. It was so quiet out here – the breeze had died down, the critters were tucked away, and the crickets were silent. Even the birds refused to sing. Everything was so calm that the humid air had become stale, further irritating him as his breathing became more labored on the ascent up the hill. Still, he couldn't help but talk to himself. "That fool doesn't know who he's dealing with."

An unexpected whisper scared him out of his wits. "Sergeant! Quiet! Come here!" commanded the voice he knew all too well.

Damn! he fumed inwardly. *Caught...*The Sergeant walked slowly into the forest, just a few yards, and saw the Inspector spying down the hill from behind a large tree. "Inspector, what are you doing?"

"Quiet! Not another word. Just watch," he cautioned.

"What are we..." the Sergeant started to say, but the Inspector turned angrily on him and mimed the words, "Shut up!" so menacingly that the Sergeant did exactly that, and turned intently toward the Inspector's line of sight. It took a moment for the Sergeant to locate, but there they were...three men at the bottom of the hill, walking along the newly formed trail that led into the forest where the car had crashed. The Sergeant could barely see what they were up to and desperately wanted to get a better vantage, but dared not say anything to the Inspector. The Inspector, however, was a man of action; he patted the Sergeant's shoulder and motioned for them to go deeper into the forest where they could hide behind another tree but have a better view. The two of them scurried across the wooded terrain, careful not to expose their position to the three strangers. They could hear their voices carrying up to them, and the Inspector was intent on finding out who they were and what they wanted.

"Sergeant, I don't want to know why you're here right now, but this is what we are going to do... We're going to stake them out until they're ready to leave. But we need to hear what they're saying before we try to apprehend them. Got it?"

"Yes, sir," the Sergeant replied, momentarily relieved to have some time to contemplate what excuse he might use for his presence in the woods.

"First we have to get lower down."

"Sir, how about if we go laterally beyond the car, make our way down to the lake, and come up from there? It's well hidden and close enough for us to hear. There's no real hiding spot up here and we risk being seen."

"Good idea, Sergeant," he whispered. The two of them entered deeper into the woods than they had intended to, but had no choice. Although the voices had become louder, they were still not clear. They could no longer see the strangers, which they took as their cue to start heading down the hill. While the descent made it easier and faster, they nonetheless paid careful attention to the forest floor so as not to trip over the many roots that protruded from the ground. The forest was tall, dense, and bright green. The sunshine filtered through in rays that lit up the thousands of leaves along their way. The humidity had remained, which created a perfect setting for the flea and tick larvae that thrived in such an environment, and encouraged the black fly population to swell to nuisance proportions, particularly along the waterfront where they tended to lay their eggs. The black flies were out in force, and the men were at an absolute disadvantage as they were prime targets – their heavy breathing from their exertion, combined with the uric acid of their sweat made them particularly appealing to the pests. The Sergeant merely gave in to their abuse, having long since given up swatting them away; it was of no use anyway, as the lake was now in sight, and the black flies were swarming. The men would be blood donors for as long as they were out there.

They came upon a clearing and what looked like a sandbar jutting out from the lake. They continued on this path back to a giant boulder and started their climb up toward the car. The Sergeant remembered this spot behind the fallen tree - it was where they had found the gun. The Inspector gave him that look again – that finger over his lips, telling him to keep quiet. *I just want to knock that finger down his throat,* he thought viciously. *One more time and I'm going to smash his head against this log.* Just the image of taking action gave the Sergeant such pleasure that it made him smirk involuntarily.

The Inspector caught the look on his Sergeant's face and couldn't imagine what could possibly be going on in his mind to elicit a smile. Maybe he was over thinking things, but his instincts were generally very reliable. He'd have to figure out the Sergeant's behavior later – one mystery at a time…

"It *must* be here, dammit!" The Rock's frustration was skyrocketing with every passing moment.

"There's nothing here, sir. I don't think they would be able to bury anything this deep, especially with these roots in the…way…" he trailed off as he caught his boss glaring at him.

"Just keep digging. Try over there," he grumbled as he pointed toward a log.

"Where, sir?"

"OVER. THERE," he yelled at the top of his lungs, as he pointed directly toward the Inspector and the Sergeant. The Rock had finally lost his cool, as his temper and irritation rose with each failure. "I'm sure it's near the car somewhere. He couldn't have gotten far - it was much too heavy. I need to find it."

"Sir? Could I ask *what* you're looking for?"

"No! You can't!" he snapped. "Dig! Just dig!"

Simms could see two men with spades working on different holes, just digging away at random spots all around the car. They were making their way toward him and the Sergeant. He couldn't be sure but the small man looked like The Rock Rothman. *Wow!* he thought, stunned. *What's* The Rock *doing here? There's definitely something more to this whole affair if the big boss had gotten involved.* One thing he was quite certain of, the Sergeant had no idea who that man was.

"Inspector, how long are we going to stay here?"

"For now, *just **watch**,*" he answered, his annoyance coming fully to the surface. "When they get too close, *be quiet…*" But the men were approaching fast, and the last word stuck in his throat before it could reach his vocal cords. The sound came out as a squeak, as they both ducked behind the log as low as their bodies could get.

Simms greedily wanted the thugs to find whatever it was they came looking for. It would save him the work - he could simply arrest them and confiscate the evidence.

There was nothing to do but watch and listen. Simms could hear the big ugly one breathing heavily as he worked-over the wet earth. He grunted unpleasantly with every dig and heft of the shovel. It occurred to the Inspector that after a few hours of digging in this heat the laboring men would need a rest, and it was clear that their taskmaster would never consider it. Neither of the workers was talking. How could they, as The Rock paced incessantly up and around the car. He had no idea what to do with himself although every so often he stopped and yelled out whatever came to his addled mind.

"Non, monsieur," they would answer, or, "Oui, monsieur." But their answers couldn't please him, nor would they until they found whatever it was that he thought was out there.

Even the Sergeant felt some form of pity for these men. *At least on a chain gang you might hear someone singing the blues*, he thought sardonically. These two were being worked to the bone.

"Try over there," the short man would scream. "What's the matter with you two? Why I even hired you imbeciles in the first place behooves me. My bubby works faster."

Louis and Gerard never changed pace, and never spoke with one another as they laboured away. Aside from the fact that they were not necessarily within earshot of one another, they both knew that The Rock would have a coronary if they even attempted to talk. The Rock had stopped pacing and had spent the past 30 minutes standing by the car watching his men work. Despite the smell that continued to linger from the passenger seat, he decided to plant himself there. He had already searched the car, and since he hadn't been there to see the body himself, he paid no mind to the fact that Otto had been rotting in that very spot just a few hours earlier.

"Where are those bloody books?" he said under his breath. *These two couldn't find their way out of breadbox, especially the big one.*

"Monsieur?"

"Yes, Gerard," The Rock snarled impatiently.

"Can we go down to the lake and get some water?" he asked, already expecting him to deny them, but hoping all the same that maybe he would show some mercy.

"No, dammit!" He couldn't stop himself then - his rage had peaked with the simple request for water and he violently threw himself out of the car and lunged toward Gerard. Despite Gerard's slight height advantage The Rock got right up into the exhausted man's face and launched into a crazed tirade. Gerard stood there, taking it all in, as The Rock's saliva splattered repulsively in his face. He couldn't even make out what the enraged man was saying, and wasn't even certain if he was speaking English. The Rock stepped back and the spray subsided, but the berating continued as he pressed on with his orders. "You keep on digging until your hands are bleeding, until the last breath in your body has been spent, until your heart explodes. You will do what *I* say, you son of a bitch. This is not..." But then the sound simply faded around them, except for the *swoosh* in the air. The Rock never saw it coming and likely never felt it. Gerard had stopped listening, and instead had focused on a woodpecker boring a hole in a beautiful pine tree just beyond his target. Before he knew it, the shovel in his hands swung back and then slashed through the air in a blinding motion. The clunk of the shovel as it bashed into The Rock temple restored the natural order of the forest.

Louis had stopped to hear whether The Rock would give them permission to get some water, and watched, as his associate was humiliated. He certainly didn't expect what had happened next. Although he was happy, even relieved, he never relished taking a life or witnessing a murder. A silence seemed to wash over the area. They were no longer obliged to dig for an imaginary treasure with a heartless tyrant cracking the whip.

"Gerard, are you ok?" he asked in his throaty French accent. He didn't know what else to say.

"Uh, yeah, I guess so," he mumbled as he dropped his shovel next to the body. "I, uh, think..." he stuttered as he stared at the body, at a loss for what to do next.

Louis approached him, towering over him like a parent and uncharacteristically placed his thick arm around Gerard's shoulder. "It's ok, mon ami, you did what had to be done." He could feel the man shaking, as the adrenaline coursed through his system, the remnants of his rage subsiding as the reality of his actions sank in.

"I, uh, don't know what came over me. It was..."

"No need to explain, mon ami. Maybe we should get out of here."

"Yes, right, that's, uh, what we'll, uh, do." Gerard was in shock. His mind had lost control and had given up to his raw emotions. He couldn't quite comprehend what he had done.

"Come with me, mon ami," Louis said quite gently as he directed Gerard toward their car which had been hidden from view behind the trees. Louis was quite composed as he was not unused to seeing people in fits of anger. He kept his arm around his associate, and the two of them walked away. Louis knew Gerard could never speak of this and would never be able to return. If word got out that he had killed The Rock, he would be dead.

The Knock that Turned Everything Upside Down

"Inspector, did you hear that?"

"I sure did," he whispered as they peered out from behind the logs. Sure enough, there lay The Rock. In a moment Simms realized that another one of the country's most notorious gangsters had been taken down. Rothman would never again be able to wield his influence over the law. Simms felt triumphant, even if it was one of The Rock's own who had taken him out.

The Sergeant readied himself to make a move against the two men, but the Inspector grabbed his arm and pulled him back down behind the log. "Let them go," he said magnanimously. "They did us a favour." In fact, he was particularly satisfied with what had just happened; he believed in a higher order, and that 'an eye for an eye' was the truest form of law. "Sergeant, in case you were not aware, I believe the man lying on the ground to be none other than The Rock Rothman. His disappearance and death ultimately serves our purpose. So we will let them go."

"Are you sure, Inspector?"

"If we catch them and parade them around, someone will want to kill them, and it could jeopardize the lives of our brothers. I will not have that crook make any more widows. Besides, in his absence his empire will start to crumble, at least if they still believe he's alive. Once they know he's dead, someone else will immediately take his place, and we'll have a turf war on our hands. This is the best way. Sergeant, any rumor of his death, could only come from one of the four of us here today. I know those two will say nothing, and I know I won't say a word. That only leaves you, Sergeant."

"No. I promise, sir. My lips are sealed."

"Good choice, Sergeant. Once they're gone let's get that body buried so no one else finds it."

The Inspector didn't see the Sergeant roll his eyes at that comment. He felt, more than ever, that there was something more to this than the Inspector was letting on. Those men had been here digging desperately for something, and he was determined now to figure out *what*, although he had a good idea.

"Then we head back to the office," the inspector continued. "This investigation is officially closed."

The Sergeant nodded his understanding and assent. Then it occurred to him that he still had one considerable issue. "My car is dead, sir."

"Don't worry, Sergeant. We'll have it towed back to the station, although I really should make you walk back...I did tell you to stay at the office. This time you can come with me, but the next time you disregard my orders I will have you removed from the force. Understood, Sergeant?"

"Yes, sir," the Sergeant lied.

"Now start shoveling behind the car. Those holes look almost deep enough to bury a body."

"Yes, sir."

"Good man." Simms knew this was far from over, but he needed the Sergeant off his back, and at the same time he needed to keep an eye on him.

Poetry in Motion

"Ok, kids. The grilled cheese sandwiches are ready, and I made some potato chips," Jippsy's mom called from behind the porch screen.

"You're the best, Mrs. R.," Butterball beamed. Butterball had recently become fascinated by her looks, and would sometimes stare a little too long. More importantly, however, he found that everything she cooked seemed to be made with love and tasted soooo good.

"Jippsy, could you come in and give me a hand? Butterball, you can grab some plates too." Jippsy and Butterball carried the sandwiches out onto the porch. They had decided to sit on the stairs at the end of the porch lined up like a row of ducks at a carnival shooting gallery.

Butterball settled in and slowly started eating his sandwich. He loved to savor every bite, especially a delicious grilled cheese sandwich. He loved cheddar cheese, but there was nothing better than a freshly baked baguette. Ohh, and those deep fried potatoes, they were so good that they even made him forget all about that crazy poem. To tell the truth, when food was involved, nothing else mattered, although he couldn't say the same for everyone else. As he looked down the line he could see that Frankie had already dispensed with his lunch; perhaps only his dog could eat faster than Frankie, he thought. Dodo had barely touched hers, but he hoped she wouldn't eat too much, and maybe she would be willing to share the rest. As they discussed the poem, Jippsy, Capri and Vicky slowly nibbled on their lunch, taking turns to speculate on the meaning of each line. Butterball only knew one thing for sure... they would going back today. But first, he had to try and get Dodo's leftovers.

Dodo was sitting right next to him, and could barely make it through half of her sandwich and hadn't touched her chips at all. She caught Butterball staring intently at her plate and smiled knowingly. She wouldn't make it easy for him, and instead waited for him to ask. It didn't take long, and he finally gave in.

"Hey Dodo, are you going to eat your other half?" he asked sheepishly.

"No, Butterball," she laughed. You could have it." And before she could even complete her sentence, it was already on his plate.

"Would you kids like some lemonade?" Jippsy's mom called from the kitchen.

Butterball couldn't resist the thought of a tall cool glass of her homemade lemonade, and despite his mouth full of food was the first to answer. "Sure, Mrs. R.," he answered, practically spitting food on Dodo in his haste.

"Ok, Butterball," she giggled, as she carried out a pitcher and glasses on a tray, and placed it on the porch. "Here you go kids. Come and get it yourself."

"Thanks, Mrs, R.," Frankie answered, truly appreciative of a refreshing glass of anything. He stood up and headed to the tray lying behind Dodo. He caught her staring at him as he poured himself a glass, and realized he was being selfish. He offered the glass to her, and she took it gladly. "Does anybody *else* want a glass?" he asked reluctantly. It was unanimous – of course *everyone* else wanted a glass. He poured and handed out lemonade to the gang, and they each thanked him sarcastically, recognizing that he merely offered out of obligation. "You're **welcome**!" he responded as facetiously as possible, then greedily chugged his drink as the others piled the dirty dishes on the tray.

Frankie belched loudly and laughed at his own nonsense. "Let's get down to business," he announced as he dropped his plate on top of the pile. He took the book from Vicky who had been studying it carefully. She hadn't shown as much interest in the poem. Instead, she was determined to decipher the symbols and notations in the black book, as she knew it would require her expertise...research.

Even though they could all recite the poem, Frankie repeated the first verse. "'Where downhill the big rock shades.' Well, we know this first one for sure...it's Big Rock, right? I guess Dutch saw it that way too."

"Agreed," said Capri. "So we have to go down to the bottom of Big Rock towards the..." she started to say, but Vicky already knew this answer and they both said, "sand bar," at the same time.

"Right, that makes sense, but how far from Big Rock? It says 'the thoroughbred runs but the 8th pole'. What the hell is that?"

Frankie! My mother is just in the kitchen. She could hear you swearing."

"Ok, Dodo," he said contritely as he rolled his eyes behind her back. It wasn't really swearing, but he didn't want her know that he thought she was being childish, and so touchy!

"It has to do with horse racing," said Vicky. "I know because my dad listens to the races, but I don't know what it means. I'll have to ask him, but he's in Montreal at the market." Many of the men in the area were in Montreal to sell their first fruit harvests of the year.

"We'll have to figure this one out somehow or wait until Vicky's dad is back," continued Frankie. "Anyone know what the rest is about?"

"They must be some sort of landmarks," said

291

Jippsy, anxious to get back to Lost Lake to start the hunt. He suggested they go back to the forest and look around, now that they had eaten and rested a little. They all agreed, some reluctantly given what had happened to Jippsy in the morning, but in the end, they were a gang, and they were all in this together.

HI mom heard the commotion of the kids moving on the porch and called out, "Jippsy where are you going now?"

"Back out with the *gang*, mom," he answered conspiratorially, and winked at Dodo hoping that would help get her onboard.

"Ok. Have fun. And Jippsy?

"Yes, mom?"

"Your dad is supposed to come home tomorrow. I hope you'll stick around in case he needs your help."

"Great mom," he answered, both relieved that his dad would be coming home, and somewhat annoyed that his participation in the hunt would be curtailed. Then he thought about his poor grandpa in the hospital and felt guilty. "How's grandpa?"

"He's not better yet, son. We're praying..." she trailed off.

"Ok, mom. We'll be back for dinner." He didn't want to seem indifferent but if he could find that treasure, it would surely help all of them.

"Ok, kids. Have fun and be careful."

"Thanks, Mrs. R.," they said in unison. She stepped out onto the porch to watch them leave. They waved to her as they made their way back to the forest.

Jippsy walked alone, deep in thought. *There are no crocodiles in these waters, what could he be talking about?* Jippsy was completely baffled by this verse. *Maybe he thought he saw a crocodile? He did call it a swampy hole, and crocs are known to live in swamps.*

The stones lining the makeshift road crunched under their feet as they walked slowly under the hot sun. They were all so quiet, each contemplating the task at hand and the meaning of Dutch's clues, except for Butterball who complained throughout the entire trek about the pains in his stomach. He realized he had eaten far too much and that this could not end well. Soon, very soon, he was going to have a problem.

Vicky was trying to figure out what Dutch had meant when he referred to the 8th pole. She knew it had to do with a race, but couldn't put her finger on it. *Does it run 8 poles? Is that the finish line? Are there 8 poles, and each pole marks a distance? If so, then how many poles are there in total?* Vicky loved puzzles, apparently much more than she loved money, as the mystery was the only thing that seemed to keep her interested in this adventure. Besides, that kind of money was just a fantasy. *No one could carry that much money...* she thought to herself. *If they did, it would weigh hundreds of pounds and a dead man definitely couldn't carry that!*

They reached the top of the road, where they could see the opening to the crash site. To their astonishment there was another car stopped along the road. The window was open, and the car was unlocked. They saw a policemen's jacket spread across the seat.

"A cop! This is getting a little dicey," Frankie said warily. He tried to mask his nerves about his altercation with the cop the day before, but the gang knew he didn't want to get in trouble with his dad.

"Don't worry Frankie, we'll take it slow and cautious."

"Ok, Jips. So what do you have in mind?"

"In case someone is actually here, other than us, we'll head through the forest. Then we'll make our way down to the lake and work backwards. Everyone ok with that?"

"Sure, Jips, whatever you say," Frankie agreed, for once happy that Jippsy was taking the lead, even though he would never admit it.

"Ok, Jippsy," answered Capri. None of the others bothered to speak up, which Jippsy took to mean they would go along with the plan.

"Keep your eyes on the ground, guys. It's pretty rough up here what with the tangled roots and rocks," Jippsy cautioned them. The ground was moist, and the leaves were wet from the previous night's rain, especially in the denser areas. The sun was filtering through in patches, causing the moisture to evaporate, but the humidity was stifling, even in the shade, and the black flies were swarming and biting. The kids were sweating profusely in the heat, further enticing the black flies to attack.

Frankie didn't care about the black flies anymore, as the heat was getting to him. He stripped to the waist and stuffed his shirt in the belt loops of his short pants, which elicited a grateful smile from Dodo, who couldn't take her eyes off of his glistening muscles. She felt as though she was being pulled in two directions. Her mind told her to be cool, he was just a boy, but her body pulled at her, made her breath heavy, and her heart beat erratically whenever she saw him like this. In fact, these feelings had become so intense that the mere thought of him – shirt on *or* off – seemed to drive her crazy.

The deeper they entered the forest, the thicker the bushes grew; the trees had all but blocked out the sunlight until the sun was nothing more than random strobes of light flickering through. Jippsy used his stick to swat the overgrown bushes but they were so strong that once he worked his way through they merely bounced back and swatted Capri – hard!

"Jippsy, cut it out! One more time and you are going to the back of the line," she ordered.

"Just doing you a favour, Capri," he answered sarcastically.

"It's no favour, Jippsy. It's actually a pain the ass." She used the same expression her mother often said to her father.

"Ok, Capri, you win. Be my guest and go ahead," he snapped, actually quite perturbed. And then he did exactly what she had suggested and ran to the back of the group. He had no interest in being anywhere near her. Besides, he figured he could keep an eye out for any kind of movement around the cop's car that seemed to have been abandoned on the road.

"I can't see the lake anymore, Capri," Vicky said. "Let's start heading down there."

"Sure thing, Vicky." Capri appreciated Vicky's sense of direction - and the fact that she was paying attention - especially since she herself was clearly distracted.

It took only minutes to get down to the lake. They had overshot Big Rock and the sand bar and had ended up at the edge of the lake where it met the other side. They hadn't heard any other noises or other people at all, and were pleased. Frankie announced that they should carefully make their way toward the car and work from there as they tried to follow the poem.

They lined up along the shore so as not to fall into the lake and made their way back to Big Rock and up the hill, where a large log managed to block them from view should anyone suddenly appear at the car. They peeked out from behind the log surveying the area around the car.

"What are those holes?" Butterball asked curiously.

"Quiet," Frankie said as he lashed out with his hand and pushed Butterball with a little more force than he had intended.

Butterball had taken enough of Frankie's abuse, and that final push, combined with the discomfort of his stomach, seemed to bring something out in him that the gang had rarely, if ever, seen. He scanned the car and their surroundings quickly, stood up and said out loud for the whole forest to hear, "There is no one here, asshole."

Capri laughed along with Jippsy. "I guess not," Jippsy remarked. Since the coast was obviously clear, thanks to Butterball's outburst, Jippsy started to make his way toward the car.

"There's a shovel over there," Frankie called out.

"One over here too," Jippsy called out from the car.

"I guess we're not the only ones looking for something here, eh Jippsy?" Butterball pointed out.

"We better get moving before they return." Jippsy realized they were in a race to find the treasure. Jippsy and Capri met back at the log each with their respective shovels.

Cristafaro Farm

"That kid," Simms remembered, as he rummaged through his desk. "Where's that book I was using yesterday? Did I leave it in my jacket?" He stood up and walked over to the corner of his office, passing the small bank of wooden file cabinets that held all of the region's case files since the Great War. Almost twenty years of information were packed into three rows of four drawers, but for Inspector Simms this case was *the* most intriguing of all. Much to his surprise, this case had essentially brought into question his true loyalty. How far, exactly, was he willing to stretch his belief system in order to achieve lifetime security? He supposed this was a dilemma faced by many men on the force, men just like him with an obligation to uphold the law, an inherently powerful position to hold, and, from his experience, seemingly easy to corrupt. His jacket was dangling from a hook on the coat rack in the corner. His hands fumbled around in the inside breast pocket, until he pulled out the small notebook and smacked it successfully in his palm. He flipped through the pages until he found the last entry: Frank Cristafaro.

He had said he was a farmer's boy who lived in the area. He checked through the Bell directory, a small book that listed the telephone number of anyone who rented a phone line in the area. Sure enough locating the name Cristafaro was easy as pie. *Not too many of those in these parts*, Simms thought to himself.

Changing times

Jippsy listened intently to his surroundings - there was something different in the air. The forest no longer had that friendly warm feeling that made Jippsy feel at peace. Instead, there was an eerie darkness that that had infiltrated the woods. His senses had become acutely attuned to every sight, sound and smell – it seemed everything had undergone some transformation. The crows had joined forces to break up the monotony, and had gathered like the scavengers they were, hovering and alighting ominously around and on the car. Had they found their lunch, Jippsy wondered. Impossible – the body had been removed and there was nothing left but the burned-out car. Their childhood playground had changed, and something told him things could never return to the way they had been. Play was over, and the serious work of unraveling a mystery had begun. He didn't realize it at the time, as he was caught up in the hunt, but Jippsy Russ had finally uncovered his destiny.

Vicky was holding the book. She recited the lines and listened as they softly echoed back to her from across the lake. She felt safer now that Butterball had broken the ice, but every now and again she looked up from the book and scanned the area, wary of the possibility that they were being watched. They all stood atop Big Rock. "'Where downhill the big rock shades'," she repeated. "Let's go down to the bottom," she decided aloud.

The sky was clear and the sun hung high enough that the kids' shadows had disappeared. Butterball was the first to observe that there would be no shade where they were headed.

"Yeah, no shade," Frankie concurred, partly out of a growing concern for the danger they could be in, but also in an attempt to alleviate the animosity between Butterball and himself. It some strange way, Frankie was proud to see Butterball gain a little more confidence as a result of his outburst.

"That's true, but it *is* around noon and the sun is right above us. That means our shadows are being cast directly beneath us..."

"Wow, Vicky! You really know things don't you?"

"Thanks, Dodo. But you know I just love to read everything. You'll see...in another half an hour we'll start to see our shadows again as the sun moves lower in the sky. The problem is we don't know what time Dutch saw the Big Rock. For that matter, we don't even know if he even wrote this for himself or maybe to throw someone off his scent."

"Hmm. That's a good point, Vicky," Capri said as she nodded her head in agreement. She was completely engaged by Vicky's logic. "So what do you recommend?"

"Well, I think we should follow it anyways. I mean, you just never know."

They sat quietly on Big Rock, waiting for the sun to lead them to their next destination. Time seemed to pass so slowly that eventually Jippsy started thinking about how refreshing it would be to go for a swim. The heat was starting to get to him, and he could feel the sweat clinging to him as it dripped from every pore. But then he remembered the morning – it seemed so long ago already - and for once his fears overtook him. Maybe I'll just wait, he thought to himself. Maybe, just this once, he had had enough of the water for one day.

"What time is it?"

"I don't know, Butterball. Relax," Jippsy said despite his own apprehensions.

"Hey, wait... I can see my shadow!" Butterball beamed.

"Then it's time," said Vicky "Let's go beneath Big Rock."

"There it is," Butterball said with wonder as he pointed to the lake. "A shadow." The shadow jutted out into the lake.

"Don't tell me it's in the lake? It figures!" Jippsy moaned with frustration. "I guess I'm going in again."

"Wait, Jips, it's not here." Vicky put her hand on his shoulder to reassure him.

"What do you mean?"

"Well there *is* the other part of the verse."

"Right. Of course..." By then he had resigned himself to jumping back into the lake. "But it may still be in the lake."

"Of course! But if you think about it, the money would probably dissolve in the lake."

"I guess, but maybe Dutch didn't think about that. I doubt he had a shovel, so it *is* possible."

"I suppose it is..." Vicky answered reluctantly.

Capri had heard enough of their ridiculous banter, and interrupted, "Ok, so, uh, why don't you go on, Vicky?" Capri stared meaningfully at Jippsy, in the hopes he would keep his mouth shut.

"Thanks, Capri." Vicky was grateful for Capri's intervention. "Ok. So it says, 'Toward the sand where the water fades,' so if we walk along the edge of the water we know the water becomes really shallow at the sandbar."

"That must be the place," Frankie yelled out as he ran ahead to the sandbar. "Come on, guys, let's have a look around here." They all watched as Frankie danced a jig on the sandbar, splashing in and out of the water.

Dodo laughed at his silliness; she was oddly relieved that he was making light of the situation, especially since everyone else had turned so serious. *This can't be good if we aren't having any fun,* she said to herself. *Even Jippsy is so serious – just like Dad during the harvest. You can't even joke around; he's always angry at the dinner table, and Jippsy's always the one who tries to lighten things up, making faces at me just to make me laugh. Dad was too serious and now so is Jippsy.* "Come on, Jips, relax. Don't be like Dad...this is supposed to be fun."

"You're right, Dodo. Let's have some fun," he answered after giving it some thought. In the end, it occurred to him that he could probably never come back to this place again. He laughed and splashed Dodo just for the fun of it, and then, for the briefest moment, they all played along, kicking up water and splashing one another. By then they were soaked anyway between the overwhelming heat and humidity of the forest and slogging through the lake along the shore. Did they forget about the hunt? Not for a second. But those brief moments allowed some of the built-up tension to dissipate, and made it possible for them to refocus on the task at hand.

Surprisingly, Butterball was the first to break up the fun. "Ok, we're here. Now what?" He clearly had no passion for the hunt. Maybe he just wanted it to be over already.

"Well, this is the tricky part. What's an 8th pole?" Vicky mumbled to herself. She had become frustrated with this line. She had repeated it over and over as though reciting a mantra in the hopes it would jog her memory. Her dad listened to the hose races all the time – she should have been paying attention. The gang watched her sink into a trance-like state, holding her breath as she concentrated. She could hear the announcer in her head, the excitement mounting as the horses reached the 8th pole, but that wasn't the finish line, she knew, it was close, though, if only she knew the distance... She mouthed the words she had heard so many times... *Here they come...down the stretch...now coming around the turn...past the eighth pole...a race to the finish line.* "Damn it!" she cursed aloud.

Her concentration was broken by the cry of a loon as it ran along the water preparing to take off. Her gaze focused quickly on the awkward bird as it lifted off the water and flew in a perfect parallel over the lake. It seemed uncertain as to what to do next – a feeling Vicky could, by all means, appreciate. She had no answer – not just yet anyway.

"Vicky, let's forget it for now and concentrate on what we do know."

"Jippsy I'm sure I can figure it out."

"I'm sure you will, Vicky, but we should continue at least with the things we do know."

"Like what, Jippsy?" Butterball asked, as he was at as much of a loss as to where this was all headed.

"Well, my dear friend, my best pal," he said affectionately as he wrapped his arm around Butterball's waist.

"Cut it out, Jips," Butterball said irately as he shoved at Jippsy's hand.

Jippsy shrugged off Butterball's annoyance and paced away. "Well," he said smugly, "we **know** that the money is hidden somewhere along this lake, we **know** there was a raft on the other side, and we **know** that Dutch couldn't have gotten very far with the weight of so much money, so we **know** that we are 'this' close to finding something that could change our lives forever," he finished as he held his hand up and indicated how close they were by closing his thumb and forefinger to an inch apart.

"Yeah, but Jips, the rest of the poem doesn't really

make sense. A crocodile? A swamp? I think Dutch was just screwy."

"You may be right. Maybe we should ignore the poem for now and just look at the physical clues. We found the shredded jacket on this side of the lake just a little ways up from here," he said as he pointed to a clearing ahead. "And we found the belt on a makeshift raft across the lake. I really think we should head back there and see if we can find any other physical clues."

Capri was getting impatient too. "I don't think we should run all over the place. I think we should just try to decipher the code or poem or whatever you want to call it - in the order it's been written - so we don't get off track. Otherwise we're just looking for a needle in a haystack, assuming there even is a needle."

"Capri...Ye of little faith," Jippsy said mockingly.

"Oh, so now you think you know things. Was there a crystal ball in that book that you conveniently didn't show us back at your house? What *more* is there Jippsy? How come you wouldn't show us the book? Eh?" Capri couldn't help but get her digs in, but she was getting angry and frustrated with his selfishness. Her body had suddenly turned from loose and warm to battle-ready as it occurred to her that he knew something and hadn't trusted her enough to share it with her.

"What's going on here?" Jippsy asked as he took a step back from the gang and raised his hands in the air in a conciliatory gesture. "Hold on a minute," he said defensively even as he knew she was right.

"Yeah, Jippsy, *old boy*, shouldn't you have shown us the book?" Frankie asked angrily as this revelation dawned on him. Dodo caught onto what was happening and stepped quickly between Frankie and her brother, as Frankie moved swiftly toward Jippsy.

"Now hold on," Dodo insisted as she raised her

arm in an effort to block Frankie's advance. She couldn't believe the sudden turn of events. In just a few short hours the gang had gone from a supportive team to an angry mob. What had happened to her friends?

"Jippsy just survived a horrible accident, thanks to you and Capri no less, and I don't think he would try to trick any of you. Get a hold of yourself. We're all friends, but just look at what this stupid adventure is doing to us. I thought we were supposed to be a gang!" Dodo's voice and attitude had become increasingly loud and aggressive as she became more and more determined to end this conflict. Jippsy was proud of her - she was showing confidence and passion. "What's the matter with you all?"

"You're right Dodo," Capri conceded. "Vicky I think you're the most levelheaded one here right now. What do you think we should do?"

"Thanks, Capri," Vicky said and smiled ecstatically.

"She's just a ten year old," Frankie said begrudgingly. "Since when do we take advice from a ten year old?"

"I'm 11 Frankie," she retorted haughtily.

"Soooo sorry," Frankie said with disdain. He couldn't stand having to listen to this little girl's advice. And then his brutishness got the better of him. "You know what? I've had enough of this."

"What are you talking about Frankie?"

"Dodo, I've had enough. This is ridiculous. The poem is screwy. This Dutch guy is just off his rocker, and we're running around like a bunch of monkeys swinging from branch to branch trying to get to the only tree with bananas."

"That doesn't even make sense," she said.

"Well, that's what it feels like. I'm going to the raft side. I'm taking this shovel," he said as he thrust his arm in the air to indicate the shovel in the air that he'd been carting around since they had left the car, "and going. Is there anyone who wants to come with me? Speak now or forever hold your peace," he finished and chuckled at his own joke. He looked from one friend to the next but they all just stared at him blankly. "No takers," he noted with dismay. "Well then, see you on the other side," he said and peremptorily turned his back on his friends and walked away.

"Just hold on a minute," Butterball called out finally. He didn't really want to get involved, but felt it had to be said. We swore an oath as a new gang to respect each other's opinions, and then let majority rule. I say we put it to a vote."

Frankie liked this idea, especially since he didn't relish the idea of being the only one to go across the lake while the others did their thing. "That's a great idea, Butterball, "he said happily as he turned back to the gang; he was secretly relieved. *That Butterball isn't so bad after all,* he thought.

"We have a choice to make," Butterball continued as he looked around. Vicky was sitting on the sandbar along with Jippsy while Dodo and Frankie were still standing. "Why don't you two sit down as well? We'll take a break, have a vote and figure out our next move based upon the group's consensus."

Jippsy raised an eyebrow at that. As this adventure was unfolding Butterball was truly impressing his friend. *He really knows how to deflate a situation,* Jippsy thought with a touch of jealousy.

Butterball had taken control of the situation. He stood before them as they all lounged on the beach. "We have two ideas put forth by two of the members. We will put it to a vote and the majority will rule. All members of the Rouge River gang will have to follow the majority.

Does that sound fair to everyone?" He could see them all nodding as they listened.

"Sure," said Jippsy.

"Ok," came Frankie's reply.

Vicky and Dodo simply nodded their consent.

Capri agreed and told him to continue.

"On the one hand we have a poem, which we are trying to decipher in the order in which it's written so we can follow a trail of written clues. We could continue on this path. On the other hand, we can search for what Jippsy calls 'physical clues' which will take us on another path. Both paths might lead us to the same place in the end, so we're simply deciding which path to take to get to where we're going. So, all in favor of Option A following the poem, raise your hands." Vicky and Capri raised their hands immediately. Butterball looked at Jippsy and then raised his hand apprehensively so as not to insult his friend. He did, after all, have his own thoughts about the hunt.

Although there was no point in asking the question, Butterball still went ahead, "All in favor of Option B?" Without hesitation, Frankie, Jippsy and Dodo raised their hands. The gang simply looked around at one another, wondering what to do next as they had reached a stalemate. It was so quiet they could hear the water lapping up along the sandbar as a slight breeze caused ripples on the surface of the lake.

Capri stood up and started to speak before Butterball could draw his own conclusion from their vote, "Thank you, Butterball. It seems we have a tie, and in the case of a tie..."

"Why are we wasting our time?" Frankie interrupted.

"Hold on, Frankie. Just hear what I have to say," she implored.

Frankie looked up at his sister. *Wow!* He thought to himself. *She's so sure and confident...and so smart...* His silence afforded her the opportunity she needed to continue.

"We can either vote again, which will most likely result in another tie, or we could split up. Just this once, unless someone wants to change their mind?" When no one spoke up she suggested that each team take a shovel just in case they find something. Frankie and Jippsy knew that Capri and Dodo didn't really want to work without one another, and were worried when Dodo stood up that she would change her mind. Instead, she picked up the shovel lying on the sandbar beside Jippsy and handed it to Butterball. Even she realized this might be the only way.

"Let's go," she said almost enthusiastically. Both Jippsy and Frankie hopped up and grabbed her in a bear hug, picking her up off of the ground.

"Well, then, Butterball, it is decided," said Frankie with a grin. "Let's get moving, Jips."

"Hold on, Frankie," Jippsy said as he held up a hand. "We at least have to make a plan." He turned his attention to Butterball. "We'll go across to the other side. If either of the teams finds something, we'll call across the lake. Either way let's meet back here in two hours. Set up a sundial on this side and we'll do the same when we reach the other side. Good luck, guys."

Chance or Fate

The road seemed to go on forever; it wound up and down and even seemed to go full circle at times. It transitioned from pavement to gravel to dirt, and if not for the rain the night before, the dirt and dust would have been kicked up from the trucks hauling the month's harvest and lumber. Simms' black police cruiser had become virtually unrecognizable as the layers of dust clung to the car. "How much further *are* these people?" he muttered to himself. He drove along, planning and rehearsing his speech. He continued along his way, deep in thought, satisfied that the Sergeant would no longer be part of this investigation yet worried that going out on his own could jeopardize everything he had worked for. The benefit, he had concluded, far outweighed the risk.

This was nothing like the city – country roads, especially private roads, often had no names as they belonged to the individual landowner. There was no way of really knowing where these farms began. Each farm blended into the next – from rolling hills of green pasture for grazing cows to endless rows of fruit trees that rose up into the hills, and of course, forests of maple trees dotting an entire side of the old mountain range. The land and soil were exceptionally fertile along the Rouge River - it allowed many families to actually thrive in the post-depression years as more and more people flocked to the city to find work. Those who remained became the food suppliers for the huddled masses.

The winding road had effectively lulled Simms into a peaceful state as the warm summer air whistled through the open windows. Simms had become engrossed in his thoughts and failed to spot the truck until it had pulled out into his path from a side road. The truck was piled high with massive 30-foot-long pine logs. As it pulled onto the road, its weight shifted as its cargo, which had not been properly secured, suddenly moved. Had Simms not been so focused on his own personal quandary he would have seen it coming, and his instincts would have kicked in. Instead, he failed to notice the truck and was equally unaware as the truck's passenger-side wheels lifted off the ground. Like a line of dominos toppled by a slight tap, the truck's sudden loss of balance caused the top log on the pile to roll off to the left and the logs sitting not-so-snuggly beneath it to follow suit. This in turn caused the truck's passenger side to further lift off from the ground, which was the final impetus the top log needed to teeter then cascade off the pile. In a moment the log went reeling across the road as the driver's slight adjustment suddenly popped the truck back onto the road with a thud as the weight of the logs was redistributed once again.

Simms' thoughts were interrupted at last by the sound of the log striking the ground. He came out of his reveries just in time to witness the truck regaining its balance and to spot the rolling pine log headed straight for his cruiser. He instinctively grabbed the wheel with both hands, and practically hammered his foot right through the floorboard as he slammed on the brake pedal. The log was so massive it managed to completely obscure the landscape ahead, and all Simms could see or hear was the immense log thundering toward him. He didn't wait for it to hit him; he grabbed the gear shift and tore it into reverse as he stepped off the clutch and accelerated in one full motion. He didn't have time to consider his options but prayed there were no other vehicles on the road as he raced the car downhill, his head swinging wildly back and forth between the log and the road behind him. The car's engine whined with the strain of racing in reverse. The tires kicked up stones that ricocheted back onto his windshield as they were deflected by the log that was bearing down on him. The stones were small but hitting the windshield with such force that the glass could have shattered but was merely pockmarked by the spitting stones. Were it not for the fact that the car had an engine, the log's weight would have caused it to outrun Simms as they both sped downhill. He needed to keep calm, to keep an eye out for a cross street or driveway, and get out of the way before the log gained on him and he was steamrolled by it.

The gravel scattered on the road was flying everywhere, and reminded Simms of the many times he'd been trapped in his family barn during rain or hail storms as they beat down upon the corrugated tin roof. He could wait out a storm; he could outlast this adversary too. "Aaaaaah!" he roared, as he finally decided it was time to try to hug the side of the road in the hope that the log maintained its current trajectory and would skim by him. He kept up his speed, down the center of the road, waiting and biding his time for just the right moment to veer off to the left, and hopefully protect his driver side without winding up rolling down the ditch. The embankment along this road was too deep to risk flipping the car over, and his calculating had slowed him down until the log was dangerously close. So he did the only thing he could...he yanked the steering wheel hard to the left and felt the car jerk quickly toward the ditch on the left. He had a matter of inches with which to play, but then he felt the car starting to lose its balance. It had two wheels off the road, but could he manage a few more inches just to be safe? He pulled the wheel sideways as his body compensated to stay upright and allowed the car to stall. He swung his head forward for a moment to gauge his odds just as the log bounced through a deep depression in the road. The end of the log was headed straight for the passenger side of the windshield but the jolt from the dip in the road forced the log to spring up and almost over the car. He ducked and heard the log graze the roof as it flew over him. He listened as it disappeared behind him. "My god," he whispered, "that was close." He breathed a sigh of relief, but his hand was still shaking as he reached to open the door. His cruiser was perched precariously on the shoulder, leaning down the embankment. It wasn't the safest thing to do, but he had to get out of the cruiser. He had no choice but to jump down into the ditch, where he rested on his hands and knees, breathing slowly in an attempt to calm his nerves.

He might have stayed on all fours longer if the sudden need to urinate hadn't forced him to stand. As he unzipped his pants it occurred to him how lucky he was to be there intact, still able to pee standing up. He took a deep breath and thanked the heavens for his good fortune. His heart was still racing and he felt lightheaded, but he was even more determined to accomplish what he had set out to do when all this madness had started. He climbed up the embankment and walked around the car to evaluate the damage. Pockmarks ravaged every square inch of the cruiser, which gave it the appearance of having been through a war. Just as he was about to open his door he caught sight of the roof – there was nothing more than a graze that ran from front to back on the passenger side, but it was damaged nonetheless.

He started the car without any problem and slowly pulled back out onto the right side of the road. This time, he vowed, he would concentrate on locating the farm and arriving in one piece. This thought had barely crossed his mind when the truck finally reached him. The driver looked at him remorsefully in an attempt to apologize, and then shrugged his shoulders as if to say, 'I don't know how it happened...'. *No harm done,* Simms tried to convey in turn. He reasoned that the driver would be short on his quota for this run and that would more than make up for the inconvenience.

He drove on slowly, carefully scanning the road for signs that he might be nearing the Cristafaro farm. The landscape had gradually become more wooded, which made it impossible for him to see beyond the trees lining the road, except for the occasional home situated immediately along the road. None of the homes had addresses or names signs so he was forced to stop and pull into every driveway and approach each home until he spotted any indication of where he was. This went on for nearly thirty minutes, by which time he had lost both his patience and his resolve and decided that he would knock on the door of the next home and ask someone, anyone, if they knew the family.

Roughly one mile later he spotted another driveway. He turned off the road and made his way up the long driveway that led up to a large lakefront home. He was impressed by the majestic landscape. Tall, dense sugar maples dotted the land as far as he could see, and the driveway cut a path between the trees that led up to the home which had been set back roughly 50 feet from a large lake on what appeared to be a peninsula. The home's view of the water was completely unhindered. Even from where he was - still several hundred feet from the home – Simms could see their view of the lake was breathtaking. An island could be seen in the middle of their bay a roughly half a mile in the distance. A canvass of lush green mountains made this one of the most picturesque settings Simms had ever seen. *These people must love seeing this view every day*, he thought enviously.

He pulled up as close to the home as he could and hopped out of the car. He was anxious, for some reason, to breathe in the air that surrounded this beautiful scenery as if somehow it might feel special as well. He walked purposefully up to the large log cabin and struck the iron lion knocker several times. He waited a reasonable amount of time, but no one answered. Just as he was turning to leave he heard the sweetest voice call out, "May I help you?" He turned his attention toward the door that had suddenly opened and the riveting woman who stood in the doorway.

"Yes," he stammered then cleared his throat. *What is wrong with me?* He wondered to himself. "Yes, madame," he continued with greater composure, "my name is Lieutenant Benoît Simms of the RCMP. I am looking for the Cristafaro residence. Do you know where they live?"

"Oh, sure," she answered.

She's so lovely and upbeat, he thought with surprise.

"You're almost there," she continued. "About another mile that way," she said brightly as she lifted her silken arm and pointed back in the direction he had been headed all along, "you'll see their driveway on the left. They live up the hill overlooking the apple and cherry orchards." It occurred to her that she hadn't asked him about the nature of his visit. "Is there anything the matter, sir?"

My god she's sweet! he thought as the purpose of his excursion seemed to elude him. "No. No, of course not. It's, uhm, merely routine, if you must know.

As perky as she was, she seemed to brighten further at his non-urgent reply. "Well, then, I spend most days here alone and would love some company. May I interest you in some lemonade?" And then she smiled in such a way that her entire face lit up and he could see nothing but the radiance of her being, as her eyes sparkled and her beautiful lips and teeth beamed at him.

Her beauty was striking, and he had to recall exactly why he was on this mission in the first place. He wanted to stay, but he needed to go. "I really must be on my way. Perhaps another time?" he asked almost pleadingly. She nodded her head in acquiescence, her smile not as bright but still warm. "What is your name, Madame?"

"It's Cooper. Faith Cooper." He smiled at the simple beauty of her name.

How à propos, he thought. "I've never heard the name 'Faith' before," he said.

"My parents were quite the bohemians in their day, I guess. They died together quite young and left me this place."

"It really is magnificent," he said almost longingly.

"Please come back sometime, Lieutenant. My offer will still stand."

"You are very kind, Madame."

"Mademoiselle, actually."

"Mademoiselle, then," he answered with a laugh and a smile.

"Goodbye, Lieutenant. Good luck and stay safe."

"You as well, Mademoiselle." He nodded to her and returned to his car as she waited and watched from the doorway. Just as he was almost out of sight he caught a final glimpse of her smiling and waving goodbye. He would definitely be back...

Despite his previous vow to keep his attention focused on the task at hand, he once again found himself distracted, but this time it was far more visceral in nature. The image of her smile, the sound of her voice, the fragrant smell of her as she stood so close to him – his every sense was being preyed upon by this lovely lonely woman. "What's a beautiful girl like that doing stranded among all these farmers? I'll definitely take her up on her offer... I bet it would be just perfect sitting with her, watching the sunset with a cold glass of lemonade, if I could just get my hands on Dutch's money that would settle it for me. Time to get back on the hunt."

Cristafaro vs RCMP

The mountains seemed to grow higher and higher as he neared the orchard that stretched out before him as far as he could see. Row upon row of trees lined the road; some were only as high as a man, while others easily grew twice or three times that height. He could see that the cherries had already been picked, while a variety of apples dotted the trees in a veritable splash of colors. Somehow, despite the summer heat, the red, yellow, and green apples hanging on the trees made him think of Christmas firs adorned for the holiday. The rest of the mountain seemed to be covered with maples. He wondered if they ever had a break... They tapped the sugar bushes starting in March and processed through to the end of June when they started to harvest cherries. After cherry season they harvested their apples well into the month of October when they finally prepared their orchards for the upcoming season by pruning and applying mulch wherever necessary. Simms knew it was a hard life to endure, that farmers were stressed by constant worry about the weather, poor crops, and pests, and that nothing was within their control - not even the success of their sales at market. No, he did not envy farmers, not one bit.

He turned the cruiser onto the gravel driveway, and immediately spotted the house, perched part way up the hill. From a distance the house appeared unassuming, but as he approached he found it reminded him of a station building on the rail line. Steps led up to a deck that wrapped almost completely around the wide stone and spruce-plank house. He was surprised to note that there were two stories, topped off with a craftsman-style roof that peaked over the house in two places, as the house was so large. Although it appeared to have been built with great attention to detail, the owner had clearly let maintenance of the house slide. A fresh paint job had been in order for some years as evidenced by the white paint chips that covered the ground around the house like freshly fallen snow. The entire porch was covered and did an excellent job of screening the home from the heat and sunlight that could render a house practically uninhabitable in the summertime. A number of wicker chairs sat idly on the porch – they were clearly hand-made, from branches that had likely been found on this very property. *How very industrious*, he thought.

He pulled his car up fairly close to the home and made his way up the steps toward the front door. From where he stood on the porch he could hear singing, similar to the opera music he often listened to on the radio or on his Victrola phonograph. He marveled at the unexpected allure the music held for him. He felt himself drawn, in some ethereal manner, toward the ebb and flow of the melody, as he could not discern the words and was certain it was in a language he altogether did not understand. He turned and walked along the porch in the direction of the music – it seemed to emanate from the trees - but he failed to spot anyone. A little bit closer to the trees and he could hear the chorus as others joined in, intensifying the volume and the spirit of the song. It was a folks song, of that he was certain; a lively working song that unified laborers by its very nature. He had never heard this particular song before, but he found it was especially pleasing. It evoked peaceful images for him, and he flashed back to his encounter, a mere hour earlier, with that lovely creature. He was about to step off the porch and follow the music up the road toward the orchard when he realized that he had been completely side tracked once again. *This is ludicrous,* he chastised himself. *I should just go to the house.* He turned back and returned to the front door.

He took a brief moment to compose himself, opened the screen door with authority, and knocked forcefully on the door. He peered through the little eye-level window but saw no signs that anyone was home. He tried to wait patiently, before trying again, but he was running low on patience, and quickly rapped on the door once again, this time even more forcefully than before. For some reason he felt bad to be intruding on this family, but then again he was on a mission and someone else's feelings were not germane to the situation.

"Ashpet! Ashpet!" yelled the high-pitched voice. The woman inside the house had called to him to wait. Although he spoke only English and French, he had picked up random words here and there that were frequently overheard around the countryside. He recognized the words and the accent, and of course had concluded just by the name that the family must be Italian. "Che?" he heard the woman's voice call from the other side of the door.

"It's the police, Madame. May I have a word with you?" He tried not to yell too loudly, but found himself talking far more loudly than usual in the hope that she would understand him better. And, as often happened when he spoke with a 'foreigner' he spoke more slowly and enunciated his words with greater emphasis.

"Polizia?" she asked warily.

"Yes, Madame. Police. I simply want to talk." He did his best to sound non-threatening but knew that recent immigrants tended to be extremely mistrustful of the police in general.

She was afraid. The police never came around

unless it was time to collect or if there was trouble. She knew they couldn't be trusted. She tried to make herself understood in English by the officer at the door. She didn't speak French, although she understood a few words, and she only understood a little English from listening to her husband and children speak with one another.

"My, ah, husband worrka," she said in her heavy Italian accent.

"I do not wish to speak with your husband, Madame. I only want to ask your son, Frank, a few questions," he said with slow deliberation.

"Frankie?" she said protectively.

"Yes, that's right, Frankie," he said as calmly as possible despite his growing frustration at having to discuss this through the door.

"Frankie good boy," she said in her stilted English. She refused to give the polizia the satisfaction of opening the door.

"Yes, sì, he is good boy," he said in the same broken manner as her, hopeful she would better understand what he wanted. "Please open door?"

"No, no. Frankie good boy," she repeated more adamantly. He turned away from the door and faced toward the orchard where he imagined he could still hear the singing. He desperately wanted to scream. *My god, if this goes on any longer I'm going to kick in this door*, he muttered to himself through clenched teeth. He took a deep breath and turned back toward the door. He knocked gently with renewed composure. He spoke slowly once again, "Madame, I am Inspector Simms of the RCMP. I need to ask Frank some questions." He was brief and to the point.

"What the hell is going on here?" rumbled a voice from right behind him. Simms turned abruptly and saw a young man, must have been around eighteen, with a scruffy growth of beard that did nothing to obscure the handsomeness of his face. He was well built, although not overly tall and clearly spent a great deal of time outdoors as evidenced by his deep tan. He was wearing a tan cowhide hat that covered his short-cropped hair and shaded his eyes, and yet he squinted with a feral glare at this stranger on his family's porch. Of course, he had a rifle leveled at the stranger so he was clearly taking aim, and at that, he was taking aim at Simms' head. Simms noticed the dead rabbit at the boy's feet. He guessed it was tonight's supper or perhaps for a special occasion, otherwise they could've gotten their meat from the local butcher. "What business do you have here?" the boy asked the stranger.

"My name is Benoît Simms, as I told this nice lady," he said as he nodded toward the door since he didn't want to risk raising his hand. I am the Inspector for the Laurentians Division of the RCMP." He needed this stupid boy to lower his rifle. "I think it would be wise of you to put down that gun, don't you agree son?"

"We paid already," he replied menacingly. "Now leave us alone."

"What? What do you mean *paid*?" It only took a moment for the implications of the boy's statement to sink in. Then he realized the boy would either assume he was a liar or a fool. So, some of his staff *were* on the take, just as he had suspected. *I'll get to the bottom of that later*, he thought angrily to himself. He refused to be side-tracked yet again – what *was* it today? "I am not here for *that*. Could you please put down the gun?"

"What is it then?" he asked suspiciously, although he lowered the gun to the Inspector's chest.

Well, at least we're communicating, he thought sardonically. "I need to ask the boy, Frank - Frankie -

some questions."

"What kind of questions?" the boy asked, nervous now that Frankie had gotten himself into some kind of trouble with the law. "You better start talking fast before you start accusing people."

"It's nothing like that. Now lower your gun," he implored once again to this boy who was not quite a man. The boy was clearly buying none of what the Inspector was selling and so he developed a plausible story from the facts of the case that he could disclose. "The boy, Frank, he witnessed an accident," he started, but then he wasn't really thinking well – it had been a long day already – and the rest of the story failed to roll off his tongue as articulately as he would have liked. He vaguely explained that Frank had witnessed a hit-and-run accident, and had seen the car and driver that had sped away, but realized as he was doing so that he was stumbling through the story like a rookie.

The boy had listened intently in disbelief. "Is *that* all?" he asked facetiously.

"Yes. That's all. Now perhaps you can put down the gun."

"Sure, Officer," he answered indulgently, "right after you take your pistol out of your pocket and put it on the porch. We have no reason to trust what you are saying is the truth."

"Ok, boy, but this is going to get you in a heap of trouble."

"Right!" he scoffed. He knew full well that the RCMP had no real power in the region.

"Now do as I say and then we can discuss anything you would like, *Officer*."

The Inspector reached cautiously into his jacket pocket and pulled out his pistol with his forefinger and thumb, slowly lifted it in the air, then bent down and placed it gently on the porch.

"Satisfied?" he asked sarcastically.

"Yes. Now what do you want to talk to Frankie about?"

"Like I said, he saw a hit and run and we need to, I mean *I* need to, talk to him."

"Well, Mr. Policeman, it just so happens that he is not here now, so perhaps you should leave my mother alone and either come back another day when he *is* here or try catching your driver some other way."

The boy lowered his rifle, walked up the stairs and past the Inspector, whereupon his mother unlocked the door and let him in, then locked the door behind him. "By the way," the boy added from behind the closed door, "next time you want money for the month, the only metal you people are going to get from us is lead."

Simms didn't know what to make of what had just happened. On the one hand he could have forced these people to cooperate, while on the other hand, the fact that he had maintained his composure might bode well upon his return. In fact, he knew for certain that the boy would have to eat at some point, and he would do exactly as that man-child had suggested...come back at a more opportune time. *Dinnertime, for instance. Tonight,* he thought to himself. *That will be a great time to return. I mean, a boy's gotta eat, right?*

With that decision out of the way he decided to return to the site of the two murders and the abandoned car. Maybe the kid was actually there again. He bent and picked up his gun, quickly replacing it in his holster, walked down the porch steps and settled into his car. He made his way back along the road, and stared longingly at Faith's idyllic property as he drove by. He started to reconsider his destination as he contemplated how pleasant it might be to spend the afternoon with a lovely bird rather than staking out a dirty country bumpkin.

He continued on, though, fighting the almost irresistible urge to stop and enjoy life a little. He reasoned that this was the ultimate riddle, the greatest puzzle he would ever solve, even if he couldn't tell anyone about it. *Was Dutch still alive? Who really died in that car? Did Dutch leave a carload of money near the crash site, or does he have it with him? Does it even exist? I could be a rich man one day and be with a woman like Faith.* The thought pleased him. Ultimately, he could either be the hero who had unraveled the mystery of this case for his superiors in Montreal – in which case someone else would surely take all of the credit, or he could find the money. He decided it would be better to be rich.

Now that he had familiarized himself with the area, the return drive to the site went smoothly and took a mere fifteen minutes. He stopped his car near the site and took no special pains to keep silent. He surveyed the scene once again, hoping something might catch his eye. The wind had picked up during the day and had conveniently whipped up the leaves and natural debris around the burial site. The earth looked as though it had never been touched.

Round 2

"Hey, do you hear that?" Butterball asked the girls anxiously.

"What's that? Butterball it's just your imagination," Capri teased.

"No. I hear something," he said with certainty.

"Come on, Butter..." Capri started to complain, before she was interrupted by Vicky, who actually took Butterball seriously.

"Shh," Vicky cautioned as she held up her hand to stifle them. They held their breath and listened, and sure enough they heard the sound of gravel crunching under the tires of a car as it approached from the road. It stopped moving abruptly, and then they heard nothing more until a car door was slammed.

At the same time, the others had just reached the other side when Dodo called out, "Jippsy, Frankie, stop! Did you...," Dodo started to ask, when Frankie interrupted her.

"What's your problem, Dodo?" he asked with a sneer. "Getting scared?"

"I heard something, Frankie," she answered as she turned and glared at him.

"What direction did it come from, Dodo?" he asked with all the seriousness this news deserved.

"It seemed to come from across the lake where...," she had started to answer as she pointed to where they had recently been.

"Just shut up, damn it," Frankie snapped in her direction. "I can't hear if you're talking!" Dodo couldn't believe how crass Frankie had become, but she did as she was told. The three of them stood still. They were a considerable distance from the site, but the lake allowed for the sounds to carry much farther than otherwise.

Frankie cupped his ear in order to funnel all of the sounds directly into his eardrum. Then he heard it...the slam of a car door.

Butterball strained to hear anything to indicate which direction the new arrival was headed, and the ominous sound of the occasional snapping twig made it clear – whoever it was, was headed their way.

We have to warn the others," Butterball whispered to Vicky. "They must already be on the other side," he added with concern as he shook his head.

"Frank Cristafaro?" called an authoritative voice.

Butterball turned immediately to the others and called, "Hide!"

"Frank, don't answer," Jippsy warned him. "*Who* is that?"

"It's that cop I told you about. I guess he wants to ask me some more questions."

"Frank Cristafaro! It's Inspector Simms. Come out now. I'd like to ask you a few more questions about the crash. Son, it's in your best interest to talk to me now."

Frankie didn't want this cop hounding him. He resigned himself to facing the man, and had turned to head back when Jippsy stopped him.

"Frankie, what if he knows about the money? You know how these police are up here. He doesn't even know for sure that you're here now. Stay here and wait it out."

"Jips, what if he comes to my home?" Frankie implored. He knows my name..."

"So?"

"So, he might tell my dad I was doing something wrong. And you know my dad...he's not going to believe *me*," he replied so dejectedly that Dodo wanted to reach out to him but held herself back.

"What are you worried about? Isn't he in Montreal?"

"Yeah, so?

"So what can he do from there? By the time he gets back this will probably have cooled down and your dad will have nothing to be angry about," Jippsy said with assurance, although he wasn't all that confident himself.

"That's true," Frankie reluctantly conceded.

"Frank Cristafaro, if you don't come out right now, we will be having a chat at your house tonight or at the police station."

Frankie was getting scared. If his dad found out that the police were looking for him, it wouldn't matter the reason, and he would get a beating just for a visit from the police. His dad couldn't afford to have the police poking around his business. His distillery was illegal and if the police shut that down they wouldn't be able to keep the farm.

"Jippsy, you know how my dad gets. If I just answer his questions, I won't have to worry about him coming to the house."

"Frankie, what if he was already there?"

"Shoot! I didn't even think about that. Oh, man, my dad's gonna kill me..."

Jippsy could see Frankie was agitated. "Frankie, listen to me. Don't answer him," he said in as calming a voice as possible. Frankie couldn't stand still. He had started to pace as he thought of the possible scenarios.

Jippsy believed that Frankie needed to keep things in perspective. "Frankie, if we find that money, you won't have to worry about your dad, the farm, your mom or your brother anymore. You and your sister will have enough money to last for generations. Trust me, Frankie. I trusted you with my life – twice." Jippsy was positive that if he could appeal to Frankie's vanity he would be able to win him over. "Trust me on this. I think you and I know what's best for all of us."

326

Frankie's face softened as his mind was made up, and his confidence renewed. "Ok, Jips old boy. You have a deal." Jippsy slapped him on the back then cringed dramatically as he pulled his hand away from Frankie's sweat-soaked t-shirt.

"*That's* the Frankie we know and love. Now we just have to make sure the others don't say anything either." Jippsy signaled the others across the lake.

"I know that bird call - it's Jippsy." Butterball tweeted back across the lake. He turned to the girls when they looked at him questioningly. "I guess we should lay low, otherwise Jippsy wouldn't have used the call."

"Good call, Butterball." Capri was impressed by his initiative and grasp of the situation. "We have to stay out of sight as best as possible. I'm sure this man is dangerous," Capri went on to say.

"It's up to you, Frankie," Simms continued in an effort to lure the boy out. I'll give you up to the count of three to come out. Otherwise we'll have to do it the hard way."

It had become eerily quiet on both sides of the lake, and abundantly clear that Frankie would not give him the satisfaction. "Very well, son," Simms called out. Frankie took issue with his repeated use of the word 'son'; it made him cringe. He turned indignantly to Jippsy as they lay quietly on the ground. Frankie couldn't help himself and pulled out his sling shot from his back pocket, secretly yearning to plant a rock right between the pig's eyes. "This copper thinks I'm his friend and that he can call me son. He's just a greasy cop like all the others."

"One." Simms didn't even know if the boy was there and he was already frustrated. *Where is that damn kid?*

"Two," he shouted out with greater emphasis. *What am I doing here...? I should have stopped at Faith's,* he thought disappointedly. Clearly there was no point in Simms wasting any more time out there.

"Three!" *Damn, damn, damn waste of time.* "Very well, kid. You made your bed, and now you'll have to lie in it. We're gonna do it the 'ard way now." His French accent – especially his difficulty pronouncing the letter 'H' - became more pronounced when he was tired or frustrated, as he was at that moment. It normally took a calculated effort to hide it, but hell, there was no one there listening anyway... He trudged away, disillusioned but his repeated failures that day. He kicked at every stone or stick in his path, like a sulking child.

Simms had no clue what to do next - he had hit a dead-end. Searching the car had revealed no usable clues; the perimeter around the car had been dug up, and they had uncovered absolutely nothing. In hindsight, perhaps he should have intercepted those two henchmen because now his only other possible witness was that kid, and he was presently nowhere to be found. *That's it! I've got to get to that kid...he saw or heard* something *and I want to know what something that is*, he thought to himself as he opened the cruiser's driver door with a frustrated yank, dropped himself in, and slammed the door in frustration.

Vicky heard the car drive off and was instantly relieved. It occurred to her that she had been holding her breath, which she expelled with a 'phew!' that resounded across the lake, and then turned to Butterball. "Attaboy, Butterball," she said with a grin. Without warning, Capri suddenly darted off. "Capri," Vicky called after her, "what are you doing?"

But Capri had zero intention of waiting for anyone's opinion, nor did she bother to let her friends know her plans. She simply took off like Superman to the rescue. "Wow!" Butterball remarked, "I didn't know she had it in her." They watched as Capri ran around the lake at lightning speed. It was impressive how she didn't make a sound, almost as though her feet never hit the ground. She showed no sign of slowing, even as the low-lying branches snapped as she blazed a trail along the water's edge. She trampled a new path, dislodging the stones and twigs that made up the ground surface that lay relatively undisturbed beneath the umbrella of the tall trees.

What the others didn't know was that she was, in fact, blinded by a rage that defied all reason and undermined any concern she had for anything else. She ran right up to where Frankie was hauling himself up from the ground, just a few feet from where they had found the book. When she reached him she was not only out of breath, but speechless as her emotions had run the entire spectrum, from fear to anger, compassion to hatred, and eventually relief and happiness. Her speechless frustration led to a solid shove. Capri's arms launched out against Frank's chest, an action that so caught him unaware that he lost his balance and landed with a thud on his backside among the leaves and twigs. Frankie was shocked, surprised actually by her reaction; he had never seen her in such a state. He jumped up quickly and grabbed her wrist just as she was about to haul off and punch him, this time aiming at his face, even though their height discrepancy would land that punch somewhere closer to his chest. She was shaking so intensely that it vibrated thru his grasp on her wrist. For once he felt an intense remorse creeping into his shallow narcissistic veneer. "I'm Ok, Capri. It's alright." He knew that their relationship was special – not just brother and sister, it was more than that. They did everything together and truly relied upon one another in a way they both knew they couldn't count on their brother or mother, or, in particular, their father. There was no one he trusted more than her. "I'm so sorry, Capri. I'm sorry.

But I'm OK. Capri, please?!" he pleaded as he pulled her in close and wrapped his arms around her. Tears were running down her face, and her body shook from the force of her sobs. He pushed her away and said her name gently. "Capri?" She either couldn't or wouldn't acknowledge. He tried again. "Capri, please look at me." He brought his hand up under her chin and tilted her head up, forcing her to look into his eyes. "I'm all right. Stop crying now. He's just some crooked cop."

Her voice cracked as she gasped for air and swallowed the sobs that broke between words. "What...about...Dad?" she managed to ask, the implicit gravity of the situation breaking her heart as she spoke the words aloud. She swiped her arms across her face as snot started to run precipitously from her nose.

"It's OK. We'll go home now, and just to make sure Mom and Vincenzo don't do anything foolish - like tell dad."

"OK. And what about the treasure?"

"There's always tomorrow. You guys OK with that?" he asked Jippsy and Dodo.

"I think after today's adventure everyone is tired, especially me," Jippsy answered without hesitation. Dodo agreed and the four of them started to make their away around the lake to meet up with Butterball and Vicky who had already decided to meet them along the way.

It took only a few moments for the gang to meet up, but by then Capri had gotten her emotions under control and wiped the tears and snot from her face. But she was clearly not herself when she finally spoke on behalf of herself and Frankie. "Hey guys," she said tentatively, "Frankie and I are gonna head home now. We have some...things to take care of," she ended wearily. Jippsy looked at the others and nodded knowingly.

Vicky was the first to answer. "OK, Capri. Should

we meet you here tomorrow after breakfast?"

"Sure, Vicky. See you tomorrow." She flashed them a wave of her hand and turned with Frankie to make their way back to the road and on home.

Jippsy seized this opportunity to keep the others encouraged. "I suggest everyone go home this afternoon, eat a good supper, and get a good night's sleep. I think a little rest will help us focus on deciphering the code, and lead us to that treasure. Tomorrow's gonna be our big day...I can FEEL it!"

"Sure, Jips," Butterball answered agreeably. Just the thought of a good meal was enough to get Butterball to agree to anything.

"Nice job on the whistle, Butterball," Jippsy added in as an afterthought.

"Thanks, Jips. See you tomorrow."

"Bye, Jippsy. Bye, Dodo," Vicky called out as she and Butterball turned in one direction and headed off.

Dodo had been watching Frankie as he and Capri walked off. She and Jippsy turned to walk home, but she couldn't resist one last peek backward to watch as Frankie's figure finally slipped out of view. "I hope he'll be alright," she said in a whisper.

"Don't worry, Dodo," Jippsy answered reassuringly. "Frankie's strong and Capri is even stronger. They'll be fine," he said with a confidence he didn't have. "I'll race you home," he challenged as he bumped her with his elbow.

"Your ass is brass, Jippsy" she answered with a laugh, and took off in a cloud of dust that blew straight into his face.

" We'll see about that," Jippsy chortled as took off after her.

Lemonade or Whiskey

Simms made his way back to the main road. He had wasted virtually an entire day just to come up empty-handed. He was tired, discouraged, and desperately thirsty. Faith's lemonade would have done wonders for him right about then. He was just about to turn south onto Route 117 when he remembered there was a gin joint just off the route about a mile in from the main road. *Now what was that exit again?* He wrapped his arms around the steering wheel and rested his head on his hands. Eyes closed, he tried to call up the exit in his mind, but when that failed he started to rap his head against the steering wheel in an unsuccessful attempt to jar his memory into action. *I'll just have to go on instinct,* he resolved as he turned the cruiser north on the route, back towards the station. He knew that the small log cabin that housed the gin joint was roughly twenty minutes away. Hopefully he'd have some luck that day and he would spot the exit.

Ten minutes later, he located the first turn for rue du Lac Ivry. It really wasn't that far from the station at all, and he hoped that he wouldn't come upon any of his men there. He turned right at an old cut-log sign that had been hung by loggers to help direct them to the logging camps. Gravel crunched and pinged under his tires as he made his way along the road. Several minutes' drive and he spotted the cabin to his right. There were several pick-up trucks, two cars and a logging truck parked in the clearing. He didn't bother to observe anything more about the vehicles other than their existence. He wasn't there on official business, after all. He officially needed a drink, however.

The simple pine cabin had been built in a remote

area that could only be reached by the road Simms had followed and that ended abruptly once the cabin had been reached. The cabin was a single-story building, no bigger than 20 feet by 20 feet, with a 3 foot deck that ran the width of the cabin. The roof had been covered in pine and cedar shingles, and overhung the deck, supported by 4 sturdy logs. Small windows along the side and front of the building gave away nothing as to the goings-on inside the cabin. They were either well shielded by the overhang, or had been covered up from the inside. The building had been well shellacked to protect it from the elements as well as the invasive carpenter ants that regularly destroyed properties in the area.

Simms approached the wooden door and peered through the small window that was at eye-level in the center of the door, but even that had been effectively obscured. He depressed the black iron latch and opened the door. The smell hit him instantly. The intoxicating aroma of beer from a keg effectively mingled with the wafts of smoke from different blends of tobacco to create a uniquely pungent yet savory scent that immediately made his mouth dry and stimulated his thirst for a drink. The door was slowly closing behind him, but the sliver of light that filtered in illuminated the smoke-filled room. The small space was poorly lit, except for the odd wall sconce and a larger fixture that hung over the bar toward the back of the room. There was no décor to speak of, and the room was essentially a square with four bare walls, an old wooden bar with a smoky mirror hung behind it, a door to the right of the bar that led, he assumed, to a washroom and storeroom, and finally a half-dozen tables and a dozen or so chairs haphazardly strewn throughout the space. Simms fancied himself more sophisticated than this, and he thought condescendingly that this was the type of place frequented by the local rabble. He would have preferred Le Chalet in Sainte-Agathe, or better yet that fancy new hotel in Montreal called the Hotel de la Montagne. He had visited the hotel during his last trip to Montreal and had marveled over the beautiful hand-painted murals intended to attract and delight the well heeled and the intelligencia. Those were elite meeting places, not a place where dirty fingernails were considered the norm, and burping contests were the highlight of the week.

He made a beeline for the bar, heedless of the other patrons who may or may not have recognized him, however he was immediately recognized by the lumberjack waiting behind the well-worn wooden counter. "Officer," he said politely as he nodded at Simms. "How can I help you?"

"Give me a double shot of rye." The bearded lumberjack placed a tumbler on the counter, grabbed the whiskey bottle from behind him and was about to pour, but Simms knew better and placed his hand over the glass. "How about you give me the good stuff, not that rot-gut that probably came from one of these guys' toilets?" He looked around the room and wondered if he was right. "What's your name, son?"

"It's Jack, sir," he answered pleasantly as he replaced the bottle in front of the smoky mirror.

"Well, Jack, find another bottle and let me see it."

"Sure, Officer," he replied as he turned toward the back door.

"It's Inspector," Simms replied smugly.

"Ok, sir...I mean 'Inspector'."

Simms appreciated Jack's earnest respect, and was rather impressed by his demeanor. He was clearly not some rugged ignoramus hell-bent on challenging authority. Maybe he was once one of the policemen's brotherhood, or had served in the army. Simms didn't know for certain, but there was just something about him. *Good for him,* he thought as he watched the man walk confidently through the door.

Simms glanced around the room from his seat at the bar, wondering about these fools. He counted ten men sitting around late in the afternoon as if it was teatime. He failed to consider that by his very presence in that place at that time he had, essentially, become one of *them.*

"Here you go, Inspector. Canadian Club, the finest in the territory."

Simms turned his attention back to the lumberjack. *Jack...,* he thought to himself, *how ironic...a lumberjack named Jack*; he smiled at his own mirth. He watched as the lumberjack/bartender poured him a double.

"Thank you, my good man." He lifted his glass, and swirled around the golden amber liquid. He bent his nose over the glass and inhaled the delicious blend of caramel and fruit. He couldn't remember the last time he had had a drink but didn't really care, as his taste buds had been awakened. He took a gulp and savored the whiskey as his tongue picked up every flavor – the creamy caramel, the lively fruit and the peppery essence, all capped off by a hint of oak. He sighed as the whiskey literally rushed the back of his throat, tearing a streak of heat along his tongue, and up into his nasal passages, then slid down his esophagus, before it eased its way down into his stomach...his empty stomach. It occurred to him, rather belatedly, that he had not eaten since the early morning. *Delicious...absolutely delicious.* He sighed contentedly. He turned in his chair toward the other patrons and scanned the room; they were a motley crew of laborers and working stiffs, some alone, others in pairs, yet they all seemed to be in their own worlds. *Probably balancing the government deficit or discussing world events,* he thought sarcastically and grinned. *More likely thinking about the next drink, or where their wives took off to.*

He swung back around to the counter, and stared into his empty glass until it dawned on him that two of the men sitting together at the table near the front had recently become familiar to him. *I know them*, he thought with excitement as a smile spread across his face, bringing a sparkle to his tired blue eyes. A plan started to form.

He tapped the bar and the bartender poured him another round. He gulped the next ounce while watching them. They were clearly in the middle of a heavy conversation, their heads nearly touching as they hunched over the table. There was no doubt in Simms' mind that they were hatching a plan – and Simms wanted to know every detail.

"Barkeep?"

"Yes, sir, ah, I mean Inspector. Yes, Inspector."

"Easy does it, son. Could you tell me what those two are drinking?" He pointed discreetly to the men at the front of the house.

"I think it's just whiskey, sir."

"Well bring over 3 more glasses of the good stuff."

"To *that* table, sir?" he asked doubtfully as he nodded in the direction of the two unfamiliar men.

"Yes, to *that* table, my good man. Merci," he added almost joyfully as he hopped off of the barstool.

Simms walked over to the two gentlemen sitting at the front table, grateful that all of the other tables were taken, and cleared his throat. "May I join you?" he asked as they both looked up from their discussion. When neither one responded he asked again, in French. "Est-ce que je peux vous joindre?"

"Oui, Officier," the smaller one responded.

Simms decided his best tactic was to revert to his

childhood dialect and continued in French. "Just call me Inspector. Everyone else does. How did you know I was from the police?"

"Well, sir, Capitaine," the man answered in French as well, "just a hunch."

"You have great instincts, my friend," he replied and smiled politely.

"Ah, thank you," the man answered warily. The bartender approached with three glasses and placed them in front of Simms. Simms then ceremoniously placed a glass in front of each of the men. Although the two men were suspicious of the Inspector's intentions they were certainly not about to pass up a free drink, especially given the day they'd had.

He lifted his glass, and the two men followed suit. "To your health, gentlemen. As the Jewish always say, L'chaim, which means 'to life'." He knew this would get a reaction, and watched as their eyes went from wary to fearful. They looked quickly at one another and then hesitated before downing their drinks quickly.

"Thank you, ah, Capitaine. I am sorry, but we must be going," the smaller man said apprehensively as they both pushed their chairs back at that moment and stood. The day's heavy labor and stress, combined with the alcohol, had made them both a little woozy. Simms stood up immediately and extended his arm to the smaller man on his right.

"Please, not so soon. Allow me to get us another," he implored then turned toward the bar. "Barkeep?" he yelled out across the room as he waved his arm. He raised three fingers and motioned for him to bring another round to the table.

Simms stared at each of them in turn then got down to business. "Gentlemen, I have a little proposition for you. I do not want to waste time discussing this at

337

length." The bartender arrived with the good whiskey bottle in hand and refilled each of their glasses. Simms could see the anxiety building, and could tell that the men were both clearly shaken. The larger man was nervously tapping his fingers on the table, but not to the rhythm of the radio playing from behind the bar. "Thank you, Jack," he said politely to the bartender as he took his leave, and then turned to his newfound companions. "This is a wonderful day, don't you agree?" Simms was quite proud of himself. He knew for certain that by the time that conversation was over those two would do whatever he asked.

"Ahh. So, what shall we drink to this time? Perhaps you have a suggestion?" He looked at both of them in turn. The smarter-looking one decided he should speak up before the other one blurted out some nonsense.

"Um-aah," he hesitated as he tried to come up with something suitable. "I got it. I got it...," he said almost triumphantly and raised his glass. "How about we drink to freedom? I hear there's a movement in Germany depriving people of their rights."

"That is quite astute," Simms replied, utterly surprised. In fact, the man's clever observation, his insight into world events, and the opinion he proffered, had effectively raised his stature in Simms" esteem. "To freedom it is, then," he offered as he raised his glass and drank swiftly once again. Louis looked imploringly at Gerard, but also raised his glass and swallowed down the heat-laden liquid.

The mood seemed to lighten somewhat. Simms decided that fear alone would just drive them away. Perhaps what he needed was to catch more bees with honey, tainted with only a mild dose of fear. He called once more to the bartender, "Barkeep, just bring us the rest of the bottle."

"Coming right up, sir." The barman wasted no time bringing the bottle to the table and placing it in front of the Inspector.

"Thank you, mon ami."

Simms grabbed the bottle, and realized that he was a little lightheaded himself. He carefully poured another round in each glass as he pronounced, "One more and then we can get onto business." Simms and the smaller man both raised their glasses once again, but the big man did not. Instead, without warning, the man pushed back from the table, practically toppling it with his weight, stood up and opened his mouth. His voice was so deep that it was practically inaudible, and his accent so unusual, although Simms pegged it to be Creole, that he was nearly incomprehensible. He steadied himself, raised his glass and made the most concise and meaningful toast. "To family!" Ironically, the big man had no family of his own, but it had long been his fondest desire to change that. Perhaps this was his opportunity, but then again maybe the copper might ruin all that.

Simms noticed the smaller man gazing up at his associate with pride. He wondered if they were related. He looked curiously between the two of them. *No. I doubt that...* Did they work together? *Probably, yet the big one seems slow.* Clearly the smaller man appreciated the toast.

"Yes. To family," he agreed as he lifted his glass and swallowed the amber liquid. *How did this become so personal?* Simms wondered to himself. *Life... Freedom... Family... I guess we'll see,* he thought with a hint of uncertainty. *Perhaps it's time to stop drinking,* he thought with absolute certainty.

"Perhaps it's time," he said aloud, "to get down to business. "My name is Benoît Simms. I am the Inspector of the RCMP des Laurentides, and you, sir, what is your name?" he asked as he turned to the larger man. Here, he had definitely caught them off-guard. They were certainly not expecting him to be the area's big boss.

"My name?" he asked stupidly.

"Yes. It's a very simple question... Do I need to repeat it?"

"No, sir."

"Well then?"

"It's - it's Louis, sir."

Simms extended his hand across the table. "Nice to meet you, Louis. And your family name is...?" Louis didn't know what else to say so he told him the truth.

"Thank you, Louis," Simms replied as the larger man's hand practically engulfed his own. "And *your* name?" Simms asked as he turned his attention to the smaller gentleman..

"It is Gerard. Gerard Liberté," he lied, and all too obviously. Simms knew this, and decided there was no purpose in pursuing that matter any further. He was sure he could get the truth from Louis or that it might just slip out along the way.

"Well, Louis and Gerard, it is very nice to meet you both. I have a proposition for you." The three men leaned in closer over the table so as not to be overheard. "As you know, Dutch Shultz's car crashed not far from here." He watched both of them to gauge their reactions.

"No, we did not know this." Gerard tried to deny any knowledge of this event, and was somewhat perturbed by his own lying.

"Well, my friend, perhaps you should listen to the radio, or better yet, why don't you say nothing until you've heard what I have in mind?" he said with rancor.

"Yes, sir."

Both men sat silently waiting for the Inspector to thoroughly ruin their day. Gerard was in fact quite mesmerized by Simms though, because, as the wind

340

picked up outside, the swaying trees allowed sunlight to filter into the dimly lit space. The light seemed to dance on the tips of the Inspector's spiky hair and appeared, to Gerard, to be flames dancing atop Simms' head. It was eerie.

"I believe there was something in the car that belongs to the RCMP..." he stated with conviction, then paused to gauge the men's reactions before finishing his sentence, "as evidence, of course. We believe it's been buried somewhere in the forest - in the vicinity of the car that Dutch used to escape. We don't have sufficient manpower to search such a large area...the digging alone will be a monumental task," he added in with the cruel intention of stabbing the knife in and then giving a little twist. "Which brings me to how you two gentlemen might be of assistance; we're looking for deputies to help us." He took in the reactions of the two men; the big one simply stared at him in disbelief, while the small man seemed to have glazed over and had the distinct look of, well, of an imbecile. Neither one of them responded.

Maybe it was the stress of the day, or maybe it was just the alcohol, but Gerard found himself gradually lulled by the tone and the rhythm of the Inspector's voice despite the fact that he was, at that very moment, Gerard's biggest problem. He had barely registered what the Inspector was suggesting, but he knew that whatever is was none of this could end well. One other thing he believed to be a certainty was that this man, this Inspector Simms, he was the devil.

"Well, gentlemen? What do you say?" he asked as he siphoned off the last few drops of whiskey from his glass and then slammed it on the table effectively jolting Gerard out of his stupor.

Gerard cleared his throat, and attempted to speak slowly in an effort not to lose his cool. "Well, uhm, that sounds, uh, very...exciting, Capitaine," Gerard stated worriedly. He didn't want to say much more or ask any questions. He couldn't say for certain that this Inspector knew about their involvement, but he definitely knew how to push their buttons. The warming effect of the booze had started to loosen up his body in a number ways. He felt his head weighing heavily in his cupped hand, his elbow pressed into the tabletop, while his legs hung almost uselessly below him. His mind was just barely intact, and he tried desperately to piece together their next move.

But Gerard's time was up, and the Capitaine's next words broke his train of thought. "Well, then, my friends, we can count on your support, then?" He smiled disingenuously as he asked the question, which was really more of an assumption of their compliance.

Gerard looked over at Louis and nodded his head reluctantly, and Louis took this as his cue to start nodding as well. Gerard looked at the Inspector and said the only thing he could, "Mais oui, mon Capitaine."

"Very well then. I would like you to do the following..." Simms laid out the details of his plan in much the same manner he would issue commands to his officers...brief and to the point. "There is a boy. His name is Frank Cristafaro. He's been hanging around the crash site. This is his address," he said and handed them a napkin with detailed directions to both the Cristafaro farm and Lost Lake. "I want you to talk to him. We are certain he is in possession of, I mean that he knows where the, um," he hesitated as he searched for the most appropriate way to describe what they were to uncover, and when the word finally travelled from his brain to his lips he blurted it out somewhat louder than he had intended, "**evidence!** is located. I **do not** want you going to his house. I want you to follow him tonight and tomorrow morning. He is a large kid. Around 14 years old. Muscular. Wavy dark hair. He looks Italian. Oh, and he carries around a sling shot in his back pocket. Do not let him see you. He will probably go back to the crash site tomorrow morning, so be sure to follow him there. Discretely. Got it?"

"Sure, Capitaine," Gerard replied agreeably. He figured he'd simply agree to whatever the man asked and then get the hell out of there when the opportunity arose. Louis didn't know what to say and decided, as usual, it was best to leave the talking to Gerard.

I'll meet you two just at the turn off to Lost Lake. Lost Lake," he repeated and tapped his finger on the napkin where he had drawn out the directions. "0-800 hours - 8:00 am that is - tomorrow morning. Understood?"

Gerard's curiosity finally got the better of him, and he blurted out, "What kind of reward are we talking about?" As the last word left his mouth he realized what an idiot he was. It was too late to take it back - at least he knew *that*. He wanted to pound his head against the table, but instead watched as the Capitaine's face transitioned from calculating and strategic to angry and contemptuous. Out of the frying pan and into the fire! Simms knew he had the bum right where he wanted him...the sucker had walked right into his trap.

Simms stood up, and this time the effect of the booze was no match for his disdain for these two idiots who had the gall to ask him for *anything*. He put his fists down on the table, leaned his head in closer to them, and bared his teeth as he contemplated exactly what he was about to say. To Louis, the Capitaine resembled a bulldog preparing to attack an intruder.

He chose his words carefully, and this time he spoke clearly and deliberately. "For starters, I won't haul your asses into jail for murdering The Rock Rothman. If you don't cooperate then Dutch's men, The Rock's men, and the police will be after you for the deaths of Dutch, The Rock, innocent bystanders, and the police officers at the bridge, not to mention those left injured on the side of the road. You will have the brotherhood across North America, the gangsters from under every little rock and the press searching for you. You will spend the rest of your, let's see...very short lives, hiding." He continued as if it was rehearsed, "The press will have your sketch in every newspaper across North America. Radio, the newest and greatest media, will be announcing your description at every news hour and commercial interruption, while tips from citizens to the police will help pinpoint your whereabouts, and you can rest assured that the curious will be searching, especially once a reward is offered. Oh, and let's not forget about the contract killers hired by the mob. I wouldn't want to be in your shoes." Simms did not mince words. He needed these two mooks and he wasn't about to let them go so easily. "Or you can work for me, receive your reward, which in your case will be your freedom and most probably enough money that you won't have to work the rest of your lives. The choice is yours. I will let you walk out that door right now and take your chances, or we can agree to do it my way. And in case you had any bright ideas, I have a terrific memory for faces."

Gerard knew he was cornered and answered resignedly, "You leave us no choice, mon Capitaine. Should we go to the boy's house now or meet you tomorrow at the turn off?"

Simms couldn't help but smile triumphantly. "Meet me tomorrow at the turn-off at eight. It's late now and the boy won't be able to, uh, uncover anything at night anyway. If he doesn't show by ten tomorrow morning then you'll go to his house." Simms had a brilliant idea. "On second thought, Gerard, perhaps you should go to the house tonight and follow the boy. One of you will meet me at eight at the turn off. And I repeat, I **do not** want him to know that he's being followed. Do I make myself clear?" They both agreed with a nod.

"Well then I will see one of you tomorrow at the turn off. Have a pleasant evening. Don't worry fellas, the drinks are on me." He went back to the bartender, paid him for the whiskey, and left him a handsome tip. They watched him walk out.

In an instant all of his suppressed panic rose to the surface and surged into Louis' face. His cheeks and nose suddenly bloomed an inflamed red, instigated, of course, by the booze, and he broke into a cold sweat. He had to get some fresh air, before...before... He stood abruptly, when he was assailed yet again, this time by Gerard, "Where the hell do you think *you're* going? Sit down! We have to make a plan."

"What do you mean 'a plan'? We already know what we have to do," Louis replied anxiously.

"No, you idiote," Gerard snapped, practically spitting at his associate, "we have to do something about this copper."

"We can't do that, Gerard," he pleaded, as Louis knew exactly what he meant to do.

"Who's going to know? Not enough manpower?! He's a dirty cop, in it for himself, and if this kid knows where the money is then all we have to do is watch him and get rid of the cop."

"Gerard," he implored, "this is wrong." Louis realized that he felt ashamed of him. "You are really starting to become just like them."

"I don't have a choice you fool," he spat angrily at his associate, loud enough that he caused some of the other men in the bar to rouse from their own drunken stupor. "Don't you see? This is our only way out. Get the money, then get rid of the cop...and the kid."

"Are you sure, Gerard? I don't like this idea so much."

"Don't be such a sap. Trust me. Let's get out of here. The kid knows something. He's the key."

Giuessepe Russo

"Jippsy, Dodo what are you doing home so early?"

"Ah, mom, just tired today. Any news about grandpa?"

"Still no word, sweetie. If you kids are hungry there's some honey that the Cristafaros brought over earlier. Jippsy?"

"Yes, mom?"

"Is everything alright with Frankie?" She was sure Jippsy would know something about what was going on – after all, they spent every waking moment together. "Mrs. Cristafaro was going on about some policeman that came looking for him. Something about a hit-and-run or a crash? I couldn't quite make out everything she said. It's really hard to follow her English - her accent is so heavy, and she was barely making any sense. Thanks to your dad I speak Italian, but her dialect is like another language altogether." Jippsy and Dodo simply stood staring at their mom, speechless. Dodo's eyes were so wide Jippsy couldn't understand how their mom had failed to notice. She was pre-occupied, of course, and this was just another one of those things.

Jippsy's throat had suddenly dried up; he tried to clear it and sound normal. "Nno, mom." He had to change the subject, and fast. "Do we have any bread left over for that honey?" he asked hopefully. He walked over to the breadbox on the counter, and lifted the lid.

"Giuseppe Russo, don't try and change the subject."

"Mom," he whined, "you know I prefer Jippsy."

"Well then, Giuseppe, why don't you tell me the truth and I'll do what you wish?" She was always too smart for him.

347

"I don't know anything about it," he lied. He was already worried that the cop was headed back to Frankie's house. "I swear mom." He hated lying to his mother, but he definitely didn't want her involved. Everyone knew that the cops here were dirty, so they couldn't be counted on to help, and Dad already had his hands full with Grandpa in the hospital. It was up to him to come up with a plan.

"Ok, then, Jippsy," she relented. "The honey's on the counter, honey," she said and giggled at her own joke, "in the paper bag over there," she said as she pointed right next to the freezer box. Just standing next to the box he could tell that they were probably out of ice. *It'll have to be refilled – again*, he thought to himself. *It's no wonder what with this heat*, he mumbled, as he wiped away the sweat that had beaded on his forehead.

He quickly assembled a sandwich, stuffed it into his mouth, and announced, "I'm going back out again, mom." He didn't wait for an answer, and turned to his sister, "Dodo, why don't you stay with mom?" Jippsy felt she had had enough.

"Jippsy?" his mom said solicitously to get his attention. "If you see Frankie, let him know his mom is concerned." She watched his face, her baby's face, to see how he would react, and she thought she caught a glimpse of something...sadness, fear, excitement? She couldn't quite make out what it was, but it was something. Her baby had grown up, and she couldn't read him anymore.

"I won't be seeing Frankie, mom," he lied once more, hating every moment of it. "He's probably out fishing," he ventured in the hope that this would reassure her. He turned and left the kitchen without another look back.

The sun was still high; Jippsy glanced skyward,

beyond the tops of the ancient trees, and the sun was still beating down with the same intensity as if it was only noon. He turned to face his house, in order to orient his body north. The sun cast his shadow to the right, and down. It was roughly four o'clock. Dodo had appeared from nowhere as he figured out the time. She was tired of the nonsense, but anxious to see it to the end. From her stance Jippsy already knew that she had no intention of staying home.

"We have five more hours of daylight. We should get everyone back together. I think this is our last shot, especially if the cops have already been to Frankie's."

Dodo nodded seriously as he spoke, but she clearly had some thoughts of her own. Yes, she *would* see it to the end, but she had one condition. Jippsy eyed her curiously as she considered what to say. She took a committed breath and then spoke. "Jippsy," she said with absolute authority, "if anyone else gets hurt, even a booboo on their finger, I *am* going to go to the police. I am not going to lose my brother or my friends to this silliness. Do you understand what I'm telling you?"

"Yes. Yes. I swear," he promised with just enough conviction to appease her.

"Ok then, what are we waiting for? Let's go!"

Butterball's house was an easy ten minute walk down the same dirt road that led to Lost Lake. As they approached the house, Jippsy called out to Butterball. He didn't want to go in just in case Mrs. Cristafaro had been making the rounds and was still visiting. "Butterball," he yelled out more loudly the second time.

"Hold on, hold on. I heard you the first time," he called from the large front window that spanned the façade of his dark spruce-board home.

From where he stood Jippsy could see Butterball's face was covered in jam. *That boy loves his food*, he chuckled to himself. "Wipe your face and come on. We have to go. I'll explain on the way." Butterball wasted no time and was out the door in a flash, the screen-door slamming behind him as he caught up with his friends. The three of them ran, and Butterball just had to keep up, as Jippsy was not wasting another moment of that day.

"Where are we going?" Butterball asked between labored breaths, although he was quite certain he already knew that answer.

"We're going to get the others right now." Vicky's house was also only minutes away, but they rushed and reached her in half the time.

"Vicky!" Butterball yelled out. "Vicky!" he called out again in a sing-song. Vicky's house was not remote, and yet she had no close neighbors. It was especially quiet where she lived as much of her parents' land had been clear-cut except for some tall old trees that stood near the road and up toward her home. There was a slight breeze that rustled the leaves and branches, but the stillness of the afternoon allowed the sound of Butterball's voice to carry right to Vicky who was standing in her kitchen alone. Her house was not very large and she lived with her parents who both worked in Sainte-Agathe cleaning rooms at the Château in the village. The summer was an especially busy time of year for them.

On her way home that afternoon Vicky had picked raspberries and strawberries from the side of the road. She had mushed them into a paste, added water and sugar, and had dropped in a few chips of ice from the icebox. The glass was already sweating in her hand, the aroma of the crystal red liquid tantalizing her. She was just about to take a sip when she heard Butterball calling her name, then saw her friends approaching her house.

She stepped out onto the porch to greet them, with the glass still in her hand. "Hi, you guys," she said cheerfully. "What brings you by?"

"We have to go...*now*," Jippsy stated adamantly.

That's what she liked about him, Vicky thought admiringly. He was a man, determined and always able to take charge. She had looked forward to savouring her hard-earned juice, but instead she merely gulped it down so as not to have wasted her effort and those delicious berries. She wiped her mouth on the back of her hand as Jippsy explained what the hurry was about.

"We think the cop was at Frankie's. We have to warn him, and that also means that we're running out of time to hunt for the treasure, so tonight is our last chance. Do you have any flint you can bring, Vicky?"

Without answering she ran back inside, where she deposited her empty glass in the kitchen sink and grabbed the starter her dad used for the oven. "How's this, Jippsy?"

"That's perfect...definitely better than rubbing two sticks together. Just in case one of those cops is following Frankie, we can use this..." he had started to say when Dodo interrupted him.

"Oh, stop talking already, Jippsy!" Dodo said uncharacteristically. "You've been listening to too many mystery and adventure radio shows. Aren't we in a rush?!" These past few days had really gotten to her. It was at that moment that Jippsy finally noticed that Dodo had started to bite her fingernails again. She was nervous, and now insistent that they get a move on already.

"Alright, then. Just forget it. Follow me and do not go ahead. If I stop, you all stop. If I get down, you all get down. Got it?

"Yeah. Sure, Jips. You're as right as rain."

"Thanks, Butterball."

Vicky pulled the front door closed, and took her place beside her friends as they took off on their final

351

mission.

They reached the Cristafaro farm in no time at all. Dodo had become unstoppable; she kept running so fast that it was difficult for the others to keep up. Jippsy had to cut her off a couple of times in an effort to slow her down. At roughly fifty yards from the house Jippsy stopped them altogether. "I think it's safer if we walk the rest of the way," he cautioned. "We have to pay attention now. Stop if you see anything that doesn't seem right, ok?" The breeze had intensified, and was a welcome relief as it cooled their sweat-soaked bodies. Butterball, for one, couldn't wait to get back to the lake. He hoped to jump in – even just for a moment – and get some relief from the unrelenting heat."

Jippsy scanned the area carefully. "I don't see any cars - you all stay here and I'll..."

"The hell we will, Jippsy," Dodo seethed as she marched forward. He moved swiftly to block her.

"You're staying here," he insisted between clenched teeth. Then almost under his breath, "I don't want any bad guys noticing you." He started to back away from her in the direction of Frankie's house.

"I don't care! I'm going." She wasn't going to give in as easily as he'd hoped, and had abruptly thrust her arms out, pushing against her big brother in an effort to get past him.

"Dodo, please! Be reasonable." He wasn't going to budge, and she wasn't going to give in, so he said the only thing he could, "What if they have guns?" He didn't want to say it out loud, and he didn't want to scare her like that, but she'd left him no other choice.

She stopped, and let her arms drop to her sides. Jippsy couldn't tell what she was thinking, but she looked as though she was...plotting. She could feel her hair sticking to her face, and the crinkle of her skin as the sweat from the heat and her exertion dried. He watched her breathe, deeply and with purpose, and the colour in her face change from pink to white to red. She could feel her pulse beating in her head, a violent pressure and rhythm incited by fear and frustration. She finally understood what they meant when she heard people say 'time stood still'. He knew something was coming, but all he could do was watch as something overtook his sister. And then she just let it all out in a steady stream. "HOW. DARE. YOU?! After all we've *all* been through these past two days," she shrieked. "If you think I'm going to back down and walk away then you're crazy. I'm not about to let some crooked cop stop me," she announced as she stepped around her brother, shoving at him unexpectedly as she walked past.

Something about her resolve managed to fortify the others. "We're going too," Vicky proclaimed as she stepped forward. Then, of course, Butterball followed suit.

"OK. Fine!" Jippsy conceded in a snit. "We all go together. Wow! You guys really *are* screwy."

Jippsy and Dodo approached the door while the others sat on the porch waiting for Capri and Frankie to join them. Jippsy knocked, and he knew from experience that Mrs. Cristafaro wouldn't come to the door, but would call out instead.

"Who iz it?" she called from inside.

"It's Jippsy and Dodo, Mrs. Cristafaro. Are Frankie and Capri here?"

"Si. Dey in," she said as she opened the door. It creaked so loudly, it was apparent that the hinges had never been oiled.

"Ah! Jeepsi, Dodo, come, come," she insisted happily. Frankie's mom liked the Russo kids. She thought they were a good influence on her Frankie, and she always secretly thought that Jippsy was a good boy who would make a good husband for her Caprice.

Jippsy stepped in and Dodo followed while the others stayed out on the porch. He spotted Capri lying on the floor listening to the radio. She was drinking what looked like tea. He caught her eye and mouthed, "Let's go." She understood right away, stood up and walked over to the radio. She turned the volume up and nodded to her friends to join her over by the radio. Jippsy could tell by the look on her face that something was wrong.

"What's the matter?" Jippsy asked as soon as he was close enough to Capri.

"That cop was here," she whispered in the hopes their voices would be drowned out by the radio.

"I know. We have to get out of here and find the treasure tonight before he comes back."

"Hey, Jippsy, old boy, what brings you here?" Frankie asked nonchalantly as though nothing were the matter. He was making his way down from the second floor, and he had changed out of his dirty clothes. "Oh! Hi, Dodo," he bubbled as he noticed her standing behind Jippsy. "So, what are you two doing here?" he asked as he joined his sister and their friends.

Dodo put her hand on his arm; she knew he would listen to her without an argument. "We know that cop who's been following you came here today. Your mom mentioned it to our mom. We're pretty sure he's after the money, and for sure he's going to come back. This could be our last chance, Frankie. We have to go. *Now.*" Her voice was firm and confident. He nodded his agreement.

"Wait a minute. I have to get my slingshot." He took off, back up the staircase taking two steps at a time. He came right back down moments later and headed straight out the door with his friends and sister without a word to his mom.

Jippsy started running without any discussion, and the gang simply fell in line like a genuine pack. Besides, was there really anything more to discuss? The treasure was somewhere in the vicinity of the crash. They had their clues and they had less than 5 hours of daylight left to figure it all out before their opportunity likely vanished for good.

"Jips, wait up! I'm getting a cramp," Butterball implored.

"No dice, Butterball. We have to get away from here quickly. Keep up!"

Gerard and Louis

"There's the house, Gerard," Louis said as he pointed to the sign for the orchard. Gerard slowed down to get a better look, and they could see a crew of workers in the groves, off to the side of the house.

Gerard craned his neck to get a better look. He knew very little about cherries and was curious about what they were doing. "It looks like they're throwing nets over the trees..."

"They are, Gerard. They're getting ready to pick their cherries before the birds do it for them. The nets help protect the trees from being picked clean." Gerard looked at his associate's burly face. He had broken into what looked like a longing grin as he watched the men working in the groves. How Louis wished he was one of them rather than in the jackpot he was in, at the mercy of the most terrible people he could imagine. *If I could only get out for good*, he lamented.

Why a Crocodile

"We have to work together now, on both sides of the lake." Jippsy always had a plan, thought Butterball, but right that moment he didn't care a damn about Jippsy or the treasure or Jippsy's plans to find that treasure. Instead, Butterball made a beeline for the sandbar and walked straight into the water fully clothed.

Jippsy was clearly unhappy to see his friend selfishly cooling off in the water when there was important work to be done. "No time for that, Butterball," he called out to him irritably.

"Sorry, Jippsy. It's hot and I need to cool off. I promise you I'll work twice as hard as the rest of you if I can just take a moment to cool off." Sometimes Butterball just made so much sense... As if on cue the rest of the gang ran right into the water without so much as discarding a shoe. Jippsy watched stonily as they delighted in the water. He relaxed as they became revitalized, and allowed their comfort to slowly chip away at his reluctance, then took his turn to run fully clothed into the water.

He realized as he soaked in the refreshing water that this was truly a significant part of his childhood – one of the best parts, in fact – and an even greater aspect of his heritage. It was an escape...a break from school and chores. To Jippsy, Lost Lake was an oasis where he had made some of his fondest memories. Unfortunately it had now been exposed to an entirely different set of circumstances. His oasis had been tainted by greedy men, who crashed into their world, and had brought death, fear and corruption along with them. They were, he came to understand, unaware, and indifferent to the awful impact they would have upon this place. Jippsy knew that Butterball's ties to this slice of heaven ran deep and that perhaps his indifference to the money stemmed from the fact that this place held more meaning for him than the improbable unearthing of millions of dollars.

When the gang felt sufficiently refreshed they hauled themselves out of the water and settled onto the sandbar. They were unusually quiet, and Jippsy was surprised to note that they seemed to be waiting for him to take the next step. He looked around the lake with a renewed sense of responsibility and commitment; this was no longer just about his friends or the money, but about something more. He gathered his thoughts and finally spoke to his friends from the heart. "I've never really been anywhere. I've driven into the city with my dad a few times, and that was great, but it never compared to this place. This is my home, our home, and I think it's the most incredible place in the world. As far as I'm concerned *we*," he said as he pointed to each of his friends, "are the rightful owners of Lost Lake. *No one* else belongs here, and these gangsters who've invaded our peaceful lake have given us an opportunity. This isn't just about the money..."

"Yeah. Sure, Jips. It's not *just* about the money," Butterball piped in incredulously.

"I'm serious, Butterball. It *isn't* just about the money. This is an adventure, and we may never have an adventure like this again. Pretty soon we'll all be headed off in different directions, and Lost Lake will just be a memory for some of us. And, yeah, the money matters whether you want to admit it or not. We...our families...could *all* use the help," he insisted, as he looked at each of his friends. "Some of us more than others," he concluded as his eyes sought out Vicky's at last.

Vicky didn't say a word but simply nodded her head in understanding.

"So," he continued, "whoever wants to stop should just go home now. I don't think anyone should stay just because we made a pact, although we started this together, as a gang, and I'd like to see us finish this together, as friends."

None of the kids made a move to leave. Jippsy had managed, in his own singular way, to appeal to each of them on some level. He was determined, more than ever, to see this adventure through to the end, and his gang, his nearest and dearest friends were there by his side.

"Well, then, I guess that makes it unanimous. Let's put our brains together, figure out these clues, not let *anyone* get hurt or in trouble, and find that treasure!"

"I'm with you, Jips, old boy," Frankie offered up.

Good old Frankie, Jippsy thought with relief. *He can always be counted on to second any motion – and to get the ball rolling.*

"Me, too" said Capri.

"Me, three" piped in Vicky.

"Me, four" laughed Butterball, which left only Dodo.

Dodo had no choice but to go along with her friends, although she was nervous about the possible dangers. "You guys know they may have guns?"

"Don't worry about that," Frankie reassured her. "We'll be long gone before they ever get here."

"Ok," Dodo answered reluctantly. "I'm in too."

"Alright," Jippsy said with enthusiasm as he clapped his hands together triumphantly. "Let's go over the poem one more time, and if we can't come up with anything new we'll grab up our shovels and just start digging. Does that work for everyone?"

This time it was Butterball who spoke on behalf of

the friends. "Let's do it!" he declared with gusto.

"Great! Vicky, you remember the poem?"

"Naturally," she said without a hint of humility. Her confident playfulness had resurfaced. She calmly repeated the poem for the gang:

"Where downhill the big rock shades
Toward the sand where the water fades
The thoroughbred runs but the 8th pole
And the trees reach across the swampy hole
The setting sun alights upon the crocodile
As I close my eyes and rest awhile

"We were stuck at the third line, if I remember correctly," Jippsy stated. "Did anyone come up with anything about the thoroughbred and the 8th pole?" They shook their heads in dismay. "Well, we're back to square one on this. We *do* know it's along the shore, somewhere in relation to the sandbar. Maybe we should just pick some random spots along that path and start digging."

"That's screwy Jippsy. We could be here for weeks! If we only have tonight then we need a better plan than that." Dodo made an excellent point.

Jippsy sighed with resignation. "I know, Dodo, I know. I was just saying...you never know...we might get lucky."

"That's true," Frankie said, eager to start something, anything at this point.

"How about the fourth line?" Vicky asked. "And the trees reach across the swampy hole." Jippsy scanned the lake slowly as he tried to piece that line together with the lay of the land. He was just about to suggest digging randomly again when a glorious smile lit up his face.

"I think I've got it. Frankie, remember the tree where we found the book?"

"Yeah, sure."

"It has to be there. That's the fourth line. Think

about it. 'And the tree reaches across the swampy hole'."
Jippsy jumped up and pulled Frankie to his feet. He
stretched his arm in the direction of the birch tree and
drew his index finger across the branch that hung out
over the lake. "Right there..."

"Hold on a second, Jippsy," Capri cautioned him.
She wanted him to calm down, and not get their hopes up.
She stood and stared circumspectly at the tree and the
surrounding area, then asked "What about the
'crocodile'?"

"To hell with that," Frankie mumbled in
frustration. "There *are* no crocodiles in this water."

"Maybe it's something that looks like a crocodile,"
Vicky added in. "What about the last line, 'As I close my
eyes and rest awhile'?"

"Maybe he was just tired?" Frankie suggested,
tired of this back-and-forth nonsense himself.

"Maybe he made a gravestone and it looks like a
crocodile?" Capri suggested.

"Maybe the crocodile ate him while he was
sleeping and the thoroughbred jumped over the moon,"
Butterball said snidely.

"Very funny, Butterball. Don't you have anything
intelligent you can add?" Vicky sneered. "Maybe the guy
hallucinated the whole thing. He could have been hurt or
tired or delirious."

"Or he just liked writing poetry."

"Ok, Butterball, knock it off!" Jippsy had had just
about enough of his pessimistic attitude.

"Fine! Maybe I'll just keep my big mouth shut." The
others simply ignored his comment and continued with
their speculation.

"Let's just assume that whoever wrote this wrote
it with the purpose of hiding something, and that they
were, as they say, 'of sound mind', ok?" Vicky's line of

reasoning made sense to the others, as usual.

"Ok...," Jippsy thought aloud, "if we just skip all the parts that don't make sense to us and concentrate on the ones that do, then maybe we can get ourselves a little closer. Let's go across the lake – together – to *that* tree," he said as he pointed across the lake, "and bring along the second shovel."

The rest of the gang got to their feet as Frankie retrieved the other shovel. Rather than swim across, they marched along the path they had carved out during their previous searches. The path, previously non-existent, was becoming rather well worn.

The Stakeout

Gerard made sure the car was at least half a mile away from the farm. "We can walk from here."

"Eh, il fait chaud, Gerard," Louis complained. He was right. The heat hadn't abated, not even a degree, and it merely added to his utter misery. He hauled himself out of the car grudgingly and trudged along beside Louis like a sulky child.

Gerard, on the other hand, could tolerate the heat, but had come to detest everything about Louis. His guttural voice grated on his nerves, his large hulking body disgusted him as he watched him lumber along, and his obvious reluctance to finish what they had started was Louis' breaking point. The rare moments when he had appreciated Louis seemed to evaporate. In his opinion, Louis was a waste of flesh draining precious resources like oxygen. He found it nearly impossible to hide his disdain, and it was only the knowledge that he wouldn't have to tolerate Louis much longer that urged him forward. "Come on, Louis, we have to get off the road. We can't afford to be seen or heard. We'll get as close as we can to the house so we can watch – and maybe hear - what they're up to, but far enough that the workers shouldn't be able to see us. Louis it is silence from hereafter. Comprends-tu?"

"Oui, Gerard," he mumbled resignedly. "I understand."

"Good."

Louis followed Gerard into the woods, where they seated themselves on the dry ground beneath the pine, maple and birch trees. They were fairly close to the front of the house, and the trees formed a sort of canopy above them that effectively hid them from sight and protected them from the sun. Louis settled in with the intention of attracting as little of Gerard's unpleasant attention as possible. From his vantage point he was able to see the cherry pickers and was amused to watch the chipmunks as they jumped from tree to tree just waiting for the opportunity to dodge in and steal some of the luscious-looking red and yellow fruit. It was, as far as Louis was concerned, rightfully theirs anyway. Louis had started to think of men, humankind that is, as a plague on this planet. Men were simply killers for pleasure, destroyers of the earth, and, all-in-all, savages despite their pretenses.

People underestimated him, he knew that... They saw a beast of sorts, and when they heard his voice it merely served to compound their suspicions. They had no way of knowing that he read, and that he read voraciously. He watched the scene that played out in the orchard, thankful for the distraction, and before too long he was caught up in a daydream. He imagined himself a writer, like Jules Verne, a talented conjurer of incredible stories. He could write about his favorite fantasy...that man would someday fly to the moon. After all, men – and even a woman – had already flown across the ocean, so why not into space? He conceived of alien beings in his mind. What color would they be? How big or small? One eye or one hundred eyes, or maybe even no eyes at all? Could they communicate as we do? Could they fly or were they bound to their planet by gravity as we were? He was grateful for these moments when he could allow his imagination to take him anywhere.

Gerard, for his part, was preoccupied with altogether different thoughts. He watched the laborers in the orchard, the lack of activity in and around the house, felt the sweat pouring down his temples, and entertained hateful thoughts about his associate, the cop, the Frankie kid, and anyone else who popped into his mind. He felt anything but peaceful. He decided to focus on something constructive...his plan to get out of this place, but to get out in one piece and on top. He thought of his family and their needs, and this reassured him that he was doing the right thing; he was looking out for what mattered most in this world – at least for him.

They sat and watched for hours, like vultures hovering near their prey, just waiting for any sign of weakness. They watched the mundane chores of the workers, as they threw nets over the trees in the orchard, and listened as the birds swooped and called and bade their time until they could claim some of the cherries as their own. Given the opportunity they would devour all of the cherries in a matter of days, but the nets ensured their failure. Louis contemplated the fate of these birds whose very survival depended upon their access to food. If man continued to win his battle with nature then how would these birds fare? Would they die off, and if they did how would that loss further impact the food chain? It was funny - ironic actually - that neither of the men considered that at that moment they were at the lowest level possible on the food chain of their professional lives.

Instead, Gerard pictured his baby, cradled in the arms of the woman he loved. *By tomorrow morning I will hopefully be rich, and that miserable cop will be dead. As for those kids, well,* he thought without an iota of remorse, *they were just in the wrong place at the wrong time.* He could wait patiently, but not indefinitely. What he *wanted* was for those workers to go back to their barracks for the night, but what he *needed* was a gun. He was positive the kid's family would have a hunting rifle at the very least, most probably in the main house. He would have to wait until nightfall before he could make his move.

And while Gerard worked out the details of his master plan, and carefully plotted and schemed, Louis sat contentedly on the ground beneath the shade of the trees and dreamed of alternate realities.

Crocodile Marks the Spot

Jippsy stared intently at the lake, mesmerized as the breeze rippled across the surface of the water toward the birch tree, and toward the marsh where he had almost drowned earlier in the day. It felt like forever ago...could it have been just that morning, or was it yesterday? His forehead creased in consternation as he tried to recall the sequence of events that had led him to this place. He followed the line of the birch tree, how it leaned out across the lake, just as Dutch had remarked. "Where did you go, Dutch, and are you even coming back?" he asked himself under his breath.

"What did you say, Jips?" Butterball asked. Jippsy had barely noticed that Butterball was standing right beside him at the base of the birch tree.

"Oh! Nothing. Look, this is where we found the last clue, so let's just start digging wherever we can around this tree. We have two shovels, and five people, so when one of us gets tired the next one can take over."

"*That's* your whole plan, Jippsy?" Capri scolded. Frankie stared at her curiously. His sister had grown over the past year. While she had always been bright, her intelligence had truly become remarkable to him, and physically, her body had become soft and shapely. She was barely his little sister anymore. But she stood there, rigid and implacably cross-armed, as she criticized their friend. Frankie didn't like this version of Capri, and *she* evidently didn't like Jippsy's half-baked plan.

"I'm afraid that's it. There's no science in this experiment, Capri. We've exhausted our ability to decipher Dutch's clues. So unless you have a better idea, this is it."

"I *do* have a better idea. It will take less effort to focus on figuring out the poem than to randomly start digging. We'll only *exhaust* ourselves if we do it *your* way!" Capri's patience for Jippsy's apish chest beating had all but vanished.

"Go ahead, Capri, figure it out. Clearly you're so much smarter than the rest of us..." he sneered as he threw the shovel at her feet.

She kicked it back toward him in a fit of frustration. "You're just a bloody caveman. Go ahead and dig... Ugh!"

Jippsy couldn't resist pushing her buttons. "Me caveman, you woman. Me hunt, you cook." The gang started to snicker despite the seriousness of their disagreement.

Capri fought the urge to strike him. She felt terribly conflicted; she could no longer put up with his presumption of superiority just because he was a boy, but she could never justify hurting him. This adventure seemed to have magnified her feelings toward him, and there was no denying that losing him would have crushed her. Unfortunately, she could no longer abide the insipid men in her life who hastily made bad decisions and exerted their will simply because they were men, and because they ignorantly believed that they were the stronger, smarter sex. She couldn't understand why men insisted upon using their brawn instead of their brains. This was especially true of her own father whose favorite saying was, 'A woman's place is in the home'. Capri knew that her mother was far more intelligent and capable than her father, but he kept control of his family through pure male bravado and violence.

"I'm just saying that I'd like for us to think it out first. Is that really too much to ask?"

Frankie had finally waited long enough. He considered himself a man of action and all this talk had resulted in accomplishing absolutely nothing. "Forget it, Capri," he snarled as he snatched up the shovel that had been kicked between her and Jippsy, and unceremoniously started to dig just at the base of the birch.

"Frankie, be reasonable," Capri implored, concerned that he had already grown to be too much like her father. But then it occurred to her that digging, or any physical exertion for that matter, might be the type of distraction Frankie needed, and so she let the matter drop and turned to the rest of the gang

"Ok, Capri," Jippsy finally relented. "We'll listen." Jippsy figured that any one of them shoveling was better than nothing, and agreed to indulge Capri this one last time.

"We know we've found the tree hanging over the lake. So now we need to figure out what he meant by 'the crocodile' and 'I lay and die'. We know he came over on a raft, and that the bag or bags must have been really heavy, right? He probably had to lift hundreds of pounds of weight, which he wasn't used to doing. He was a gangster, after all, and might not have been used to such heavy labor. That means he wouldn't have been able to go very far without a great deal of effort. Maybe he was lying down because he was tired or because he was hurt? Or what if...oh!" She realized at that moment that she was onto something. "What if he could only see 'the crocodile' **when** he was lying down?" A smile spread across her face as the obviousness of this clue dawned on her.

"Jippsy," she ordered, "lie down just in front of the tree." Jippsy had a feeling she was onto something too and didn't hesitate to obey her immediately. He lay down on his stomach at the foot of the tree, which meant he was staring across the lake at the sandbar. "What do you see?" she asked with excitement.

Jippsy scanned the area closely, hoping to see anything that resembled a crocodile. "Nothing," he finally declared with disappointment. He rolled over onto his back, oblivious of the twigs and debris that stabbed at him through his shirt. He stared up through the trees, squinting as his eyes focused on the sun which had dipped low enough in the sky that it no longer penetrated the mass of leaves above him. Something about the setting sun triggered a thought. "It had to be pretty late by the time he made it over here. What's that line about 'the setting sun'?

"'The setting sun alights upon the crocodile'...Vicky answered. "So he's lying down as the sun is setting. What if whatever he's referring to can only be seen at sunset?" Vicky postulated. "Which means we won't be able to find the treasure until it's dark."

"That's preposterous!" Butterball spluttered.

"That's impressive, Butterball," Frankie teased as he continued to shovel. "How do you know such a long word? Did you also know that Constantinople is now Istanbul?"

"Very funny, Frankie. You're a real Abercrombie, aren't you? We can't all be as smart as you, can we, Frankie?" Butterball had finally had enough of Frankie's constant wisecracks. He pushed his way past Vicky and Dodo and got right up and into Frankie's face.

Frankie laughed at his nerve, but stopped shoveling. "I can take you down with a stare, **Butter**ball."

"Go ahead, gorilla boy." Butterball didn't flinch. He would never back down from Frankie again. Jippsy hopped up when he realized they might actually come to blows. He wedged himself between the two of them.

"Hey! Guys! Come on... Calm down. Now's not the

time for this. We're all in this together. Everyone's opinion counts. Let's just get through this." Much to Jippsy's relief the two boys each took a step back. Frankie went back to digging around the tree and Jippsy turned to address Butterball. "Butterball, it makes sense. Dutch was in the woods hiding out all afternoon, dragging the money along with him. There were people all over the area up until nightfall, so that's the only time he could have hidden anything so large. I'm telling you, he's lying down, he's looking up to heaven, and it's the setting sun that points the way to the crocodile."

"Jippsy, are you saying that we wait until tonight to continue searching?"

"That's exactly what I'm saying, Dodo. Don't you see? It all makes sense."

"Honestly, Jippsy, sometimes your imagination is just too much for me."

"Well, then, I guess you'll just have to believe it when you see it." Jippsy hated constantly being second-guessed by his little sister. She had accused him of being a daydreamer one too many times, but at least he was figuring things out.

"Dodo, why can't you accept that my imagination is what's helped unravel these clues? I'm not making this stuff up! What have I ever done to make you question me?"

Dodo rolled her eyes at this. A bird flying overhead caught her attention; she watched as it circled just beyond the lake near the car wreck. To everyone else it was just a crow, waiting and hovering, looking for its next meal. But to Dodo, who was normally rational, it was a bad omen that made her skin crawl.

"Well, Dodo?"

Dodo simply shook her head and answered, "Nothing, Jippsy. Absolutely nothing."

Jippsy smiled triumphantly. "Trust me. I won't let anything happen to you, Dodo."

"It makes sense to me, Jippsy," Vicky offered up in the hopes it might help his cause.

"You see, Dodo? Even Vicky agrees with me. I think..."

"Except...," Vicky interjected, "what are we going to do in the meantime?" The rest of the gang turned their attention from Vicky to Frankie, who had been digging around the birch.

Frankie felt them staring at him. "Feel free to stand around and watch while I dig up the treasure alone," he scoffed as he continued to shovel.

Jippsy contemplated the night to come. Butterball looked longingly at the lake. Vicky and Dodo suggested they pick some berries while they wait, and took off into the forest. Capri stared at Frankie with a smirk on her face. "Really, Frankie? Are you going to dig up the entire forest?"

He stabbed at a new patch of earth. "You have a better idea, Capri?"

"No. Not really," she admitted.

"Well then, grab a shovel."

Cristafaro Residence and Mama

Gerard looked at his watch for the hundredth time. Seven p.m. He sighed loudly. The hours had passed slowly and painfully. The men had grown stiff and uncomfortable on the rough ground.

"I feel like roots are growing out of my ass," Gerard grumbled.

"Very funny, Gerard," Louis answered as he sifted hopelessly from one cheek to the other.

Gerard slapped Louis' thigh. "Let's go, Louis. We can't sit around here like this any longer." Gerard stood and stretched himself out in an effort to loosen the muscles and joints that had stiffened as they watched and waited.

"Sure, Gerard," he said as he used a tree trunk to haul himself up.

"You let me do the talking."

"Of course, Gerard."

They had only moved a few feet when Gerard thought he heard voices. "Stop!" Gerard cautioned as loudly as he dared, but Louis bumped into him, knocking him into a tree.

"What? Sorry, Gerard," Louis croaked apologetically.

"Watch out, you big oaf! You just about knocked me to the ground. Didn't you hear me say stop?"

"Sure, Gerard." *Sure, Gerard. Sure, Gerard.* That's all he would say from now on...

"Why, Lord? What did I do to deserve this?" Gerard's frustration was not only directed at Louis, although he didn't particularly care for him. Gerard felt as though he had been subjected to a series of unfortunate circumstances, each begetting an even more dire fate. In general, Gerard was dissatisfied with every hand life had dealt him, except, of course, his wife and child. Even when he had choices, he felt as though he was constantly choosing between the lesser of two evils, and that even then he made the wrong choice. *How am I ever going to get out of this, when every move is even more dangerous than the last?* He wondered to himself.

Gerard surmised that the stress of the past few days had caught up to him at last. He must have imagined the voices, as there was clearly no one in sight. *Can't afford to lose your mind, Gerard*, he told himself. *You're too close to the finish line to trip now.* He just had to get through the next few hours and everything would be fine. But he needed to stay alive, and to do that he also needed Louis to stay alive...at least until he found the money.

They approached the house cautiously and stopped by a large sumac shrub. "Louis, stay here behind these bushes. If I get into trouble... Well, you know what to do. Ok?"

It was no surprise when Louis merely answered, "Sure, Gerard."

Gerard tentatively made his way up the steps and stopped to compose himself once he reached the front door. He knocked purposefully, but not forcefully, on the screen door. "Hello?" he called out softly as though he were a door-to-door salesman making a sales call.

"Who iz?" the woman called from behind the door in heavily accented English.

"Madame, my car broke down up the road. I would like to use your phone to call for assistance."

"You go. No phone," she replied curtly.

"Please, Madame. It's getting late and I have nowhere to go." Despite his reprehensible intentions,

Gerard found himself astonished that the foreign lady was so...mean. *Why won't she let me in?* he wondered, ironically offended. He leaned his head against the door in frustration.

The lady didn't even bother to respond. *What kind of people behaved so unneighbourly*? He didn't know what else to say. "Madame, please, I..."

"Go. You go..." she pleaded from inside the house.

The door opened without warning and he suddenly found himself at the wrong end of a rifle, which hovered mere inches from his nose. "Perhaps you didn't hear what my mother said." Gerard slowly took a step back as he raised his arms – a natural instinct by then – and looked beyond the gun's barrel to take in the youthful face that matched the young male voice that had reproached him.

He cleared his throat, which had suddenly dried. "Sir," he croaked, "I am lost."

"Well, then, perhaps you best go back to where you came from."

"No. Um, you don't understand. I must get back to my family." Gerard thrilled at the prospect of getting the rifle. Somehow, he had managed to turn an inauspicious event into something positive. Maybe things were finally looking up for him... He had come here for the rifle, and there it was, ready for the taking. He realized they wouldn't have to terrorize the family after all. He backed up a few more feet, cautiously reaching the edge of the stairs and descending backwards off the porch. He was happy to see that the young man followed him. Gerard could see the intense concentration on the young man's face as he squinted at him over the rifle's sights. *This kid looks a little too eager*, he thought appreciatively. Gerard knew he could bait him, and that, if they found it necessary to kill him, no one would ever find out. The stakes were too high for him to back down, so he did the only thing he could. He decided to goad him out past the porch.

"Sir, you don't understand. I can't leave." At least that part was true. "I'll never get back to my family, and my child is sick." He hated the fact that he had to use his child as an excuse; he was by no means superstitious, and yet he worried that lying about the health of his child could somehow bring about negative consequences. But his hand had been forced and he was desperate. He reassured himself once again that he had no other options, then continued to plead his case. "Won't someone help me, please?!" he begged as he covered his face, and started to sob into his hands. All along, he continued his backward trek down the stairs and toward the bush where Louis was waiting to back him up.

"Vincenzo, you going to hurt him. No gun. You come in," the lady pleaded. It was exactly the distraction Gerard needed. He un-cupped his hands from his face and made a move toward the boy. He was just a dumb kid trying to protect his family, but Gerard was a man who needed to protect his own. The boy stumbled back, and caught his heel on the bottom stair. He threw back his right arm to stop his fall, but he was too late, and his body hit the stairs with such force that it sent shock waves through his torso from his tailbone to the base of his skull. His left arm couldn't bear the entire weight of the rifle. The butt of the gun slipped over his right shoulder and managed to strike the third step as the boy reeled backward. The rifle had been modified for hunting wild game, and had a hairpin trigger, the slightest movement near the trigger, or in this case a major jolt to the rifle, would suffice to fire off a round once the rifle had been cocked. The boy still had a firm grip on the rifle with his left hand as it fired straight toward the only target in his path - Gerard.

In an instant he fell backward to the ground, deafened to the surrounding chaos by the gunfire, and dazed by the rush of blood as it pumped and pounded through his heart and ears. He felt no sharp pain...just the sheer exhilaration of adrenaline. *I'm not shot. I'm not shot,* he repeated over and over again.

The boy recovered quickly and didn't waste any time getting back up on his feet. He heard his mother shouting in Italian, but even he couldn't understand what she was saying as he was more accustomed to speaking English. "It's ok, mom. Nobody's hurt," he called over to her. He turned his attention back to Gerard, who had not quite regained his footing, when he noticed a shadow moving in quickly from the corner of his eye. It was no shadow, but a beast of a man who suddenly appeared from behind the sumac bush. In a fluid motion the man took a deliberate and practiced swing at the boy, as his mother watched and screamed gibberish from inside their home. The man had managed to land his blow precisely on the boy's right. The boy immediately released his grip on the rifle and it clattered to the ground right at Gerard's feet. The boy hadn't had an opportunity to re-cock the gun.

Gerard reacted quickly and grabbed the rifle. He facetiously thought of what wonderful hosts the boy and his mother had been thus far, how they had been unwilling to help a man in need, and happily turned the tables on them as he leveled the rifle at the boy's chest. The mother, meanwhile, kept yelling and screaming. "SHUT UP ALREADY!" Gerard yelled in a fit of anger. The mother stopped yelling and instead resorted to what sounded to Gerard like prayer. *Shut up,* he thought with amusement. *Now **that** she understands,* he thought mockingly. "Shame on you, kid! You could have just helped us," Gerard chastised. He loved the idea of keeping up the pretense of being stranded strangers just a little while longer.

Louis simply stood there watching the kid writhe in pain on the ground, barely able to move his arm. He waited for a nod from Gerard before bending down to pick him up. The mother threw open the door and ran down the stairs to her boy, fearful that the beast would further harm her baby. She tried to push Louis away.

"Mama! Mama! Ashpet," the boy begged between clenched teeth. The boy had enough sense to know that the man was offering a hand. His mother stopped and stepped back as Louis bent down and hooked his left arm under the boy's left arm and gently hoisted him to his feet. "You will be ok," he reassured the boy. "I did not break anything."

"Anyone else in the house, boy?" Gerard asked menacingly. He already knew he wasn't the boy they were looking for.

"No. No one."

"You sure, boy? If I go in the house and find someone else there, you'll be digging a grave with your good arm," he promised as he pointed the gun at the mother.

"I said no one," he tried to yell, but the pain forced the words out in strangled spurts.

"You go to the cops, kid, and your mama gets it. Capiche?" Gerard was sure the kid would do as he said. Boys and their mamas... He practically grinned just thinking about it.

Ten Holes

Frankie had already dug a hole in every possible clearing near the weeping tree. He was working on his tenth as the rest of the gang looked on. Frankie seemed to be on a mission, and while the rest of the gang were just as determined, they could see no point in blindly digging without any particular bearing. By the third hour Dodo stepped up to Frankie and placed her hand on his arm. He stopped shoveling long enough for her to appeal to his common sense. "Frankie, I think you made enough holes. Why don't you rest? You'll need your strength."

His frustration was evident – the tension in his jaw and the wild look in wild eyes said it all. There was a sad desperation there, as though this was his last opportunity before devastation struck. Every thunk of the shovel as it hit the earth hammered home how weary he had become. The only problem was that he didn't know what else to do.

"Frankie, come sit with us," Capri implored as she waved him over. The others had spent the last few hours talking and gathering firewood so they would have light when they needed it as the sun when down. The daytime sounds of the forest were gradually slipping away only to be replaced with a different kind of noise. The creatures that roamed the forest during the day had settled and become quiet. As the evening approached, their priorities shifted from food to shelter – their best means of defense against the predators that came out at night.

The forest had this way of coming alive at night. It transformed into a symphony led by the sound of the male crickets as they rubbed their hind legs to attract any interested mates. The crows were winding down their hard work fighting over the last food discoveries of the day as the bats emerged from their caves to begin their evening hunt. The moon had started to edge its way up into the sky, and the wind had receded, imposing a welcome calm amid the trees, as, during the daytime, the rustling of their leaves was the white noise of the forest. Hoots and howls harmonized to weave a melody that resounded throughout the forest. There were red foxes nearby; several days earlier Jippsy had spotted a den burrowed into the steep embankment that led down to the lake's edge, not more than half a mile from where they waited near the fire. Although they tended to avoid contact with humans, the foxes were sometimes spotted in the area as the woods were full of berries and small prey. They could be disruptive to the farmers' livestock and crops, but generally harmless if unprovoked. Jippsy knew the light cast by their fire would keep them safe, although he wondered if perhaps Dutch might have been attacked by one of the many predators in the woods that night.

As Frankie turned to start yet another hole he finally surveyed the results of his unsuccessful labor. He hung his head in defeat and walked resignedly over to where the gang had settled in beside the fire. He sat down hard next to Dodo who scooched over to make room for him. The ground was dry and warm from the day's heat, and the rising humidity failed to cool the air. Frankie's heavy breathing had attracted more black flies and mosquitoes than he could handle. Now that his hands were no longer wrapped around a shovel he was swatting and scratching at their incursion. Despite the ongoing heat, he had no choice but to sit near the fire.

"How much longer, Jips?" he practically whined. He could see Butterball on the other side of the roaring

380

fire, slapping at the air.

He had made it his personal vendetta to kill any bug that flew near him. "For Christ's sake, this is screwy, Jips. I'm getting eaten alive."

"Stay near the fire, Butterball. They don't like the smoke."

"They also don't like lemons or oranges, or any kind of citrus for that matter."

"Vicky, where am I going to find lemons or oranges around here? Sheesh! I'm just saying..." Butterball scoffed as he fought the flies.

"Just forget it, Butterball." Vicky answered crossly. "Stop acting like a monkey," she admonished as she watched his flailing arms cut through the air. She had become absurdly irritated with his attitude.

"Me, a monkey? Eeeh eeh eeeh eeeeeh eeeh eeeh," he mimicked as he scratched at his armpits. Everyone laughed - Frankie the loudest. Butterball simply continued the charade.

"Stop, stop, you're killing me," Frankie pleaded as he rolled on the ground and held his stomach.

That was Butterball's cue to step it up even more. "Eeeeh eeeeh eeeh," he continued, as he crouched on the forest floor and swung his arms over the ground, dragging his knuckles along the bits of leaves, stones and earth. He danced his monkey dance around the flames. The others had joined Frankie, rolling around on the ground. Butterball could see the reflection of tears as they rolled down their faces. "Stop! Stop!" was all he could hear amidst the laughter. Even Butterball couldn't keep a straight face as he continued to entertain his friends, and he certainly had no intention of stopping. Their laughter was contagious and much needed after all.

The unexpected laughter had reenergized Jippsy. He jumped up and walked away from the fire and the laughter, and headed to the water's edge. The sun had not set entirely, and instead cast upon the lake a mirror reflection of the mountains and trees. He scanned the lake slowly clockwise from where he was standing. Something – he couldn't put his finger on it – had caught his eye as he peered across to the other side of the lake. He thought he saw...no, it couldn't be...another pair of eyes. He looked long and hard; he didn't want to blink, as his eyes had to readjust to the dimming light every time he did so. No, he couldn't make it out... The only thing that stood out was the white bark of the birch trees.

"What is it, Jippsy?" Capri asked as she put her hand on his shoulder.

I can never figure out this broad, he thought to himself. It was something he had heard on a radio show once. "I thought I saw something across the lake, over there," he answered as he pointed almost directly across the lake to the left of Big Rock. The others slowly came along, and he had hoped someone might see what he had, but he seemed to be the only one.

"I would say another half an hour or so and the sun should be down low enough to start our search." The gang returned to the fire to wait it out.

The gang sat quietly around the fire, each immersed in their own thoughts and struggles with the day's events, not to mention the unwanted attention of the pests that seemed determined to make them as uncomfortable as possible. The sun held on with such determination, refusing to set, as though it knew these kids were up to something. In a magnificent display, the sun's last rays streaked over the horizon, casting the mountains as a blackened backdrop, illuminating the few clouds hanging overhead in shades of blue and purple, and the skyline just over the mountains in pink, orange and yellow. It was glorious and breathtaking as the sun cascaded below the horizon, and the first stars appeared in the sky. The gang might have been in awe of the beauty that existed all around them, but their ability to appreciate what nature had to offer was obliterated by the task that brought them all there.

"Ok, guys, it's time." None of them had even considered the fact that it was after nine pm, and their families had absolutely no knowledge of their whereabouts. It wasn't unusual for any of their parents to be away overnight in the city on an errand, and so their children's absence wasn't necessarily observed. Besides, they always came home eventually, albeit a little more tired and dirty, but always safe and somewhat more educated each time.

"We can't split up so we'll go as a group," Jippsy instructed, naturally taking over command of the gang. "Frankie, you have one shovel, if you're still up for it. Can you grab the other one, Capri? I'm going to settle back down under the tree and look for what Dutch saw the other night. It was only two days ago so the moon should be about the same." He did lie down, but couldn't see anything other than the moon's reflection off the lake. He rolled over to try another position, but still saw nothing.

Vicky watched as Jippsy maneuvered himself on the ground beneath the tree. She could see the consternation on his face, and she figured it couldn't hurt if she lay down on the ground as well. Her short overalls were already a mess and smelly from the fire - cleanliness was definitely not on any of their minds. Hunger, however, seemed to be a hot topic, especially where Butterball was concerned. Vicky could no longer tolerate his incessant questions and badgering – he had been at it all evening long... *When are we doing this or that? What was that noise? When can we eat?* And, of course, the ever-famous *I'm hungry.* They must have heard that one at least once every fifteen minutes for the past three hours. By Vicky's calculations he had whined about being hungry at least a dozen times. It didn't help that they were *all* hungry, and that his constant reminders simply played on their nerves. Vicky lay down on her back and strategically adjusted her position by ninety degrees until she had come full circle. Nothing stood out and so she decided to try 45 degree shifts. Again, she came full circle without noticing anything special.

"Hold on, guys," Jippsy suddenly called out. "I have an idea. Let's each try a different position and then rotate a quarter turn, say, every fifteen seconds. Frankie, you stand. "Sorry, buddy," Jippsy laughed.

"It's ok, Jips, old boy. All part of the fun."

Capri you get on one knee," he continued. Vicky quickly understood what he was doing.

"I know...I could sit on my knees," Vicky prompted, as if reading his mind.

"That's exactly right."

"I'll sit, and Butterball, you lie down."

"Why do I have to lie down?"

"Fine," he answered with frustration. "Dodo, you lie down. Butterball, go to the edge of the tree and look out over it. And try not to fall in."

"Thanks, Jips."

"You're part of the gang, Butterball. You're not just here for comic relief."

"Ok, Jippsy, old boy," Butterball quipped, once again making fun of Frankie. "What am I looking for?"

"Come on, already Butterball," Jippsy sputtered angrily. *How could Butterball be so stupid sometimes*, he wondered to himself. "The crocodile shaped whatever," Jippsy seethed. "Got it?"

"Yeah, sure," he mumbled.

"Ok, Vicky, you time us. We'll rotate clockwise

every fifteen seconds until we've done a full rotation. Butterball you'll have to go on the other side of the tree. Start by looking straight over it. Ok, everyone?" He was about to give Vicky the go-ahead to start timing when he felt compelled to add in one last motivation. "This will probably be our last chance before that cop shows up to harass Frankie, so let' really pay attention. Anyone sees **anything** that looks like it makes sense speak up right away."

"Wow, Jips! You really have to work on your speeches," Capri said with annoyance.

"Whatever you say, Capri! Everyone ready?"

"Ready!" they all called in unison, except for Butterball.

"Sure, Jips. Not too comfortable on this log, though."

"You'll be fine," he said to Butterball patronizingly. "Ok, Vicky, start counting."

"One Mississippi, two Mississippi, three Mississippi," she counted.

"If anyone sees anything that even remotely resembles a crocodile, stop us, remember your position, and we'll investigate. If it's nothing we'll continue from where we left off."

"...fourteen Mississippi, fifteen. Ok, everyone, rotate."

She repeated her count and the rotation three more times, until they were all facing the side of the lake from where they had crossed over. The moment Jippsy made his last turn he thought he saw something but then discounted it immediately. *My mind's just playing tricks on me – wishful thinking...* But he had nothing to lose, so he leaned closer, with his arms wrapped around his knees, to get a better look. He could hear Butterball struggling alongside the tree as he did his best to balance himself against the trunk without falling in. Jippsy figured Butterball had the best view from where he stood.

"Hold on, everyone," he called out with excitement, although he had his doubts and didn't want to get the gang revved up for nothing. He moved closer to the tree and sat down in the same position he had been in. He shook his head, got up, and took a few steps over to where Butterball was struggling to stay upright. His heart had started racing as he approached Butterball. He could see the moon reflecting off of something along the shore and lay down to get a better look at the shore line. "Butterball, do you see something down by the lake from where you are?"

"No, Jips, just the moon reflecting off the water, and a couple of trees that I can make out from the light.

The others came down to the shore, anxious to see what Jippsy was looking at.

Jippsy pointed across to the shore where a tangle of trees had been lit up by the moon's glow. "Could that be it? Could that be what he was talking about?"

Vicky lay down beside him and peered closely at the tree. "Is that the crocodile?" she asked as she pointed to a jumble across the way that had, indeed, the distinct look of something scaly. "It sure looks like a crocodile's tail. What are those...?" she trailed off as she squinted to focus in on the object in question. "Are those roots growing over a rock? That has to be it! Jippsy, you found it!" There was no doubt about it.

Once they knew what they were looking at it had become so obvious. "He must have been writing his poem from right here. It all fits...we found the book right under the tree, the tree across the swampy hole, the code for night, the crocodile," Vicky blurted out. She couldn't contain herself. She loved when a puzzle came together.

"Come on, Vicky," Jippsy said enthusiastically as he

grabbed her hand and hoisted her up.

"I can't believe we found it... We might have unraveled Lost Lake's greatest mystery," she chattered as the gang hastily made their way around the lake toward the 'crocodile'.

They were out of breath by the time they made it around, but they were too thrilled with the prospect of finding the treasure to waste another moment. Jippsy started handing out orders. "Ok, Vicky, Frankie, this is the spot," he panted as he pointed at the water's edge where the 'crocodile' was best illuminated a few short steps away from the tree.

"Here you go, Jips, old boy. Dig away!" Frankie handed the shovel to Jippsy.

Jippsy was grateful that Frankie fully appreciated the importance of what was happening. Capri and Jippsy stabbed their shovels into the ground, and encountered no resistance whatsoever. Dodo and Butterball ran back to the fire to get them some extra light. They brought back the sticks they had left at the fire's edge and some pine that would burn brightly, although far too quickly. Someone would have to get more pine soon, but neither could bear the thought of leaving as their friends started to dig.

They both worked quickly to scoop out the earth. They hit no roots or rocks, just soft earth covered with dead leaves. They met no resistance at all – which was a great sign.

They didn't have to dig for long before Jippsy felt, and the gang heard, the most promising *Thump!* of their lives. Jippsy's shovel had struck something and couldn't go in any further. It was hard, but not earth-hard. It was solid. Then Capri's shovel landed with the same heart-stopping *Thump!*

"Oh my god!" Capri called out as she dropped to

her knees and started to dig at the earth with her hands. Jippsy, Frankie, and Vicky dropped and cleared as much earth away with their hands as they could as Dodo and Butterball stood in awe of the scene that was playing before them as they lit up the area with their makeshift torches.

Frankie ran his hands along the top of the hard surface they had unearthed. He burrowed like a mole, digging around to locate the very edges of their discovery. Mud, dirt and leaves had been strewn everywhere. Jippsy used his shovel to enlarge the hole which was taking the shape of a large square. The exertion of digging had set his heart racing at the craziest pace. "Hold on!" he shouted. He didn't want to interrupt their progress but felt they might do better to work with a plan. "Frankie, you and I will carve out the outline. Dodo, Butterball, jab your torches into the ground and start moving the earth away from those two sides of the hole. Vicky, Capri, you two move the earth away from the other two sides. Once we've loosened it up enough we'll try to pry it up with the shovels. Let's go."

They managed to dig the earth away faster than Jippsy had anticipated. They could finally make out not just the shape but the details of their treasure. Jippsy stopped digging and took in the sight of the case; he couldn't believe his eyes. Despite the dirt, the buckles on the valise still shined in the moonlight – they glittered, in fact, as the flames from their torches jumped and danced. It was a magical moment for him and he wanted to savor that feeling of triumph. He realized that at some point this adventure, at least for him, had ceased to be about the money. While he had appreciated the rush of the chase, dissecting the riddle, hunting for something hidden from everyone else, what had truly delighted him, what would become his ultimate reward, was the conquest. *I've done it*, he thought smugly. He breathed deeply and puffed up his chest. He imagined himself a prize fighter, the Joe Louis of treasure-hunters. Lost in his reverie, he jabbed the air repeatedly with his fists, knocking out his imaginary opponent.

"Jippsy! **What** are you doing?!? Keep digging!"

That snapped him right back into the moment. "Right! Sorry," he mumbled in embarrassment and went back to clearing the earth from the valise. The shallow grave had been excavated sufficiently to reveal the entire case. They were anxious to open it then and there, but decided it would be best to remove it from the hole and maneuver it toward the fire.

"Ok, guys, Frankie and I will get our shovels under it. Stay where you are and try to hoist it up and out of the hole while we pry it up. Jippsy knew it was going to be heavy.

"Ready? One, two, three – heave!" Frankie and Jippsy weighed down their shovels as best they could, and used leverage to raise the valise out of the hole. "All hands lift." They lifted it, but only slightly. Capri managed to lift her corner out of the hole and rest it on the edge then went about helping the others.

"Ok. Frankie and Jippsy go around to the other side and try lifting and pushing toward me. Dodo and Vicky can you get the shovels under the case on each of your sides and try to raise the case out of the hole? Butterball, come around next to me and try pulling with me."

Frankie and Jippsy started chanting in unison. "One, two, three, pull! One, two, three, pull!" They chanted together over and over. They worked together, chanting and moving the valise inch-by-inch. Most significantly, they encouraged one another all along.

"We're getting there!"

"Come on – don't give up!"

"Almost there...keep going!

"One, two, three, pull!"

"Ok, guys, one more time and we should have it out." Capri announced.

"I need a break," Butterball moaned as he fell back on the ground.

"Butterball, get back in here," Capri commanded, and to everyone's surprise he dragged himself up off the ground to rejoin his friends.

"Forget 'it, Capri!" Frankie yelled angrily.

"Pull!" they all yelled with an unprecedented resolve. And Capri was right - it was the last effort needed to dislodge the valise from its hiding place. They wanted to collapse on the ground, and indeed, Butterball did, but Frankie and Jippsy wasted no time and grabbed the handle of the valise, which easily weighed hundreds of pounds in their opinion, and dragged it, inch-by-inch toward the fire.

"Jips, this bag is heavy! I can't wait to see inside," Franking said gleefully as he hefted the valise.

Me. Oomph. Neither." Jippsy struggled with the weight of the bag, anxious to finally drop it near the fire and crack it open. He wished he was stronger, that he could have lifted it up and over his head and run toward the fire like Hercules, but he was just a mortal kid. Then again, he was about to be a mortal kid with a ton of money; maybe he couldn't be a god, but with all that money he could certainly live like a god. The thought put a smile on his face just as they reached the fire.

"We made it," Jippsy blurted out as they both let go of the bag at the same time. The rest of the gang were already waiting by the fire. They had wanted to help, but there was nothing more to be done until the valise could be opened.

Jippsy knelt in front of the case, and noticed his

hands were trembling. He had spent the entire day exerting himself and straining his muscles, but this was nervousness, pure and simple. He unclasped the first buckle, and noticed that the second buckle had already broken off. He attempted to open the clasp that held the top and bottom of the case together, by squeezing the mechanism, but it wouldn't budge. He bent down to get a closer look. "Capri, shine that torch down here, would ya?" Moments later the problem with the clasp became evident. It was locked, and they certainly didn't have a key. "We need a key," he said desolately. "Does anyone have a knife?" he asked without looking up at his friends. They looked at one another blankly. "Ok," he answered for himself, "no knife."

"Let's try to break it open," Frankie suggested.

"We can't... Then we'll have nothing to carry the money in."

"Who cares? We'll just bury it again," Frankie retorted, but he wasn't smiling.

"Hold on! Let me see it," Butterball insisted. After all, he was used to get into things his mother tried to keep from him. He knelt down and eyed the clasp. It was a simple lock – a type he had successfully opened many times before. His mother kept a small jewelry box in her room that he used to unlock whenever she was out and he was bored. As luck would have it, his pants button had popped off the day before and his mother had not had a chance to sew it back on. Instead, his pants had been held together with a safety pin – who would have thought that the extra weight would finally come in handy?

Vicky watched in shock as Butterball reached down to unfasten his pants. "Butterball!? What are you doing??"

Butterball simply laughed as he smugly answered, "You'll see."

"Come on Butterball," Frankie insisted impatiently.

"Don't get your knickers in a wad. Could you shine that torch down here again?" He jiggled the pin in the lock, his tongue partially protruding from his mouth as he concentrated on the task of freeing the money. It was so quiet that they would have heard that pin drop had it slipped out of his hand. "I think I've got it," he said tentatively. And just like that, the first clasp clicked open. He inserted the pin into the next lock and before the gang could even register excitement over the first lock, Butterball sang out, "Ta Daa!" as the second lock clicked open.

They leaned even closer over the valise as Butterball flipped the top open with a sweep of his hand. The fire still burned brightly enough to light up the trees in golden tones. The torches had started to fade as the dry brush burned away, but the moon had started to rise, casting that extra bit of light down into the opening where the kids now stood, speechless, their mouths wide open as they gaped at the unimaginable fortune of green bills that were stacked neatly in the case.

"That's Benjamin Franklin." Jippsy recognized his face right away although he had never seen it on money.

"Yeah, I know who he was," said Butterball who recognized his face from a magazine he had once read. "He was the guy that invented electricity."

"Well, sort of. He was actually..."

"Vicky?" Capri stopped her.

They circled the valise and reached in to touch the money. In addition to the hundred-dollar bills there were bundles of fifties and twenties, adorned with the faces of Presidents Grant and Jackson, stacked into the valise alongside the Franklins.

"Wow! How much was supposed to be here, Jippsy?"

"Well, in the book he said thirteen million."

"Screwy!" Capri couldn't think of anything else that would aptly say it all.

"It's more than screwy. It's out of this world...like 'Flash Gordon' out." Jippsy noticed that a number of black books like the one they had found by the lake had been tossed into the valise as well. He counted them quickly (eleven more black books) while everyone grabbed bundles of bills. They flipped through the bills, fanned themselves with the stacks, and laughed at the prospect of being wealthier than any one of them could have ever imagined.

Jippsy was as excited about the cash as the others, but he was far more interested in the possibility that the black books held clues to something more. He was no math genius but he was pretty sure that the valise they had uncovered didn't have thirteen million dollars in it. If the rest of the money was hidden somewhere out here then he knew the best way to find it was to read through the black books until he figured it out. He couldn't afford to let the others take the books, and set about pulling them out of the valise while the others were distracted with the money.

"Hey, Jips, what you have got there?" Frankie bounded over, curious to know what Jippsy had found.

"Oh, these? Just more of those black books with crazy notes in them," he answered as casually possible. He made light of tossing them aside as though they meant nothing.

"Ok, Jips, you're the only guy I know who would rather be reading when you could be swimming in dough. Knock yourself out."

"Frankie you have such a way with words - you should consider becoming a writer."

"Are you kidding, Jips, old boy? Ha! I don't have to

do *anything* anymore," he said as he started to juggle with three bundles of money.

Jippsy didn't want to cheat his friends and swore that if he did find anything, they would, of course, share it with him. He just couldn't take all of the bickering and hassle that came along with the gang. It had proven nearly impossible to come up with a simple plan because everyone had their own opinion of what to do or what made sense. As he thought it over he did recognize, however, that had it not been for them - Vicky especially - they might not have found the money at all. He glanced over at Vicky, her red hair glowing like the flames of the fire, her face radiant with happiness, her dazzling smile lighting up the dark. He really liked her. He breathed deeply, and embraced what the others had already come to know...they were rich!

He calmly stacked the books somewhat out of sight behind a bush, and left them behind to join the gang for a dance around the fire. Jippsy wanted to share in the revelry and simply enjoy the moment, but his thoughts kept returning to the black books and how he could most effectively hide them. He considered that perhaps the most obvious plan was the one with most merit, so maybe he should just slip them back into the hole where the valise had been buried and come back for them later. Satisfied with that simple plan he changed gears. "Who's going to count it?" he asked rhetorically. Each and every one of them knew that Vicky was the best candidate for the job. "I think that's a job for...Vicky," he added magnanimously as he dramatically extended his arm in her direction.

"Thanks, Jippsy," she replied sarcastically, as she secretly relished the idea.

"Yeah, Vicky. You should count it." Butterball was excited and wanted to join in on the conversation.

Besides, he didn't want to get saddled with the job.

They each took a seat around the valise, either on the ground or on logs they had pulled over to settle in for a lengthy chore. Vicky sat to the left of the valise so the firelight could help her distinguish the bills. Jippsy looked happily around at all his friends. The hunt was over, and the rush of adrenaline that had coursed through their veins earlier had been replaced by a lightheaded rapture as they each maneuvered the possibility of fulfilling their deepest desires.

Vicky had, as anticipated, been the best choice to count the money. She devised a system whereby she separated the paper-taped bundles into stacks by denomination. There was a large stack of 20's, an equally large stack of 50's and a smaller stack of 100's. She made sure that the bundles were all comparable in height, and counted several of the bundles to determine how many bills were in each bundle. Vicky stacked and counted, separated and counted, flipped though and counted, and then recounted twice, three times.

She was grateful that the bills had been split into bundles of 200. She counted exactly 124 bundles of the 20's, 133 bundles of the 50's and 73 bundles of 100's, scratching her count into the dirt at her feet just to keep track of the bundles. She hadn't accounted for the possibility that the bundles weren't all of the same denomination, although the thought had occurred to her so she had randomly flipped through every fifth or sixth bundle just in case. At the end of forty-five minutes she proudly proclaimed, "Three million, two hundred and eighty-six thousand dollars. That's what's here, unless the bundles aren't all two hundred bills apiece or have different denominations stacked in them."

Frankie whistled through his teeth as Jippsy registered immediately that the other ten million was still out there.

"Three million, two hundred and eighty-six thousand dollars...divided by six..." she calculated out loud, "carry the four...um...ok, that leaves us with five hundred and forty-seven thousand six hundred and sixty-six, with sixty-seven cents left over."

"You can have my sixty-seven cents, Vicky, just for counting so much," Butterball offered generously as a giant grin spread across his face.

"Oh my god," she blurted out as she realized that they had just found more money than her family could make their whole lives for several generations.

"'Oh my god' is right," Capri said in a daze.

"We're *rich!*" Frankie roared as he jumped to his feet. "Rich, Capri. We can get away from Dad." He was overjoyed at first, but his emotions pitched and rocked from lighthearted to vengeful, from heavyhearted to optimistic and unstoppable. "We're rich," he said seriously for the first time. "We can get out of here, Capri," he said as he pulled her to her feet and hugged her. "We're free! We're rich!" For once, no one wanted to interfere with Frankie's mood. His joy was infectious and what he had to say was as relevant to his friends as it was to his sister and himself. But something had been bothering Jippsy as the evening had worn on and the reality of what had happened started to sink in.

"I hate to mention this," Jippsy interrupted the raucous gang, "but how are we going to get this all out of here?"

"Let me see eef I could 'elp you wit' dat." The gang turned toward the sound of the unfamiliar voice to see two men standing in the clearing, one with a rifle pointed directly at them, the other a giant. The man with the rifle continued to address them in heavily accented English. "Hmm... How about if I just take it off your hands?"

Dodo almost fainted but was luckily still seated. Capri was right behind her; she leaned forward slightly and placed her hands slowly on Dodo's shoulders for support and to reassure her. Butterball was completely catatonic...he didn't even flinch. Jippsy was the only one who spoke, pleadingly. "You, you can't do that. Listen, there's enough here for everybody. Please?" He tried to appeal to his humanity.

"Oui, that is probably true, but I think I – we, that is, and he nodded toward Louis - will just take it all, and if you kids don't help, I *will* kill you." He said it so nonchalantly that they believed him. Louis, however, could not stand for that idea.

"Gerard, êtes-vous fou?" Louis whispered in his ear. Was he crazy? "We can't kill a bunch of kids," he continued in French.

"Arrêtes, Louis." While they only spoke French with one another, the kids all understood what was happening. After all, everyone in the Laurentian Mountains spoke French, among other languages.

"We have to get the money. Now shut up. This is the only way," Gerard answered as he talked from the side of his mouth. "Now just follow my lead, and **don't** let any of them move."

"Alors, everyone, come back over here. The first one who tries to escape will get all of you shot, believe me. I have done this before and will not hesitate a moment. Just in case you get some idea, you two come over here," he insisted as he pointed toward Capri and Dodo. "Well, come on. A couple of pretty women...come over here."

Dodo was terrified and couldn't move.

"Leave them alone!" Jippsy snarled, ready to charge the man with the gun. He could feel his blood boiling; his anger was palpable. He had to do something –

he had promised Dodo they would be safe.

"Are you going to stop me, tough guy? Move over here, girls, or he's the first to go. Capri helped Dodo get up, as anger welled within her. She could barely breathe as she contemplated what was happening and how she could fight back. She wanted to attack them, and tear them limb from limb. The giant terrified her, like some monster from one of the fairy tales she used to like to read, but the adrenaline coursing through her system had set off a fury of such proportion that, in her tired and desperate state, she honestly believed she could fight him somehow. Besides, she figured, once they had what they wanted, what would stop them from killing them all anyway?

The girls walked around the fire. Louis immediately pushed them to the side with his enormous beefy arms and cautioned them. "You stay and be quiet, and nothing will happen." His voice was so low, but he spoke confidently and somehow managed to sound reassuring. "You move, and then something will," he said in perfect English, but for the hint of an accent. The girls listened and obeyed.

Gerard continued his orders, "The rest of you will drag the valise with you. We will take the whole night if we have to. Les filles," he called to the girls, "at the front, lead the way. The boys, you had better pull with all of your might. If you stop, I shoot someone. If you talk, I shoot. I don't need all of you, and really, I don't need any of you, but it will go much faster like this so I'm willing to spare your lives in exchange for help. I think it's fair, eh? Do you think it's fair?" he turned and asked Louis who was not accustomed to rhetorical questions.

"Well, um, sure," he answered, somewhat confused.

"Well, then, now that we all agree, shall we?" he

stated rather than asked as he smiled a wicked smile. "Push or pull...I don't care how you get it there...just get it done."

Jippsy raised his hand.

"Oui? Do you have a question?"

He nodded. "Go ahead this one time."

"How can we work together, if we can't speak with each other?"

"Very well - you can talk. Of course we want to work as a team, don't we?" he laughed to himself.

"Um, sure, yeah," Louis agreed.

"Not you, Louis!" Gerard fumed as he shook his head. *How could this man be such an imbecile?* he wondered.

"However, if you attempt anything funny at all the first girl gets it. You can run, kid, but their lives will be on your shoulder. Capiche?" Gerard knew Frankie would pick up on that one.

"Ok, guys," he said calmly to his friends, "forget about anything else. Let's just do as they say. I don't want anyone getting hurt."

"Sure, Jips," the girls agreed at once.

"Ok, Frankie?" Jippsy was worried about him. He knew what he was thinking...if he could just pull out his slingshot, he could hit him right between the eyes. He looked Frankie square in the eyes. "I'll get you out of the house, Frankie. I promise. But you can't do anything – anything at all - to jeopardize their lives." They couldn't stall anymore. "Come on, guys, we'll work together," he said loud enough for the thugs to hear him clearly. "We'll pull, and you two," he said as he pointed at Butterball and Vicky, "will push. We can do this." He noticed the look on Butterball's face; he was on the verge of tears. "We'll be fine, BB, just fine. Then he turned his attention to Vicky. "Keep your eyes on me, ok? Don't look up at them or at anything else, got it?" Vicky nodded her head timidly.

After several minutes of trying to move the valise along the ground through the shrubs, it was obvious this tactic was not going to work. Jippsy told them all to stop, and raised his hand again to get Gerard's attention. He knew it was a risk, but if they continued this way without any progress the thugs would only grow more aggravated They had moved beyond the firelight and they path was light only by the moonlight.

"Sir, this will take forever. What if we just carried some of the bundles?"

"Sure, kid, if you think that will go faster, let's try it your way."

"It would be better if the other girls helped as well," he said tentatively.

"Of course," the thug replied condescendingly, "The more, the merrier, kid."

"So, les filles, go help your friends." They quickly removed over half of the bundles from the valise and split them evenly between the girls, Jippsy and Butterball. They closed the valise and Frankie managed to turn it on its side and use the strap to drag it along the ground. Vicky showed the gang how she had tucked the bundles into her shirt then lifted up the hem to create a carrying pouch. The bills were wet and still fairly cumbersome for them to manage, but they headed off along the path they had carved out with the girls in the front, then Butterball, Frankie and finally Jippsy at the back. He wanted to make sure the thugs would have to deal with him rather than any of his friends. He also wanted to distract them in case they knew to look for the black books.

Louis led the way and walked slowly. He cautioned Dodo about the terrain, and every root or rock in her path. He seemed genuinely concerned about her welfare, and tried in his own way to reassure her that they wouldn't hurt them.

"Which one of you is Frank?" Gerard asked out of the blue.

Frank spoke up immediately. "What about it?"

"Well, Frank, I met your mom and your...I guess he was your brother. Nice people," he said mockingly. "Your brother is not very sure-footed, is he?"

"What do you mean by that?" Frankie asked as his rage started to build once again.

"Nothing, except that we had the misfortune of meeting him."

It was a good thing Jippsy stood between Frankie and the thug with the gun. There was no telling what would happen if Frankie lost his cool. Jippsy tried to change the dynamic by changing the subject. "You guys aren't from around here?" he asked aloud, then spoke quietly to Frankie. "Easy, Frank. Please,'" he pleaded.

"How can I put this? I wouldn't come here if my life depended on it, which it doesn't. But you...you're life does depend on it, so shut up! You will talk when spoken to only."

They walked casually around the bend of the lake as though out for a leisurely Sunday stroll. The moon had peaked above them and easily lit their way.

Gerard decided to switch to French. "I will tell you a story. There was a man named Dutch Schultz who had the misfortune of doing business with another man named The Rock Rothman. If you think Dutch was a bad man, then you never met The Rock; he was even worse. An evil man, with ice in his veins, who called the shots." Gerard couldn't have explained why he felt compelled to tell his story to these kids. He didn't figure they understood him anyway, but perhaps in the retelling they might appreciate why he had to do what he was doing. Besides, he wasn't going to let them leave and repeat his story.

"We worked for The Rock, and he didn't help our families. He was greedy and only helped himself to more and more and more. You and all of you farmers also worked for The Rock - it was your fruit that he bought to ferment into all sorts of liquors. I bet your mom and Dad have a distillery at their farm too, don't they Frankie?" He had the most absurd desire to taunt Frankie for his family's rude behavior and supposed shortcomings. "It was The Rock's money that controlled the fruit and wheat business in the region. He paid for your houses, your farms, the food on your tables, and because of you, Dutch Shultz and Rothman ran the cities."

In the retelling of his story, Gerard had worked himself into a frenzy, had talked himself into a conspiracy to justify, perhaps, what was going to happen. He convinced himself that these kids weren't merely innocent bystanders, and that their deaths would save the good folk from servicing evil. They would be the martyrs and Gerard would be a hero.

"Well, times are going to change. It's time for payback now, and The Rock, he's resting in a dirt field face-down eating maggots," Gerard spat from between clenched teeth, "and Dutch, hmh, well, who cares? You kids, you're just a part of the machine, and I hope you learned something today. Pigs. Get. Slaughtered. That's right...pigs get slaughtered," Gerard ended on a moral note.

They reached the sandbar across the lake, and something about the poem came to mind. Dutch had made a reference that, as he thought about it, must have indicated something on this side. But they had moved quickly along the path and were nearing the road. That meant the end...but what next? Jippsy had to think of something fast. He whistled their bird call to Butterball who promptly answered back. The gang all knew the sound, and Jippsy had to prepare them.

The climb with the money had become more difficult; they needed at least one hand free to help support them. Dodo, who was first, slipped repeatedly, and dropped the bundles each time.

"I can't!" she finally blurted out in frustration, and then covered her mouth quickly as she realized that she might have jeopardized their lives.

"What's going on up there, Louis?" Gerard called out in French.

"The kids keep slipping," he shouted back.

"Sir?" Jippsy turned to address the thug with the gun.

"What now?" Gerard asked gruffly.

"What if we just make a chain and pass the money up to the top?" he suggested.

"You're a smart kid," he remarked, clearly impressed. "What's your name?"

He hadn't wanted to say his real name, but couldn't think of anything else fast enough. "Jippsy," he replied curtly.

"Jippsy? What kind of name is that?"

"It's um..."

"It's a rhetorical question, kid. Gypsy, eh? Gypsy what?"

"Jippsy Russ." He never referred to himself as Russ, but he figured it would be better than saying 'Russo'.

"Alors, Gypsy Russ. Let's continue with your plan."

Gerard called out once again to Louis. "The kids will form a chain and pass the money up from here. D'accord, Louis?"

"Oui, Gerard."

"Kids, leave your money here on the ground and

403

then spread out along the hill. You, Gypsy - I *like* that name - you stay back here with me. Louis, stay up there and have the girl drop the money where she's standing and move up the hill a little so that she can pass to you. You, Frank, you go next. And bring that valise with you." Frank was happy to be next to Dodo, where he could protect her, and started to make his way up the hill, dragging the valise along behind him. "You too, chubby," Gerard said to Butterball as he waved him along with the rifle. Butterball knew he was chubby, but hated when anyone else pointed it out or insulted him. He didn't bother to hide his hatred for the man; it was written all over his face, and Butterball was an open book. "Don't think about it, kid," Gerard said menacingly. "You'll never get your revenge. "Ok, you," he said as he pointed at Capri, "you're next."

They passed the bundles of money up the hill along the chain, a dozen or so bundles at a time. Dodo piled them neatly at the top of the hill. Jippsy stacked and passed the bundles as slowly as he could in the hopes that he could formulate a plan before it was too late. The reality of their situation had started to sink in, and the thug's rant had served to validate Jippsy's worst fears. The moment the gang had laid eyes on these thugs, there was no way they would be allowed to leave these woods.

"Let's go, kid," Gerard insisted as he nudged him with the rifle. "We'll all walk up together. You carry the last few bundles. Everyone move!" he shouted up the hill. "Then we'll continue to carry the money to the car," he said to Jippsy.

We are now in the home stretch, Vicky thought to herself. It was that thought that finally nudged her memory. *That's it!* she realized. She remembered her dad recounting close races at the track, about horses coming around the bend passing the 8th pole, then into the home stretch. She recognized that it didn't matter anymore anyway. There was nothing she could do, except try to accept her fate. She reasoned that the thugs couldn't get them all, or maybe they wouldn't get any of them. *I know Jippsy has a plan,* she hoped. *He wouldn't have risked being caught whistling if he didn't.*

Come on Jippsy, what's the plan? Vicky wondered. *I know you've been thinking about one this whole time. The whistle's the sign, I know, but* when?

Come on, Jips, old boy, what do you have in mind? We have to get out of here. Maybe running is worth the risk, although I'd rather kill this bastard. Don't EVER talk about my mother ever! He felt his jaw starting to ache. He had been clenching his teeth in frustration since the thugs had shown up.

He whistled. That's the sign. But what does he have in mind? Chubby! God, how I hate that! He's probably the ugliest son of a bitch I've ever seen. Boy would I love to smash him one right on his mug.

Disgusting, vile man, Capri thought to herself. *What kind of woman would want to be with that ugly pig, leering at me and Dodo? Maybe that's how we can get them...let our womanly charms reel them in, and then a shot between the legs and he's down for the count. The rest is easier, a few kicks to the head, and maybe one in the gut. Come on Jippsy, I want to make mincemeat out of this sad excuse for a man.*

Jippsy, you can do it. I've always had faith in you. It's always been the two of us, and Mom and Dad, and our family can overcome any kind of adversity. We need to get out of this, and I need to stay strong.

Jippsy and Gerard were the last two to ascend the hill. Jippsy stumbled, and his arms wind-milled as he fell forward. "Careful, kid. You might get yourself killed," Gerard taunted, then laughed at the irony.

As Jippsy struggled to right himself he whistled and yelled, "Run! Now!" As if anticipating his command, they each obeyed promptly and scattered in different trajectories toward the road, as though it had been planned. Jippsy moved swiftly and rammed his shoulder into Gerard's gut. Gerard has successfully been sacked, like a quarterback, and the impact sent the gun flying in the air, but not before it fired off a single bullet as a result of the impact. The force of Jippsy's tackle sent Gerard tumbling down the mountainside and back toward the lake where this had all begun. He watched as the rifle flew through the air, as the ugly man tumbled down the slope over mud and stones. He hoped the thug would continue to tumble and fall right over Big Rock. *Wouldn't that be ironic? If the man who worked for The Rock fell over Big Rock and drowned.*

Jippsy had lost his footing again and slid alongside Gerard. He tried to dig his heels in as he grasped at random tree limbs and rocks. His legs and hands were covered in cuts now and would have been burning were it not for the adrenaline coursing through his system. He caught a lucky break as his heel jammed painfully into a rock, and he managed to stop his descent. He flipped himself onto his belly and grabbed for the closest branch to haul himself up. He could hear Gerard as he continued to tumble downhill, and redoubled his efforts to quickly scramble uphill. He had nearly succeeded in reaching the road when Louis appeared, out of the dark, like some massive moving tree, and grabbed him about the waist, his arms pinned around his body. There was no give, and Jippsy's torso was trapped in a bear hug, his arms unable to move. He tried to slide out of his grasp as he bounded up and down, but Louis simply tightened his hold.

"Let go of me," he pleaded with the giant. "*Please.* You can keep the money. I swear I won't say anything. I know you're a good one, Louis," Jippsy coaxed and used his name in an attempt to appeal to the giant's humanity. "I will never say anything."

"I know," Louis finally answered reluctantly. "But I have to be sure." His deep voice vibrated through Jippsy, trapped as he was in the giant's hold, and elicited waves of fear.

He knew his friends had escaped, and yet, he had no idea how he would escape from the situation at hand. Even if they wanted to help him, they still had no gun, or weapon of any kind other than Frankie's slingshot if he hadn't lost it.

The moonlight continued to diffuse through the forest. They heard Gerard before they spotted him shuffling slowly up the hill. As he neared, Jippsy could see the thug holding his head. He moved his hand across his forehead searching for blood or debris or both.

Gerard was fuming. "Where are they?" he roared. "I'll get you kids. I will. I swear it. If I ever lay eyes on any of you again, you're dead! You hear me, Frankie? Jippsy? Dead!"

"Over here, Gerard," Louis called through the trees. Gerard had found the rifle on his climb back up the hill. Just beyond the pile of money, cloaked by the darkness afforded by the trees stood the giant, with their enemy detained tightly in his grasp.

"*Where* were you?" he bellowed at his associate. He didn't want to hear the answer; he merely wanted to humiliate him for not doing his job.

"Right here, Gerard," he replied innocently.

Gerard blew out a gust of air in exasperation, but perked right up when he noticed that Louis held one of the kids firmly in his grasp. "Well, what do we have here? Ah! Gypsy, you little bastard. You're going to get what's coming to you," he vowed as he waved the rifle in his face.

"Let him go, Louis. If he runs, I'll shoot him on the spot. You're going to finish the job that our friends aren't here to do. Now pick up the bundles," he spat at Jippsy, with the rifle just inches from his chest. Jippsy noticed that Gerard's hair was matted with blood.

"Louis, grab some bundles and help him."

Jippsy picked up a small armful; he was in no rush to see this to the end. "You can do better than that, kid," Gerard reproached him. "Louis, load him up with more bundles. I want to do this fast."

Louis did as he was told, then grabbed as many bundles as he could hold. Louis and Jippsy labored up to the road; although it wasn't far - maybe a hundred paces or so – this extra exertion after the events of the past few days took its toll. Jippsy definitely wasn't used to hauling that much weight and he was exhausted as they plodded through. It had been an incredibly long and arduous day, and he was still not out of danger. In fact, his situation was rather dire as he was his enemy's only remaining target. They continued to haul bundles up to the car until all of the money except one small pile had been loaded into the boot. Only then did Jippsy notice the second car just ahead.

I'm surprised we didn't notice it earlier, he thought to himself. *Did they come in two cars?* They really had just about finished, and once again Jippsy's ultimate fear started to plague him. *They're going to kill me.* Louis dumped his latest armful of bundles on the ground, and Jippsy followed suit. When Louis turned to head back to the last pile of bundles, Jippsy remained in place.

"Let's go, kid. Move it! One last load to haul, he reluctantly turned and headed back to the pile. They loaded themselves up with as many bundles as possible, and still there were bundles lying on the ground, but it was impossible to carry anything more than what was already loaded in their arms.

Gerard could see their dilemma and finally relented. "Ok. We'll come back for those."

They returned to the car and dumped their bundles on the ground. Louis opened the boot, and quickly started piling the bundles neatly into the empty space. Jippsy merely stood there watching as the bundles disappeared from the ground, and he thought of the bundles like grains of sand slipping through an hourglass. His time might very well have run out...

"That's the end of the line, Gypsy. I kind of liked you, except for that tackle." Jippsy looked warily into Gerard's cold eyes. He noticed a significant amount of blood streaming down his forehead and along his cheek. Jippsy grinned, satisfied that he had at least inflicted some form of pain upon this monster.

Gerard raised his rifle and pointed it at Jippsy's chest. He cocked it, and, with an indifference saved for pure psychopaths, was about to pull the trigger. Jippsy had run out of clever ideas. Sure, he could run, but then he would certainly be shot in the back. "Please, I..." he started to beg, just as Louis leaped forward.

"You can't do this! You can't kill a kid," he yelled at Gerard just as his associate's finger depressed the trigger. The rifle's report echoed through the forest, terrifying its denizens who bolted in the night. Bats scattered from the trees in a flurry, and foxes howled their unrest, as both diurnal and nocturnal creatures unsettled themselves from their hideaways.

The bullet pierced flesh just as Gerard's head snapped backward. Jippsy heard the crack of the thug's skull and watched as his lifeless body fell to the ground. Jippsy instinctively patted himself down in search of blood or pain. *I haven't been hit...did the rifle backfire?* he wondered. He felt dizzy and closed his eyes as he took a deep breath. When he reopened his eyes he finally noticed Louis writhing and wheezing painfully on the ground. In the moonlight Jippsy could see the black blood as it oozed out from his stomach.

"Help me," the giant moaned deeply. Jippsy looked over to Gerard's still form – he wanted to be sure he didn't move again. Jippsy was in shock. He wanted to run, but his feet were glued in place. His tortured mind flashed back to some of the awful events he had witnessed that night and experienced over the past few days. It had suddenly become impossible for him to focus and think clearly.

"Help me?" the voice croaked again, almost as though the giant was drowning. Blood spluttered out of his mouth. "Pray for me. No heaven...for me. Maman, I am coming home," he said with great difficulty as every breath drained away one last bit of life. He thought of the generations of his family that had sacrificed their lives for freedom from slavery, and who had helped others escape to freedom via the Underground Railroad. He hoped his salvation would lie in his own sacrifice, as he saved a young boy's life.

Jippsy had heard his pleas, and understood the significance of what this man had done, in the end. "You saved my life," he whispered as he grasped the man's enormous hand in his own. "That will get you into heaven. I know it will," Jippsy promised him confidently. Louis tried to smile, but he could not. He stopped trying forever.

"Jippsy," Frankie asked tentatively. "You ok?"

"Frankie? I've never been so happy to hear your voice..." They hugged, relieved that this nightmare was over, and everyone was safe.

"Thank god you're ok, Jippsy."

"That was you?" Jippsy asked with admiration.

"Yup! Not bad, eh," he asked with a laugh as he

licked his chops. "He would have killed you, Jips," he added seriously, "and I couldn't let him do that, now could I?"

"Your aim *is* impeccable, Frankie. Thanks. Now let's get the car – it's loaded up with the money."

"I know. I was watching, just waiting for my moment."

"Where are the others?"

"They're right up there. Everyone's ok," he answered as he pointed toward the road at the top of the hill.

"It's ok. Come on down," Frankie called up to them. "He's ok."

Dodo almost fainted right then and there. Instead, she ran down the road as fast as she could, her vision clouded by tears of relief that flowed uncontrollably. She was running so fast that she feared she wouldn't be able to stop her momentum, but Jippsy caught her just in time and she jumped into his arms. The rest of the gang came barreling down the hill just behind her.

"Let's go, guys. We'll just take the car. The keys are still inside."

"Not so fast," another unfamiliar voice ordered from the direction of the car. "I will be commandeering this vehicle on behalf of the RCMP," it continued. In all the chaos they hadn't even noticed him, but that did explain the presence of the second car.

"You kids will be heroes," he exclaimed. "You caught two notorious gangsters and uncovered Dutch's fortune. You'll all be famous across North America. Now, I'm going to need everyone's name."

Jippsy spotted the man's pistol on the inside of his jacket. "Could we see some identification, Officer?" Jippsy asked warily.

"Of course, my boy," he answered reassuringly. He

reached into his breast pocket, and handed Jippsy his badge. "Here you go." He also took out a small pad and pen. "What are your names?" They each answered in turn as the Officer pointed his pen at them.

"Caprice Cristafaro."

"Frank Cristafaro."

"Victoria Doncaster."

"Robert Fried."

"Domenica Russo."

"And you, son, what's your name?"

"You can call me Jippsy Russ."

Epilogue:

The following evening...

He knocked on the rustic door with his heart in his throat. He hoped she was home. To his great relief the door opened, and he smiled at the sight of her. "Hello, Faith. Do you remember me?" He asked like a nervous schoolboy.

"Of course, Benoît. Have you come back for your rain-check?" she asked sweetly.

He breathed a sigh of relief and nodded happily. "Well, if your offer still stands, I thought I'd take you up on that lemonade."

As she closed the door she noticed the car in the driveway. "Wow! That's quite a fancy car, Benoît. No more cruiser?"

"That's right. No more cruiser, Faith. I'm retired."

She smiled approvingly. "How about we take our lemonade on the lakeside veranda?"

"Sounds perfect..."

"Mom! Dad! We have something to show you,"

Jippsy and Dodo called out as they made their way into their kitchen where their parents sat talking quietly.

"What is it?" their mom asked as she strained to make out what her children were cradling in their arms.

"*This...*" Jippsy emphasized, "is just part of it," he said with a huge grin as he and Dodo dumped the contents of their arms on the kitchen table between their parents.

Their mom and dad were speechless. "Where...where did you get this?" their father asked incredulously.

"We found it, Dad. It's ok. The police know all about it. It's ours to keep and to use as we need."

Despite - and because of - the injuries he had sustained during the war, he had met and married the love of his life. And despite the fact that economic times had been tough, he lived on a fine, productive farm, and had been blessed with two incredible children. And now that his father had been injured in an awful car wreck, and they were in desperate need of money to pay for his care, good fortune had smiled upon him once again. He dropped his head into his hands and started to sob tears of pain and tears of relief. Jippsy watched as his mother's eyes filled with tears at the sight of her husband sobbing. He watched her soothe and reassure his father. "It's ok. We'll be ok," she whispered lovingly.

Then she turned to address her children. "I love you, Jippsy. Thank you. Dodo," she cooed as she pulled her close, "I'm so proud of you both!"

Jippsy recalled how they had returned to retrieve the last few bundles left at Lost Lake, and how he had returned this morning, alone, to gather up the rest of the black books. All thirteen were now safely hidden in his room. He looked down at his mother who seemed, somehow, so much smaller than she did just a few short days ago. "You're welcome, Mom," he mouthed to her.

The telephone rang. Jippsy took three quick steps and picked up the phone. "Hello?"

"Jips, old boy, I'm in New York," Frankie's voice crackled on the line.

Jippsy smiled excitedly, much to his family's curiosity. "What are you doing *there*?"

"I'm going to try to join the Marines. I think it's the best thing for me. Capri's with me. She's going to start school here when the summer's over. I just wanted to tell you... Well, I just wanted to say, 'Thanks' is all. For everything."

Jippsy's smile faltered at the mention of Capri's name, but then brightened again, nothing short of radiant, as tears finally welled up in his eyes. "You're screwy, you know that?"

Writer's Notes

Although Dutch and the rest of the money was never found. You can be sure someone will continue to try someday. It may be Jippsy. Jippsy will assuredly lead an adventurous life and I hope you will follow along.